My Eyes Dance

With liquid eyes flood my soul

That I may be able to discern

Not only what is good

But what is excellent

Mark Nwagwu

BookBuilders • Editions Africa

ISBN: 978 978 8088 98 1
E-ISBN 978-978-921-191-

Published in Ibadan, Nigeria by
BookBuilders • Editions Africa
2 Awosika Avenue
Bodija Estate, Ibadan, Nigeria
gsm: 0805 6629266

cover illustration: Chidozie Daniels (my grandson)

Other publications by the same author

Forever Chimes, 2007
I Am Kagara, 2017
Helen Not-of -Troy, 2009
Kat Man Dew, 2012
Helena Venus, 2013
Time Came Upon Me, 2019

This work is dedicated to the
memory of our daughter,
Mrs. Onyemazuwa Fern Eseka
11 January 1971 to 20 November 2006

FOREWORD

Mark Nwagwu's *My Eyes Dance* is a novel of character and a novel of ideas. The character around whom most of the action accretes is Chioma Ijeoma, and the ideas surrounding most of the themes are about African ancestor worship and its attendant idea of totemism.

Mark Nwagwu, a renowned professor of molecular biology and a scientist of note, created the character of Chioma with a subtle hint of Mendel's atavism. Chioma, a great granddaughter of Pa Akadike of Okeosisi becomes the carrier of the ancestral genes by receiving an ancestral 'walking stick' that has a mind of its own and tries to influence Chioma's actions at important moments in her life. Chioma led a life of exceptional virtue and is everything one admires in a human being. She is an artist *par excellence*, a painter, a philosopher, a brilliant academic, and her celibate life in the Opus Dei, influences for the better many followers who are fascinated by her abstemious life at The Nesbit Study Centre of the Opus Dei. She is in every way a saint if we consider the adage that a saint is a person who does the ordinary things in life extraordinarily well.

I just said that *My Eyes Dance* is a novel of ideas. The ideas are about the African concepts of totemism and ancestor worship. Ancestor verneration is an important contribution to the African novel by Chinua Achebe. Camara Laye in *The Dark Child* extends ancestor worship to totemic myth in the black snake that guides and often speaks to Laye's father, a goldsmith. And totemism is manifested in the 'animal' or 'tree' ancestor one worships. Mark Nwagwu's 'walking stick' handed to Chioma

FOREWORD

by Pa Akadike, her great grand father, is a form of totemic myth which guides Chioma at important stages in her life. This makes Chioma the Igbo culture-heroine of the novel. And since, in totemic myth an intimate relationship exists between favoured human beings and their "animal ancestor" or "tree ancestor" in a mysterious way, the totem becomes Chioma's alter ego, the projection of her life-drive which keeps her in contact with her profession and her society. The walking stick, Chioma's totem, is a carry-over from Mark Nwagwu's first novel, *Forever Chimes*.

The belief that the living and the dead belong to the same category of beings and are in constant communion with one another is referred to as ancestor worship. In *Things Fall Apart*, Achebe tells us:

> The land of the living is not far removed from the domain of the ancestors. There was coming and going between them, especially at festivals and when an old man died, because an old man was very close to the ancestors. (p.115, Fawcett edition)

As I mentioned earlier, in *The African Child*, Camara Laye's ancestor worship manifests itself in the 'animal ancestor' his father worships, in totemic myth. The little black snake speaks thus to Laye's father: 'Lo, I am the guiding spirit of thy race,' and when Laye's father decides to reveal his special relationship with the snake (his totem) to his son, he admits:

> If these things are so, it is by virtue of this snake alone, who is the guiding spirit of our race. It is to this snake I owe everything (The Dark Child (New York: Farrar, Strauss and Giroux, 1970, 25-26)

Thus, Mark Nwagwu's use of totemic myth has a long ancestry in African literature. What Nwagwu does is to carry the African philosophy of totemism and ancestor worship to a new level, the internationalization or rather globalization of the concept. The concept has now crossed the Atlantic, riding high on the wings of philosophy, in the hallowed halls of an American university. *Ex Africa semper aliquid novi.*

The extraordinary life of Chioma Ijeoma is one packed with lodestars of genes. Anything she touches turns to gold. Each time I think of Chioma and the impact of her impeccable life on others, my mind runs to that popular song, number 48 in the Catholic hymn book, "Bring Them In" whose chorus goes thus:

Bring them in, bring them in,
Bring them in, from the fields of sin
Bring them in, bring them in,
Bring the wandering ones to Jesus.

Always on a high moral horse, always with words of advice with high moral content, with a virtuous life worthy of emulation, those fallible, even sinful people around Chioma are inevitably influenced to live a more virtuous life whatever their religion. Mike, who abandoned his Hindu wife for the more fleshly Doris, returns repentantly to his wife, Sutapa. Bia is successfully urged to save Nkemdi from reproach by marrying her properly in the church having recklessly put her in the family way; Susanne the promiscuous, finally goes to confession and receives Holy Communion. The exquisite, incomparable beauty, Geneve, a mega star entertainer finds Chioma's simple life at the Nesbit Study Centre so attractive that she wants to join her. Mark Nwagwu in the character of Chioma, convincingly creates a role model; and only few readers will doubt Chioma's positive impact on the life of others. Chioma must have been an ardent student of Boethius whose *Consolation of Philosophy* preaches that happiness cannot be found in such transitory or ephemeral externals as wealth and power, but in goodness and in God, for true blessedness can only be found in God. The character of Mike who returns to his wife after delivering a lecture on Eros, instructs us not to set our hearts on such ephemeral things as sex and infatuation

My Eyes Dance also is a story of sin and repentance, offence and forgiveness, confession and salvation. How one young woman of great virtue, through moral example salvages others, props the weak and leads everyone who knows her to a life of virtue makes for high comedy. It reminds theologians of the theory of *Felix Culpa* (the happy fall); that man falls to rise to a higher level, for the greatest saints in the church were once great sinners: Mary Magdalene and St. Augustine, for example, *My Eyes Dance* is certainly an uplifting work of fiction.

The journey of American students to Okeosisi in the company of Chioma, to Igbo heartland, is like a leap, back into the womb of myth. But the Igboland they arrive at, pursuing the meaning of *Chi* as a name and as a philosophy is a glamorized Igboland, bereft of nastiness and all primitive and depressing encounters. It is an Okeosisi with a tennis court, a swimming pool and a basketball court in a private home. And the Igwe's palace in Igboland rivals the palace of the Oba of Benin. And the kitchen out of which the visitors fed, and from which different varieties of sumptuous dishes were served, could shame a five-star hotel. But this is fiction and no eyebrows need be raised.

My Eyes Dance is a patriotic work of fiction. It posits that there is nothing wrong in African beliefs and customs; that indeed, our customs and beliefs have something attractive enough for other people to copy, and that African philosophy contains moral and ethical aspects that other races could live by. The Igbo of Nigeria need to be grateful to Mark Nwagwu for selling Igbo culture and traditions in the international cultural market.

Mark Nwagwu's *My Eyes Dance* is a serious and highly philosophical novel that teases us out of thought.

Charles E. Nnolim, NNOM
Professor of English, University of Port Harcourt

PREFACE

This book is a sequel to *Forever Chimes*, a novel by the author which describes the life and times of Chief Akadike Okeosisi of Okeosisi, the great-grandfather of Chioma, (the main character of *My Eyes Dance*), from her birth to her graduation from Georgetown University, Washington, D.C., USA.

A walking stick endowed with magical powers by the gods from time immemorial, had been handed down through the first son of Okeosisi families, generation after generation, finally ending its life in the hands of Chioma, who gives it a female identity and names it *Uzo*, 'The Way'. *Uzo* eventually disappears and the novel ends with Chief Akadike literally dying in Chioma's arms.

Although it would be helpful to have read *Forever Chimes*, the characters, personalities and events that are recalled from there are presented herein in sufficient detail for the reader to follow the story with ease.

ACKNOWLEDGEMENTS

I acknowledge with profound gratitude the assistance I received from Rev. Fr. Boniface Okafor, who read the original manuscript, made corrections, again read the revised manuscript, and made further corrections.

Professor Charles Nnolim read the manuscript, suggested improvements to the style and content, and, of his own volition, wrote the foreword. I thank him most sincerely for his critical input to this work.

I am immensely grateful to Dr. Ayobami Kehinde: he went through the manuscript with a fine-tooth comb and took great pains to complete editorial revisions in limited time.

Dr. Victoria Okoje guided my thoughts on Chioma's character and behaviour. Her assistance is greatly appreciated.

My publishers, BookBuilders • Editions Africa have provided me with a literary family, a home where my spirit finds vivid expression.

Destiny's Dance

come, let's be on our way
run
to where we once belonged
meet our souls
merge with the spirits
dance
in blissful embrace
of our destiny
with the saints
from here to eternity
souls cold
rest ... less

come, let's be on our way
to find our beginnings
where we once knew ourselves
souls on fire
rest...more

From: *Helen Not-of-Troy*, 2009, a collection of poems
by Mark Nwagwu

ONE

Perhaps, you best find yourself in losing yourself. And amongst my people, the Igbo, we best lose ourselves in dance. I can hear my great-grandfather calling me: Chioma, Chioma, Chioma. It is not a bland call. No; he is actually calling me on talking gongs and I make out the beat to mean Chioma, Chioma, Chioma. And my eyes start to dance.

August 2005, University of Maryland

After my Pa passed on in 2001, I took a break from my studies to spend more time on my paintings — having been appointed artist-in-residence at Georgetown University - with the hope of returning to the University of Maryland for my Ph.D. later. It was left for me to commence my graduate studies at the University of Maryland, College Park.

Today, Monday, 15 August 2005, I was waiting outside the door of Dr. Dwight Campbell, Dean of the Graduate School, University of Maryland. I cannot imagine what he was thinking asking me to teach a course on *The African Spirit*. I could not imagine it, but Dr. Campbell is one of those who believe that to know who you are, you have to look deep within yourself, be introspective, reflect on what is going on in your mind, dig down to your roots. He has a rather romantic view of the African and believes that Africans have a complete grasp of life and what life's all about.

1

He had told me, "You Africans know who you are, you are so steeped in your culture that you have become your ancestors, who never die. Your parents leave a permanent imprint of themselves in your souls and practically give all of themselves to you, their children. They lead you through the past into the present and leave you powerful tools to deal with whatever the future may bring. You are never in doubt as to your invincibility, once you remember who you are and can call upon the spirits of your ancestors to come to the rescue."

The door finally opened and Dr. Campbell dressed as usual in his navy blue double-breasted blazer with four golden buttons on the cuff of each sleeve, a colourful tie - gold dots on a blue background- and a pair of beige trousers, looking very much the Dean of the Graduate School, invited me into his office with a bemused smile.

"I got your letter. . .." I began.

"Good." Still smiling, he perched on the edge of a desk, a curious twinkle in his eyes. He appeared to be waiting for me to acquiesce in his plan. I would not give him that satisfaction, though. Never one to beat around the bush, I launched my first torpedo.

"I cannot imagine how you expect me to teach a course on the African spirit. I do not even know what it means! I am an African, yes, but that's as far as it goes. I'm just a painter trying to pursue my studies in philosophy as a graduate student. This does not add up to much, really. How can you ask me to teach a course based on my meagre experience as an African just because you have read my life's story as a great-grand-daughter of Pa Akadike of Okeosisi, and you think I have completely married my Igbo attributes with the best of American culture? How many people out there care about such things?"

"You might be surprised."

"I will probably make a big fool of myself. Those students could tear me to bits!"

"Ah, Chioma, that's exactly the point. We want you to make a fool of yourself, if you please. We think it would help the rest of us bigger fools be humbler yet. After all, you're one of our best, an 'Investigator Without Borders', and you may rightly decline to teach the course. And nothing would be amiss; after all, by your appointment, you can carry out your studies as you please. All I am doing is simply trying to persuade you to put your talents to good use and help our students to make every possible use of your brains.

"We know you would not make a fool of yourself, surely. As we see it - and I can tell you this as truthfully as I can - the Igbo, like many Africans, have what is best described as the Communion of Saints, whereby you live in constant touch with your past, your grandparents, your noble ancestors, who have passed on to a happier life in the heavens of their aspirations."

"Mr. Dean, writing an essay is one thing, teaching a course is another."

"Chioma, I never said it would be easy, but we know once you set your mind to it, you will come up with a whole new way of looking at humans so that we will merge, black and white. Can you help us? The University of Maryland is counting on you. And you'll always have our full support, even if, as you say, you make a fool of yourself. But I doubt that will happen."

I crossed my arms over my head in a state of perplexed despair. Yes, I was excited about the thought of teaching a course on the African spirit, but HOW?

* * * *

The University of Maryland was one of a few universities in the United States experimenting on a project termed, 'Investigators Without Borders', which involves researchers who could investigate any problem of their choice in the area of their specialization, without any intervention from the authorities for a period of three to five years, their contribution to knowledge being evaluated at the end of the third year.

Fifty of us from across the country had been invited to apply for this status at the University of Maryland, all from the top schools in the United States, from Harvard to Berkeley. I was still at Georgetown University as their artist-in-residence after graduating in 2001. We were each given a month to write an essay on a topic of our choice related to our Ph.D. programme to be examined by scholars from other universities, including Nobel Laureates.

It was a challenging exercise, but I was able to turn in a one hundred-page treatise on Paul Klee, his sense of human tragedy and the striking interrelationships between Klee and African thought. He was profoundly interested in nature and laboured tirelessly to penetrate her secrets.

As he saw it, humans are soaring, creative, imaginative; but at the same time, are weighed down by their selfish pursuits and desires. To be able to translate these diverse and tragically opposing views into his paintings is, to me, the enduring success of Klee's masterpieces.

Exploring my African heritage, I sought the human and spiritual virtues in Klee's work, knowing how much he laboured for purity and temperance in art. In particular, his presentations seem to be child-like caricatures, yet they are profoundly captivating, making the soul readily penetrable.

Friday Morning 11 a.m. Georgetown

The president of the University of Maryland at College Park, the amiable and affable Dr. James Mansfield, called to ask me when I would be free to see him. I could not believe what I had just heard. Somewhat confused, I blurted out that I would be able to see him whenever he wanted me to.

"Ah, Chioma, you must give me a specific time. Dr. Campbell tells me you are right now doing a huge mural in their Hugo Martins Concert Hall and that you spend countless hours on the canvas, pleading not to be disturbed. So, when can you descend from the heights of your painting and come down to us, please?"

Dr. Campbell was a professor of Anthropology at Georgetown, and was being sought after by College Park. He had engineered my artist-in-residence appointment and was greatly interested in both my African ancestry and my paintings. And he was the one who had asked me to apply for the Young Investigator's award. It then struck me that the telephone call must have some bearing on my submission for the award. My mind became fully awakened, and I excitedly told the president I would see him the following day, anytime after 12 noon.

"You must be intensely busy, Chioma. It seems your only free time is during weekends. Tomorrow is Saturday, Chioma, and I'm sorry but I won't be able to come to my office. But you could join my family for a barbecue at 2 p.m. or so. We've never met, but don't worry, you'll be at ease with my children. I have a daughter just about your age, she's a medical student at GWU and she would be glad to meet you. So what do you say?"

Grandpa Maduka, had taught me never to accept an impromptu invitation unless it was for an exceptional reason. Since I could meet with Dr. Mansfield during the week in his office, I did not see this occasion as one that qualified as 'an exceptional reason'. In a more settled voice, I politely declined the invitation and suggested to Dr. Mansfield that we meet the following Monday morning.

****

"Tell me, Chioma, do you see any links between Paul Klee and African myths?"

That was Dr. Mansfield firing the first salvo before I had time to straighten my aching back. I thought my essay had addressed this question and, perhaps, all he wanted was to hear the words directly from me.

His was a large office, I suppose it was the largest office I had ever been in. It must have measured something like fifty feet by fifty feet. The president's table was far in the left-hand corner of the room, set at such an angle that it formed a triangle with its ends abutting on the left wall of the room and the wall adjacent to it, leaving just enough room on the right side of this arrangement for his exit. The result of this arrangement was that I found myself looking at the president and at the same time at the meeting point of the right and left ends of the wall.

Since nothing, say a painting or a picture, could conveniently be placed at such an awkward point, his imposing countenance was all that confronted me.

Both sides of the wall had huge Pela windows, and right now the sun poured in from the left windows. The curtains were drawn, so a full view of Dr. Mansfield's face was boldly before me. This setting had immediate impact on me and, totally oblivious of the question I had been asked, I blurted out:

"Dr. Mansfield, your seat is at the meeting point of the east and the west. At any time of the day, the sun would be right on your face, as it is now. Perhaps, this is meant to give your visitors a clear insight into the workings of the University of Maryland at College Park."

"You make a big jump, Chioma, from the sun to this university. No one has ever pointed this out to me. So, do I take it that it explains the relationship between Paul Klee and African myths? Is that what you're saying, Chioma?"

Of course, that was not what I meant and the president himself must know that. What was he up to then?

Dr. Campbell and two others —a lady and a gentleman — whom I presumed were also university professors invited to give me a good drilling, were comfortably seated in a leather settee, within easy hearing distance. I was totally dumbfounded, not knowing what next to say. Perhaps, I had already said too much! So, I kept quiet, waiting for Dr Mansfield to continue speaking while I listen. And that's exactly what happened.

"Chioma, we see that you adore Paul Klee, your essay was scholarly, excellent; you presented us with a creative account of his works and its parallels with African myths. Nobody before you had seen Paul Klee in that light, but then no African has yet evaluated his works from a distinctly African scholarly perspective."

I found my voice.

"Thank you very much, sir. Yes I love Paul Klee and I show him off any chance I get and the essay gave me a unique opportunity to merge my ideas on myth in African thought with his brilliant brush strokes. I am happy you liked it."

I did not say more. Dr. Mansfield, leading the way, invited me to join Dr. Campbell and the other guests, Dr. Agnes Cassidy, professor of philosophy and Dr. Brian Westwood, professor of literature, both at College Park. They were members of the committee that had assessed me and had just heard my exchange with the president. They were all smiles, seems I had not disappointed them— they wanted someone fiercely independent and creative. My reply to the president, they told me, said more than I could imagine and immediately gave them a clear indication of my personality. Naturally, I was delighted. Dr Mansfield then gave me my letter of appointment for three to five years as an 'Investigator Without Borders' beginning in May, 2005.

"Congratulations, Chioma. We hope you will be happy here and share with us your unique African appeal, both personally and academically. Again, congratulations."

"Thank you, sir, thank you very much. You all make me so happy I pray that I live up to your expectations."

The appointment meant that I could do my Ph.D. under conditions entirely of my own choice, including picking my own supervisor. I even had my own parking space on campus!

****

"Mr. Dean, my country, Nigeria, is infamous for one thing: '419', ie scams and corruption. Where then is my credibility?"

"Yes, you guys out there may be as corrupt as hell, greedy, self-serving, all the vices are there. You call it '419', we call it 'scam'. But all these pale into insignificance in comparison to your awesome power — yes, awesome indeed — of co-existence. Tell me, how do the Yoruba live in harmony with the Hausa; the Fulani with the Kanuri? And how do the Fulani and the Hausa live with the Tiv; the Igbo with the Nupe? How do you guys manage to live so peacefully together after a terrible civil war? We never thought you would be able to get together again. But here you are, in spite of all your awful military governments, you still band together and are now the envy of all of Africa when it comes to oneness and togetherness. Look at the gruelling life in Lagos and tell me how it is possible for people to live in such huge numbers, skin next to skin, in abject and hopeless poverty, yet you pull it all off and smile and laugh and dance? How do you do it? Tell me, how do you do it? Did Fela not sing '*Ai be Africa man, original*'?"

"Well, Mr. Dean...."

"No. No more of this Mr. Dean stuff. Call me Dwight."

"You know, Mr. Dean, I would never call you by your first name. No. Always it will be Mr. Dean, or Dr. Campbell."

"You see what I mean! You say the African in you will not let you do this or that. What about the American in you?"

"Well, Dr. Campbell, I hate to spoil your illusion, but many Europeans have the same custom!"

"This is America! Suppose I told you that your addressing me as Mr. Dean or as Dr. Campbell is like immersing me in a bathtub of ice and then suddenly pouring scalding hot water on me; now, how would you feel? "

"Well, Dr Campbell, I would simply say that that's your own funeral, none of my business; because you are indeed Dr. Campbell as well as Mr. Dean. And I'm sorry I can't get you out of your bathtub of disquiet."

Undaunted by my somewhat rude reply, Dr. Campbell sallied on: "And you can dance! Man, can you dance! You live in the spirit, internalize your pains, your sorrows, and all this explodes in your dance. Wow!"

"You are wrong, quite wrong. We are filled with love, but love does not win wars! The British colonialists had superior arms and were able to impose their rule on us. In the long run, we 'forgave' them and accepted the new creation of The Commonwealth. I'll give you some points for Lagos. No one — I'm sure, no one - can tell you what makes Lagos run. It's indeed a classic case of the face of agony finding strength and hope in the human heart."

"Well, there you have it. You've got the whole thing summed up. But when it comes to confronting us colonialists, I don't think it was a matter of you submitting to a stronger force. For, if there was any force at all, you had it — the force of nobility and love. Look at Mandela: he does not hate the white South Africans, whom he calls his sisters and brothers."

"How many Mandelas do we have in the world? Apartheid created him and his character shone for all to see. If there was no Apartheid, perhaps, Mandela would have gone unnoticed."

"Yes. I grant you that. But, surely, Mandela is not just a case in isolation. Look at the brilliance of Kwame Nkrumah when he challenged Africans to form The African Union over fifty years ago.

"The idea is that you study the African and teach us what it is to be truly human, a person not defined by anything external to himself or herself. You said as much in your thesis proposal, suggesting that you will explore the African, particularly the Nigerian, and come up with new ways of wholesome living based on the African spirit."

"What I am trying to say, Dr. Campbell, is that I need to go home and conduct my research before I plunge into a course on the African spirit."

I thought I was making myself clear, but I could see that my arguments were rolling off the dean like water off a duck's back. He was still insisting that I teach a course on something as nebulous and abstract as the African spirit.

"Chioma, Chioma, stop fussing. We see you have been making arrangements to spend some time at the Obafemi Awolowo University in Ile-Ife. You tell us that at Ife, you'll research on the African ethos, the African spirit, the African perspective on life; that indefatigable, indestructible elan that goes on and on whatever rains may drench you; though avalanches bury you, slave ships trap you, and slave masters brand your bronze skins with fire and iron. Whatever evils you suffer, you're filled with love. One of your great poets, Niyi Osundare, has given us a line that could serve as the signature tune of the Nigerian:

"My question, Africa, is a sickle, seeking ripening laughter in your deepening sorrows."

****

I left Dean Campbell's office wondering where exactly I stood. Well, I did not agree to anything yet, did I? The dean was a savvy professor, quoting my own poet to me, and telling me to bounce my ideas off a classroom of undergraduates!

The African Spirit: Unlimited in Time and Space, my proposed Ph.D. thesis, was still very much a cloud of ideas floating around in my head. If I did agree to teach this course, it would certainly give me a crucible in which my ideas could be cooked and refined. Or perhaps, destroyed!

Here, I trust my art to help me out, for it has opened up my soul to the heavens and to the African spirit unaffected by life's passing phases; art freed from the skin of experience and the vanishing-skein of the body; art freed from the boundaries of self and grows tender loving tendrils, reaching for the dense uncharted spirit of the other in whom it finds meaning in self-giving. Apart from my paintings, I know little else about the African soul. That I am African and that I have a soul myself does not help much.

* * * *

May 2004, Georgetown University

One day - I think it was on the last day of the final semester of the year - I had just finished a painting, *Onyinye*, the last of a series of seven paintings in the Bryan and Leslie Gossett Hall at Georgetown, in 2004. Dean Campbell called me to his office.

"Chioma," he said, "I'm taking you with me to College Park next year."

I looked at him wondering if he would use this imperative tone with an American student. Being the polite African young woman, I did not contradict him straight away.

"Sir. . . ," I muttered, pretending that I had not heard him well.

"I've been offered a position as Dean of the Graduate School," he continued, "with the freedom to develop a research project on the future of man on this planet, scientifically and socially. My particular interest is in the social sphere and I would like you to come with me to do your graduate studies and to teach a course on the African spirit. I intend to build this research project with you leading the way, and with the African spirit as the foundation."

I could not believe my ears. I had made up my mind to go to College Park for my graduate studies entirely of my own accord, after spending three years or so painting to my heart's content.

I was struggling to be as African as I could possibly be, after the tenets of my great-grandfather, and here was this man, from nowhere, telling me he would like me to accompany him to his new position. Well, I was not particularly perplexed for I knew that professors have been known to take their graduate students and staff with them to their new positions in a new university. However, Dr. Campbell was not going to take anyone else and I was not even his student. Suppose things do not turn out right and my studies do not tell us anything we do not already know, how would this man view his work? Would he blame his failure on me or would he just let it pass? I was frightened at the thought.

"Dr. Campbell, you cause me bitter pains more than you can ever imagine. I . . . "

He did not let me finish.

"Fantastic. Knowing you as well as I think I do, I thought you may be frightened. So, I'm right about you. Your fright shows that you are humble and sincere. That's all I need for now."

"But, Dr Campbell . . . '

"Ah! Don't worry, Chioma, I shall write College Park tomorrow to say I'll be with them in summer, 2005."

T W O

October, 2005

I taught my first class on the African spirit on Monday morning at 10.00 a.m., October 10, 2005. It was unseasonably warm for mid-autumn, so I wore one of my Nigerian tie-dye indigo dresses with matching black shoes. In case the weather turned unfriendly, I wore a jacket my mother gave me when I was a junior at Georgetown. It was my goodluck wear: once I put it on, I became cheerful and felt like dancing to Fela's Afrobeat, dreaming of my days as a child in Lagos.

My lecture was scheduled to hold in Room 37 of The John Babbidge Jr. Building on Apple Close, located in a quiet part of campus. The original wood had been preserved, creating a pristine, bucolic atmosphere. I felt the cool refreshing wind brushing my face and, as I walked, a lone local bird, not one of the brave and adventurous breeds that migrate to the tropics in the winter, twittered loudly, perhaps asking me the first questions of the day. I smiled.

I went to my first class petrified at the idea of standing before a room filled with first-class brains. How would I fill their minds with words from my untutored and recondite mouth? Well, I started my class with an introduction.

"Good morning, everyone. My name is Chioma Ijeoma and we shall spend thirty hours or so exploring philosophical presentations of the African spirit."

A painting that hung above the board gave me back my confidence. It was done in my favourite colours - crimson-red, sandy-brown and indigo.

"What's so good about the morning, Ms. Joma?"

"What's your name, please?" I asked this student who had mispronounced my name, without paying sufficient attention to how I had introduced myself. In fact he was looking over his shoulder at another student, a girl in a body-hugging stretch blouse. I felt hot inside and, perhaps, my pride was rearing its ugly head right now. Not pronouncing my name correctly after I had introduced myself irked me, and I felt I should let this student feel the sting of my tongue as I have always believed that Americans treat our African names rather discourteously. I thought better of it and found sufficient composure to continue with my class.

"Ms. Joma, my name is Gregory, Greg for short."

"Thank you, Greg."

I took some time to teach my class how to pronounce my name correctly.

"I am Ijeoma, pronounced I-Jay-Aw-Ma. You lengthen the "I" then proceed to "JAY", "AW" and "MA". So, could you please repeat my name, Greg?"

"I-I- J e o ma. Ms. Ijeoma, I think I got it right this time. I'm sorry for the error. My mind was somewhere else at the time."

"Yes, I think so too. The charming student by your side seemed to be all you cared about."

This produced wild laughter, just as I had intended, to make the atmosphere more convivial so that I could continue, more relaxed.

"Well, Greg you have now given me the substance for this lecture, namely distance, space, time."

"I had said, 'Good morning, everyone,' and Greg here asked me what was so good about the morning. Let us begin with what we would consider as usual, simple courtesy. Is there a philosophy there? Is there something in there that reveals our humanity to us, something that makes us know ourselves better and understand what the universe is all about? Let us now delve into what I call 'classical philosophy' with its foundations in Greece, in Aristotle, flowing into Descartes' era, the Enlightenment School, to our own so-called post-modernist era.

"I am an African by birth, and by cultural heritage, as transmitted to me by my parents, my grandparents and my great-grandparents, all of whom I knew and most of whom are still alive. But I have lived here in Maryland for the past seven years. Somehow, the thick, protective hide of my indigenous African culture is slowly and inexorably being sliced away by the prevailing and daunting American way of life. But when I say 'Good morning, everyone,' and you don't respond in a similar friendly manner, my African spirit wells up to a storm that only my education can stultify.

"Distance, space, time: are these philosophical concepts with bearings on my greeting, 'Good morning' and the response, 'What's so good about it?'"

There was no response. No one said a word. It seemed I had raised issues that the class had not given much thought to. It then struck me that the simple things were often the most difficult concepts to discuss objectively.

THREE

My Pa (my great-grandfather) gave me the name, Chioma, a few weeks after my birth in 1983. It means Good Fortune. He died in 2001 in my arms, my feeble arms, now made noble by his glorious death. The joy of the fantastic news I had told him left him needing more air than his frail lungs could contain, so he breathed his last. The news was too much for his tired heart. I did not know he would die from what I told him or I would have kept my mouth shut. Well, how do you keep the truth to yourself?

My great-grandfather, Akadike, my Pa, loved nothing more than the truth, even though he liked to believe in the dynastic life of the Akadikes running into eternity. In a way, my new life runs into eternity. I have stirrings in my heart that propel me to flood evil with good. I am enthralled by the universal call to holiness as given by St. Josemaria, urging us to be holy wherever we may be: in the lecture hall, in the office, on the farm, in the performance arts, in sports; in fact, in any honest human endeavour. He taught that we do not need to leave wherever we are and join the priesthood, or a religious community such as a monastery, in order to serve God in holiness. I am particularly prompted to sanctify the ordinary things I do by doing them well, with a lot of generosity and love; to do my best work each and every time.

This really sets my mind ablaze - doing the same ordinary, everyday things; transforming these humdrum activities into joyful encounters with God.

St. Josemaria's message fills me with indescribable joy and fully extends all that my Pa has handed down to me, turning them into instruments for seeking sanctity. Pa always said to me: "Chioma, don't walk, run; don't run, dance to your destiny."

****

I would like to know myself better; for, I believe, the search would be of immense help in my course on the African spirit. I know humans are created to live in two worlds - in the world of sensation and objective knowledge, and in the world of the spirit, of the soul - the very core of the human being; a world that transcends mere knowledge. This is the world of the sage, the poet, where the human being takes flight - as Klee believed - seeking to escape the limitations of his own body.

As I see it, Africans live comfortably in, in close proximity to, these two worlds, readily travelling from the one to the other. But feeling their powers limited by life's practical experiences in the material world of knowledge, Africans seek a new existential reality in the world of the spirit that supplants what is 'knowable' by practical reason. They erect their mansions on foundations of the spirit. Has this any bearing on my own life, or on the life of any African woman living in the perplexing social transformations of the United States?

So, where do I begin this search to know, as fully as I can, who and what I am? Can I truly study myself and hope to find the truth about me? Maybe I should study someone else and from that vantage point gain insight into my own self.

Ah! That reminds me of this great mathematician friend of my grandfather Maduka's, a classmate from his days at

University College, Ibadan. He says that when he is dealing with a small problem that seems unsolvable, he immerses - no, 'embeds' is his exact word - it in a bigger problem, then starts solving this new creation of his, and *voila!* the small problem disappears as the bigger one is solved.

This is where Angela comes in. She is a dear friend of mine, the one to whom I pour out my joys and sorrows, who helps me embed my insignificant troubles in the larger issue of seeking holiness in the midst of the world. Perhaps, I get ahead of myself. What about the demons that afflict me, demons of pride in particular? I tend to be impatient with people who I regard as not quite bright; I am also rather intolerant of 'reality of the situation', which some people plead to explain away their wrong deeds. Right from my childhood, I have always wanted to do things my own way. Add to this, I do not readily brook criticism and tend to be rather full of myself. I keep struggling against these defects and others with varying success. Admittedly, some days are better than others.

Is this too much? Are my expectations too grand, dreaming the impossible with all my defects? That is the whole point - to dream huge dreams, our shortcomings notwithstanding, and then to struggle to turn the dreams into torrents of love. Well, stay with me a while and you might see whether or not I succeed in this venture of total self-giving.

But first I need to sort out a few matters of culture, for I am so many things in one - American, African, Igbo. No, I do not put it right. I am an African, I know. I am Igbo, I know. I am not American, I know. I just live in the United States. But a world of ideas and knowledge has turned me into an endless competition of fragments of cultural diversity. At any given point in time, one fragment reigns supreme, then its influence subsides, only to rise again, contesting for space with another fragment that had made its presence felt.

****

Let me recount my ancestry more fully, as handed down to me by my great-grandfather, Pa Akadike Okeosisi, for that was the pivot of my childhood experiences.

I come from a long lineage, immersed in the gods of the heavens and of the earth. Legend has it that my great-great-great-grandfather founded our town, which since his time, has borne his name, Okeosisi, literally meaning 'a huge tree'. In fact, the name was used to describe a man for whom no description would suffice, no matter how superlative. Colossal, gigantic, titanic, monumental, ineffable - these are mere words.

Okeosisi encompassed the entire universe: it was a cosmic reality wrapped in the blood and soul of one man. Where I come from, there is only one Okeosisi and there has never been another. Only our family goes by the name, an eternal reminder of our dynasty. And there are now over a thousand of us in our village, all from the same ancestors, from my great-grandfather, Akadike Okeosisi down to my own grandfather, Maduka Okeosisi, but only one family bears this name to this day.

We are told that in any given generation, only the first son of the first wife of an Okeosisi may bear that surname. That was how my great-grandfather came to be Akadike Okeosisi and my grandfather, his first son, Maduka Okeosisi.

As a child, I could not pronounce the name, all that my infant tongue could make of Okeosisi was 'Kosi' which rolled out more easily from my lips. When I learned to read and write English, I substituted 'Cosy' for 'Kosi' but my great-grandfather would have none of it. I asked him if our legendary patriarch, the first Okeosisi, was not known for his homeliness, warmth, informality and friendliness - was he not cosy

I was duly informed that the priestly Okeosisi was fierce and feared, brave and boisterous, ebullient and engaging, all at the same time. He could be cosy if he so desired, for he was a man who strenuously laboured to achieve whatever he set his mind to. I asked if he was a politician and was told that indeed, he gave his best and served the whole community without reserve. He was, thus, all things to all men that his purpose might be achieved.

Towards his own people he could have an attitude of bonhomie, but to outsiders he was a warrior who gave no quarter whatsoever to the enemy and would fight to the last drop of his blood. In fact, he died leading his people to victory in the War of the High Noon. When his death was reported, the earth went black in the afternoon and the town of Uduma sneaked in, and in the darkness attacked Okeosisi

The name Okeosisi came from the spirit world of the gods themselves, from a life in the forest trees where the gods lived. It is the forest which nurtured the past pristine culture of the people.

The largest and tallest tree in the forest was Okeosisi. It was regarded as the most benevolent of all creation, reaching up to the clouds. Its top was seen only once a year, at the beginning of the yam planting season, and only by the man with the largest yam farms. He and he alone received this uncanny ability from the gods to see the top of Okeosisi. You can, therefore, imagine the struggle, at the beginning of this dynastic time, amongst all the men in the village to be the one who would earn this prodigious honour straight from the gods.

My ancestors, in the lines of their first sons, for umpteen generations, were reputed to have retained the prize for being the proud owners of the greatest piles of yams stacked in yam barns stretching to over a hundred metres in length and about the same in breadth. Imagine a barn larger than a football field, filled with yams and nothing but yams. For this reason, if no other, my ancestors were found worthy to bear the name, 'Okeosisi', beginning from the earliest, who was reputed to have lived for over a hundred years at a time when humans had not learnt how to count beyond one hundred.

I had promised my Pa that I would seek holiness in the midst of the world, living a celibate life. This was unusual in Okeosisi. Every maiden dreams of the day a prince charming would come calling at her father's house to ask for her hand in marriage; so my case was quite special. It got many tongues wagging. No woman of my age, with a rich family history and a heritage such as mine, would ordinarily be expected to choose to live as a single woman all her days.

No one understood my deepest yearning to dedicate myself to God, living entirely for him. Of course, one of the enduring customs of African people is their penchant for self-sacrifice; whereby the interest of the community is paramount, of greater significance than any personal desires or ambitions. But even in this context of the supremacy of communal interests, a young woman is expected to get married and have a family of her own.

Well, actually my wish to dedicate my life to God is nothing so special after all. Among the early Christians, there were quite a number of women and men who, for supernatural reasons, lived as ordinary lay people, giving all of themselves to help cultivate a Christian culture of morals and virtues in a happy, human society. This mode of living with a supernatural outlook, is extant today.

FOUR

June, 2001

I returned to Nigeria to see Pa Akadike in June, 2001, to tell him my recent experiences at Georgetown University, Washington, D.C.; and of my wish to live a life of celibacy and total self-giving to God in Opus Dei. I had thought I would be married to Bia, the young Ghanaian man who had fallen desperately in love with me and with whom I had hoped to have seventeen children! I had left the U.S. without Bia knowing anything about the incredible happenings in my soul, nor about my travel back to Okeosisit.

The morning after my arrival, I woke up early and before I went to Mass in the morning, I helped to sweep the large compound, beginning with my great-grandmother's kitchen. It was locked so all I could do was sweep the narrow veranda where my Ma sat when the smoke revolted and drove her out of the kitchen. It was the beginning of the rainy season and the grass had started growing here and there, especially behind my Ma's kitchen. I picked a few banana and orange peels off the ground and threw them into a drum reserved for this purpose; it was already half-full. My Ma was particular about the cleanliness of her surroundings and would make sure the refuse was eventually transferred to a compost pit in a farm just behind the compound. I realised that I could not sweep the entire compound before going to Mass and so I stopped halfway.

This was just about when my Ma stepped out of her room to inquire about the noise even though I had tried to be as quiet as possible. Before I could answer, she looked up and saw me. I ran straight into her arms.

"Good morning, Ma," I greeted her.

"My sweet child, God bless you this morning and every morning for as long as you live. But what are you doing sweeping the compound? You arrived only yesterday. Why, I have girls here who help us. Please don't do this again. It's not so bright yet, you should be in bed."

"It's okay, Ma, I only wanted to clean your kitchen for you, and I shall always do this. I also swept the front of Pa's house, and that's all I've done so far. It keeps me close to the land and I enjoy it a lot."

Ma would have none of it and asked me to go back to bed saying that there were other things I could help her with when I came back from Mass.

****

After a breakfast of my favourite boiled yam and beef stew, which I had not had for over two years, Pa said he would like to take me to a site on one of his farms. I did not know what the purpose of the visit was and I was very afraid my Pa might just pass out on the way since he was ninety-six years old and frail. He insisted that we go, but not by foot. One of the young men in the compound, a distant cousin of mine, Chudi, drove us in his car until we were just a few feet away from the intended spot. Pa got out, stretched, lifted his hands in thanksgiving to God and prayed silently. I did not hear him and he did not want me to hear him.

We walked for a while until we came face to face with a huge, very old palm tree, with a canopy of large bunches of palm fruits. It was the grandchild of the palm tree Pa had planted for my mother when my grandfather, Maduka, had brought him my mother's umbilical cord.

It was the custom in Okeosisi that the umbilical cord of every child be safely delivered to the head of the family, who would bury the cord with a palm nut which, in time, would grow into a full palm tree, known as *Nkwu Alo,* the palm tree of the umbilical cord. Very close by, Pa had planted one for me from one of the palm fruits from the tree of my mother's umbilical cord. As to what happened to my own cord and whether or not any of my father's relations planted a palm tree for me, no one knew with any certainty. It was for this reason that Pa had planted one for me, but without the cord accompanying the palm nut. My tree was now two years old, quite young and stout, and had not yet started bearing fruit.

Chudi was agile and with his *ete,* the loop used for climbing the palm tree, he went up and cut down one head of palm fruits from one of the progeny of my mum's *Nkwu Alo.* Pa had moved me with him to a safe spot so the fruits would not fall too close to us. A bunch dropped and not one fruit was dislodged from the bunch by the fall. Pa shouted for joy, and said that this meant that I would live a long life; that I would be strong, and that however I fell - if I fell at all - I would not shatter; and that I would face my problems and overcome them. He was thrilled and laughed uncontrollably. He tried to talk but he choked on the words, and so he stopped. There was so much he wanted to tell me but he did not have the strength to continue. He sat down for about half an hour without saying anything. Then he stood up, supported by his walking stick and aided by Chudi.

Pa gave me a palm fruit and asked me to eat of it and give him the rest. I did and he ate the rest. Then he asked me to take a fresh palm fruit from the bunch and hand it over to him. I did so. Pa then walked further for a while, a distance of about twenty feet, then he made a depression in the ground and asked Chudi to dig a hole there and plant the fruit. He called the fruit *Zim Uzo*, literally meaning, 'show me the way' or 'pathfinder'. Pa blessed me in the fruit and told me that I would always find my path in life; that I would never be lost; that all the glitz and glitter of this world would not choke me and snuff out my virtues. Then we drove home, but not before he stressed that this was to be our special 'Meeting Point'.

Of course, I did not know what Pa meant by 'Meeting Point'. But it did not matter then.

Back at the compound, Pa was shaking as he sat, and I feared that I may be seeing the last of him. But no, he was shaking with joy, not pain. He stood up, moved his body, moved his legs, and then started singing and dancing. Everyone, including my great-grandmother, Ma Nneoma, came out to watch. The great Akadike had not been seen to move his body to any rhythm for ages. This must be a special occasion for him. What was going on? We wondered but we dared not ask as we watched.

I saw my Pa as I had never seen him before. He stood ten feet tall. No, twenty feet was more like it; for he was as tall as the palm tree of my mother's umbilical cord. And he was as solid and as erect. He looked like a god. What was going on?

I wondered. Were my eyes playing games with me, or were they taking me to another world inhabited by tree-men? Palm trees do not walk or dance. There was Pa, not only dancing but actually gyrating, and at ninety-six! He suddenly stopped singing and the music he danced to must be one played by the spirits, not meant for human ears. Pa took me in his arms and I felt tall, at least, my face was at the same level as his, and my hands moved in synchrony with his.

Pa danced with me turning me round and round. Then he steadied me, sat me on a stool nearby and, wonder of wonders, proceeded to dance alone again even more vigorously. Ma Nneoma was perplexed and tried and tried but could not get Pa to stop dancing.

Then he must have heard a bell ringing in his ear for he said, "Who's ringing that bell. What does he want?" Right then we knew that all was not well with Pa. I held him by the waist and started crying. Pa stopped dancing all at once. He could never bear to see me cry and had told me when I was a child that for as long as he lived, I would never cry—that he would never live to see me cry unless he was no longer Akadike Okeosisi. I knew he was not dying yet, at least not now, while I still had tears in my eyes. He wiped them away and held me firmly to his chest as if he wanted to feel my heartbeat. And he did.

"My Chioma, I'm well. Please don't cry."

"Okay, Pa, I'll stop crying. But you frightened us all and we began to fear the worst."

"Chioma, you left America to come and see me and be with me, having travelled thousands of miles. Don't you think the Good Lord will keep me, at least, until you leave? No, the Good Lord will spare me yet."

It was evening and Pa, clearly worn out by all this frenetic activity, trudged to his *obiriama*, the outdoor hut of a living room typical of Igbo homes, where the family meets, visitors are received, meetings held and feasts celebrated. He asked for water. He drank his fill from his big cup which holds about a litre of water, palm wine, whisky or whatever else he might choose to drink. He always used this cup, *iko*, a natural product made from the gourd of a climbing plant. Somehow, the family was able to anticipate how far to fill the cup, depending on Pa's mood — whether it was one of anger, or celebration, and whether to serve water, palm wine or anything else. If palm wine, his *iko* was filled to the brim, and if water, just halfway.

Pa drank the water and wanted some more. Then he asked Ma for boiled yam with fresh palm oil and some dried fish peppersoup.

"Udo," she said, (my great-grandparents fondly called each other, 'Udo', meaning peace) "do you want to eat everything in this world all at once? You want yam, and peppersoup too. This is a bit too much. Why don't I just give you boiled yam with palm oil? Peppersoup will be too hot for you now. You're already sweating. You're an old man, you know. You must calm down. We know your dear Chioma is here and she makes you so happy. You're doing things you haven't done since you were seventy. But you are not seventy now. You are almost a hundred and all your dancing and so on is a big worry for me. I'm not young myself. Please, my loving husband, great Akadike of Okeosisi, Lion of the Forests, my very own Peace, God be with you. We beg you, for now, just try and slow down a bit so that you can pray for Chioma when she's going back to America."

"Okay, okay, Udo, give me what you can. The water has cooled me down," he said.

"Thank you, Udo, thank you. And thanks be to God," she replied.

After Pa had his boiled yam with palm oil, we sat with him for a while before he turned in for the night. Who knew what would happen that night which seemed so pregnant with vast forests of lively and delightful destinies?

Morning came and Pa called me to his room. We were alone, just the two of us.

"Chioma, my very own child, I had a dream last night and I saw you. You were with me and whatever it is you want to tell me this morning before you go back to America, I already know. You told me everything in the dream. And that you may not doubt me, it has to do with your decision to go and live in a place called Nesbit Centre. You told me everything and I have only given you this hint so that you might know that what I saw in the dream was really true. There are three things I want to tell you and please promise me you will keep them all the days of your life."

"Pa, you know me: you know I always do what you tell me, and this will not be an exception. I'll do what you ask of me."

"Very good, my child, I know there will never be another Okeosisi quite like you, for you have been set apart for a life in the spirit world and in the world of humans transformed by the same spirit. You will see what others do not see and be able to do with relative ease what others cannot begin to attempt."

"Pa, please don't talk like this. You frighten me and make me think you're saying your last words to me."

"Don't be afraid, Chioma. Now please listen and listen very carefully. You're going to suffer and suffer greatly. I want you to accept suffering, for the path to true happiness passes by the way of suffering. Remember, the palm tree I planted for you is called Pathfinder, the one that leads the way. Well, my dear, the way for you is suffering.

"Chioma, my very own, you know you belong to me just as you belong to God. And all through your life, you've been very close to me and have always paid heed to whatever I told you. More than that, even though you now live in America, you are still as African, as Igbo, as you were when you were with us here in our country. You've not lived in Igboland at all, yet you have assimilated the culture and nuances of our people, particularly those that have to do with respect for your parents and elders, hard work, sincerity and steadfastness. When an Igbo man gives you his word, you can be sure he will keep it no matter what may happen."

With '419' so prevalent in Nigeria, and with *Ndigbo*, as active participants, why did my Pa say this? Did he not know what was going on? Sure in his days, what he said was true, but not in 2001. But it was neither the time nor the place to contradict my Pa, so I kept my opinion to myself.

"Well, Pa, you taught me all that. I'm only trying to live as you would like me to live, and not disappoint you."

"That's right, my dear, but life is full of treacheries that you cannot begin to imagine. You're a loyal friend. I've seen how you stand by your friends Nwanma and Buihe: you always come to their defence whenever anyone attacks them. Do you understand what this means? It means, my dear, that you must choose your friends carefully. Once you call anyone your friend, make sure, make absolutely sure that he or she is someone you'll be prepared to die for. Choose your friends carefully.

"I know you won't be married because marriage, as you said, with all its joys and grandeur, is not for you. You've chosen to live a life of apostolic celibacy, giving yourself completely to God, to serve him with your entire mind, all your strength, all your heart, all your body and soul. This is a huge task that calls for unimaginable grace and assistance and, of course, suffering. You will suffer a lot for your friends."

"Please, Pa, pray for me, then; pray for me fervently for, as you have rightly said, life is full of treacheries, of unknown land mines of sin and betrayal lying in wait for us. Please, Pa, pray for me."

"You know only too well, Chioma, my own little girl, that you will ever live in my heart; and my life, as long as I have it, is one continuous prayer for you, rising to the presence of the Almighty that you may live out your dream.

"Finally, above all, love. Open up your heart to everyone, and love. Love without ceasing. This would also involve suffering, for there's no love without suffering. The measure of our love is the measure of the extent to which we suffer for the one we love. Of course, love calls for friendship and loyalty. So there you are, I have given you all I can possibly give you on this earth. My prayer now is that when I die, I shall be able to make it to the presence of the Almighty so that I can help you even better from there in the Communion of the Saints."

I listened intently to Pa, with all the fears of a child looking at a loved one whom she might not see again. His talk of seeing me in a dream filled me with the premonition that something momentous was at hand. Everything he had said was exactly what I had wanted to tell him. Lost in total astonishment, I simply repeated what my Pa had said

"Pa, you have indeed given me everything a father could give his child; and, as you have said, you saw me in a dream spending my life in total self-giving to God, serving him on earth as he wants me to serve him, wherever he wants me to serve him, and in whatever capacity he wants me to serve him. Thank you, Pa, and may you live many more years for me so that I can learn more from you, so much more."

"My dear sweet child, my own very own, my Chioma, God bless you. God be with you. God...."

"Pa, Pa, Pa," I called out but Pa gave no response. He had passed on to eternal joy while he held my right hand. He was warm. He wore a smile on his face. His life was complete. It was Saturday, June 9, 2001.

FIVE

After I had managed to tell my Ma Nneoma that Pa had passed on, I called my mother on my cell phone and told her what had happened. Then she told my father, who then called my grandpa living in Enugu after his retirement from Obafemi Awolowo University, Ile-Ife.

My Grandpa Maduka, the first son of my Pa, arrived the following day. He was driven in his car by his loyal driver of over ten years, Bolarinwa, whom he had brought with him from Ife. His ash-grey Toyota Camry had just come through the gates when I ran out to the car, opened his door, buried my head in his lap and wept uncontrollably.

My grandfather was everything to me. I was so fortunate to have such a wonderful man as my grandpa. He must have been a tremendous lover for he had irretrievably fallen in love with my grandma, Adiaha, on their first meeting and they were married six months later.

Grandpa studied at the University College, Ibadan, and, in fact, lived with grandma off campus, in Mokola. After graduation, he took his Ph.D. at the renowned University of Uppsala, Sweden; my grandma was with him. Then off they went to the States for his post-doctoral fellowship, finally returning to Nigeria in 1976. My parents — my mother is Grandpa Maduka's daughter — were married not long after, in 1982. Of course, all this was history to me and my siblings. Grandma, whom we saw more often back when we were younger and she came to Lagos to take care of my mother, childbirth after childbirth, in true Igbo tradition, regaled us with tales of her life at Ife with Grandpa.

As a child, I wanted very much to be like my grandma and make someone a good wife just as she did. Grandpa would never let me rest on my oars, ever challenging me to greater heights, above all, to seek sanctity in all I did. Oh, he is ever so charming. A professor of organic chemistry, he is a true scholar in the old academic tradition, with interests in the arts, music, literature, sports and all things interesting. He is well-read and never stops reading. I think I owe much of my talent in painting to my grandpa.

He is as Igbo as you could get. He satisfactorily married his Western education with his noble Igbo heritage, very much like my great-grandfather, his father. He wanted me to be as Igbo as ever in America - in culture and outlook, taking the best that my new environment in the States offered, never forgetting my roots. So, here I was with my loving grandpa to perform the obsequies of my Pa, his dear father.

When Grandpa arrived a day after Pa Akadike had passed on, before Uncle Obidike had time to inform him, the compound broke out in uncontrollable weeping and wailing. They were all caught off guard and wondered just how my grandpa could have heard of Pa's death so quickly. If he had said that he had heard it from my side of the family; that is, from his daughter, Onyebuchi, my mother, they would have had my scalp. Grandpa put their minds at rest when he told them he had heard of it through a source in the village, Chief Kalu, an old man loved and widely respected. No one dared ask how this chief himself came upon the news. This was not true, of course, but my grandpa had apprised Chief Kalu of how he got to know of Pa's death and how he planned to use the chief's name to save me from apparent vilification.

I wept uncontrollably in my Grandpa Maduka's embrace. He held me close, as if his life depended on the measure with which he grasped me. I did not see his face, as we each looked over the other's shoulder, but I felt his sobs, if not his tears. Then he pulled away from me, wiped my face with the palm of his right hand and we headed for the family *obiriama*. Grandpa, much like my Pa, sat me on his lap. He always carried me like a child. He had sat me on his lap ever since I could remember and this mournful occasion was no exception. In fact, the sadness made me look all the more like a child needing all the consolation she could get. We were wrapped in each other's arms for a long time, neither of us saying a word. When he felt that I was better at peace with myself, he left me to be with my great-grandmother, my Ma Nneoma.

A day after he arrived, I told my grandpa that I had to go back to the States and return to Okeosisi two days before the burial. Grandpa listened to me attentively and then replied:

"Chioma, you don't know what you're saying - you would leave Pa here in a cold mortuary without the benefit of your company!"

I was taken aback by these words. I did not know what to say. Was I being insensitive to the situation? I waited for Grandpa Maduka to continue.

"Papa wants you to be here until his funeral ceremonies are over. In fact, he wants to see you everyday until he is buried. That is to say, you will spend time with him at a place he said both of you know very well - he called it your special 'Meeting Point' - talking to him, singing about his life. He said we need not worry about what you'll say, as he would guide you through that. There's more, but you now know you'll not be returning to Chevy Chase in a hurry; at least not until after Papa's burial. I'll tell Oke and Buchi that you'll be here till they arrive, and then you'll go back to the States with them."

This was more than an earful! It became clear to me that Pa Akadike intended to live on through me, with his soul living in my soul, two of us becoming one! I was beginning to better understand the meaning of "Communion of the Saints". I surprised myself by what I said next.

"Grandpa, I thank my God I was born into this wonderful family, and I am eternally grateful to my Pa, to you, to my parents, for all the values and the sense of being you have all inculcated in me. You see, Pa has just given me all the ingredients of joy and peace in seeking holiness in the midst of the world. He wants me to be in this world but not of the world. He is united with me so that I would continue life in typical Akadike style. Ah! I'm a happy woman! And I shall live a life of virtue in apostolic celibacy. This is as wonderful as it gets."

"Chioma, what are you saying? Am I to understand that you will start with the means of formation that would prepare you to be a faithful of Opus Dei on your return to the States? Is that what you are saying?"

"Precisely, Grandpa, that's what I'm saying."

"When did you come to this decision? And how? Have you told your parents? Who else knows?"

"Well, this is really a long story. I could well write a book on this. No one else knows. The first person I told, the only one who knew and took this message to his death, was Pa. I believe it was the unbearably thrilling joy of hearing that I would live a celibate life that caused his heart to collapse. Pa died in great joy; he has passed on to heaven, there to sing hosanna, hosanna, to the Lord."

Grandpa laughed hard.

"So you 'killed' Pa!"

He continued laughing. I joined him, given my new role in Pa's passage to heaven.

"Now it all makes sense. That's not at all unusual, after all he's ninety-six years old and his heart, as robust as it was, could just go kaput at any time, especially were he to hear something as astounding as your choosing a life in Opus Dei. All that your dad, Oke, told me was that you were sitting with Pa when he died. That's all I knew. We're lucky he lived so long. Now let me tell you my own story of you and Pa, all based on what he himself told me. It's a long story, though."

"Please, Grandpa, go on. This is all like a dream to me."

"Like yours, it's a long story, and like yours, I might have to write a book just devoted to this story, for it's as noble as it's marvellously inspirational. Well, let me cut it short and just give you the gist of it."

"Grandpa, please don't cut it short. Write a book if you like but please tell me everything. Ever since I arrived here about five days ago, everyone has been calling me *Agunwanyi*, *Omekannaya*. And when I tell them that I don't understand what these words mean, they say, 'Don't worry, one day you will know.' It seems that day has arrived. Please what do these words mean? I have a faint idea, but as you know, my Igbo is not so good."

"Chioma, you make me laugh. You're so forthright. Let me first disgorge my mind of what Pa said of you and what he saw in you. You know, he gave you your name, and he chose it carefully. He said he had an enduring dream of a girl born into this family through his granddaughter, Onyebuchi, your own mother. He had seen that this girl would be great, greater than any other person of her generation. Above all, the gods had ordained this child as a child of the heavens belonging to the gods themselves.

"Well, you know, by the time you were born Papa had become a Christian, a Roman Catholic. But he had had this dream for a long, long time - even before I was born. When he converted to Christianity, he realized that the gods of his dream were symbols of the Almighty God and therefore, he paid greater attention to the dream. Of course, you have proven the gods right, or shall I say, you have proven that you're a child of God and that you're eager to serve him with all your will and your strength and you have put the talents he endowed you with to immeasurable use."

"Grandpa, I believe what you are telling me because they have happened and are still happening. But, Grandpa, I shall keep reminding you of my disabling defects, monsters out to get me, if I relent in my struggles for the virtues."

"Well, let's leave your demons, your errors, aside for now. Pa saw all of them too before giving you this role you're now to play. Briefly, Papa believed that the Almighty God has chosen you to serve him in a special way. Papa read this to mean that you have been set apart to accomplish many things, not limited by the ordinary traditions of Igboland. He believed that you will change history; or, put differently, that a whole new history would begin with you and that you would forge new traditions with your total self-giving."

"How is one young woman going to be able to do all this? Am I Joan of Arc? I'm sorry; I just need my faith to be stronger. Oh God, increase my faith."

"Don't worry. You're now the Forge, where characters are formed : that is why it can be understood if you're called, *Omekannaya* .Literally, it means someone who does things exactly like the father. You know, ordinarily, a man may be assumed to be just like his father, so you don't usually find a man being called, Omekannaya. It is reserved for a woman who bears the name of her father with great pride and acts just like her father. It is, thus, a great honour for a woman to be given that name.

"Traditionally, it deals with mere earthly actions. But raise your eyes and look up to heaven and then ask yourself, what does it mean if I, Chioma, act like my father in heaven, and do things the way he does? It's in this light that Papa wanted us to set aside the hallowed age-old Igbo traditions as they affect your position in this family. And he wants to make the statement that a woman of merit, imbued with inviolable virtues, can do anything she wants to do in Igboland, within bounds of course."

"So, Grandpa, what is it that Pa wants me to do?"

"I've already told you some of it; such as, you have to be with him till he's buried. But the important point for you to grasp is that Papa believed so much in you that he wanted you to take over the Akadike dynasty, not through having children in marriage, as I learnt you had planned - and not through living the religious life of a nun, like St. Theresa, as wonderful as that is - but through giving yourself completely to serving the Almighty God in your daily ordinary professional life and fulfilling your daily Christian duties as an exemplary Catholic. And he strongly believed that this was the highest attainment for any child of his, male or female."

"Grandpa, you're turning this into more than it's meant to be, I'm sure. I'm human. I'm weak. And my mind wanders from one thought to the other, seeking a firm iroko tree to alight upon. Alas! Iroko trees are not easy to come by. So, my mind continues in flight. And maybe you don't see all my pitfalls, my pride, my hotheadedness, irascibility, impatience, intolerance, and so on. All you see are my academic achievements and my paintings. No, Grandpa, I need a lot of formation. I am hopeful my life in Opus Dei, if I'm accepted, will help me struggle better to live the virtues, in the ordinary circumstances of my daily life."

"Chioma, my dear, you don't have to worry too much. Yes, I sense it when you're being unduly difficult, bent on having your own way, being unsympathetic and all that. You know, we've had lots of talks on this and I can see you're truly struggling to be better. I pray this continues. Pa died in your arms holding on to his love for you, the best gift he could have given to anyone in his life."

"Grandpa, it may be so, but I was just a child in his arms. And all my life he's borne me in his arms, lifting me, and swinging me around and around. Nothing in my life gave me as much joy as having Pa lift me. When he died in my arms, I was totally devastated at first. I wondered who would bear me and lift me up? Who? I felt lost."

"Chioma, you've said it excellently. The greatest joy you ever had was to have Papa lift you. And what do you think he's doing now? You always sat on his right hand, his mighty strong right hand .What do you think he's doing right now if not lifting you to the high heavens to be unspoiled, unsullied, as sparkling and as delightful as a diamond? You now see why you are *Agunwanyi, Omekannaya*. Oh, *Agunwanyi* means a lion of a woman, an invincible woman .You are all this and more.

"Pa easily surmised that the dream he had must have some spiritual significance, after he became a Catholic, and should not be dismissed as a mere wish of the gods of his ancestors. As you can see, he was right. And that's why he died in your arms. What other evidence do you want?"

SIX

Grandpa asked me to accompany him to inform Igwe of Pa's passing. Pa had taken me to Igwe's palace when I was only ten and I cannot quite remember what it looked like then. But judging from the age and looks of some of the buildings and walls, I would say much of the structure of the old palace was still in place. There were three rows of walls around the palace: first a mud wall, about four feet high and nine inches thick, an ardent reminder to all that Okeosisi was one of the few towns in Igboland that had a traditional ruler of its own before the colonial incursion into Nigeria. Legend has it that cannons could not penetrate this mud wall, and that it had been built by the spirits that watched over Okeosisi. I wondered how this craggy-looking wall survived the heavy rainfalls of the land, not to speak of cannon fire, but I had learnt not to ask too many questions about what the spirits could, or could not, do.

Abutting on the mud wall, was a modern brick wall about nine feet high and nine inches thick, with a roll of electrical wiring along the top for security, a massive iron gate, barring any intrusion, in which the insignia of Igwe was engraved.

Grandpa rang the bell and the stern face of a security guard appeared in an opening in the side door. Since we had an appointment, he had been directed to let us in when we arrived.

Grandpa knew his way around the palace and made straight for the main two-storey mansion standing a hundred foot high in the centre of the grounds. It was as massive as it was aesthetically inviting. We passed through two large halls with tiled floors, obviously for large gatherings. We were finally ushered into a smaller room, in elegant beige furnishings. There were four high-back chairs in the room, one bedecked with jewels, definitely Igwe's. There were also a set of Kano leather cushions, four seats and a three-seater settee. The room was so cosy, so intimate, made for quiet, pleasant conversations. Grandpa told me this was where Igwe received his closest friends, in an atmosphere of moderate pageantry and royalty.

We were gracefully ensconced in our seats, Grandpa and I chose to sit in the settee. Drinks were served while we waited. Grandpa had his favourite Gulder and I had a Coke. I had time to study one of the paintings: it was the one I had given to the *Ikemba* I through my Pa. I felt great!

Twenty minutes or so later, Igwe Ikemba II made a majestic entrance, dressed in a white long-tailed, long-sleeved shirt with a folded red handkerchief tucked into the breast pocket, blue trousers and shiny black shoes. To complete his royal costume, Igwe wore three strings of coral beads around his neck and a simple red felt hat; in his right hand he held his traditional whisk. His royal fan, richly-feathered bore his title and insignia and was resting at the foot of his chair, together with what seemed to be an elephant tusk. One of his chiefs accompanied him. Grandpa identified him as Chief Ogadinma, the head chief of Okeosisi. We rose briskly with greetings of I-GWEE, I-GWEE, I-GWEE. Igwe responded by shaking the whisk briskly. I duly genuflected in warm respect. Then Grandpa greeted him, singing his praises.

"Eze, Lord of all Kings; Face and Power of Okeosisi, Killer of Lions, King anointed by the god of Life, Light of the

People; Fierce Lightning of the Skies; Big Soul of Man, I salute you. I greet you. I honour you. Forever and ever I shall serve you with all my strength. I shall fight any fight, climb any mountain, cross the oceans, to bring honour to you, Great One, and to Okeosisi, great land of my birth, land of giants."

Igwe smiled responding to the greetings by briskly shaking the whisk. Before Grandpa continued his speech, we were presented with two kola nuts from Igwe. Grandpa was given one and the head chief, Chief Ogadinma, proceeded with the ceremony of breaking the other kola nut, with loud prayers, invoking the intercession of the ancestors. The kola nut broke into three cotyledon, a sign of majesty and distinguished accomplishments. Igwe was pleased and seemed more attentive to Grandpa's address.

"Igwe, fabulous Igwe, marvellous Igwe, The Big Heart of our people; Great Igwe, priceless Work of the gods, the Legend of Okeosisi, we are here to inform you that my father, Chief Akadike Okeosisi, has been transported to the heaven of the Almighty God to join the Communion of the Saints. Proud Ruler of all of Okeosisi and beyond, including all of Ijeobi, I bow before you.

"With me here is my granddaughter, Chioma. Some of her paintings hang in your palace. They were given by my late father to Igwe Ikemba, your late father."

"Pa Akadike is the Legend of Okeosisi; Great Warrior; strong and powerful; the tallest iroko tree in our glorious forest; the most courageous son Okeosisi has ever produced. The history of our people is all wrapped up in his personality. He was a wonderful man. My father loved him and proudly decorated him with the highest honour of Okeosisi as the foremost chief in his cabinet. The colonial government could not help but show their deep respect for this valiant voice of his people. Oh! We will miss him. His life will be fully celebrated. The ancient spiritual drums of Okeosisi and our brave, victorious guns will all boom in his honour. Make all the necessary arrangements and keep me fully informed. All my chiefs will come to the funeral. Akadike deserves no less. So go on and may the Almighty God give you the strength and the fortitude you need at this time. I have heard quite a lot about you, Chioma, my daughter. Okeosisi greets you warmly and is proud of you. Keep up the good work in the States. And make sure you come and see me before you go back."

"Great Igwe, all would be done as you have directed. It will be a mammoth celebration, the likes of which Okeosisi has never seen. We thank you. I shall come with Chioma to see you before she returns to the States, "Grandpa Maduka heartily replied..

SEVEN

The day of Pa's burial began with a funeral Mass at Christ the King's Cathedral, Okeosisi. The Catholic Bishop of Okeosisi the Most Reverend Anthony Okoli, preached the homily. He told the congregation that he had a friend in Baltimore, Maryland, in the United States, Dr. Jerry Finecountry from Bonny, a former classmate of his from primary school through secondary school, who was now a physician at Johns Hopkins. They saw each other once a year; both taking turns to travel to visit each other year after year. He had just returned from visiting his friend and Jerry had suggested that they watch the movie, 'Meet Joe Black'.

"Well, I agreed and, indeed, it was a learning experience for me. What struck me was the character, 'Death', or Joe Black (played by the actor Brad Pitt), who had come to take the chairman and chief executive of a top media company, Mr. William Parrish. Wherever William (Bill) went, there was Joe. And so Joe accompanied Bill to board meetings, although he was not a board member, and was never introduced to other members of the board. So no one knew who he was, except Bill, of course. At a board meeting to consider an offer by a competitor to buy Bill's firm, Drew, one of the board members, said, 'We all know the deal is as certain as death and taxes.' Joe Black had not heard this expression before and so wondered aloud, 'Death and taxes? What an odd pairing!'

"I'd rather not go into all the details of the movie for they really do not concern us here but toward the end, Mr. Drew got the board to force Bill out and to get him to take a mandatory retirement at sixty-five. Bill was to turn sixty-five not long after this board meeting. This was where Bill played his ace, for he got Mr. Joe Black to reveal to all the members of the board, to Drew's total consternation, the details of how Drew had been cheating on his taxes. With this revelation, Drew had to resign from the board, and Bill got to keep his position as chief executive. Drew turned to Joe Black and said, 'And who would've thought you to be an IRS (Internal Revenue Service) agent.'

"Joe gave it back to him: 'Death and Taxes.' The joke was on Drew who did not know that Joe was Death.

"My dear people of God, Chief Akadike Okeosisi told me years ago that work, any kind of wholesome work, was an avenue for sanctity; and that everyone is called to be holy. He said there are millions of ordinary people on earth, and there must also be millions of ordinary people as saints in heaven. He said he paid his taxes; that he paid his dues; that he worked hard, and that everything he did he offered to God. So as he paid his taxes on earth, he also made investments in heaven to be enjoyed after death.

"Death comes to us all, but if you have made your investments in heaven, through the offerings you made to God while still alive, then death becomes an avenue for you to reap your rich dividends, the richest dividend of all - to see God face to face."

The casket containing Pa's body was driven from the church to the grave site. It was time for the 'ashes-to-ashes — dust-to-dust' ritual. In respect of my Pa's wishes, I threw in the first soil from the 'venerable' area of my 'palm of birth', the Meeting Point for Pa and I; then Fr. Ben, Ma Nneoma, Grandpa and the rest of the family threw in some sand, according to age. The whole Akadike clan was there.

****

"Will you marry me and be the mother of our seventeen children, nine girls, eight boys?" I turned, not believing my ears or the words I thought I heard. He repeated himself, this time in a more assured manner as though he knew my answer would be yes.

"Will you, Chioma, take me, Bia Thompson, to be your wedded husband, from this day forward…" I could not let him finish these words of marital union, for I was totally confounded.

"Chioma, you seem to have forgotten. Who was the first person to raise this issue of marriage? You. Who said she wanted seventeen children? You. Who said the children would comprise nine girls and eight boys? You. So, come on

Chioma. Let's get on with it. You know when you left Chevy Chase to come to Okeosisi to see your great-grandfather — at least that's what your dad told me — I was so thrilled I could not eat for two days. I was sure you had gone home to tell the old *baba* about our plans.

"Bia, this is neither the time nor the place for you to talk like this. Here we are, at the grave side of my Pa, and all you can think of is marriage. You can see the coffin has just been laid in the grave. Can you not wait till the burial is over?"

"Chioma it's a long story that will use up a good-night's sleep to tell. Well, it will wait for now. I'll give you some time to grieve and be sorrowful, for our sorrows do give birth to new joys, undreamed of, unimaginable joys. I return to the States in two days time. So you have the rest of today to weep, tomorrow my love will flow all over your face and wash away all your tears. And we shall be one."

****

"My Pa, my great Pa, the earth of my *Nkwu Alo* that you named *Zim Uzo*, 'Show Me The Way', or 'Pathfinder', now finds you and will show you the way to your heavenly inheritance. And now I know why this bit of soil is priceless to you. May your good soul rest in peace." These were my last words to my Pa as I threw the soil on his burnished mahogany coffin.

****

I went to see my Pa every day before the burial, to be with him and talk to him as he had wished, at the place he had chosen, Our Special Meeting Point, beside my *Nkwu Alo*. I

drove myself there in a Peugeot station wagon my grandpa
left at home for running errands. Fifteen years old and it was
still going strong. I declined my grandpa's offer for Chudi to
drive me there as I wanted to be with Pa alone, with no other
family member present.

The first day, I arrived at our Meeting Point and found the
ground around the palm tree Pa had planted for me from my
mother's *Nkwu Alo* strewn with dry palm branches that had
fallen from the tree over time. I cleared an area around the
tree and sat down. It was morning, around 9am. The sun was
up, but clouds drew a curtain over the rays, shielding them
from view.

I really did not know what to do, what to say, when to
speak, what my Pa would say to me. Would he be the one to
speak first and then I reply? My mind was racing as these
thoughts weighed on it. I sat and waited for promptings from
my Pa. After a long wait, I thought I should break the silence.

"My Pa, my own Pa, my one and only Pa, here I am to be
with you and keep you company for a while. As you know - I
think where you are now you would know - in the beginning,
I had protested that I did not want to come here everyday
because I had wanted to return to the States. There's a
painting, roaming in my mind, not knowing how to take form
and appear on canvas. So many thoughts are going on at the
same time in my mind, and I had wanted to go back and
begin the sketches for this painting.

"But now I'm so happy to have this honour of being with
you, to talk to you, for I have so much to tell you so that you
can help me. Pa, Pa, are you listening? You haven't said a
word. Please tell me that you are or show me a sign to let me

know. Or do you want me to keep my big mouth shut and listen for your voice?"

I kept my big mouth shut. My Pa said nothing to me for over an hour. So I left and drove back home. I shook with fear all the way home. My throat was dry and I was ready to burst into tears. I could not find my voice even when I wanted to express my inexplicable pain. Here I was, going through an experience I would have described as a horrific experience if it had not involved my Pa. Whatever may be the fate of the dead, I was sure my Pa would not want to frighten me, at least, not on this day, my first visit to say hello to him. So what was the meaning of all this?

Grandpa eagerly awaited my return and was with my great-grandmother in the *obiriama*. He must have sensed the tumult in my mind or I must have looked like a ghost to him for he rushed out and held me firmly. He discovered I was actually shivering, weeping. I told him Pa had abandoned me, or was simply testing my faith.

"Don't worry. Don't worry at all, Chioma. I'm sure that in time Papa will talk to you at length and explain his absence or should I say silence today. It seems a mystery, but then we'll know and it will no longer be a mystery. Papa will lead us to the truth; he always has, and he always will."

I took some comfort in Grandpa's words and regained my composure. I felt wonderful. In fact, because my family had shown me so much love, and sometimes love comes with tons and tons of mysteries, I awaited what might confront me with a good measure of confidence and courage. As long as it came from my Pa, I would be able to handle it, I told myself.

I visited my Pa the following day as early as 8 a.m. in case he had thought I was late the first time. I just could not sleep that night, and I wanted to meet my Pa and stay with him till he revealed to me what was going on. I felt that I might just leave for the United States if he said nothing on this second day. But my Pa said nothing in response to all my pleas. However, I did not leave Okeosisi. Rather, I went back home and started wracking my brains about what Pa might have in mind. And I came up with an idea: Pa must have sensed that his death would fill me with so much sorrow and pain that for the rest of my life I would like to forget he ever died in my arms; and he had insisted that I stay with him just so I would remember. It occurred to me that, with the passing on of my Pa into eternity, research on my Ph.D. thesis with the inconceivable title of *The African Spirit Unlimited in Time and Space* had commenced. That Pa wanted me to grieve as much as I could, to mourn like I had never mourned and to be completely immersed in death and dying, so that I could speedily arrive at my final destination, in the resurrection.

With this insight in mind, I went to see Pa the next day. Still, he said nothing to me. Day after day after day until the seventh day after his death, when he woke up, as it were, and recognized me at our Meeting Point.

"Chioma, how are you?" my Pa asked me.

"How do you expect me to be when you won't talk to me and yet you want to see me; is it fair? Why are you treating me like this, Pa?"

I started crying, giving free rein to the deep anxiety that had been welling up in me all these days. Then I remembered what my Pa had told me that he would not live to see me cry. Well, he was no more, and I could cry, couldn't I?

I heard my Pa laughing, having read my thoughts.

"Do you think that I do not have life in me now and that you can cry? Well go ahead, cry; if you believe that my life is over, go ahead and cry to your heart's content then and I'll just lie here and keep quiet."

I tried to gain control of myself now that Pa had beguiled me into accepting his living death. He was dead, surely, but I believed that he lived on in the Communion of the Saints and so I should not cry. I responded to this assurance:

"I'm sorry, Pa, I won't cry anymore. No you're not really dead in the sense we know it, for I'm still alive and you live on in me."

"That's my wonderful girl. You're my own Chioma, sent by the gods to bring the Akadike life cycle to a heroic conclusion. Now let me put your mind at rest."

If you thought my Pa's words could be heard by one and all, then you are wrong. Pa was not actually using 'words' to talk to me: Pa's face appeared in space, about five feet above the ground I looked deeply into his silent, solemn face in the distance, and I could hear him speak to my heart. I listened to his voice in spiritual joy.

"Now, my dear, let me tell you a story," Pa continued. "There was a man crossing a river. Not a river but a stream, in fact. When he started crossing, he could see the bank on the other side, not more than a minute's walk and at no point was the stream more than ankle-deep. As he stepped into the stream, he noticed that it was suddenly growing bigger, broader, but still not deep. He started crossing and what used to be a stream steadily grew into a river, bigger and deeper. He noticed that if he tried to return to his starting point, the river went deeper but if he continued he could keep his head above the water.

"He was afraid and asked himself what this strange turn of events could mean. He wondered, 'How could this stream whose bottom I could see, with its stones and pebbles and plant-life suddenly turn into a river? How could this stream which I have crossed so many times before grow so gigantic that I'm being swallowed up. I can look across and see the same old trees, and the buildings are still the same. In fact, everything is the same except for the stream that has become a river!'

"Towards the end, just as he was about to step out of the river, it grew even deeper and the water rose up to his neck. He was drowning and tried to swim, but he couldn't, he did not know how to swim."

'Is this the end of me?' he wondered. 'What's going on? I'm done for!'

"Then he heard a voice from the river, 'Come to me and I'll save you. The crossing which you thought would take you no more than a minute has taken you the better part of the day, and worse still, you're about to drown and die. Don't you think this whole thing is strange?'

'Did you say strange? This is all a mystery to me,' the man replied.

"Again he heard the voice: 'Come to me and I'll save you. I'll carry you across the river to your destination on the other side.'

"Unbelievably, the man was not pleased at all, and pleaded with the voice: 'Why don't you just change the river back to a stream instead so that I can then cross to the other side on my own, without you showing off your magical superhuman powers? Please, I beg you, just restore the stream's normal size and proportions and I'll be fine. You created this whole mess, so why don't you solve the problem, and I'll be fine.'

"By this time, the man was berserk, but he would not go with the wishes of the voice from the river.

'Okay, have it your way,' the voice responded indignantly, 'I'll show you who's the boss here and you will taste my powers fully and, I assure you, it will be a bitter meal for you.'

'Do whatever you like, I won't come to you and have you carry me across. You won't manipulate me and dictate to me. Call yourself whatever you like. I've found myself in this mysterious situation. You're not the origin of mystery. If this is the work of God, then all is well and good. Let it consume me because then my drowning, nay my death, would be part of the great mystery of the universe. So let me die.'

"And the man died!"

Pa did not say one more word. His face was still there. He did not communicate anything more to me. I called him, "Pa, Pa." But he would not answer. Then, I realised I was on my own.

Pa must want me to try and make meaning of all he had told me. But where do I begin?

EIGHT

I went to my Pa the following day. I greeted him and sang his praises as I had never done before. I did not know where the words came from but listening to me, you would think I was singing to my God. And why not, we see God in one another, do we not?

"Pa, please tell me the meaning of the story you narrated to me yesterday. Why did the man drown? Why did he die? He did what his conscience told him to do, what he thought was right; why then did he die? There he was, engulfed in a mystery - the stream growing bigger and bigger and deeper and deeper and taking so much time for him to cross and just as he was about to step on land, the river grew even deeper and drowned him! This was a mystery, beyond human comprehension. I would have done exactly what he did."

Pa spoke and my eyes sparkled. I mean I felt my eyes sparkle since I could not see my own eyes.

"You said two things, Chioma. One, that you would have done exactly what he did."

"Yes, Pa, I would not yield to anyone giving me commands, especially after the person had set up what I consider a total mystery."

"Yes, I believe you would do just as the man did. But there was something else you said, I don't remember what it was."

"Pa, I said that too much of his time was taken up crossing the river."

"Yes, that's it. Did you say 'time'?"

"Yes, Pa, I said so."

"Well, now, you have it: time embedded in mystery. Let me tell you another story similar to the one you've already heard. It's about a palm wine tapper. He climbed up a palm tree, made a hole in the tree and began tapping wine. The good wine flowed out till it filled the two jars he had brought with him. Still, more wine flowed. He plugged the hole and went home to get more jars.

"He brought all the jars he had - four of them - ready for the river-like flow of the palm wine. On his way to the farm where the palm tree was he heard a voice:

'You will need about twenty jars more, each as big as my mouth.'

"He did not know what to make of this but he did not heed the voice and simply continued on his way since he did not have twenty jars neither did he know the size of the mouth speaking to him. He climbed up the palm tree again, unplugged the hole, and was able to fill all four jars. The wine continued gushing out of the tree, but there was nothing he could do. He sealed the hole, went home and invited his relations and friends to a palm wine party.

"While they were at the party, the mystery palm tree walked over to the scene of the party and gushed some more, wine flowing all the way to the ground. Everybody ran away, cursing the man who had invited them. But the palm tree ran even faster than they did until it stood in front of the crowd now held spellbound by fear and bewilderment."

'Good people of Amakohia, I greet you,' it shouted loudly, over and over again, till its voice was heard by the entire village. The villagers came running to the source of this spectacular greeting.

'I made Duru, your son, your renowned palm-wine tapper, an offer I thought was irresistible but he turned me down. I'm here to reward him.'

"He said nothing further and the people were all bewildered. 'Since when do palm trees walk? Since when do palm trees talk?' they wondered."

Pa went quiet and I did not want to press him to speak. I had learnt that his protracted silences contained hidden messages of wisdom. When Pa said nothing more after an hour or so, I left.

****

"Chioma, my sweet child, let's talk about time. What is time? Tell me. Oh, before I forget, Duru was rewarded with six jars of palm wine every week, for the rest of his life from the same tree, now ageless."

That was my Pa speaking again. I went to see him the following day, rather displeased with myself that I could not make out what was going on in my Pa's mind since I had prided myself in having acquired his soul. So where was his soul now? Was it still in me or had it gone back to its original owner? How do I answer Pa now that the two of us were of the same mindset, thinking along similar lines? What is time?

"Pa, the issue of time is a timeless proposition. Time is a creation and could be considered a mystery."

What my Pa meant I did not know, but I trusted he would teach me what he wanted me to know about time.

"Chioma, you see, the man crossing the river, Dibia was his name, what he thought would take one minute to do ended up taking not only a minute but a whole day to do. And he still died! Let's deal with the first part of that story, that is, time. You know you have two genres of painting: those that take you a short time to create are products of the times you and your *Chi* work in unison. Two of you have met, I was told, and your *Chi* has a female personality."

"Yes, Pa, so it is. As for the two of us meeting, I thought she lived in me, or rather that I was a manifestation of my *Chi*."

"You're right, of course; how silly of me. It's not a case of the two of you meeting, rather she lives in you and has lived in you from the day I named you 'Chioma'. So let's continue. Where was I?"

"You were going to talk about time, Pa."

"Thank you, my dear. You don't know it, but those of us on this side need you mortals to remind us of things. Forgive me, I digress. Now where did I stop?"

"Pa, you keep going round and round. Please tell me what time is all about before we use up all the time I have for this visit just going around in circles."

"Forgive me, my dear. Yes, when she lets her genius - I mean your *Chi*, of course, that is your genius - flow into your brush, you turn out work that is simply breathtaking. And all this happens in a flash. You don't feel time passing. Other times, she just leaves you to your own devices. That's when you find your work tedious. The works are good but they are not the masterpieces which people admire, for which you are renowned. Sometimes, though, the worst can happen when your *Chi* turns her back on you and bids you goodbye. That's when it takes you forever to do your work. Your work is somewhat grotesque, even though people might admire them and pay a high price for them; like your *Anyanwu*, one of those you painted when you were distraught and on the way to losing your faith. Time and your *Chi* work together. In fact, with your *Chi* you live in eternity."

It was only a few days to my Pa's burial: in fact, we had only two days to go, and Pa had not responded to further ardent urgings to speak to me for the past ten days. I was in my room, feeling quite depressed, when I heard my Pa's voice asking me to come and see him.

Pa told me another interesting story.

"A man named Dimkpa had a large piece of land. As large as several football fields put together. One day, after he had planted eleven rows of yams on the land, he felt tired and wanted to go home but his son, Chilaka, persuaded him that they should plant one more row, bringing the number of rows to twelve.

When they returned to the farm the following day, they found that a fresh row of yams had been added, this one longer than those they themselves had planted. He was bewildered and asked Chilaka: 'Did you return to the farm to plant a new row of yams?' His son said that he did not.

'How come we have thirteen rows then, instead of the twelve we planted?'

'I don't know, Papa. Perhaps we didn't count correctly and we may have made a mistake.'

'   'Yes, my son, that's possible; but as you can easily see, the extra row is quite different from the ones we planted: not only is it longer but it's also broader. How do we explain this?'

'Somebody must be helping us, Papa.'

"They worked on the land and planted another thirteen rows of yams. Making twenty-six rows altogether, including the one from an unknown source. Father and son went home afterwards.

"They anxiously returned to the farm the following morning. Unimaginably, there were now two extra rows of yams, each longer and wider than the ones Dimpka and Chilaka had planted the day before. They were beside themselves with fear. Who could they tell? How could they explain what was going on? What could it mean? Should they go to the oracle to find out, or should they just continue? Should they mount a guard on the farm at night to see when this person, or force, came to carry out his duties?

"Dimkpa did not know what to tell his son in order to calm his fears. Like a good father he took courage and said to him, 'Chilaka, my son, let's not be afraid. Whatever is going on would soon reveal itself. Let's continue with our work and see what happens.'

"Dimkpa decided that he would take a cue from this invisible means of support and planted fifteen new rows of yams for he reasoned thus: 'When we planted twelve rows, he gave us one extra, making thirteen. When we planted thirteen rows, he gave us two extra, making fifteen. Now let me plant fifteen rows, and see what this spirit would do.'

"They rested on Sunday and, therefore, did not go to the farm. The following day, Monday, with their hearts in their mouths, Dimkpa and Chilaka, his son, speedily made for the farm. And there, before their fervid eyes, were six new rows of yams. Dimkpa did not say anything to his son, having sternly warned him not to say anything about all these occurrences to anybody. He believed he had understood the source and the reason for the mysterious rows of yams. They did not plant any new rows that day and went home.

"To the farm they went the following day, Dimkpa smiling cheerfully to Chilaka's consternation. He could not understand how his father could feel so joyful when they were faced with indescribable events. But he had faith in his father, and he started smiling too as he looked into his dear father's face."

I had been listening studiously to Pa because I found the story captivating. Then he asked me what I thought Dimkpa saw when they went back to the farm and how they may have solved the mystery. I had no idea whatsoever, but I suspected that Pa felt I could solve the riddle and so I gave it a try.

"Pa, let me reason this out with you. There are three possibilities, perhaps four even. Let me deal with the fourth one first because I think it's the most unlikely one: they found that all the rows of yams had disappeared. I doubt if this was how it was, so let's consider the other three. First, they found that things were exactly as they had left them the day before and that no new rows of yams had been added. Again, I don't think that this was what happened. Second, they may have found some new rows of yams had been planted by the unknown being. Again, I don't think that this was what happened. Now to the last possibility: I think they arrived to find that all the mysterious rows of yams had vanished leaving them with only the fruits of their own labour. I think that's what happened. So, Pa, which was it?"

Pa said nothing. He kept mum for a long time, and I left, not knowing what to do. I wondered when he would give me his answer.

NINE

"Chioma, *nwam*, tomorrow you will lay me to rest in the grave of my ancestors, your ancestors, and you will see me no more. So I thought I should spend the rest of the time with you listening to you telling me anything you want to tell me and to ask me anything you want to ask me. I, on my part, want to hear about your childhood in Lagos; your years in primary school and the years at Afikpo. I want to fill in the gaps in my knowledge of you."

Pa did not often speak to me with that striking Igbo word, *nwam*, my own dear child. Since I did not speak Igbo very well, all our conversations were in English. I guess, on this occasion, Pa felt he would miss me a lot and wanted me to know it.

"Pa. How can I tell you so much in just a few hours? You know our stories go on endlessly, and we never quite seem to finish. For the past three weeks, we've been going back and forth on three stories. And now you want to hear my story of about fourteen years. You know today is Friday, so it's the only day we have left. Your burial is tomorrow, Saturday, June 30.

"You see we've already used up about half an hour without getting anywhere. Why don't you start, and we'll see how far we get. I'm all ears."

I told Pa stories he already knew. Where he was now, all knowledge was available to him, at least knowledge of the past. I supposed, however, that he wanted to hear it all from me, in my own words. And I obliged him, starting from what I could remember from my first day at school, at St. Paul's School, Yaba. There were two events I thought would interest him: so I started narrating them, but he stopped me.

"My dear I know all that. What I would really love to hear from you are your foibles; the things you did wrong at Afikpo; your childhood offences."

"Pa, why didn't you tell me, and I would have saved you the trouble of listening to stories about my life in Yaba. What are my faults? Pa you know all of them. I tend to be impatient with people whom I consider dull, lazy and insouciant. And, sometimes, my pride gets the better of me."

"Tell me, my little one, what does 'insouciant' mean? The word did not exist in my time and I never heard it."

"Pa, you're just pulling my leg: 'insouciant' means, carefree, unconcerned."

"Thanks, my dear. You know, nobody here where we are is insouciant or lazy. Such people are somewhere else—where you and I would rather not be."

"Pa, why do you want me to tell you about my offences, my mistakes? Surely those who share the heavenly places with you no longer sin or are given to sin. They are the ones who have made it through life's turmoil and temptations and now live in heavenly splendour."

"You're right, my dear. I only wanted to hear you voice your own guilt. Now I'm satisfied. Confessing one's sins is a sign of humility. You know humility is the truth. I am reassured that you will make it through life. Know yourself, know your limitations, know your strengths, confess your sins, and you'll be fine. God bless you, my dear. Oh, Dimkpa and his son discovered that all the yam rows planted by the gods disappeared; so they were left with only the fruits of their own labour. So the last possibility you proposed was right."

I meant to continue telling Pa of my other faults, but he asked me not to speak further as I had said enough. These sounded like the last words of a father to his child. So I left Pa and went home.

This was our last conversation. I felt like a lost soul.

TEN

The homily of His Lordship at Pa's Funeral Mass weighed heavily on my mind, and I dwelt on it in the few days I had left before returning to College Park. I also had to work out something else that gnawed away at my mind: the question of Bia, who would not let me be and would not take no for an answer. He stayed in one of my grandpa's guest rooms in the main house. As this was his first visit to Okeosisi, Grandpa gave him the best treatment. He had a bedroom with a hot water bath-cum-shower, white towels galore and matching white bathrobe and white bathroom slippers, which were more than I, or even Grandpa himself, had. Only Grandma had something similar. This must have given Bia the confidence to want to marry me quickly without any delay. Little did he know that I was not going to be his bride.

Grandpa Maduka's house was built when he returned to Nigeria from the States. An L-shaped, one-storey building, with a sloping roof on the west side, it sits within shouting distance of Great-grandpa's own house. When you walk in through the front entrance, you step into a reception room where you wait to see Grandpa. The waiting is brief if he really wants to meet with you. In that case, you would be taken to one of the main living rooms. And if you were close to him, one of those to whom he bares his soul, you would go

ahead to a different living room - the love den, where
Grandma reigned supreme; not in the kitchen, but in the love-
den. This was where Grandpa and Grandma usually sat,
Grandma often sitting on Grandpa's lap, very un-African, if
you ask me. The lap is meant for carrying babies among the
Igbo, not wives. But then you need to know my grandpa and
my grandma: their love deserves some telling. But let me first
take you through Grandpa's home.

The sun rises to greet the kitchen with warm rays of a
good morning eagerly awaiting Grandma to come down and
pull the blinds for its first rays to fall on the coffee-pot.
Grandma had perfected this to an art: she places the pot in a
particular position for the sunrise to bathe the whole pot in
beams of light. Of course, this means that from one time of the
year to another, she has to gauge the right position in which
to place the pot for the sun to fall on it.

Actually, Grandma and Grandpa go to Mass every
morning, so Grandma has to get all this setting-of-the-pot
right before they leave for Mass. By the time she comes back,
the whole kitchen is flooded with the sun and coffee-making,
and coffee-drinking can commence. Grandpa's is usually
black, without sugar and Grandma's black with sugar, two
cubes.

The kitchen is at the end of the longer stem of the L, the
other one contains Grandpa's and Grandma's study, a vast
room with two tables, side by side, to accommodate their
owners who sit opposite each other, so Grandpa can gaze
into Grandma's liquid eyes.

Next to the study is the opulent guest room now occupied
by Bia. On the top floor, there are six bedrooms, a large one
for my grandparents and one for each of their two children,

my mother and her brother, Ugonna, my uncle. After marriage, they retained their rooms. Their children: myself, my four brothers and sisters and my three cousins - eight of us altogether - take up the remaining three rooms. We neatly sort ourselves out except that I tend to spend the longest time in the shower, much to the chagrin of the 'gang'.

We had all come to Okeosisi for the funeral ceremonies of Pa - all of Pa's children, grandchildren and great-grandchildren. There must have been over fifty people in the Akadike compound, all well-accommodated in eight houses. Pa Akadike's house stood in all its majesty and vigour, made all the more striking at his death; having been fully refurbished for the burial ceremony. Pa's *obiriama*, the traditional 'welcome house' where relations and visitors were received was a whirlwind of frenetic activity. From dawn to dusk, the people of Okeosisi and surrounding villages came in to greet Great-grandma and other members of the family. They were entertained with food and drink, while the drummers seemed tireless in the traditional renditions.

Of course, Great-grandmother, Ma Nneoma, did no cooking herself; but her kitchen, with the gracious assistance of our relations, kept her legendary delicious cuisine rolling out, non-stop, from the first rays of the brilliant golden sun of the day, until the dreamy moon rose to light up the dark earthenware pots.

Large slices of *ugba*, made from oil-bean, thoroughly mixed with *eketeke*, palm oil expressed from tender uncooked palm nuts with pieces of stockfish nestled unobtrusively in the paste made an irresistible dish. This was not all; in fact, it was only the first course of what would be a sumptuous meal. And why not? Pa's death was a landmark event, unequalled in the history of Okeosisi. If you wanted to eat more, or if for some unusual reason *ugba* was not your thing, then you would be served *ofe*, a soup cooked with vegetables of the same name; *ofe* containing *sungu*, dry sardines, the bones carefully removed, some crayfish, well-ground and a bit, just a bit of stockfish. Experts at eating the soup, who do not want to eat much of the cassava meal, *fufu* but who want to enjoy the *ofe*, make a deep groove in a bite-sized ball of the cassava meal, immerse the ball in the soup and skilfully guide the fish and stockfish into the groove. All that is left is to simply toss the whole ball into a welcoming mouth. Before the ball is swallowed, the tongue would have artfully selected the fish, the best part of the meal to chew and savour. Palm wine is used to wash everything down or, if you were a teetotaller, then you might go for ordinary water, from Ma Nneoma's large clay pot. For the burial ceremonies, Ma's relations had loaned her some of their own clay pots to help out.

Various soups and stews were prepared for every imaginable taste: *onugbu* soup for Anambra indigenes; *ofe owerri* for Owerri indigenes, *achara* for our Bende relatives; and *okro*, *ogbono*, and *egusi* soups for cosmopolitan dwellers from Enugu, Port-Harcourt, Aba, and Calabar. Grandpa Maduka also ensured that his colleagues from Ife had a choice selection of Yoruba foods: catfish peppersoup and stew; bush meat stew; *amala* with *ewedu*, *eforiro*. *Jollof rice*, fried rice and beef stew complemented the indigenous cuisine from Grandma's and Ma's kitchens. Professional caterers provided all sorts of dishes for other guests who were entertained in the premises of a secondary school nearby. Drinks of all kinds, ranging from beer to burgundy; whisky to white Bordeaux, gin to sherry; soft drinks to malt drinks to non-alcoholic grape wines flowed non-stop.

Visitors who relished it were served *mpataka*, a meal made from boiled cassava, which was sliced into chewable bits, soaked in water for two days or so and the water drained. *Mpataka* is usually eaten with coconut, with much more *mpataka* thrown into the mix than coconut.

My Pa's obsequies, climaxing with a display by over sixteen majestic masquerades, marked both the nobility of the human kind and Igbo culture.

****

Bia did not have an adventurous palate, and stuck to familiar staple like *jollof rice* and pounded yam.

"Chioma, so much happened in the week before I came here. When I did not see you at Mass on Sunday, I figured that I should call at your house. So around 5 p.m., I was at your house. Your dad was home in the den with Ngozi and Akachi. When I asked after you, he told me you had travelled to Okeosisi to see your great-grandfather. I was relieved to find out you were okay, and I stayed with your dad for over an hour."

"What could the two of you have been chatting about for upwards of an hour? I didn't know you and dad had so much in common."

"Come on, Chioma, men share a lot of interests. If the worst comes to the worst, we can always talk about sports, the latest scores, be it pro-football, tennis, basketball, or even golf. I think we talked golf."

"So what else happened? You talked golf, that boring stuff, for one hour plus?"

"Well, it was your dad who started it."

"Started what?"

"He asked me what I thought about large families."

"And what did you say?"

"What could I say? I didn't know what he was leading to, and so I didn't know how to answer."

"Why didn't you just tell him the simple truth as you saw it?"

"What kind of simple truth is it when I had no opinion whatsoever on large families not having given it much thought? Well, I quickly managed to give the sort of answer an African father would like to hear."

"Which is what, if I may ask?"

"I said that large families come by the grace of God and that we should never stand in God's way if he wants to give us many children. After all, the children belong to him, not to us. Parents are put there to take care of them and watch over them for their Supreme Maker."

"Did you say all this, Bia? Did you say all this?"

I was very impressed by Bia's reasoning. I had also thought of having a large family before I realised marriage was not for me; and that I wanted to live a life of apostolic celibacy.

"I went further: I told your dad that if I had the chance, and by the grace of God, I myself would have a large family; that I was totally disgusted with the stifling materialism now so pervasive in the Western world, particularly in the United States. I told him that I was totally fed up with the hedonism that seems to rule the American family. I said that I would rather return to Ghana, to Legon, to lecture there. My Ph.D. programme is almost over: I'll be defending my thesis in the fall. Or I could even go to your Ibadan. You have a first-class Department of Biochemistry at Ibadan. It has produced more Ph.D.s in Africa than any other department on the continent. What do you say, you and I live here in Nigeria and pursue our dreams here, working at Ibadan?"

I was going to say something, but Bia would not give me the chance. He was in total control of the dialogue and wanted me to listen to his every word and just go along with him. I had never seen such confidence in a man, not even in my legendary great-grandfather, Pa Akadike, who, to me, was a mountain of poise and self-assurance.

But then, I had not come along in his youth, and I was not there when he proposed to my great-grandmother. I am sure he would have given a greater performance than Bia's. Fortunately, Bia did not let me say anything or I might have — just might have — yielded to his enormous pressure. By not letting me speak, he unwittingly gave me time to gain full control of my feelings and emotions. I must admit, I am truly fond of Bia, and if I could have fallen in love with any man, it would surely have been Bia.

"Something bizarre happened to me recently, before I came here," Bia continued, "I had a dream. A walking stick was walking towards me as I lay in bed. It was a huge stick, about ten feet tall. It had a smooth body with protruding knobs here and there. I counted them. They were twelve, and as it approached me, in bed, the knobs grew longer and sharper as if they would suddenly stretch out and pierce me. I awoke from sleep, breaking out in a sweat. After recovering somewhat from the scare of this nightmare, I lay down again and slept. And there was the stick again telling me to hurry up and travel to Okeosisi, and that if I wanted to marry you I must get to you before you left Okeosisi for the States, or else all would be lost. It—was it really 'it', or did it have a human body, like a woman's? I recall now, she had twelve breasts, feeding her seventeen children; all struggling with this breast or that to be fed at the same time.

"I was dumbfounded. I had never seen such monstrosity before. She repeated the statement that I must hurry to Okeosisi, to see you before your return to College Park; that you had something to tell your Pa, and that once your Pa heard it, he would pass on in indescribable joy; that you would have made up your mind not to marry me and that you would dedicate your life to God in apostolic celibacy as a professional lady. Of course, I had considered the whole thing preposterous. Then she said that she would come to my aid and help me convince you to accept my proposal. It was a long dream, it lasted all my sleeping hours."

I felt very sorry for Bia and called on St. Josemaria and all the saints to intercede for me in this difficult and stressful moment when Bia's eyes spoke of nothing but pure, ardent love. I kept quiet and let him continue, allowing time for the saints to muster their strengths and help me out.

"I was in a dilemma," he continued, "about what to tell my parents. What would I say was my reason for wanting to travel to Nigeria? Well, I braved it and told them I wanted to see you, and that I would be travelling that afternoon on Air France's Washington-Paris-Lagos flight. My mum did not ask me too many questions, but my dad would have none of what he called 'nonsensical nonsense.' Mum prevailed on him to let me travel and by 7 p.m. Washington time, I was airborne and on my way."

I found my voice.

"I think I know what you're talking about, Bia, and who the walking stick represents. Yes, it's a 'she' quite all right, but I have never seen her in the manner in which you have described. Anyway, I'm absolutely certain she won't be able to help you as much as you would have liked. Perhaps, you'll see the walking stick in another dream and, this time, it might direct you as to what next to do with your life."

"What's all this? What could it mean? Are we meant for each other or are we not? Why do we see the same image but in different forms? Is our love to be thrown this way and that? What do you mean you know about the walking stick? Have you also seen her in a dream? Was she the one who put the idea into your head that you would have seventeen children?"

I did not know how to proceed, because the story of the walking stick was an integral part of my birth as a great-granddaughter of my Pa, and I was not about to let a non-family member into this age-old secret. Still, Bia had been close to me, and I had to find some way to assuage his yearning.

"Yes, Bia, I saw the walking stick in a dream, but she vanished without saying a word to me, and she had only two normal breasts and was not breastfeeding any babies. She was alone."

"Let the gods and all their walking sticks hide their heads in shame then. I take my destiny in my own hands and now formally put the big question to you: Chioma, will you marry me?"

ELEVEN

As soon as I saw Bia, even before he said a word, I knew what he had in mind—that he had come to propose to me. Now that he had talked about his dream at length, I knew he referred to the walking stick Pa gave me when I turned seventeen. I had given her a female identity and always treated her as such. She had the magical powers to grant me any request I made if I rubbed her seventeen times, as long as the request was for something good. I gave her the name, *Uzo*, meaning 'The Way'. Bia did not let me speak but immediately composed a symphony of love.

"Chioma," he said, "not to have loved is not to have lived. Love is everything. Humans were created to love and for love. Giving oneself completely to another is the greatest joy there can be. There must be this person without whom you feel your life is dry and barren. She is like living water onto your soul. She looks at you and you are transported into paradise. For you and for you only, her soul and spirit sit in her eyes; you see her and you immediately enter into her soul. That's how I feel about you. I was created for you and you for me. I don't understand what is happening to me. My whole person is on fire. I look into the distance, and I see you dancing, your limbs floating like dry leaves in the harmattan wind. I come near you, breathe in the air stirred by your silky hair and my heart is set ablaze with flames of wholesome desire. I listen to your voice and my ears tingle. What am I to do? Please save me, Chioma, tell me you are mine and save me."

What do I do now? What girl would hear all this and not be moved. Am I not a mortal, flesh and blood? God, help me. Come to my aid, angels of heaven.

"Bia, you leave me breathless. Your words, in another setting, would have been true symphony to my ears and would have sent my head spiralling in clouds of passionate love. I thank you. I thank you immensely for you have made me realise even more the significance of the new vocation to apostolic celibacy God is calling me to. Indeed love is everything and a life without love is a life of abject misery. My heart is now elsewhere. I've given all of my heart, my soul, my mind, my intellect, my love, to my God."

"Come on Chioma, what are you telling me? Surely you can marry and still give all your love to God. Are you saying you won't marry me? What's wrong with you? Are you saying you don't love me? What do you want me to make of all this? Please speak, Chioma, speak, before I collapse."

I thought he would actually collapse for he stood up from the high-back chair and began pacing up and down the room, flailing his arms in utter bitterness and pain. His eyes were misty, and his large eyeballs seemed to grow even larger. Bia was not himself. First I must calm him down and then tell him what I had to tell him.

"Bia, let's go and see what's happening in my Pa's *obiriama* and then we can come back and try and sort this whole thing out. I think there's a dance group from Calabar, my great-grandpa's people from Port Harcourt might be here. And they might even bring some *Ekpe* masquerades. It would all make for an unforgettable spectacle for your Ghanaian eyes."

"Don't give me this cultural stuff. I didn't come to Okeosisi for fun and games. I came here for you."

"Well, as you can see, you have come at a very awkward time. What do you want me to do? My Pa was buried just this morning, and I have a lot of work to do and ceremonies to attend to. So, let me be for a while and then we'll continue talking later in the evening. You are here for a couple of days more, so we still have a lot of time to ourselves."

Just then, Grandma, Adiaha, on my mother's side of the family, came into the room and asked me to join her in welcoming her parents from Port Harcourt, that is, my great-grandpa Chief Etim Henshaw and my great-grandma, Chief Eno Henshaw. I took leave of Bia and left with Grandma. I was not myself. I felt very sorry for Bia and did not know how I could help him out of his present state of despondency.

I loved Bia, and I knew I would always love him, but as a friend, and not in the way lovers love. That was, of course, out of the question. So, was there any middle ground between the love of Eros and the love of Agape? I do not think so. Eros is either pure Eros or it is something else altogether. What Bia wanted from me was that all-consuming love that takes full possession of the body and soul finding fulfilment only, and only, in that one person in whom all of life is manifest and in whom one becomes totally absorbed losing one's individual identity and acquiring a new self in the soul of the beloved. Of course, I could not give Bia this kind of love.

How to comfort him and console him weighed heavily on my mind, especially as he was my guest and, in answer to the gods, had come all this distance to offer me all the love his heart could contain. I could not find any easy way out. I had to tell him what my life of a vocation in Opus Dei would entail as charitably as I possibly could.

The whole compound was, as expected like a circus, with so many dance groups piping, drumming, singing and dancing. Bia accompanied me everywhere to the delight of my parents, grandparents and relatives who saw in him the makings of an ideal husband who had come all the way from the US just to be with his friend, Chioma, and her family, in this massive celebration of my Pa's passage to eternal rest. He kept asking me all sorts of questions each time alluding to the children we would have. Bia was a man who did not take no for an answer. Well, he would be in for a shock. And a shock, indeed, it was.

TWELVE

I had to face Bia, to tell him exactly how it was, in words kind and sincere, considerate and faithful. This was my first opportunity to present Opus Dei to anyone, and I had to do it with all the faith I have in God.

After dinner, I took Bia to the veranda outside Grandpa's study. There was still music and dancing and drinking and talking and singing and loud noises everywhere, so it was difficult to be heard. I tried the rooms in the guest chalet, but these were all filled with my relatives and their relatives and friends, and their clothes and boxes. There was no space anywhere, and whatever space there was, was filled with sounds and echoes of the sounds. But since it was necessary for me to put Bia's mind at rest, we decided to make do with the veranda.

"Bia, I'm sorry there's all this noise around us making it hard for us to have a quiet conversation here. But tomorrow is a full day for me, with so many rites that I have to perform here and at my Pa's mother's birthplace at Ukam. You know Pa delegated so many traditional rites to me, instead of to Grandpa, Maduka."

"Well, Chioma, what's there to talk about? You've shoved me off using Opus Dei as your lame excuse. Well, go on, go to your Opus Dei and leave me alone."

"Bia, don't be unduly difficult and obdurate. Things are hard for me right now, and I need your understanding."

"What is there to understand? Tell me, what do you want me to understand?"

"Well, since you put it that way, what makes you think that because you love a woman she would love you back? Do you think love is a *quid pro quo* arrangement - give me and I give you back? Is that what you think?"

"Please don't upset me, Chioma. You were the one who asked me a year ago if I would consider being the father of your seventeen children. Or have you forgotten?"

"No, I've not forgotten, and I'll never forget that. What about you, what did you say when I broached the idea to you? Remember, you told me I must be out of my mind. And what did you do after that? Nothing."

"What was I expected to do, rush off to the altar?" He asked.

"No, but you could well have professed your love, as you did today. We stayed friends, yes, we kept on seeing each other, yes, we were the best of friends, yes; but there was nothing there that spoke of heart and soul being bound together. You were you, and I was me. And now you come here and expect me to fall for you."

"Well, Chioma, I'm all ears. Just go ahead and complete the demolition. You've already shaken the very foundations of my being. I'm no more than a mere shell of what I once was. So, please, mercifully demolish me."

"Bia, please bear with me. I'm human. If you cut my skin, I will bleed. You've just made a cut, please do not continue, the sight of blood curdles my spirit."

"I didn't know you were human. I thought you were an angel, an Akadike goddess from the high heavens, flying through this mortal world on wings of genius and mild generosity."

"What do you mean by 'mild generosity'?"

"Oh! So you are a goddess, you're from the high heavens, you only think that 'mild generosity' does not quite present you as you truly are. Well, well, well, God help us."

"Bia, if you continue this way, I'll just stop, and you can return to the US with any idea you like. What I am, is what I am and nothing you say can change that. So I'm not bothered one bit. If you call me a 'goddess', that's your word not mine. If you say I'm an angel, flying on wings of genius, again those are your words, and you are allowed to say your piece. So go ahead. If it makes you feel good to be sarcastic, on this occasion, I can't stop you."

"I'm sorry, Chioma. I'm very, very sorry. But how do you expect me to feel? This is the most painful moment of my life. I'm exhausted, and there's nothing left in me. How can you expect me to be understanding and accommodating and pleasant? How could I be? Am I not flesh and blood?"

"Oh! Only you, and no one else, can be flesh and blood? Well, I grant that if I were in your shoes, I might have felt the same way and reacted just as you did. I might have even done worse. But that's beside the point now. You have made a huge sacrifice to be here at the beckoning of the gods, or what you call the gods, and I am sure the gods will, in their own way, bind your wounds and repay you.

"I'm a normal person and am not free from the foibles of human nature and the inclinations of the flesh. You are right here with me, and we could easily find a way to gratify our sexual appetite. But even if I did not live a life of apostolic celibacy, you would still not have me, and no man would, until he married me. That's one level of consideration."

"Well said, Chioma, why don't you marry me then and satisfy your sexual appetite as you call it?"

"That brings me to the second level of consideration, namely, my sexual appetite. It is just that, an appetite, at the control of my will. I determine what I want to do, and it's not my appetite that tells me what to do. In everything, it is always first things first. The first thing is always that I'm a child of God and with the help of His grace, which is ever there, I shall serve His will first, and mine second. Granted, God calls many to the marriage vocation in *Opus Dei* and, in fact, the majority of people in *Opus Dei* are married women and men. Nevertheless, God has made me realise that he wants me to dedicate my life to him, with complete availability for whatever the apostolic needs may be, anywhere, anytime. And so here I am completely free to serve, as my apostolic celibacy makes it possible for me to do."

"Chioma, I get it. You know I too don't have any knowledge of any woman. I'm still in the pure state of my baptism. Oh! of course, I sin, but I've never taken a girl to bed."

"So what did you have in mind when you were coming on so strong with me? To take me to bed, in Grandpa's home while you are his guest, my guest, on this mournful yet festive occasion of the funeral of his father, my great-grandfather?"

"You're damned right. What's so wrong with going to bed with the girl you have just proposed to?"

"Is a proposal, marriage? A proposal is an intention, given some formality of expectation of fulfilment, and until it is fulfilled, it remains only a proposal. No. it's not right to go to bed with anyone who's not your wife, or husband, not even with your fiancée. No. Bia, I hope you never go to bed with anyone who's not your wife."

Bia left Okeosisi the next morning in a huff, but he was civil enough to express his profound gratitude to all of us. He then bid goodbye to my great-grandmother, Ma Nneoma, my great-grandparents, Pa Etim and Ma Eno, my grandparents, Maduka and Adiaha, and my parents, Okeadinife and Onyebuchi. He was not his usual bubbly self, and they observed that all was not well with Bia. They did not ask him any questions and simply put it down to the sadness and solemnity of the occasion. Only I knew the riot in Bia's heart. I kissed him on the cheek with all the gentleness I could muster and waved to him as he was driven out of the compound to Port Harcourt from where he would catch a flight to Lagos and then, by midnight, on to Washington D.C.

THIRTEEN

I could not get Pa out of my mind, no matter what spiritual device I used to direct my thoughts elsewhere. I could hear my Pa's voice and my mind swiftly went back to my days with him at our Meeting Point. All those thoughts flooded my soul.

****

Here I was, at Georgetown, about six thousand miles from Okeosisi, and I began to consider the significance of this distant separation that took me away from my indigenous culture and way of life. Yes, I could go back and forth from one place to the other, totally at ease interacting with everyone I met, in one place or the other. I was now frightened as to who I was!

****

July, 2001

It was time for me to start my programme of formation at Nesbit Study Centre, Washington, D.C. I attended the monthly days of recollection and weekly talks with my spiritual director, Dr. Angela Davenport, all to guide me in the path of vocation and mission in Opus Dei: to strive for personal holiness in my professional work and in the fulfilment of the ordinary duties of a Christian. I was moved to learn that in addition to spiritual and doctrinal formation, there was also cultural and social formation that emphasized our role in the world. It brought to mind some of the things my parents had taught me, right from childhood.

I carefully studied books by St. Josemaria, the Founder of Opus Dei, and was particularly taken with *Christ is Passing By*, making me feel He is right outside my door waiting to be invited in or seeking me out to follow him.

"Do your work well and the world will be at your feet." That was what my father taught me from as early as I could look straight into his eyes. He would take me in his arms, throw me up in the air a number of times and each time he would tell me whatever he thought I should do in life. Of these, three canons or so stayed with me into adulthood: never be thrown off course by your mistakes, your failures. Just pick yourself up and do all you can to be better. Always seek to be better than you are, for there are no limits to excellence. We can all be better, no matter how good we are. Another tenet was that if I did my work well, it would attract many people some of whom may become my friends.

I was therefore thrilled when in one of the talks at Nesbit, Angela kept driving home the point that my work would be the basis of my apostolate of bringing people closer to God; and that I should sanctify myself, sanctify my work and sanctify people with my work. I had been brought up to do my work well and with all the acclaim and fame I had attained with my paintings, I had little difficulty bringing more and more people into my life as my friends. In fact, I could not cope with all the attention my work received. Of course, friendship is a two-way relationship, but at least my work gave me the excellent opportunity to draw people to me, and then we took it from there to see how things developed. Many of the friendships turned out quite right so I was able to bring my friends to the means of formation at Nesbit.

It was so wonderful to learn that my paintings in Georgetown, for which I was paid a salary, and other works I had sold in a number of auctions, could be a means of sanctity as I offered them to God. As I painted them, I kept in mind that my talents were not my own but gifts to be used for God's glory. I found this captivating, and once I understood my particular role in life as one of selfless service to others, my paintings gained stature in an increased sense of total presence of God in all that I did. This fascinated me: doing what you did with God in mind all the time with the aim of imitating Jesus who did all things well.

Living in the presence of God thus pervaded my work; not only my work but also my relationships with others. I got to realise that whenever I placed my own interests first and sought only my own way, I suffered setbacks and slid into ugly pride, brashness, thinking my way was the only right way, giving little or no room to others in my company. This of course irritated many people, and I easily lost them as friends, all of my natural talents notwithstanding. Naturally, this caused me a lot of pain and embarrassment when I was on my own and took time to examine my conscience. I suffered greatly when I remembered that my abruptness had cost me a number of valuable friends. Well, I was now struggling all the more to change.

"Live in the presence of God and you will find that you're marvellous and everyone will love you. Live on your own strengths and you will find that you are a bore, a worrisome irritant."

That was my mother's counsel whenever I told her about one incident or the other that brought my self-centred character to the fore. Angela had counselled me times without number to remember always that I was a child of God and that I should, therefore, act accordingly.

I danced and did not stop dancing as my everyday working life began to mesh so nicely with my spiritual desires. My work led the way, and my paintings wore heavenly colours. I took my time with my friends and gave them more attention than I used to, listening to their stories, whether or not they were interesting. In all, I struggled to forget myself and to seek the good of others. My joy was infectious. My life assumed added significance as I struggled to be natural and sincere, filled with a gigantic optimism that all things worked well for those who loved God. I did not have to leave my station in life, to do anything extraordinary. I only had to live as I always did, but this time I invited my God to be close to me in everything I did so that I could offer him a smile and make him somewhat happier. He was my closest friend and I was always talking with him on almost anything that came to my mind. Oh, he is a tremendous lover ever caressing me with kisses that lift me up and give me mountainous joy. Of course, every now and then I slipped into my comfortable egotism; being more difficult than necessary, even obnoxious.

My demons were still with me, and, just when I thought I was making good progress and had put them to flight, they would rear their ugly heads and remind me that they had a lot of bite left. Fortunately, the struggle never ended, and I could begin over and over again. Optimism welled in my heart, and it was written all over my face. My friends gathered around me and I found myself animated and challenged.

The journey to holiness was moving at good speed. However, some of my friends found the programme rather demanding. When I discussed my formation with a close friend of mine, Susanne Capello, an assistant professor of

jurisprudence at Georgetown, she poured out her mind
directly.

"Chioma, what are you saying? All that I'm hearing
sounds like a return to the age of dogmatic instructions
compelling everyone to act according to a given set of rules
and doctrines with little room for discourse and freedom of
expression. What do you mean by formation?"

"You speak of 'the age', Susanne: in fact, this is the age.
Now. Today. Every age has its presence in our todays."

"You can't be serious, Chioma. Our todays are not our
yesterdays. No, we've outgrown all that. Will one have to
become like a pillar of poured concrete—solid and immovable
instead of being a free spirit, ever in motion challenging any
firmly held beliefs?"

"No, Susanne, it's not like that; and I'm quite serious,
because I'd like to share some thoughts and ideas with you,
all of them old, all of them new. And we have a chance to talk
about them. That's all."

"The way I see it, you are a fossil, lost in time like the
dinosaurs. Why get fossilized, Chioma? Why do you want to
degenerate into the dumps of doctrine and dogma?"

"Come on, Susanne, get serious. How could I be
fossilized, as you say? Surely, you know humans combine
several attributes all at the same time; and in their freedom
make choices as to who they really want to be."

"That's exactly the point I'm making, Chioma. In our
freedom, we make our choices. What I am is acted out in all I
do. Isn't it?"

"It's not quite like that Susanne. Before we start all the
social engineering of our character, we need to know who we

were created to be. For me, for you, for all of us, we are created to be children of God, to be like our Creator himself. You are a Christian just as I am, so you understand me clearly, or don't you?"

"Chioma, I know all that; yes, our Creator wants us to be like him and yes, there's so much we can do in this context. But does this mean we are to abandon giving full rein to our spirit to explore the universe? Is that not what Georgetown sets out to achieve? Does formation not mean being poured like concrete into a pillar?"

I laughed at this.

"Why are you laughing? You tell me you're serious and that you want to share some thoughts with me and here you are laughing. Now, I'm the serious one."

"Okay, suppose I agree with you and say that formation means being poured like concrete into a pillar; does a building not need pillars to hold it up? The stronger the pillars, the more solid the building, so that winds may blow and tornadoes may strike yet the building stands. Or do you want to be like the house built on sand?"

"Don't give me that old biblical stuff about the house built on sand. You know quite well that's not what I mean.

"That's exactly what I think you mean, Susanne."

"Well, you're quite wrong. I see formation as the antithesis of the pursuit of knowledge without any boundaries, without the confining armour of doctrine and Mosaic law. Descartes changed all that and gave us freedom of thought."

"You can't be serious, Susanne. After all these years at Georgetown and with all the freedom to pursue knowledge,

to seek the truth about all of creation, can you say that we are
stifled and lose our freedom when we live according to
certain moral truths about humans and society?

"Here we go again—'moral truths'; what are moral
truths?"

"Let's not go round and round in circles. I realise the
whole issue of what constitutes moral truths is a big
philosophical area that we cannot fully exhaust in this short
time we have together. We can always continue our
exploration."

"Chioma, please leave me out of all your exploration. Let
me just live my life as I see fit."

"Well, Sussane, if that's how you want it we could stop
here and now and you go your way and I mine."

I did not think that I was making much progress with my
good friend and I was quite distressed. My countenance must
have shown my concern, for Susanne immediately asked me:

"Chioma, what's wrong? You look like you're before a
firing squad, with total abandonment to all that confronts
you."

"You're right, 'total abandonment' is the way to put it, for
I don't know how best to approach the question of formation
in the virtues. I am at a loss as to what next to do."

A voice within me urged me not to give up, that I was
indeed making good progress, as long as Susanne was willing
to listen. I gained in confidence and continued.

"Let's look at this issue of formation this way, Susanne.
Here at Georgetown our minds and intellect have been so
well built up that you and I can freely make those choices that
fully express our human nature in union with our Creator."

"Well, I've never heard of someone seeking formation, as if one were an empty sack in need of stones to hold one up. Do you really think that Georgetown has taught us as much?"

"You've said it so well, Susanne, beautifully indeed. I could not put it any better. We are all empty sacks in need of solid material to fill us up and hold us up so that we can stand tall. Yes, some of us have more filling than others, but we all basically start life as children in need of solid food to give us strong bones and strong muscles to build up our bodies."

"Chioma, don't take me back to my childhood. Of course, mum and dad taught me what's right and what's wrong. They gave me solid food, if you put it like that. But Georgetown is different. It has taught me to question all I thought I knew."

"You know only too well that we are not born with all the knowledge we could acquire neither are we born knowing everything we need to do to attain fulfilment. Yes, Georgetown has taught us a lot and we now know better how to seek the truth about things material and immaterial and make our choices."

"Well, if you put it that way, I think I get what you mean. I just don't like being told what to do now that I'm an adult. Whatever suits me is what I do and if it is agreeable with you, fine; if not, then so be it."

I was pained by this line of reasoning that has thrown humanity into dire straits, and I realised that I would not get far with Susanne. Still, I felt drawn to her, with the thought that, now she had bared her mind so openly, we might be able to share more and more of each other's aspirations. It seemed some of my friends were getting farther and farther away from a life of virtue, trusting only in their own ideas and beliefs, erecting them as inviolable truths. To them, it was a case of 'my truth' against 'your truth'. And this is wrong! I loved Susanne and did not want to lose her friendship, whatever happened. I put aside my sorrow and found some words of comfort.

"It's not quite like that, Susanne. You know we may falter when all we have to go by is our own judgment. We just might be in error and need guidance to the truth. We cannot be the authority on what is true."

"So, who then is the authority, Chioma; please tell me I'm all ears."

"I'm not talking about scientific truth here. That can be more readily established by humans and we have been created to explore the earth and have dominion over it. And science, with technology, teaches us truths about the universe. But we cannot take this to the domain of our soul, the very essence of our being that makes us humans and not mere animals."

"Who's talking of animals?"

"Well then, Susanne. You and I are not mere animals. We have souls; our soul hungers for spiritual food, and we should go for it. Let us then be more ambitious and seek what is the best for us humans: we should not be satisfied with mere fleeting pleasures."

"You're my dear friend, Chioma, and nothing must come between us. You have covered a lot of ground in philosophy, and Georgetown has not seen the likes of you. So, why don't we say we'll continue some other time? I really want to hear more about this sensational formation of yours. Perhaps, you'll take me to your Nesbit Centre so that I can see what it's all about. At least, I can take an academic view of formation, and we could discuss it more intelligently."

"Wow, sensational, you say. Very soon, I just might be eating formation out of your hand. Fantastic, we'll go to Nesbit, then; I'll let you know when."

****

It was Sunday, 16 September, 2001, the first Sunday after '9-11', that unimaginable day of evil so preposterous that the devil himself stirred in disbelief, in horror. Two of our professors at Georgetown died in the attack, Professor Tom Huston, who had taught me four courses right from my freshman year; and Gary Findlay, a professor of medieval history.

Susanne and I were on time for the 10am Meditation, that began the monthly Day of Recollection. The mood was sombre and solemn, utterly sad and despondent. There were about twenty of us, many dressed in black. I wore a white blouse and a navy blue skirt. Susanne wore a similar outfit as if we had both planned to do so. Her skirt was inches shorter than mine, and she had on a long-sleeved blouse with lace embroidery.

The Day of Recollection is really what it implies: a day you endeavour to recollect yourself; to take stock of where you are, where you are going, and to open your heart, mind and soul to the spiritual guidance you need to keep to the path of sanctity and to help you to struggle ever more resolutely in the battle against your own shortcomings and defects, be they cultural or spiritual. One is thus enabled to seek holiness with every ounce of energy one has and to do battle against one's weaknesses. I always tried not to miss these means of formation that strengthen my spiritual muscles, and give my lungs much-needed moral oxygen.

Rev. Paul Carter, an African-American priest of Opus Dei who was also a professor of oral literature at Howard University gave the first Meditation of the morning. He looked bright and cheerful as if to lift up our hearts to join him in an extraordinary act of faith. After recalling the horrendous events of the previous Tuesday, he told us of a Yoruba proverb I loved so much; so appropriate at this time of unsurpassable sorrow and mourning. According to the proverb, a burnt palace takes on added beauty when it is rebuilt.

Fr. Paul spent the next thirty minutes training our minds on evil, on our defects; to see our defects as palaces that needed rebuilding, after being burnt down. As I understood it, our defects destroy us not with fire, but with filthy acrid sin. It is in the rebuilding of our human and spiritual virtues with unyielding, steadfast, valour and consistency that we gain new beauty. Fr. Paul termed it 'holy intransigence'. After the Recollection, Susanne took me on:

"Is this part of what you call formation? Wow! I think this is fantastic, appealing directly to my very core. I felt he was talking to me. With this, I don't have to spend any more time on my psychiatrist's couch; it costs me thousands of dollars without any significant change in my sexual promiscuity."

What was going on? Was this the same Susanne, my good and amiable friend! I did not know she was sexually promiscuous, in her own words. Why should she be telling me all this?

She had more on her mind and she continued, revealing her innermost thoughts and fears: "I don't have to be a slave to my defects, whatever they may be and however massive their appeal. I can now rebuild myself with 'holy intransigence', never giving up in the effort not to indulge my sexual appetite. The good priest said we should begin, and begin again. It's simple for him; he's a priest, isn't he? What does he know about my uncontrollable tendency to indulge my desires? What am I going to do? One thing I know for certain my psychiatrist is history. I won't see her again."

I could not believe what I had just heard: Susanne saying she will fight her desires with holy intransigence. What pleased me most was that she grabbed on to this expression which was as graphic as it was inspirational. I was thrilled beyond words confirming even more firmly that we must never give up on our friends, however hopeless it may seem. My joy was boundless. How could the Meditation have had such an impact on Susanne that she had resolved to seek a change in her life? The Holy Spirit surely works!

"Susanne, this is simply unbelievable: you're going to fight your defects with holy intransigence. May your wish be granted. You've hit the nail right on the head. You can now see why we need formation. I did not know you had a problem with what you referred to as 'sexual promiscuity."

"How could you have known? I never told you. I just lived my life as I saw fit; but the more I sought joy in sexual intimacy, the unhappier I became. Sex seemed to gain control of my life, and after some time I just didn't care any more."

"I'm sorry to hear that, Susanne, and even more sorry that you have been receiving therapy running into thousands of dollars. Well, you've said it; it's all in the past and now you can try to begin to drown evil with a lot of good as you rebuild the burnt palace of your beautiful soul."

Over a period of more than three years, Susanne accompanied me to Nesbit from time to time, and I was truly beside myself with indescribable joy that Susanne was able to confront her inadequacies. I kept in mind what I had learned a long time ago at Nesbit: that it was far more important to understand than to be understood. And so I gave her all of my time whenever we were together. I could not have imagined that she had such severe moral problems with sexuality. But here she was, confiding in me, no holds barred, as if I were her trusted psychiatrist. I was in a trance, as it were; nothing could have prepared me for all that was going on, and it was only the beginning.

One Thursday morning, when I usually had a class with some students offering art in their degree programme, Susanne gave me a call and asked that we meet for lunch at one of the university cafeterias close to my office at College Park. I was surprised; she only lunched on campus when something weighed heavily on her mind. I suspected it was not the lunch that she was after but something weightier, far more important.

She said she had gone to her psychiatrist, Dr. Christine Pearson, that morning and for the first time, after over twenty weekly one-hour sessions, she had looked at her psychiatrist and seen nothing more than a woman with feet of clay - an ordinary person, who, in spite of superior clinical knowledge and reputation was unable to reach Susanne's soul. She felt that her sexual profligacy was so deep-rooted that only a thorough cleansing of her soul would provide any succour. And for the first time, she understood that her defects lay in herself and that only she could defeat them with the grace of God.

She sought more: she wanted to go to the Sacrament of Reconciliation and start a new life as a Catholic; as at Confession she could tell the priest whatever was bothering her, sin and all. She felt she had to do something better than attend weekly one-hour psychiatric sessions at two hundred dollars an hour, at the end of which she simply went back to all those men and continued where she had stopped. Yes, she did make some effort, following Dr. Pearson's promptings and counsel. But she never ever felt that sexual intercourse with someone who was not one's spouse was a grave offence. It was just the profligacy of it that Dr. Pearson tried to help her with. She felt that she needed over one hundred sessions before she got over her promiscuity, and she could neither afford the expense nor could she be sure that in the end she would be able to resist men's sexual advances.

Susanne was weeping, and I felt great sympathy for her. I had to be strong. She had confided in me beyond the bounds of ordinary friendship. I could not have expected this outcome. I listened to her telling me one horrid story after another, and in the end I could see my way clearly as to what to do. This was the beginning of one of the most exhilarating experiences of my life. On Jan. 16, 2005, after attending doctrinal classes with some priests at the National Shrine of the Immaculate Conception, in Washington, D.C. and at Nesbit, Susanne received her first Holy Communion at the Church of the Ascension on Massachusetts Avenue, close to Du Pont Circle. Angela and I were with Susanne at Mass, and afterwards she took us to lunch.

"Chioma, Angela, you have helped me to a new life. For the first time in my life, I know what happiness is: to have Christ actually living in me in all his majesty in my miserable soul, now flooded with bounteous of joy. Oh! I feel like I rule the entire universe. I feel so powerful. Oh! This leaves me speechless."

"Well, you did it all yourself, Susanne, with the help of God. We'll ever be at your side."

"Yes, you will literally be at my side for I shall now be attending all the spiritual means of formation at Nesbit. And who knows, God might have something in store for me yet."

We were speechless, Angela and I.

****

My last days with my Pa and our conversations after he had passed away continued to fill me with unfathomable joy. He was always on my mind and it seemed he brought with him the whole Communion of Saints to assist me. Somehow, I found myself becoming more and more immersed in things of the spirit. My paintings received fresh vigour, and ideas which I had had difficulty conveying on canvas were now more approachable and more readily portrayed.

My duties as artist-in-residence filled up all of my waking hours, and I was beginning to contemplate the virtues as I worked. Of far more significance was my more acute perception of my defects and shortcomings; huge demons out to consume me. What in the past I considered mere wrinkles in my personality garb, no more than unavoidable side-effects of my talent, now stared me in the face with the ugliness of a beast. My formation in the human and spiritual virtues was taking deep root in my soul, and I found that I could easily integrate all the cultural formation Pa had given me into keenness in seeking sanctity. Everything was of one piece.

I was in this vivacious mood when I visited one of my friends, Constance Ferguson, a personable lady - gifted, affable, something of a social climber - a quality I had difficulty accommodating. She had been a year ahead of me at Georgetown and had come in on a programme for mature students. Having graduated at the top of her class in Economics, she now worked in the U.S. Congress as an assistant to a senator from her home state of Virginia but she still lived with her parents. Whenever I asked her why she lived at home, she would parry the question and that would be the end of the matter. My paintings drew us close together, and our friendship grew stronger as the years passed. I liked her simplicity, although she moved in the higher echelons of society. Well, she worked amongst the most powerful people in the country, so, perhaps, all this influence went to her head. Who would blame her, anyway? She was my friend, and that was all that mattered to me.

"Chioma, how are you?" Connie embraced me warmly and would not release her hold for over a minute, leaving me short of breath but exceedingly happy.

"I'm so upset that you had not bothered to call me since you came back from Nigeria, and only called after I ran into you and threatened not to talk to you again. And you say we're the best of friends! Anyway, I was relieved when you said we should get together."

"I'm so sorry, Connie, it's just that the whole world seems to be whirling round and round at top speed, and I'm trying to find my feet again. I've been coming home late, and I'm swamped with work. Still, that's not a good excuse; you're my friend, and I'm here to put things right."

"Well, you're here and I shouldn't be harassing you. What may I offer you?"

I joined Connie in the kitchen and helped myself to a Diet Coke. I felt I had treated her badly and continued with my apologies.

"Please, Connie, don't be too upset. You see, the pace of life in Okeosisi, the little town in south-eastern Nigeria, where my great-grandfather was born is slow and peaceful, no mad rush from here to there. My Pa has left me, so I find myself in two worlds at the same time, each seeking supremacy."

"Come on, Chioma, this confused state you're in won't do you much good. You have not come back to the real world we live in."

"I think I'll be alright. Right now, my Pa's world seems to be winning over this fast-paced materialistic society. There is so much joy in my heart, Connie, and it all flows into my hands as I paint. It seems there was a side of me that I did not know existed and which my Pa's death has thrown to the surface. Connie, I have a feeling you will be seeing a new Chioma, and you will like her a lot."

"Well, that's great! Let's go to my room, Chioma, I have Bondde's new album and I'd like you to listen to it. I'm sure you've heard of their lead singer, Geneve, who made history last year with the best-selling album of all time, *I am all yours*. You know, she said she got the title from the motto of Pope John Paul II, who said those immortal words on his election as Pope."

"Yes, Connie, I know Bondde very well. My brothers always bother me with Geneve did this, Geneve did that."

Geneve was at her best in the new album, her voice as soft and mellifluous as it was strong and vibrant, picking just the right moment to rise, or fall, as into a slumber, or rise to a crescendo. Her voice was an ingenious work of art, a singular gift to humans that they may sing in unending glory to their Creator. I listened to her and was transported to marble halls of heavenly delight.

I had been in Connie's room many times before but had not taken any particular notice of just how impeccable it was; the sheets brilliant white, the windows clear and bright, each ray of the golden evening sun reflected off the glistening surfaces of the superbly polished wood furniture. I sat at ease on the deep-pile rugged floor, my legs folded, right over left, gladly sipping my drink.

"You're sitting on the floor, Chioma, instead of in your usual cosy seat up there by the bed; why the floor?"

I was not aware that I was on the floor.

"Connie, your room is just perfect, everything clean and in its place. I simply sat on the floor so I can better bask in the comfort of this unusual elegance. Has it always been like this?"

"Come on, Chioma, you're putting me on. You've been here umpteen times, and this is the first occasion you took any notice of my things. What has come over you? You're so into yourself, into your own world of your studies, your art, your writings, always busy; with little time for the rest of us mortals."

"Please, forgive me."

"I've often complained about your nonchalant attitude towards those you call your friends. I even wonder why we're still friends. So, has your trip to Nigeria, ending in your Pa's funeral celebrations changed you?"

"I think you're right, Constance: my Pa's passing on has had a profound effect on me."

"I was always hoping for that, that you may change and be the charming person hiding inside you. May your Pa's soul rest in peace in the knowledge that his sweet daughter is turning into a tremendous person."

Connie knew me inside out. She was right, but not quite: I was even worse. My smile and laughter were only meant to save me from uncomfortable situations when my otherwise intemperate character got the better of me, no more. They were not genuine, but people didn't know that. All people were interested in were my art and my ideas on knowledge and philosophy. And once I gave them the benefit of my brains, they were satisfied. Now, I was seeing things more clearly. Why, I was becoming more sensitive to my pitfalls, my impatience, my irritability and was eager to make amends. The sessions with Angela and the memories of my Pa, both in his lifetime and in his death, had a profound influence on me. I could feel that.

FOURTEEN

I had been to rock concerts before with my friends from Georgetown and some of the rock stars were my favourites. Amongst them were Bondde, Flags Flying and Green Bays.

When my younger brother, Zoputa, heard that Bondde would be coming to perform at the Coliseum in Washington, D.C., he would let me know no rest with his importunate insistence that we attend. I was not in the mood for rock concerts at this time when all my thoughts were on Nesbit Centre. I just could not see myself sitting there in the crowd shouting and screaming my head off in wild excitement.

This was not the time for excitement. Then, a voice inside me said, "Why not? Do you know what you might gain from the concert? Or if you gained nothing, do you know what you might offer to someone you meet there?"

At first, I did not pay much heed to this voice but, it was unrelenting. I finally yielded, believing there might be some merit in its suggestion. So, I told Zoputa I would go with him. He was excited and thanked me profusely.

There were other groups warming the air, whetting the appetite of the fans before the appearance of Bondde. The fans were getting impatient and rent the air with shouts of "We want Bondde! We Want Bondde! WE WANT BONDDE!." But not yet, two more bands came on the scene and were booed, without let-up. It was all well-orchestrated; all in the game plan. The unbelievable screams could be heard all the way to the White House, I was sure. No wonder there is not much rock entertainment in Washington: no one wants to make the President deaf!

Their lead singer was still the same beautiful, svelte, Geneve. I believe that the Almighty God took particular care to create her, to make her the best of the best with the finest body he could bestow on a woman. Geneve was exceedingly exciting, and men would swoon and faint just to see her. Her first song, *A New Me*, was one from the album, *Bonded*, released two years earlier, not the best of her repertoire, but she still held her fans spellbound with scintillating smiles and glittering looks. The world would stop for her!

You should watch her dance. God created her that she may glorify his name in dance. As long as humans lived on earth, hers would be the lithe movements that would be celebrated for all time. And she gave us our fill. I stretched all of my five-foot-eight-inch height, urging my toes on and on to extended lengths like a ballet dancer, trying to peer over the heads in the crowd before me, since we did not get good seats. Zoputa was too lost in the whole extravaganza to pay much attention to me. As long as he could see me, standing there next to him, he felt satisfied.

I started thinking; oh I started thinking about what this fantastic woman could do for young African-American girls in the US and for girls everywhere on this globe. When they watched this dazzling star with chocolate skin, would they dream to be the best in whatever they did, in whatever motivated them and in whatever purpose God put in their hearts? I believed Geneve would change those who watched her, those who watched her with the right intentions, the intention to be entertained by a child of God created to give humans the light of joy and delight; for I believed her heart was pure and that what we saw in her dance was the fantastic and terrific expression of a clean soul uncluttered with earthly, bodily pleasures.

The question for me then was, how do I get Geneve to fulfil the mission I think God has given her, that is, to glorify his name with her body and soul in dance, such that the purity of her soul completely flows out of her as her body spins inspiringly in dance?

Surely rock stars, like anyone else, can live a life of virtue, for rock music, by itself, is wholesome, and all things wholesome can be offered to God. It seemed I had set a huge task for myself: to get into Geneve's mind and find out what went on in there. But first I have to gain her trust as a friend. How do I go about this? I decided there and then to see her after the concert, as I did not know when next I might have such an opportunity as this to see her perform. Of course, I could be wrong in all this, my imagination might be wild, not having any bearing on the truth; but I must find out how wrong I was, if that was the case.

After the concert, I went backstage in search of Geneve's dressing room. Many fans were milling around hoping to catch a glimpse of her if she came their way. But come their way, she did not. So, after lingering for a while, they began to disperse. When the number had grown lean, I began the journey past one security guard, then another, and another, showing them my identity card from Georgetown as Artiste-in-Residence. This got me past the less formidable stops but not any more. As I approached what must be Geneve's room, I was peremptorily stopped by two tall athletic-looking African-American men who said I could not proceed any further without an appointment.

Of course, I did not have one, they should have known that. They just wanted to get rid of me but I would not let them. I showed them my College Park card but this was not enough. Then I produced my New York Museum of Modern Art card with one of my works clearly engraved in it, introducing me as Artist-of-the-Museum. One of my greatest paintings, *Looking at You*, created when I was sixteen, lived at this Museum. Whenever I look at the card, and the image looks back at me, I am enthralled as I contemplate the painting, a surreal work that fills me with all the mystery of the Akadike dynasty. And this occasion was not an exception.

One of the guards, the taller of the two, looked intently at me as if to make sure it was my photo on the card. Then he asked,

"Did you go to Georgetown? You seem so happy. Did you like the music so much?"

"Yes, I was at Georgetown. I feel so happy because of the painting in the picture. It's all about my great-grandfather, and the thought of him now he's no longer with us fills me with great joy. And yes, Geneve's music is phenomenal."

"I think I know who you are. Is it your painting that decorates the wall of The Augustine Auditorium?" I said it was.

"Wow! Hey, brother, this is some special woman, man, special, and I mean special," he said to the other security guard.

"I think I know you, your name was in all the college journals: you were the first on the Dean's list, the first in literature, the first in philosophy, the first in sociology, you were the first in everything, giving a whole new meaning to the word first. We were so proud of you, all of us Africans and African-Americans; here was a girl who could beat them hands down with a lot of room to spare."

If I could blush, I would have. I did not want him to continue this way, and so shifted the focus of the conversation to him.

"Please who are you, if I may ask?"

"Please go on and ask and I'll tell you. I'm Bob Franklin and my buddy here is Ahmadu Kojo, from Ghana. We work for a security company, which sends us from place to place to keep the peace. I graduated from Georgetown last year. Ahmadu and myself, we work with Ms. Geneve as her bodyguards while she's in the District. Ahmadu graduated from Maryland College. What can we do for you? Just say it, and it's done."

"I really would like to meet Geneve. I want to do a painting of her and get to know her better."

I threw in the "I want to do a painting of her" bit because I thought that this might open doors for me. It had opened doors for me on different occasions before: first, when I wanted to meet a famous unapproachable writer; then a rather raucous woman activist, and also a Supreme Court judge. It always worked. This time, though, I was not so successful with that line.

"Why do you want to paint her? She wouldn't want that I'm sure. She's been photographed too many times, and she's everywhere on magazine covers, in the tabloids, in everything. But surely you'll meet her. I daresay she hasn't met anyone like you yet. Oh, yes, we'll take you to the manager, and he'll take it from there. Please follow me, but tell me a little bit about your great-grandfather and why you are so thrilled about his death."

"I'm afraid it's a long story, Mr. Franklin."

"Please call me Bob."

"Ok, Bob, my great-grandfather loved me so much and gave me so much. I meant everything to him."

I followed Bob up the stairs as we talked, then downstairs, and then up again, like a roller coaster, until we seemed to come back to where we started, all in the name of security to make Geneve safe.

"Please wait here," Bob said when we finally got to what I considered to be Geneve's dressing room. He gave my card to her manager. I heard voices and then a shout and out ran Geneve herself to hug and kiss me and pull me to herself.

"What's going on?" I asked myself.

The room was riotous - gowns, dresses, cosmetics, shoes - oh so many shoes - were strewn all over the floor.

"Wow! You are Chioma, here in the flesh. I can't believe it. My brother at College Park won't let me have any peace all because of this woman the students call "Good Fortune", and they all want to be like you. I have one of your paintings, you know. Jane, please get us drinks. Chioma, what would you like?"

Was I dreaming, or had I been kidnapped? Where was I? Is this real? I had been scheming about how to meet this God's-gift-to-the-world-of music-and-dance, and instead I was the one being serenaded, as it were. I had to be fast with my answer. But what do I drink? I was thirsty and would have liked a large glass of water, then some dry white wine, but I was afraid that if I asked for wine, I might be offered the champagne Geneve was already drinking, and I do not like champagne at all. So I asked for water.

"What do you mean, water? Let's celebrate. When will I see you next? Tell me, what would you really like? We could have dinner right here. Just say it and it's done."

"It's so late, it's 1am already. Well, I'd like some white wine, but water first, please."

"Ok, let me see. Jane, what white wines do we have?"

"Oh, Gene, we have some of your favourites—*Pouilly-Fuisse*, *Montrachet*, some Alsace, *Beaulieu* and *Clos du Bois.*"

When I heard that *Pouilly-Fuisse* was available, I knew that would be my choice, and I asked to have it after some water. Grandpa had taught me a lot about French wine, and he and Grandma Adiaha drank some of the choicest brands. But how did this star know so much about wine? My curiosity did not last long.

"Seems we're two of a kind. I love whites I mean white wines, of course. If you go for *Pouilly-Fuisse*, then you've got me because that's my first choice any day, although it costs an arm and a leg these days. My dad grew up in the Beaune region of France, went to school there, and took his degree from Strasbourg. I was born in Beaune and we returned to the States when I was fifteen. I am well-versed in French wines, and Jane, my manager, makes sure I'm kept supplied wherever we go. Gosh! We need to get together and talk. But where can I find the time? Gosh!"

Jane brought in some water, a bottle of *Pouilly-Fuisse* with a side plate of prawns, clams and crabs and set the tray by my right, between Geneve and myself. Geneve started taking off her clothes right there before me. I made to walk over to where Jane stood near a window with a view of the Washington Memorial, but she asked me to stay where I was. Well, she did not take off everything; she still had her underwear and her bra on. Well, it did not matter. This made Geneve all the more approachable. There were only the two of us with her in the room and two others in an adjoining room, all women. How could she be so relaxed with me? What had her brother led her to believe about me?

"Cheers! Here's to a great friendship."

We clinked our glasses and then I felt I could say a word or two. With all my gift of self-control, I could not help myself. I started babbling whatever came to my mind in words of ecstatic praise.

"Geneve, you are fantastic. You know that. Your record sales and the media say it. You are a great pride to all of us Africans and African-Americans, and you are a woman, a star, the likes of which the world has never seen and may never see again. The day God made you, he created only you and you alone. He took a look at you and he said, 'Yes, this is my greatest work of art, the masterpiece of all my creation.' And then he rested all day; he did no other work. You make us so proud, and you're not only such a superb singer and dancer, you're an intellectual, a music graduate with three novels under your belt. Your latest, *Show Your Face*, has sold over a million copies and you're well on your way to becoming a major writer of the 21st century! Incredible! I'm here simply to say hello, to make your acquaintance and I hope I can get to know you better."

"Get to know me better," you say. Chioma, Good Fortune? Well, you'll know me as well as any human can know me. I hope the same applies to me, that I'll get to know you as well as anyone can."

"Easy, Geneve. It's a deal."

I had never been that close to a star. I was dazzled by Geneve: she was more brilliant than diamonds, filling my heart with a throbbing joy that kept on welling up, never really subsiding, leaving me longing for more and more of her sparkling presence.

"Please, Chioma, you'll do me a painting. I must bring you to my home in Westport, Connecticut and you'll do something that lifts the place up, something with your remarkable brilliance and simplicity that speaks the language of purity and love. I'll give you all my numbers and contact addresses so that wherever I may be, you'll have contact with me. And it won't be a one-way affair. No, I'll keep in touch, and whenever I can't, Jane will stand in for me.

"Come to think of it, why don't you do the lyrics for my next album, all seventeen songs on the album? The music will be ready in six months or so. In fact, if I had my choice, I would say, let's work together."

Things were moving too fast for me. How could I have hit it off incredibly well with this wonderful star in so short a time?

Of course, I agreed: was it not a huge honour to do a painting for Geneve and to write the lyrics of her songs to boot? It was past 1 a.m. and I had to tear myself away from this magnetic personality.

When I left Zoputa, I had told him to wait for me in the foyer; close to the swinging door that opened into the parking lot where we left our car; and that if I was not back within an hour or so, he should ask any security guard to take him to Geneve's dressing quarters where I had headed. They may not take him there, but, at least, they would know where to begin searching for me. Like the reliable and ever faithful brother that he was, he waited patiently for me. He seemed restless, though.

"Did you see her, I mean Geneve? Did you see her? Did you get to talk to her?" Zoputa asked. Too eager for an answer he continued: "Wow, big sis, Chi, here we are, mere mortals, and you get to spend so much time with the exquisite Geneve."

He opened the door for me, and we walked towards the parking lot.

"Come on, Big Sis, why do you keep me in all this suspense?" Zoputa, as well as all my younger siblings, always prefaced my name with "Big Sis" or *Nda*, as a sign of respect. According to the hallowed customs of Okeosisi, '*Nda*' means my beloved elder. I did not know how to begin as the whole evening had been one huge bombshell. As I tried to recall everything, it occurred to me that I really could not recount what had happened. It had been lightning-fast and stunning.

"Yes, I met Geneve. Yes, we talked. Yes, we celebrated with choice white wine. Yes, she is now my friend and I, hers. Yes I...."

Zoputa had had enough of my yeses and cut in.

"Ok, ok, what's next? You say she's now your friend. When do you get to meet her again? Will she ever come to our house? Will we ever meet her? How can I meet with her, just the two of us?"

"Do you want to be with Geneve, just the two of you?"

"Yea, wouldn't that be astronomically fabulous and monumentally mountainous?"

"What does all this mean? Where did you get this way of speaking?"

"Big Sis, this world was not made for the likes of you and Geneve. To you, everything is so ordinary. To the rest of us, certain things like meeting Geneve is like arriving at the top of the Mount Everest of human joy and delight."

"Zoputa, you're my own brother, and you're saying all this. Am I not just like everybody else, my paintings and grades aside?"

"No, you're not like anyone else I know. You're way too much. But then, you're my sis. So, I guess meeting Geneve should be no big deal. I don't think she's all that greater than you. Come to think of it, what really matters is that you're my own sister, and you're always mine to keep for as long as you live. And I love you so much. Yeah, that's what counts. Geneve or no Geneve; what counts is how well you live your life. So how soon can I get to meet Geneve?"

FIFTEEN

August, 2005

My soul was aflame, and I was certain I wished to seek admission into Opus Dei. I shall never forget the date, Friday, August 19, 2005, when, after over four years of attending the spiritual, doctrinal, cultural and apostolic means of formation given and fostered by Nesbit Centre, I had a chat with Dr. Chelsea Morgan, Director of Nesbit Study Centre. That same day, I wrote to the Bishop Prelate of Opus Dei, Bishop Javier Echevarria, as follows:

Dear Father,

Imbued with the grace of God, I wish to ask for admission to Opus Dei as a 'numerary'. Although the great majority of the members of Opus Dei are married people, I realise that I have a vocation of apostolic celibacy in Opus Dei. I desire to completely give myself, body and soul, to God, in the service of all souls; eager to sanctify myself in my daily work and in the fulfilment of the ordinary duties of a Christian. I have been going to the Nesbit Centre for means of formation for the last four years. I am moved by the life of St. Josemaria and pray that I may be able to turn all the circumstances and events of my life into opportunities to love my God and to serve the Church, the Pope and all souls with joy and simplicity, lighting up the paths of the earth with faith and love. With the intercession of the Immaculate Mother, the Most Blessed Virgin Mary, I wish to dance in step with Our Lord Jesus Christ, wherever he may take me, praying that, I may be able to discern not only what is good, but what is excellent in his eyes. I look forward to a favourable consideration of my request."

If accepted, I would need to move to live at the centre so I could attend the programmes of spiritual formation and so better serve the church and *Opus Dei*. I had long talks with my father and mother. Mum was extremely delighted but Dad took it too hard. Yes he wanted me to live at Nesbit, but I knew he would miss my daily presence in his life a great deal.

"Chioma, my little girl," that's how dad always addressed me when he had something of great import to dispatch, "you're taking a very important step in your life, perhaps, the most important step you will ever take. Living a life of apostolic celibacy is not easy; it is fraught with perennial difficulties that only tons and tons of the grace of God would help you surmount. You will face fierce temptations, such as you cannot imagine because the evil one will come after you ferociously with all the daggers in his vast arsenal. You are pretty. You are charming. You are bright and you are pleasant. Men will not leave you alone. They'll never leave you alone. And you will have to develop surreptitious ways to keep them at bay. Obviously, you can't do this on pure human energy: you need God's guidance all the days of your life. Your art will also pose problems for you as you may begin to explore all kinds of ideas in your eager and unquenchable thirst for knowledge. You are rich, thanks to the sales of your paintings, and this can be insidiously used by the evil one to trip you and make you lose your hold on chastity."

I was listening attentively to dad. I took in every word he spoke just as I did my Great-grandpa's. I had always known I needed the grace of God to be able to do anything worthwhile, but now I felt like getting down on my knees and resolutely praying that the evil one may keep a long distance away from me.

"Lord, please help me," escaped my lips, and dad smiled and then continued with his advice.

"But I need not tell you, you know this already, as a 'numerary' you are a bride of God and he will always be the perfect groom to you. So we need not worry unduly. Just stay close to him and he'll always lift you up and bear you over any mines, or caverns, or craters, or gorges of sinful lust and passions. Everything Pa Akadike said about you is unfolding: 'you will fly high like the eagle', he said, 'and you will dazzle the world with your brains.' Now God calls you to a vocation in *Opus Dei* to the greater glory of His name. Can you beat that? Is that not flying high, to the Almighty? Furthermore, the prelature of *Opus Dei* gives its members systematic, constant and sound formation on spiritual, religious, doctrinal and apostolic development. I now know why Pa Akadike died in your feeble arms. His eyes saw what they had never seen. His ears heard what they had never heard. His heart and soul saw what God had prepared for those who love him, and he died to take possession of God's promise."

Believe it or not, when Dad said these words, I wished I could pass on and join my Pa Akadike, that great man. Mum weighed in with similar views:

"Chioma, you know I was the first person who asked you to go to Nesbit for help during those dark days, long gone. And now God wants something more from you - to give yourself completely to him and to the service of other people. It is not your success that is called into play here but your sense of generosity, your ability to abandon yourself completely to God. Don't ever forget that you don't need to be brilliant to go to heaven. You don't need to be a star to serve God in Opus Dei. All you're asked to do is to strive to live your life as an exemplary Catholic, a consummate professional and to spread the faith through the energy and passion for excellence you bring to your work and the loving fulfilment of your daily Christian duties. Your work and the way you live thus become tools for seeking sanctity, turning everything you do into ways and means of getting to know God, to get closer to him and serve the Church.

"Pay great attention to your work, Chioma, my dear. Your work would draw others close to you, as it is doing already, and now it's left for you to use your work as a vehicle to bring all your friends closer to God. That's what you'll be doing at Nesbit and more, there's always more, for our formation never ends, and we can never give enough of ourselves to God."

Mum seemed sombre, so I moved to her seat and hugged her firmly. It was now clear to me, if I ever needed any proof, that my parents, grandparents and great-grandparents have rigorously and lovingly sought to transfer to me all the rich values of both the Igbo and the Christian culture: the best a child could ever dream of. I held mum as if my life depended on it. She turned to look at me, freeing herself from my hold to continue:

"Now on to a practical subject - children. You know, when you think of apostolic celibacy, you tend to think only of giving up your sexual appetite and sublimating it for the love of God. One consequence of this is that you won't have children. And I know you love children. A man can have children right into his old age. You cannot. Therefore, be absolutely certain that your love for children is sublimated to the love of God. Make quite certain in your mind that you can see any child you meet as your own child. I'm being rather foolish, am I not? Of course, it's not by your power that you'll be able to live a celibate Christian life. It is by the grace of God. And in your ascetic struggles, you'll discover the true joys of life, the joy of the cross. Without pain, without suffering, you will not discover your true self; you will not penetrate the mystery of God's love. So, my dear, you are near us in space and you are ever near us in spirit. You will always have us."

****

Early one morning, before 5am, when I usually wake up to get ready for Mass, my eleven-year old sister, Ngozi, ran into the room sobbing and dived into the sheets. I put on the lights and asked what the matter was.

"*Nda,* mum tells me God has called you to a vocation in Opus Dei to serve the church and all souls. I am so happy. Go wherever you please because it is God who takes you there. And he has told me that he would take care of me even better if I just stop crying and let you go. He said you would never want to hurt me and that if going to Nesbit means hurting me, you wouldn't go. So the tears you see now are tears of joy. I'm so happy. You've made me so happy. Oh my God, how can I be so blessed with this wonderful sister?"

Ngozi kept on crying, and soon I joined her. It became a symphony, Ngozi taking the higher notes of the violin and I more like the cello. Dad and mum rushed to my room fearing something grave may have happened.

"Chioma, what's this? What's going on? What happened?"

We wailed even louder, with my voice rising to match Ngozi's high notes. Then, simultaneously, we burst into wild, uncontrollable laughter; the kind that makes you hold your sides to stop your ribs from cracking. Believe it or not, Ngozi started singing, then stood erect and stamped her feet on the wooden floor in what could only be called a dance of the spirits. She seemed possessed, by what, of course, we did not know. She pulled me to herself with the energy of a prize fighter. I had never felt such massive power before. I joined her in the dancing, what else could I do? Dad and mum just stood there, speechless, utterly bewildered. The stamping and shaking-of-the-waist continued for a while yet but soon gave way to unheralded silence and Dad could get a word in.

"Could somebody please tell me what's going on before your mum and I drop dead?"

Ngozi started dancing all over again to a tune she was singing:

Nda Chi's my own sis

my sis is going to Nesbit

there to glorify God

in all she does

great! wow! great!

God be blessed

God gave us Nda Chi
Now he'll keep her

for me

for me

for me

The '*for me*' continued in rhythms of unspeakable delight. And it was the turn of dad and mum to weep. By now the whole family was in my room.

"What's all this jumping and singing and dancing?" Akachi asked.

"Will Geneve be here later today? Is that why you're all in this merry mood?" Zoputa wanted to know.

Ngozi started singing another song:

Come to my nest

I'm a bird

and I'll give you eggs

laid by Nda Chi

soon to hatch at Nesbit

into hens of glory

singing to the Lord

Who put this idea into her head? What's going on? Then I heard my Pa's voice again:

"Chioma, don't forget you're the end of the Akadike dynasty as I knew it, as my forefathers knew it. But now we have a new beginning as you can see. The dynasty continues in a new light, blazing with God's grace. What awaits you at Nesbit is more than you can possibly imagine. Let me just say that a whole new world will live in your paintings, in your work of teaching and research; more than this, you're going to live in many souls, too many to count. So go on, go to Nesbit and bring more souls up here so we can continue our celebration."

"Are ghosts talking to you?" Mum wanted to know.

"You are right, Mum. Someone you know very well was talking to me, not a ghost. Do you know any ghosts?"

"Don't tell me Pa Akadike is at it again. He won't let me rest, always reminding me of this and that, never letting me be, especially when I'm inclined to do something silly. Isn't this what the Communion of Saints means? That we're in constant union with our dear ones who have left us here on earth only to watch over us from heaven?"

"What are you two talking about? Don't tell me you're planning one of those your surprises again."

"All is well, Dad, nothing is amiss. In fact everything is just fantastic," I replied.

"Now, don't flatter me; are you saying I'm fantastic? No news there, your mum never stops telling me that I'm wonderful, terrific, amazing."

"Dad!" that was me calling dad to order. He kept on reminding us just how wonderful he was. After all, with a woman as charming and as graceful as his wife, mum, what other qualification in life did he need to demonstrate his character and mien?

"No, Dad. By fantastic I mean that this is a great morning like no other in the history of the family."

Ngozi saw this as a good time to tell the family the whole story of this unusual morning. Turning to me she added:

"*Nda* Chi, I'm only a little girl, and I don't really know anything. But one thing I know is I love you. I love you very much. And we all love you. Wherever you may be, I know that God would not only be with you, but would be using you to do all the wonderful things he expects from the rest of us because he wants the world to respond to you. What's left? All we need to do is follow you, just follow you and we're well. Go ahead and here we come."

Mum started singing and dancing as the rest of us watched her steps:

> *Come with me*
> *let's follow our own Chi*
> *Chi, go on we're coming*
> *just don't run too fast*
> *for our steps may be too slow*
> *for your fast God's-own pace*
> *Come with me*
> *Come with me*
> *to walk the way*
> *that God lights up*
> *in our own Chi*
> *let's go*
> *let's be on our way*

SIXTEEN

My dear friend, Sutapa, and I meet frequently at *Brightwave*, a restaurant with a lively bar on College Avenue, the main avenue in town. Characteristically, she likes margaritas any time of the day and I, my favourite glass of white wine. Well, it is not quite "any time of the day", for we have not been there in the morning or at night or during school hours. It's just that whenever we were there, Sutapa would order, "One margarita, please", and so the margaritas kept on coming.

Sutapa had a throbbing tale to disgorge from her troubled chest.

"Hi, my sweetheart, what will it be today? The usual?"

"Yes, the usual, Peter, the usual will do," replied Sutapa.

"And you, my pumpkin, what will it be? Our Chardonnay's inviting. And it's a brand new bottle, unopened. What do you say, a glass?"

"No, Pete; I think today I'll join Sutapa for my first margarita."

"Wow! Miss Chioma, what's the occasion? You are having your first margarita."

"Nothing out of the ordinary; believe me, nothing."

"Okay then, two margaritas it will be."

"Chioma, ever since you could drink, I've been trying to get you to down a margarita every now and then, but you wouldn't. Why today? What's up?"

"Well, Sutapa, I reckon today you've something really awesome to unload, and I figured I should give you all the support you need, on every front, margarita and all."

"Two margaritas here, ladies, and some ham sandwiches. Never mind, it's all on the house. Today is the twenty-first anniversary of our opening, and we're giving our regular customers a real treat. Have fun."

"Mighty thanks, Pete," we both chimed in appreciation. "Cheers."

"Cheers to you, Chioma. Where was I?"

"You were nowhere, Sutapa. You hadn't said anything. So you can begin anywhere you please."

"Chioma, I don't know how to begin this long, tedious story of an event of such monstrous proportions that even the devil himself would hide his face in shame."

Sutapa was nonplussed. An exquisitely beautiful lady with long charcoal-black hair usually tied in a bun at the end, she usually exuded confidence and serenity. But not on this day. Hers was the look of someone who had spent a long night weeping and pondering over life's excruciating pains. She did not wear a sari as was her wont, but donned a sleeveless denim dress that had seen many scorching summers, two buttons long gone revealing her athletic legs as she swayed this way and that in apparent anxiety. Her hair was ruffled, and the whole mass carelessly cascaded down her shoulders. Her shoes, sandals, rather, were well worn, almost like bedroom slippers that had been abandoned and then rediscovered. Only one thing sat comely on her - her brilliant head firmly and elegantly standing on her steady and loyal neck. Otherwise, all else was dross and disarray. How could this be? I was astounded.

Sutapa was on her third margarita and still not much had been said. Realising that the drinks were going fast to our heads, we quickly ordered dinner. Sutapa, had veal and mashed potatoes and I, duck and rice. For wine, I persuaded Sutapa to try *Meursault*, a favourite of my mother's. Suddenly Sutapa erupted:

"Mike has left me: he just upped and went last Tuesday. And do you know where he is now? With our very own friend, Doris!"

All I could manage was "Oh my God! Sutapa, how can this be?"

****

Sutapa and Michael Caldwell, close friends of mine, had been married for seven years and had two children: a boy, Devan, fondly called Dev, and a girl named Tara. Of Australian descent, Mike was thirty-five, just three years older than his wife. One of America's more popular artists, he met Sutapa, an Indian-American, when he taught art at George Washington University, Washington, D.C. Sutapa was then a post-doctoral fellow in microbiology at the same university. She had taken a graduate course in viruses and Mike had come in to give a series of lectures on the fine architecture of viruses and, after that, she bade viruses goodbye. What she did not reckon with was that Mike would later invade every cell in her alluring body and take over her life, much like the unstoppable viruses.

Mike's lectures gave viruses a life no one could have imagined: he turned these vile, disease-provoking invaders into objects of expansive beauty and elegance. To us, the victims, the virus is completely an unwelcome guest. But indeed, unknown to us, we have been so constructed by Mother Nature, our body cells are delicately and exquisitely designed to welcome the virus and provide it with life-giving nutrition. Mike showed from his works just how much the virus illustrates some of the basic principles of painting, reminiscent of Escher's symmetry.

Sutapa fell hopelessly in love with Mike, so much so that her proudly conservative parents were worried. As they saw it, their charming and thoughtful daughter was getting more and more unhinged, unbalanced and preposterous, seemingly mired in selfish and fruitless pleasures. She did not pay any heed to what they said, and nothing mattered but Mike. It was Mike this and Mike that; she spent lots of time with him after classes, evening after evening. She grew rebellious against any parental advice, and was riled by any talk of prudence and chastity. She was simply uncontrollable. Just nine months after their first meeting, she and Mike had a full-scale Indian wedding with all the traditional festivities.

I first met Sutapa at a lecture given by one of the world's greatest minds, Professor Subhash Sen, Master of Trinity College, Cambridge, U.K., an Indian Nobel Prize Laureate in Economics. I sat next to her and after exchanging greetings we agreed to meet after the lecture.

Sen talked about commodities and capabilities; that it was not what you had (commodities) that was important; rather it was what you did with what you had (capabilities). This was to be the manifesto that would bind Sutapa and me in a world of giving our best at all times.

For reasons I would never understand, she confided in me right from the start and effortlessly fed me a rich diet of her life with Mike and just how much she had fallen for him, as if he were the only living man on earth. I grew very fond of Sutapa and was close to her although she was older than me. Slowly and decidedly, she came to take a deep look into her soul, steadfastly rinsing out tiny smudges of selfish desires to reveal its original core of sterling chastity. Raised as Hindu, Sutapa tried to live according to the faith, but gradually succumbed to the American way of life. Mike was an ardent follower of Mahatma Gandhi, and his doctrine of simplicity, peace, and a contemplative life, having spent his formative primary school days in Hyderabad. They seemed the perfect example of married life. Then the bombshell hit.

"Mike moved out ten days ago. He came home yesterday to take the last of his things stating clearly and strongly that I should not expect him back, that he would be filing for divorce in due course. Nothing could have prepared me for this deep, soul-wrenching pain. I didn't see any warning signs. I thought we were doing fine and that all was well; in fact things couldn't have been better. Our sex life was active, fresh and fulfilling, and our children, Dev and Tara, love and adore their dad."

I was totally dumbfounded by this revelation, my mind seized up: how could this happen to two people so much in love? I finally stuttered: "Do the children know their father has left you for another woman? Do they know? Have you told them?"

"How can I tell them? Let that blundering bastard tell them. How can this be happening to me, Chioma? What did I do to deserve this?"

"Come on, Sutapa, don't use such foul language to describe a man you are still married to and whom, I believe, you still love. Please don't ever let such silly language slip from your lips. It does not sound like you at all."

"Well, say what you like, the man is a big fool. Yes, a big fool. To have left me, he must be the biggest fool on earth."

"Sutapa, let's forget about Mike for now and worry about you and the children."

"How can this be happening to me, Chioma? What did I do, or not do, to deserve this?"

I was searching for some words of comfort when our food arrived, although by then neither of us felt like eating. The waiter sensing some crisis left us quickly without his usual banter and happy wishes of 'bon apetit'!

The anguish of my dear friend welled up in me and the duck became impossible. Here was a seemingly ideal marriage, blessed with two beautiful children, how could Mike have done this? Sutapa's eyes grew redder and redder, and I could only imagine how her heart was faring if her eyes were any indication of her feelings. Nothing in life could have prepared her for this unprovoked betrayal. Sutapa resumed her story, tears flowing freely from her swollen eyes.

"You know, Chioma, Mike was to me the perfect husband. From the first time I saw him, I loved him even though I did not let him know this. I thought it was just the sort of crush one had for a teacher, the sort that would not keep you awake at night, nothing much to it. He grew up in India, and had a true and abiding taste for our customs, particularly the spirit of devotion, oneness and unity that pervades family life."

My friend was sorely in pain and I gave her all the time she needed to disgorge this huge load from her troubled mind. She drank some *Meursault,* flicked her hair backward and continued.

"Trust is so dear to us, and although my parents have now lived in the United States for the past forty years, they're still very much Indian in their way of life. Crass materialism is not for them: a life of the spirit is the driving force of their being. And I've acquired a lot of this myself. Well, perhaps, not as much as my parents would have liked. You yourself know how I am, rather rebellious and very independent, wanting my own way not minding what my dad and mum may say. This is America, and whether you like it or not, we all become slowly, dare I say, inexorably, drawn to the rapids of the culture of individualism."

Sutapa was in dire pain. I wondered what sort of a world we live in, in which lovers are not true to each other. What is it about human nature that makes us such pitiful victims of our passions? I felt both rage and sadness at all I was hearing. Sutapa continued her love story.

"I was drawn to Mike like bees to nectar. He brought to the fore niches in my heart I never knew existed. He revealed me to myself and showed me what I truly am. I became completely immersed in him, and my world with him was simply overpowering. How do I form this into words, my God? Now, look at me. What did I do wrong? What could I have done wrong? What do you see in me that suggests that Mike has reason to leave me, to betray our love?

What could I say? How could I assuage my good friend's feelings of helplessness? Well, I've been well tutored at Nesbit to listen lovingly, especially when someone was labouring hard to unburden her heart. I sat silently, but I was sure Sutapa could read the look of disconcertedness in my eyes.

Slowly, she regained her poise and tried to lead me through her Hindu culture.

"You know for Indians marriage is sacrosanct, a sacrament ordained by Destiny. It's inviolable and indissoluble just like your Catholic marriages. Mike and I walked the seven steps that signify our journey through life together as one, each step a sacred marital vow."

I was captivated by this narration and my interest in the story must have helped Sutapa gain her confidence more and more. She continued:

"You can see that this is detailed, and we, Hindu don't enter into marriage just for the sake of having a wife or a husband or a wedding certificate to warm our hearts. A wife or a husband is not a piece of furniture, an embellishment, a showpiece, a selfish contrivance to solve one's problems. No. Marriage is a true blending of two souls to become an indivisible whole. Mike knew all this. I know I'm stubborn, and the American way of life has surreptitiously, like osmosis, crept into me, although my parents have brought me up in the strictest Hindu customs and traditions and I've done my best to abide by them."

Yes, I would agree that Sutapa really tried to be as Hindu as she possibly could and I told her so. But she still did not think that there was anything wrong in being fully American and continued along that line.

"Well, I was born here, wasn't I? What could anyone expect, a full-blooded Hindu girl? Impossible. What I know is that I brought to my marriage the finest customs of my people and, as you yourself can easily guess, similar traditions are found in other cultures and religions. Could Mike have married me because I am Indian and solely for that reason? Doris is also Indian-American. What does he see in Indians? How did I fail him as an Indian? Oh! God help me."

I felt the pain of my sweet friend and did not know what words could console her. This was not the occasion for a lecture on marriage and what could go wrong. However, I thought I must lift up my friend's spirits and show her the bright face of nature. What do I do? The waiter came around and refilled our glasses but not before asking, as all good American waiters do, "Enjoying your meal? Is everything okay? Is there anything else I can get you?"

"We're fine. Just fine," I lied, as all good customers do, too.

I continued as calmly as I could, in case the waiter had sensed that something was amiss and had come to offer us a smile, some relief.

"Sutapa, as you've said yourself, I know you quite well, and there's nothing in your character that I find either offensive or off-putting. In fact, you are my idea of a cheerful, balanced and energetic personality. I've never seen you moody or depressed. You're cheerful in the face of all sorts of trials and tribulations. You have a beautiful soul which it shines forth to give you a charming and friendly disposition. I could go on and on. Above all, you're my close friend. So, even if there's anything untoward in you, I might not readily see it. Still, I know you're a fantastic person. The way I see it, something you just cannot put your finger on went wrong. And it may be something quite complex, not easily searchable.

"Perhaps, even Mike himself may not be able to tell us why he's doing what he's doing. Would you like me to have a chat with Doris? Who knows, she might be the one leading Mike down the deceit trail, ensnaring him with her beguiling charms of no enduring substance, only passing pleasures."

Sutapa started sobbing again. I was distressed. It was getting too unbearable for me.

"Sutapa, please don't cry and don't be sad. We pray that Mike comes to his senses and returns to you soon."

"What are you saying, Chioma? Re.... what? Did you say r-e-t-u-r-n? That is to say, to turn around and go back to where one once was? Is that what you mean by 'return', that he would come back to me? Come back to me, Sutapa? Am I a house? Am I a farm? Am I a car? Yes, you can return to your car, or your farm, or your house. You could even return home, if all you did was simply go out with the intention of coming back. But Chioma, you do not, repeat, do not, return to a human being whose soul you snubbed and abandoned. It's not a case of leaving something in the cupboard and then coming back for it, returning to collect it; or returning to your locker to get your sneakers. And as you know only too well from your own ugly experiences, when you go to get your things, when you return for them, they may not be there. They may have been stolen. Even your home, you might return and it might have been burnt to ashes.

"No, Mike cannot RETURN to me," Sutapa stressed. "He can come back. He can visit, he can do whatever he likes, but he cannot return to me because I'm not the same Sutapa he left behind. Whether or not I know it, I have changed. My soul is changed. My spirit is changed. Even my body is changed, as my thoughts now draw lines on my face leaving me looking dry and forsaken. I'm sorely wounded. No Chioma, just forget about Mike returning to me. There's no longer a 'me' for him."

"Well, Sutapa, let's just say this is not a good time for us to do anything drastic. I'll come in and help with the children for a week or so. I'll come in the evenings and help them with their homework, and help you too. Don't worry. Above all God is looking after us."

"Come on, Chioma, just leave God out of this. I'm too angry. Where was God when Mike was flirting with Doris? Why did God let it happen?"

"Sutapa, without knowing it, you may have found the answer to this travail. If God let it happen, it can only be for your own good. Do you think Mike is so good for you? If he is, why did he leave you? Do you think he's such a wonderful man? If he is, why did he leave you? You say you had a healthy and fulfilling sex life; well, if it was so healthy and fulfilling why did he leave you? You say he's a good father, that he loves Tara and Dev: if he's so loving and caring, why did he leave his children? Perhaps God is on your side and wants you to take a closer look at Mike, and fix a few things that may have gone wrong. Remember, God wants us to have good marriages because it is through good and loving families that a just and peaceful society can emerge on earth. The path to a just and peaceful society has loving families dotted on both sides of the road."

"To make matters more painful, Chioma, Mike went for Doris: Doris of all people; someone who has enjoyed the hospitality of my home. She came and spent weekends with us, and we all had a great time together. I didn't know I was unwittingly digging my own grave. God help me."

Lunch over, I walked Sutapa to her car, and then drove behind her till she got safely home and then I was on my way.

I had to talk to Doris. I believed that talking to her would yield good results, but you never know in life how things may turn out. Something may just happen, something not foreseen or even foreseeable. Not quite knowing how to proceed, I left it all to chance. But I have lived long enough to know that what we call "chance" is really God working and in this case God really needed to work, and fast too.

****

I ran into Doris on my way to give a lecture. She, too, was on her way to lectures. Although she was Indian-American, she was as American as they come. A friend of mine and Sutapa's, she was a frequent guest at the Caldwell residence at 237 Marlborough St., Bethesda, nestled in one of the finer parts of this heavenly suburb. She was a doctoral student in economics, and we often got together to hear her tell us the right paths that developing countries should follow in their journey to make life a lot more liveable for their people.

She was a Subash Sen apostle and often began her conversations with 'The gospel according to Sen' says you should approach some problem this way, and try to do so and so. In time, Sutapa and I both became strong adherents to the Economics of Subash Sen.

Pretending to know nothing of what was happening between her and Mike, I asked how she was, and she said she was fine. Well, I guess she must be fine now she had managed to get Mike into her bed. She seemed to be in a hurry and was not in the mood for small talk. Still, I acted out my own part, which was to treat her as I normally would.

"Doris, where are you rushing to? Could we meet for coffee after your lecture? Mine will be over by 4pm and we could grab a bite at *Garfield's* too."

"I'm sorry, dear, today is a bad day. I'm all choked up with work. Let's make it tomorrow, that's if it's okay with you."

Still acting my part I said, "Sure, tomorrow would be fine. What time?"

"Let's make it lunch, 1pm"

"Great. See you then tomorrow, 1pm"

I had an engagement at 1pm for the following day, but I could not pass up a chance to have a chat with Doris and see if she would bring up the topic herself. Ordinarily, I would have begged off and excused myself. But not this time: all was at stake.

SEVENTEEN

Here I was, surrounded by mounting problems. Bia was still troubling me, saying he would never give me up and that if I did not marry him he would never marry, as I was the only girl for him; and that just being friends was not satisfactory - he called it 'disinfected love', lukewarm and drab, like a pitcher of spit. He said he wanted the real thing, which meant only one thing, having me all to himself.

My dear friend and confidant Sutapa was suffering malady after malady from a marriage gone sour. Mike and Doris were living in undisguised sin. How could I help myself and help my friends too?

I went to my class on 'Mind and Memory'. The whole world seemed dreary. What do I do to restore my spirit of cheerfulness in all things? How would I be able to deal with this gloom? How do I return to my erstwhile world of joy and peace? Not today, do I hear my mind tell me? Well, the class could begin.

What do I see before me? At last count there were only thirty students enrolled in my class. Now there was standing room only: there were over a hundred students in a room meant to hold no more than fifty students or so. This had the immediate effect of lifting my spirits, sending me into a spiral of joy and recollection of self. I knew who I was, a child of God, and today I would be just that, a child, making all the mistakes of a child with the good humour of a child, trusting in the goodness of her Father to guide her and put things right.

"Good day, everyone; what's going on here? How come we now have so many students? Are you all validly registered for this course? I thought registration ended last week: what's going on?"

The class erupted in loud laughter. Doreen stood up and spoke for the class.

"Ms. Ijeoma, we're all duly registered. Some of us went to Dean Campbell requesting for the extension of registration exercise for PHL 217 and he exhilaratingly agreed."

"He exhi....what?"

"I said, Ms. Ijeoma, that he excitedly agreed."

"He excitedly what?"

"I mean he happily agreed, to put it simply."

"This is where we begin our lecture: you used two words, 'exhilaratingly' and 'excitedly', which you realise are both subjective, simply indicating your own personal observations or feelings or attitudes. Can you tell me, what was going on in the good dean's mind when you asked for an extension of registration?"

Doreen volunteered an answer.

"Of course, Ms., none of us could tell what was going on in the dean's mind. There were about twenty of us there at the time but I guess I was the one right in front so I could see his face clearly, his eyes, his lips, and I could 'sort of' and I mean, sort of, in the strict sense of 'sort of' tell what he might have had in mind."

"Good talk, Doreen, but can the expression, 'sort of' be understood in any strict sense?"

"Ms. Ijeoma is that not what philosophy is all about? To understand the meaning of things in the strictest possible sense?"

"Thank you Doreen, thank you very much. You hit the nail right on the head. To understand the exact meaning of things is what philosophy is all about. Correct. Now we can proceed. What then is the exact meaning of this large number I see before me? Before a foray into this exercise, let me just tell you something about the 'meaning of things'.

"Before I came to this lecture, I was what you may describe as 'depressed'. I'm not sure that 'depressed' truly expresses my state of mind at the time but it is a word you all clearly understand. At least it's a word very much in use in this country. So, let's say I felt depressed. I could tell you why, but that would not be necessary anymore because you have all been brought up to appreciate the perils of depression. However, immediately I stepped into this class and saw this massive number of people, my depression took flight, and my spirit was once again buoyed by feelings of joy and peace. My tranquillity returned. So, what does that make of my depression? What kind of depression was it that did not last for more than seven minutes, that is, between the time I first noticed the feeling and the time I walked into the class? Does this tell you anything about the state of my mind in any way?"

There was no response. Of course, everyone has days when one feels that all is not well; days when one could say that one is depressed. Did The Beatles not sing *Yesterday* to recall just that experience that makes us long for our yesterdays? I rephrased the question:

"Can you separate what you experience from what your mind tells you or what lies before you? Can you separate what you see from what you think about? Does what you feel have any bearing on what you see?"

This got everyone going. Hands rose here and there seeking to provide answers. I thought I should give Doreen a chance. I know her to be flighty, easily changeable, not steadfast, not believing in the highest human values. To Doreen, all was dross, or, as she would put it, 'horseshit'.

"Yes, Ms. Ijeoma, I know my feelings don't have much to do with what lies before me; they spring from nowhere and just take control of me. The question then becomes how do I respond to these feelings?"

"But you're the one who so aptly described Dean Campbell's feelings when you told him that many of you wanted to register for PHL 217. Can you then please tell us how you were able to surmise the dean's feelings?"

"But Ms. Is this not psychology, dealing with feelings? Is it really philosophy?"

"Ah! Doreen you have brought up a hot topic right now, 'consilience', a word coined by the eminent Harvard insect behaviour biologist, E. B. Wilson. According to this view, all is material, all can be reduced to the laws of physics; all things that exist owe their existence to evolution, mind is matter; and everything can be explained because everything is connected. Can you believe this? That mind is matter! Just to complete this frame of thought, as many of you know a good number of universities now have a whole discipline devoted to *Mind, Brain, Behaviour*. And as you might already know, I was brought here to explore this whole question of the meaning of things, how the mind and memory work to give meaning to things, and it is believed that the African might have something unique to contribute in this respect if you could conceive it, that some novel concepts of philosophy would emerge from my studies! Of course, I don't think that anything novel would come out of the whole thing. Let's get back to where we were, namely, how do we know our feelings?"

A voice in anonymity yelled out, "If I like it, I know how I feel. If, therefore, someone shows they like something then I would know how they feel. To like means to feel, and to not like means to not feel."

I did not know what to make of this line of reasoning, but I immediately realised I had introduced a topical, burning issue at the heart of student behaviour - calling into play how the mind impacts on behaviour. I felt that I had to steer the discourse in another direction, but I must do this deftly.

"Please, please, we're getting ahead of ourselves, let's proceed with one concept clearly defined and understood - that of the dispositions of the mind that enable us to know our feelings. Remember, I told you that before I came into this class, I was downcast, that is to say, I was in a certain frame of mind such that I was not feeling particularly happy. My mind was at work before my feelings came into play. The mind is the key. It's ever at work, or I would be a mindless being, that is, someone who is not able to think, construct images, make choices about things, and more. It is in the area of this 'more' that, I hope, my Ph.D. thesis will make a solid contribution. This is where you will meet the African who would give more to the present Western thought on the human being. Have I helped you at all today? Is there something new you have learnt?"

"You won't believe this, Ms. Ijeoma, but this is the first time we're being challenged way beyond our capabilities on issues we simply take for granted - what one might consider the ordinary things in life. What we're learning is that there is nothing ordinary, as such, in our experiences; that everything we see, think of, is a philosophical issue at the level of resolution using our minds and intellect. But please don't ask me if the 'mind' is the same as the 'intellect'."

"Well, we shall stop here for today and continue the next class to give more meaning, if we can, to what we call the 'mind'."

****

My next class was simply unbelievable! I think the whole university was there, Dean Campbell was seated right in front.

EIGHTEEN

I met Doris for lunch at *Nathan Hale*, eponymously named after the great martyr of the American civil war from

Coventry in New England. Whenever I felt I needed a place with a quiet ambience that allows for soul-to-soul conversation, I went to *Nathan Hale*. Slightly more expensive than most restaurants in the Bethesda-Potomac-College Park vicinity in upper class Maryland, it was just the right place to meet with Doris, whom I considered sufficiently world-wise to appreciate a place of such impeccable standards.

I had been with Doris to the Nesbit Centre twice. She knew that the residents lived the simplest mode of life devoid of frills, thrills and excesses. Everything at Nesbit was beautifully elegant, comfortable and inviting, attending more to the contemplative soul.

Doris liked Nesbit but could never, for the life of her, understand how normal, healthy, charming women, with alluring bodies worth dying for, most of whom were professionally successful, could choose a celibate life in the midst of a world of flowering beauty and mirthful delight. Yes, she would admit the world of the flesh was not so pleasant; still, to live the single life, even if one completely gave oneself to God, was anathema.

"What ever happened to good healthy sex in happy marriages?" she always asked me

"Chioma, I thought we were to meet at *Garfield's*, why did you choose this high-brow place? This is my first time here. The price must be way beyond what we can afford. What are we going to do?"

"Come on, Doris, we're not that poor. Look over there, behind the salad bar; do you see that painting hanging there? Go over there; get closer and see if you can make out the name of the painter."

"What are you trying to tell me, that it's one of your works?"

"Just go over, okay, I'll go with you. Let's go then."

We walked over to the wall behind the salad bar and there hung my *Anyanwu*, one of eight paintings from a dark period of my life, when I lost my faith and all interest in my soul. I did not name it at the time, but when I finally saw the light, I gave it the name, *Anyanwu*, meaning sunshine.

"Wow! Chioma it's indeed one of your paintings: it's signed in your unmistakable signature, ChiakadIKE. I don't recognize it as one of yours, though. It's not done in your usual fresh tones conveying thoughts of heavenly delight and movements ever rising to the skies. There's a tree, I can see, with branches and large bunches of nuts tucked in between the stem and branches. This is a massive painting. It must be about ten feet high, almost touching the ceiling. What is it all about?

****

I heard a voice. It was a voice I had heard before.

> *"Chioma, you see what I mean. Here I am at Nathan Hale far, far away from my origins in Okeosisi in the days of your great-great-great-great grandfathers, right down to your great-grandfather, Akadike. And you were to have thrown me into the fire once you returned to your active Catholic life. Now I'm preserved in this painting, and you spend hours and hours talking about me. You see, I miss you. But this way, you remember me each time someone walks into the restaurant, looks into your gorgeous eyes, and tries to ensnare you with loving lies. But you never*

*believe them. Good. I just want you to know I'm on
your side. Today, no one else will come over to you;
it doesn't look like they will. So, enjoy your lunch
with your friend. It seems you're the one to
inveigle her with all your fine wine and lamb chops
to boot. Bon appetit!"*

That was *Uzo* speaking to me, the walking stick which had
lived with my ancestors for as long as there had been an
ancestor and which Bia had seen in his dream. That is to say,
it had been with the family for ten generations or so, my
great-grandfather, Pa Akadike, being the last great custodian
of this heritage with the power to do good if its head was
rubbed seventeen times. My Pa had passed it on to me when I
was seventeen years old with strict instructions on how to use
it to great effect. I brought it with me to the States and had
completely forgotten that it ever existed. Oh, I gave her a
female identity for she was my soul-mate. To pay me back in
my own coin, she got me to make a painting which I did not
ever remember painting. And then she disappeared with the
reason that she knew that I would get rid of her when I came
back to my senses and returned to Mass and the Holy
Sacraments. The painting I made then, *Anyanwu*, now hung
here at *Nathan*.

****

Apart from wanting to impress her with my predilection for
sophistication and poise, I had brought Doris here purposely
because of the story behind this painting.

"Let's order first and then we can settle down and talk."

"Hi, I'm Dave. How are you fine ladies doing? What can I get you to drink?" Dave, the waiter, wanted to know as he handed us the menu.

I knew I would have my usual white wine and asked Doris what she would like. She left the choice to me and, since she also loved white wines, I ordered a bottle of *Pouilly-Fuisse*. She pinched me and whispered,

"That's expensive," to which I replied, "I know. It's my treat. It actually won't cost me anything. It's all on the house."

"Well, that's a very fine choice," the waiter continued, "seeing that the house special today is fish, canapé provencale, red snapper with shrimp and mustard mayonnaise, cucumber and cherry tomato garnish. For dessert, we have nesselrode pudding. Alternatively, you could have grilled lamb chops, cherry tomatoes in dill, toasted protein bread and for desert pineapple with kirsch. And if this is not to your taste, you could order a la carte, as on the menu."

Thus ended Dave's suggestions for a pleasant lunch.

"Thanks, Dave. We'll have both: fish for me and lamb for Doris, my friend here."

"Doris, you asked about my painting hanging over there. I can tell you most truthfully that I really don't remember doing that painting. Yes, the hand that did it was mine but it was not my mind, or my intellect. It's a long story, it's about my life, and we don't have the time to go through my life right now."

"Well, let's make a start. Then we can continue one lunch after another, one *Pouilly Fuisse* after another, from one restaurant to another, till death do us part. We're now united in your life, Chioma, yes, I think we can joyfully relate to each other."

This whole 'unity' idea weighed heavily on my mind: was Doris serious about this, that we could both be one, given her present state of debauchery? How could my life blend with hers unless she gave up Mike? I don't want to judge anyone, least of all Doris. She's my friend. I must work this out with her so that we can both strive to live a life of virtue.

The wine arrived well chilled, and I had the first taste. It was dry and smooth with a rich inviting flavour, cheerful and compelling, everything a *Pouilly-Fuisse* should be. We walked over to the salad bar and served ourselves.

"Doris, let me make the story of *Anyanwu* brief by saying, first, the title means 'sunshine'. I gave it that title to remind me of a dark period in my life when I abandoned my faith and sought refuge only in my own abilities. I had begun to wonder about the purpose of humans believing in a God who sits in his place, wherever it might be, while so much evil goes on in the world."

"I've always wondered about this God who allows so much evil. I didn't know you fervent Christians also have similar doubts."

" Well, Christians are ordinary human beings, too, Doris and they may go through periods of drought in their faith. Only the grace of God saves us all and fortifies our faith. My experience is thus not unusual: I thought that I should take my life in my own hands and be guided by reason and propriety only. The whole point of religion and the sacraments was lost on me. This went on for almost a year, and my parents were worried about me, my mum in particular, as I had stopped going to Mass."

"Chioma, you know I'm not a Catholic. I'm not even a Christian. So what you call your 'dark days' seem to me to be the ordinary way of life. I believe in myself and take from the world whatever it offers me that I find suitable. Yes, I make choices, but they are not based on any religious text but rather on my own conscience as to what is right or wrong."

I was relieved to hear that Doris had a robust sense of what was right and what was wrong. And I saw this as a window to return to my telling her about my earlier life of darkness that produced *Anyanwu*.

"Here's to you, Doris, dear."

"And to you Chioma, our own Paul Klee."

"So let me ask you, if I may, I thought you were Buddhist and that you lived by the principles of Zen."

"Yes, Chioma, they're just principles to guide you and nothing more. They are not dogma, like your Catholic dogma. You know my mum is a converted Catholic, and she's trying very hard to carry us all along with her. But I think we're simply too heavy for easy transportation from one religious life to another. As for me, as I said, nothing holds me to any particular religious thought."

We had a few more sips of wine, and then lunch arrived. Doris's lamb was temptingly hot pink, the cherry tomatoes, like little bubbles, adding a touch of romance to the colour. The red snapper was steaming hot, well garnished with shrimps and looked cheerfully divine. I was greatly satisfied with myself for having chosen *Nathan* on a day of fish and lamb. With grace and joy, we dove into our meal.

"You see, Doris, what I was saying about my dark days was that sometimes we do things without being in full control of our actions. We just go with the flow of things, carried on by the currents of whatever we're doing. The danger, Doris, is that we can be swept to forlorn islands of grief and pain. And then we're sorry in the end."

"I don't see anything special here, Chioma, it happens to all of us. It simply depends on what you want to call it; some might call it, 'learning experience', others, 'life's sobering experiments', and others, like you, call it 'darkness'. But don't forget, after darkness comes daylight. So why are you so afraid of the dark when you know daylight will come?"

"That's exactly what I mean, Doris, daylight may never come if we don't live to see the day. That dark night might just be our last night that never sees the day."

"Come on. Cheers! Let's enjoy the wine, Chioma. Let's forget the dark days and return to the painting."

"You observed it's not painted in my usual freestyle eliciting images of gaiety, of joy, of exuberant living. So, when you see *Anyanwu*, you know something must have been off when the work was done.

"How can I tell that anything was off, as you put it. Aren't you artists weird, some sort of 'gods' in your own world?"

"What would you say is weird about me, Doris; or what sort of god do you see in me?"

"Well, you are an okay person, Chioma, as far as I know, but then, when you start painting and you entered into your depths, would you say that you know who or what you are?"

"That's exactly the point I'm making, Doris. Generally I'm fine but on this occasion of *Anyanwu*, I just don't know what happened, how I came to paint that work. It was Jeff, a dear friend of my grandpa's, living here in Chevy Chase, who liked the works so much and explained to me its relationship with the god of divination in Yoruba culture called *Ifa*."

"Now you agree with me that you artists enter into another world when you paint. What, or who, is *Ifa?*"

"Oh, Doris, let's enjoy our lunch without much digression. As I said Ifa is the god who tells us all things about everything that is to happen or what may have happened, and teaches us how to avoid dangers, and the evil actions of our enemies, and so on. Of course, it is more than this, more complex too."

"So what did this Jeff do to help you back to normality?"

"He got me to mount an exhibition of all eight paintings, and you know what, they were all bought within an hour of their presentation to the select invited guests. The proud owner of *Nathan Hale* saw courage, honour and fortitude in *Anyanwu*, hallmark qualities of the hero Nathan Hale himself, and bought it at a very good price."

"Wow! Jeff is a great guy; he put you in the public eye."

"You're correct, Doris, Jeff has done a lot for me."

"What else did the owner of this fine restaurant do?"

"Mr. Gordon Anders, the proud owner of my painting and this restaurant, went further; as part of the purchase, he offered me a lunch-for-two, once a month. Anything we wanted we could have for as long as he owned the restaurant with *Anyanwu* invitingly displayed. That's why I suggested we come here. The whole lunch, *Pouilly-Fuisse* included, is on the house. So, in a way, darkness does turn into light. But we should not force the hands of the gods on this."

"Come on, Chioma, forget the gods. Here's to us." Doris raised her glass and we toasted to ourselves. Then came the bombshell.

"Chioma, you might know this already. Anyway, since you've said nothing about it all afternoon, let me bring it up now: Mike has moved in with me and is planning to file for divorce from Sutapa."

Of course, Sutapa had already told me all this, but I continued with my pretence and told Doris she was awfully disingenuous, especially as Sutapa was her friend, and she had often enjoyed the hospitality of their home. I was visibly distressed. I wondered if Doris would draw any parallel between what I said about darkness and sunlight; about my giving my painting the name, *Anyanwu,* in sharp contrast to the image it depicts or suggests; and, above all, about right and wrong, good and evil, seen in the images of light and darkness, respectively. And I wondered if the name *Nathan Hale* meant anything to her.

We continued with our lunch, enjoying every bit of it. All I could manage was, "Oh, that's a great pity." I could not leave this matter here. All of my Opus Dei spirit was ablaze. I invited Doris to give a talk on 'Conscience' to a focus group led by Susanne. I told her Susanne trained as an attorney and taught at Georgetown; that her group was purely informal and the members all spoke their minds freely and openly with the sole aim of helping one another through the difficult times they may be experiencing. She jumped at the chance of meeting Susanne of whom she had heard so much, especially concerning her fights for minority rights and gender equity. I told Doris I'd get back to her after obtaining Susanne's consent.

I was terribly upset and hoped that the talk and the focus group might help Doris take a critical look at her affair with Mike and get back to her original freshness.

NINETEEN

It was time to have a heart-to-heart talk, at Nesbit, with Angela to whom I had completely exposed my soul. Life's problems were mounting again, and I needed a breath of fresh air to revive my dying dreams.

Angela is a full blooded American. It is said her parents came on the Mayflower, but no one really believes that. Her family is at least six generations American, her great-great-great-great-great-grandfather having come to the eastern shores of America in the eighteenth century. The first Mr. Davenport established a home at Westport, Connecticut, and to this day his house sits on over twenty-five acres of choice land. The family has maintained it, with each successive generation adding this building or that, and there were now seven homes on the property, each a huge mansion. The ancestral building stands alone in the front, commanding a superior air of history and tradition. Angela had taken me there once, and from time to time, she visits her grandparents who live in quiet refuge in bucolic Westport.

"All my dear friends are having problems, and I don't seem to be able to help them. More than this, their problems have become my problems. Even worse, I think I feel the pain more than they do."

"Fantastic," Angela replied, a broad smile all over her angelic face.

"What's fantastic about it, if I may ask? And why this huge smile on your small face?"

"Are you sure, Chioma, are you sure that Washington is not getting to you, and you think it's your friends' problems that have suddenly shaken your otherwise tranquil soul? Will going to Westport help?"

"No, Angela, baring my soul will do, and, if after this, I still feel rotten, then we could seek Westport's fresh air. It's this whole question of marriage. You know Sutapa, my dear friend; I would say she's my closest friend. She is having problems with her husband Mike, and he has now left her for Doris, another friend of mine. You don't know her. She's Indian-American like Sutapa but she's more worldly than Sutapa, and perhaps more alluring too. Or, maybe, I think she's alluring because Mike has seen something he did not see in his wife in her. Mike has moved in with Doris and has filed for divorce. Why is life treating me this way? I cannot bear to see families falling apart. And their children, Dev and Tara, are taking it sorely. Why are some men jerks?"

"Come on, don't use that word, 'jerk'. It is unseemly and sullies your delightful lips. Let's just say that Mike has not been listening to the promptings of his soul for, whether Christian or not, God upholds families and is ever on the side of wives and husbands and gives them all the grace they need to live in love and fidelity. It's just that while some cooperate with the grace they receive and live worthy lives, others, and I daresay, Mike may be in this unsavoury category, row their marital canoes with oars of selfish desires. From what we know of Sutapa, she seems happy and content with her marriage and has never given us cause for worry. Has she in the past weeks, said anything to you or done anything that suggests danger in their union?"

"Nothing Angela, nothing of the sort. But then, you know it's the friends who're often the last to know if anything is wrong with a marriage."

"So how do you plan to proceed to help Sutapa and Doris?"

"I don't know, Angela, I don't know. I wish my brains would help me here, but I find that I'm not able to handle all these problems anymore. I was with Doris last week, and I didn't get far with her. Before our lunch, I already knew that Mike had moved in with her, but I didn't let her in on this; so before we parted she came out and told me herself."

"Where did you girls lunch? You must have taken her to a swell place."

"You guessed right. We went to *Nathan Hale* where my painting is displayed and where I am a guest of the house once a month. Doris didn't tell me more than that, and I left it at that too. I've invited her to give a talk on 'Conscience' to a focus group organized by my good friend, Dr. Susanne Capello. You remember her; she teaches jurisprudence at Georgetown."

"Oh, yes, I remember her; she came here for doctrinal formation in preparation for Holy Communion."

"Of course, how could I forget? Her group meet every fortnight, and they are into a lot of social and family issues. I think they would like to listen to Doris since she said she's guided only by what she considers right and wrong. I would like to hear what she has to say about the rightness or wrongness of living with a married man and ruining a happy marriage."

"When is the talk, and where? I'd like to come if I'm free."

"It will be on the second Friday of next month, and they usually meet at the basement of the Goldman Building at Georgetown. It will be at 7 p.m."

"Ah! Sorry, that's a dreadful time. I have to be at Nesbit for some talks at that time. If it were earlier, I would have joined you. Anyway, you'll tell me all about it."

"Back to where we were: you know the kind of life we live - a contemplative life of joy and peace in the midst of the world, always cheerful, not brought down by life's debacles - has a lot of pain and suffering. But it is precisely the struggle to face and overcome this suffering that produces joy and peace. It sounds like a paradox, but it's real and you know it as I do. You have a sensitive heart and you are hurt by little things and you feel pain easily. Still, you're calm and give us these fantastic paintings all singing alleluias to God. Well, you'll be able to help your friends because you feel their pain. Pray, pray hard and then put your mind to it and, with God's help, you'll be able to come up with some assistance for Sutapa and Doris. I think it's Doris who stands more in need of help because she doesn't seem to know what she's doing."

"You've got it, Angela, she doesn't seem to know what she's doing. That's why I took her to *Nathan* where my painting *Anyanwu* hangs. I took her through the dark period of my life when I made that painting. I thought Doris might be prompted into thinking of this period of her life as a period as dark as mine. But she didn't see things that way."

"Of course, she won't feel like she's in a dark period. The way she sees it, she's having a ball, the time of her life, a life filled with sunlight, gaiety and laughter. Oh yes, she's feeling happy and romantically satisfied. But I can tell you, one day, she'll wake up and Mike won't be there for her, having returned to Sutapa, not because Doris isn't beautiful and alluring but, in fact, it would be precisely because she's beautiful and alluring. It sometimes happens that the reason men marry women are the selfsame reasons they give when they seek a divorce, or just want to change partners. The qualities of being a mistress, a fiancée or a girlfriend, are not quite the same as those required in a wife."

"What are you saying; that men come to hate what they once loved? Is that it?"

"Yes, indeed, it happens. Men come to hate what they once prized highly. A man falls in love with a girl because she's freewheeling, a free spirit, living a life of total abandon, not caring about the details of dedicated living. After marriage, he wants her to be a solid rock of fidelity and order, predictable, highly organized. He doesn't get his wishes, however, because he wants something which she is not. Or, when they were boyfriend-girlfriend, she was always seductive, scantily dressed, showing much skin, dancing the latest steps, and then after marriage he wants her to be stolid and conservative. And when he does not get that he cries foul and heads for the divorce court."

Angela and I continued talking about how we could help Doris find herself again and live a wholesome life. We agreed to see how her talk went and then take it from there. As for Sutapa, her stability and peace of mind depended on Doris's final decision. Angela, ever compassionate, ever understanding, had put my mind at peace.

Since I had about a week free from teaching, I spent the time in the studio painting images of love, youth and fidelity. But I felt rotten. My own problems I can deal with, for the solution lies in the problem itself. I really felt like going to Westport but did not have the courage to face Angela again and tell her I had changed my mind. She would not like that. After all, I had the chance to say yes, but I did not. I felt miserable and could not shake off the feeling.

TWENTY

It was a Saturday morning. I had gone to my studio on Connecticut Avenue and 18th St., Washington, D.C. to pour out my thoughts and feelings on love, unrequited and fulfilled, the sort of things my good friends, Sutapa and Doris must be experiencing, respectively, at that time. In the corridor outside, studiously inspecting some reproductions of my paintings on the wall, were three girls. I walked past them, and as I was opening the door to my studio, one of them ran to me.

"Are you Chioma Akadike Ijeoma?" she asked.

"Yes I am," I answered.

"You are Ms. Ijeoma, the Nigerian student who broke all records at Georgetown University and is renowned for her angelic paintings?"

I did not know how to say a straightforward yes to encomiums, so I simply repeated that it was I.

"I'm Funke, and my friends over there are Amaka and Nkemdi. I'm a freshman at Georgetown, and don't know what

I'll major in yet but I'm inclined toward architecture. Amaka is a junior studying computer science at GWU, and Nkemdi, also a junior, is a physics major at College Park. We have heard of you and wanted so much to meet you; and so we made inquiries and were told that we stood a good chance of meeting you in person if we came here on a Saturday morning before noon. In the alternative, we were told to go up to College Park where you teach. And finally, since you enjoy the rare distinction of being Artiste-in-residence at Georgetown, and have an office in the Stanley Cohen building, we were told we could meet you there if we came on the first Friday of the month after 2 p.m. Well, the first Friday of the month is about a month away, and we didn't want to wait that long to see you. So, here we are."

"What can I do for you girls? From your names I can tell you are all Nigerians like me. Let's go inside."

We entered the studio. There were some finished and unfinished works and some of my favourites which I keep to myself on the wall. The girls were excited.

"My goodness, Ms. Ijeoma, you're something else. All these are products of your own hands?" Nkemdi asked.

"Yes they come from my hands quite all right; but I think it is more than that. I'm limited but I do try to re-produce on canvas the magnificent images I see in my soul."

"Ms. Ijeoma," said Nkemdi, "we have no clue what you're talking about. We know nothing about paintings and the meanings they convey, neither can we begin to imagine what goes on in the minds of painters as they paint. We really have a lot to learn from you. Aren't we lucky to have found you?"

"Oh, don't worry you're going to learn a lot, and you're going to help me learn a lot too. But let me quickly add here,

that with the eyes of faith, we can capture the image of God.
What schools did you attend in Nigeria?"

Funke came in to bat:

"We all attended Owerri Girls' Secondary School, but at
different times. I am the oldest, I graduated in 2001, Nkemdi
and Amaka in 2002."

"That's wonderful," I continued: "Owerri Girls' Secondary
School used to be a Catholic school and I think that even after
the government took over Catholic schools some of them
retained their Catholic foundation. With faith in God we're
able to comprehend mysteries, though not fully. I think God
works in our souls where he speaks to us and with faith we
can see him, live with him and dance with him."

"Please, Ms. Ijeoma, this is too much for our little heads.
Let's just enjoy these paintings and then you'll train our
empty minds to be able to capture the true image of God as he
wants us to know him."

"Fantastic, Nkemdi, you know reality can best be captured
as images. So let us continue. Just forget the paintings for now
and tell me what I can do for you."

"Yes," Amaka said, "we're all Nigerians. That's why we are
here to appreciate your wonderful accomplishments in this
godforsaken land."

"What makes you say that, Amaka?"

"Just call me Ama, Ms. Ijeoma"

"Why do you describe this great country as 'Godforsaken'? You live here and school here, and this country has
so much to offer you. You should be grateful. You know
America is called God's Own Country. Haven't you heard
that?"

"I'm sorry, Ms. Ijeoma, if I've upset you. It's just that we were told that if we wanted to retain our African-ness and our rich Igbo traditions, we should stay close to you.

"Who told you this, your parents?"

"No, Ms. Ijeoma. Our parents are not here." That was Nkemdi speaking.

"Oh! Ama, you talk about your rich Igbo traditions. What about mine? Do you think that because I lived in Owerri all my life I have all of a sudden become one of you? Granted my mum is from Umuoji, and my dad is no more, so I spend all my time with my mum. Well, go ahead, call me Igbo, just don't forget I'm an Owu girl, that is I'm Egba, with the Alake as my king. And though I'm more fluent in Igbo than Yoruba, I'm still my father's daughter, and proud of the great Egba Kingdom."

"Don't mind Funke, Ms. Ijeoma, she's been with us for as long as we can remember, right from our primary school days. Her father has prime property in Owerri, and during the war, he sided with us and just like our parents did, he ran from here to there to escape the rampaging army. Of course, we were not born by then, but our parents told us everything about the war."

"We came here through the American lottery system. We were lucky and gained admission into the universities where we are now."

"That's wonderful. You must be some of the best students from your class in Nigeria then. Well, Owerri Girls' is a good school. Who pays your fees, your parents?"

"Yes our parents are responsible on paper," Ama responded. "Our tuition and board are paid from a scholarship fund provided by the Umuoji Development Union, Lagos branch. And GWU has come in with a tidy sum for me as scholarship stipend, and I share this with Funke and Nkemdi from time to time."

"So, how can I help you maintain your African-ness?"

Before we continued, Funke quickly stopped me.

"Oh, please, Ms. Ijeoma, let me say how grateful I am to the Umuoji Union, Lagos branch, for paying my fees since it's my mum who's from Umuoji. The three of us, Ama, Nkemdi and me are inseparable. Our parents watch over us and assume collective responsibility for all of us; that is to say, if anyone of us is in need, any of the parents who can help readily does so. When Nkemdi's dad took the matter of my education to the Union, he had little difficulty convincing them to come to my assistance because many of them knew my dad in person from Owerri or had heard of him. They see me as one of their own in true African spirit."

Nkemdi continued, "Well, we were on the web and read what one Dr. Jeff Cooper wrote about you and your family, your total absorption, if it can be believed, into your great-grandfather, Chief Akadike Okeosisi, an amazing man himself. He described your ancestry, how you have adopted your family traditions, your determined African spirit and, of course, your talent in art. He went on and on and we could not believe our eyes. So here we are, for you to guide us, build us up, and guide us to marry our African-ness with the American way of life."

"Nkemdi, I hope I do not disappoint you but Dr. Cooper is prejudiced in my favour and says all sorts of wonderful things about me, much of which I don't deserve. I would even say he's as Igbo as you can get being a close friend of my grandpa's and having lived in Nigeria for a year. Right now, he's back in Nigeria, living in Pa Akadike's compound at Okeosisi. He makes trips to Nsukka, spends two or three days there and then returns to his base in Okeosisi.

"Well, now you know where to find me. I'll give you my numbers, and I'll also have yours. That way, we can all be in contact with one another and we can then best help one another."

"We hear you live at a residence for professional women. What sort of place is this Nesbit Centre? It sounds so un-ordinary."

This was our 'un-ordinary' Nkemdi wanting to know more about me. I guess these girls really wanted to get together with me and I decided to accommodate their wish.

"No, Nkemdi, I've been going to Nesbit these past few years, but I do not yet live at the Centre. I live with my parents and hope to move to Nesbit in due course. I can't tell you exactly how it is. You just have to go there and see it for yourself. But let me tell you that Nesbit is not a 'place' as much as a home, where one lives within a family of God's own children in a cheerful Christian atmosphere in which heart, body and soul can truly reflect the nobility of the human being. Home is where you live out your dream. So, I'll bring you to Nesbit; in fact, next Sunday would be a good day. It's our Day of Recollection. You might like the talks and Meditations, or periods of personal prayer and self-examination. They are directed by Opus Dei priests in the oratory of the Centre."

"Yes, we hope to enjoy the talks, Ms. Ijeoma."

"Well, it would be wonderful if all three of you could come. But please let's leave out this "Ms." bit. You know, here in the US people are less formal and call one another by their first names."

I was only testing their regard for African culture and they truly obliged my curiosity.

"Ah! Miss, but we can't just call you by your first name. We are Africans and we don't do that, whatever they do in the US notwithstanding. But please what time is the talk?" Funke spoke for the group.

I was truly satisfied. "I'm sorry I did not tell you. It begins at 10am. After that, we'll have a barbecue in the garden. Please come and, oh, bring your friends, all your friends. You will have to pay a little something to help us run Nesbit. Ok?"

"Very Okay," Funke responded. I saw them off to the lift and returned to do some painting. A knock on the door interrupted my thoughts.

"Can we stay and watch you paint?" Nkemdi asked.

"Oh, I'm so sorry, Nkemdi, but right now I want to sit for a while and gather my thoughts before I commence my work, and this could take a long time. It might take me two to three hours before I begin to paint. And your staying would not help me at all because I need to be all by myself."

"Well, we thought you look awful, your eyes are red and puffed up. Although we have not seen you before today, we do not think you look yourself; you are somewhat unhappy."

That was Nkemdi not taking no for an answer. What do I say? Before I could say anything she continued.

"Something must be wrong because you have a long, weary look on your face. Why don't we go and get some coffee at Starbucks across the street? What do you say, Ms. Ijeoma? Although you don't know us well, we know about you. We'll take care of you. Is that not the African way of helping one another?"

We went off to Starbucks and I had a great time with the girls. I immediately took to them and told myself I would stay close to them and be of assistance as much as I could.

****

I shall never forget the date of the day I started living fully at Nesbit, Wednesday, 22 March, 2006. I had stayed there off and on for over a year, so my residency did not come with a bang. It was not meant to: for, indeed, my vocation in Opus Dei is based profoundly on my professional work and on my social and cultural life at College Park where I teach, and Georgetown where I do my painting. This is what Opus Dei is really all about: to sanctify my work, that is to offer God my best efforts; to sanctify myself in my work, to seek holiness in all I do, and to sanctify others through my work. And for me, the academic profession, as well as my panting, gives me a tremendous opportunity to live my vocation fully in the ordinary circumstances of my life.

At the centre, I am in the unique and immediate position to demonstrate to my female friends, at first hand, the joy and fulfilment that come from living the Christian vocation better and better in our steadfast struggle for holiness. The programme for spiritual formation, in which I directly participate, guides us and leads us along the path of the Cross to the Kingdom of God. I cannot adequately convey the joy I have when I return to the centre at the end of my day's work and immediately run to the arms of our Lord in the Tabernacle, in the Blessed Sacrament, and have him hold me firmly and lovingly. I whisper sweet words to his attentive ears; or sing him a song, tell him of all the troubles and *wahala* of the day; or just sit there in his warm embrace!

Yes, I could live at home, quite wonderfully with my parents and family, but now in addition to being with my new family of numeraries, all of us living out our Christian vocation in our professional life, assisting one another and others who come to the centre in the path of holiness, I go to bed at night knowing that our Lord lives next door to me in the oratory, truly, physically and substantially present in the Eucharist. What joy! What peace! I feel that all of creation lives in me; as I would be totally available to serve my God, and all his creation in love, wherever Opus Dei activities may take me.

TWENTY-ONE

I invited my new-found friends—Nkemdi, Funke and Amaka to Doris's talk at Susanne's focus group, and they all gladly came. They wanted to be exposed as much as possible to American culture and I thought they would have something to gain from a talk on 'conscience' by an Indian-American.

"Before we start talking about 'conscience', which I'm supposed to discuss at this get-together, let me first tell you a true story that happened just two weeks ago."

I had introduced Doris to the audience, and she now commenced her talk.

"Chioma had kindly taken me to lunch at The *Nathan Hale* restaurant in Bethesda. Some of you may have read about it in The Washington Post where it always appears on their Weekend Guide-to-Restaurants' column. It's a posh place, very intimate and inviting. I had heard that one of Chioma's paintings lived at *Nathan*, but I had never been there to see it. So when she invited me to lunch, I knew that I would be killing two birds with one stone, have lunch with her and see the painting called *Anyanwu*, one of the landmark paintings in Maryland, talked about by all, acclaimed by the connoisseurs.

Where was Doris taking us to, I wondered. Perhaps, that was how she got Mike, taking him on vast seas for which he had only weak and feeble oars. Anyway, I was all ears.

"Once a month, Chioma is allowed to bring a guest to *Nathan Hale* for lunch, free of charge; this way, she would be able to talk about her painting with any guest dining there who wanted to know more about this masterpiece. And many a guest had gone there just to meet Chioma, on the day listed in the Post.

"There was something new happening in my life of which Chioma was aware, but she cleverly avoided bringing it up during our lunch. The husband of her best friend, Sutapa, has left his wife and moved in with me. That's what everyone thinks, and I was certain Chioma had lunched with me in the hope that we could discuss this matter, and to see if there was a way Mike could be persuaded to return to Sutapa. Chioma said nothing about this; instead, she talked about the dark period of her life when she painted *Anyanwu*, which, by the way, is the Igbo word for 'sunshine'. She contrasted the meaning of *Anyanwu*, sunshine, light, brightness, energy, vigour, redemption, resurrection, with the dark nights of her mind when she did the painting, in the hope, I believe, that I might somehow view Mike's rendezvous with me as darkness."

I had not been with Susanne's group before this day and was not sure whether or not I could butt in from time to time,

such as the times Doris referred to me. Since everyone else
was quiet, I took a cue from them. I had thought they would
interrupt the flow with questions, from time to time. Since
they did not, Doris sallied on.

"I did nothing to help her in her ploy to draw something
out of me about Mike. After lunch, she asked me here,
requesting that I talk about 'conscience' because I had told her
that I was guided in what I do by what I think is right and
what I think is wrong. I'm sure Chioma would give me one of
her masterpieces just to get me to give up Mike and make him
return to his wife, which is precisely what I have done, and
I'm not asking for a painting."

I was not sure I had heard Doris right. Did she just say
that she had given up on Mike, after a brief six-week affair? I
did not know whether to jump from my seat or shout for joy. I
thought of asking her to repeat what she had just said, but I
felt I should give her all the support she needed and so I kept
quiet. Doris now looked straight in my direction and
continued.

"You see, Chioma's a bright young woman, assiduous and
ingenuous too. She would give her life for her friend. To her,
friendship is everything. Now, I wonder if Chioma still wants
me to talk about conscience. I think what she would like to
hear now is how I managed to get Mike to return to Sutapa."

I could not believe what was happening. How could Doris
have read my thoughts so well? Did I leave any clues to
suggest all that she has revealed? How could all this be
happening: if I am as ingenuous as Doris would have us
believe, how could I have missed her eyes and what they
said? I pride myself in being able to look into people's eyes
and make out what might be happening in their minds, and

here I am, not knowing what to do. My spiritual strength must be at its lowest ebb for me not to be able to understand the world I see before me.

I gave free rein to my spirit and decided to go along with Doris; she says she has helped Mike to go back to his wife. What more could I ask for? After all, that is exactly what I wished for—that husband and wife should live together in love.

"Well, well, I have astonished my good friend, Chioma, and now she's dumbfounded. But I can look at her eyes and see into her mind. Yes, I can tell she wants me to continue now, since she knows I won't be a hypocrite, telling you one thing, while I run off and live a wild life with someone else's husband."

We all laughed, a few side remarks here and there, and we were quiet once again.

"Let's go back to the reason why I'm here. So, what's conscience? As Chioma sees it, and I give her credit for her faith, she wanted me to use the occasion of my talk to look at my soul using the bright lights of my conscience, to come to my senses and end my affair with someone else's husband. I have used words that lead us to a better understanding of what conscience is all about. I have used words like, 'faith', 'soul', and 'bright lights'. Let me now introduce another expression, a statement credited to Uthman Dan Fodio, and used by a Nigerian newspaper, *The Guardian* as its motto: "Conscience is an open wound: only truth can heal it." Thanks to our conscience, we are able to judge whether our actions are good or bad."

This made me glad: Doris had introduced the subject and at the same time brought the attention of the audience to one of Nigeria's finest papers.

"Uthman Dan Fodio was a religious leader who introduced Islam into Northern Nigeria. *The Guardian* is a popular newspaper known for its intellectual flavour. Chioma reads it quite often and introduced it to me.

"I think we can now proceed with our discourse. I think the most important word here is 'truth', what is 'truth'? As you might know, a big problem faced by the world today is how to define 'truth'; I don't intend to go into all the different connotations given to this erstwhile simple word, 'truth', on which the whole concept of right and wrong is based."

It is just as well that Doris did not delve into the complexities of 'truth' or the talk would have lasted all evening. She did not say more on this and went on to aspects of right and wrong we were all familiar with.

"Parents teach their children what is right and what is wrong, at least they teach them what to do and what not to do. As they grow up, the children begin to find their way in life and to challenge their parents as to what is proper and what is not, based on their own life's experiences which, they say, is quite different from those of their parents. That is to say, to them it seems everything is relative, relative to the circumstances, to the environment, to the prevailing culture. There are no absolutes anymore. There's no absolute truth. Truth is that which an individual considers as truth. So now we have 'your truth', 'my truth', 'their truth'. Of course, this is nonsense. We do not create truth. Truth is determined by the reality of things as they are independent of us."

Some people in the group seemed to take exception to Doris's use of the word, 'nonsense'. There were hisses and some disquiet, but Susanne requested that everyone wait till the end with any disapproval.

"I have a conscience; we all have a conscience. My conscience speaks to me. I would answer to my conscience. What she wants from me then, is to let my will act according to the dictates of my conscience. It's very important for the will to conform to one's conscience. It is thus essential to have a well-formed conscience so that truth may always prevail; and so that when we do wrong, we know we are doing wrong, and not try to wish it away as a 'relative' good, following a misguided notion of truth. I think this is really what Chioma wanted from me. I hope I haven't disappointed her.

"To complete the discourse, let me add that conscience is our intellect which we apply to judge the morality of our thoughts and deeds. If or thoughts and deeds conform to human dignity, they are good; but if our thoughts or actions are not in conformity with human dignity, they are bad. I think that's all I have to say. Thank you all."

Susanne opened the talk for discussion but not before this brief remark: "Well, Chioma, as you can see, Doris has saved you a lot of trouble. Your problem is now solved though not exactly as you had planned."

Nkemdi threw a bombshell: "Why worry about conscience when we can be guided by knowledge? To me, knowledge is all that matters. I have come to the United States to gain knowledge in this knowledge-driven world with all its scientific and technological advances in the way we gain information, process information and live according to knowledge-driven information; to use what is useful, whatever enlivens the spirit and gives the individual maximum freedom. That is the world as I see it, the truth of the world we live in."

I felt ill at ease but kept quiet. Arlene, an Australian, a sophomore at the American University majoring in anthropology, came to the rescue.

"Of course, truth exists, and there's no such thing as relative truth. Things are the way they are in reality and not the way we feel about them. No matter what I may feel to the contrary, the truth is that I am a woman and not a bear! We once thought that the earth was the centre of the universe. But Copernicus put all that in the wastebasket of errors. At the time that knowledge prevailed, it was accepted to be correct. But then superior scientific knowledge showed that it was not true. Science has elucidated the truth about nature in so many ways."

I did not know which direction her contribution would now take, as a number of scholars see science as a god, that makes all things knowable, and, in time, would make all things known. I listened with intense apprehension. Arlene then dazzled us:

"But, of course, not everything can be explored by means of scientific tools or scientific paradigms: we do not study love in the laboratory, neither do we inquire into friendship, courtship, marriage, celibacy, with the tools and methods of science. And, yet, marriage is true, as is love, as is celibate consecration of oneself for the kingdom of God, that is, apostolic celibacy.

"Can we live without air? Can we live without love? These questions are not at all similar. We cannot live without air. We need air to live. But we most surely can live without love; that is to say, if we are not loved, it will not of itself be the cause of our death. We would still live, but it would be a shallow life not worth much. It would all depend on the one whose life is without love, what he or she wants to make of that life. Truth does exist. What happens to the food we eat? It is digested and fed into our blood for living. One cannot deny this. We cannot deny that our heart is beating now: that is a fact."

I was very relieved; my heart had resumed beating at its normal pace. Arlene kept us all relaxed with her talk; but I wondered where all this came from. It was turning into heavy academic stuff, not light conversation at all and she was not done yet.

"The objective truth of our humanity does not inquire into variable personal nuances, but into what makes us human, the nature of the human being and of the universe, the interrelationships between humans, and between humans and their world. Here, revealed truth from the scriptures, the word of God, is indispensable, and as much as we can raise questions about it in our studies, in our minds and in our thoughts, our very nature as humans moves our intellect to accept revealed truth. For our humanity is bound up in our oneness with our Creator, who has revealed himself to us, having made us for himself."

Nkemdi would have none of this. For her, revealed truth is handed down to us as dogma, and in her book, there is no such thing as dogma. She believes that humans can come to a complete understanding of themselves and their world using the tools of science and reason alone, guided by knowledge. The entire universe is knowable, she proclaims, and when we know all things we will discover that the so-called dogma was only meant to keep us at a subhuman level, not much higher than the animals. Humans have their life in their hands, and they can determine what to do with it. She believes it is all relative to one's own perspective.

Susanne was invigorated by the discussion which was blowing this way and that like the wind. But she tried to direct the wind in the direction of objective truth, revealed truth, and the unrepeatable mystery in each human being as a child of God, reminding everyone of what Doris had said, particularly the bit about every child being taught by her parents what was right and what was wrong. Surely the knowledge of right and wrong establishes some standards which in time become habits, and we would like to acquire good habits and avoid bad ones. All this has bearing on the truth, which is not created by the parents but is determined by the reality of human nature. Humans are rational creatures with intellect and will, capable of acting with freedom and responsibility.

Susanne continued, "Doris said Chioma should have come out and told her what was on her mind instead of trying to lead her to a confession, or some hypocrisy. Again, this is related to the truth. She also talked about conscience as an open wound. Wounds are real and need healing. No one likes to be injured: we all want to be healthy and wholesome. The same thing applies to truth. Truth heals wounds. Life sees many injuries, so many things that do not work out: oversized egos, depression, falsehood, defeat, lost loves, failed relationships; so many things do go wrong and only when we can face the truth about ourselves and our experiences, our relationships, can we ever hope to be able to solve our problems. Lies do not solve problems: only the truth does. Truth does more; it is the stuff of which life is made."

After the talk, we meandered to the coffee table and helped ourselves to cold cuts, cheese sandwiches, soft drinks, coffee, and other simple fare. I promptly offered Doris my apology and she drew me to a corner where we were alone, undisturbed.

Again, she surprised me.

"Chioma, you must wonder how I could have read your mind so perfectly. No, it's not the work of God: it's the work of my evil, inquisitive mind. I see you making notes all the time, and I'm forever wondering what it is you are writing."

This was true: I scribble a lot into a note pad I have with me, mindful that if I ever lost it, I was done for; but I was not prepared for what Doris had in store for me.

"That time, at lunch, when you went to the 'ladies' to wash your hands as you always do before meals, so that you can feel at ease eating your bread and whatever else you felt like eating with your hands. Well, when you went to the 'ladies', I took out your notebook and read what you had written about me, about the lunch, about your doing apostolate work with me, and how you would get me to speak on 'conscience' to enable me to look at myself and see what evil course I pursued in living with a married man, whose wife was a dear friend of mine.

"And more, you held me up as someone whose friendship you would always cherish and who, therefore, you would hold dear and always assist no matter what. I was quite touched. I was moved to search my soul. I never thought I had a soul worth searching. And I didn't like what I saw. That's when I decided that I would rather have the wholesome joy of your friendship than the hopeless love of another woman's husband, who, by the way, snores a lot. And I can't stand a man who snores!"

My shock subsided, and I was somewhat more relaxed after Doris had put my mind at ease. She then wanted to know how I could live a life of chastity.

"Please, tell me, Chioma, how do you plan to live a life of celibacy? Look at you: you are a beautiful woman, you have a charming and pleasant personality; you're friendly and genial and on top of all it all, you're gifted. College Park says you can do whatever you like for your Ph.D. thesis, no questions asked; they pay you a great stipend, a stipend you don't even need as your paintings have made you a fortune and still sell for tidy sums. Your paintings have sold for close to a million dollars by now. Yet you want to stay single. Has no one ever seduced you?"

"Well, Doris, you could use the word 'seduced' because you're very much in the world - given to seduction. You see, seduction leads to pleasurable follies that may end in sin. And where there's sin, there is no beauty. I have had certain feelings for Bia, a nice man who would do anything to marry me. But I have been led into a life of the greatest beauty and splendour, by the songs and flowers of my Tremendous Lover, playing violins to my heart, serenading my spirit into a a new world of freshness and bounteous joy.

"Let me quickly add that all the earnings from my paintings and my salaries, apart from covering my personal needs, frugal as they are, all go towards the upkeep of Nesbit, and for the apostolic works of the Centre as we usually source funds for our activities."

"What do you mean by you want to live a celibate life with all the love you say you have experienced, or is it a new kind of love?" Doris asked.

"Yes, Doris, it's a new kind of love."

"Is it the kind where a man tells you he's madly in love with you, can't live without your company, tells you that you have the erotic smell of gardenias and frangipani, that he wants to kiss your feet and drink *Meursault* from your shoes, swears on his mother's grave that he will ever remain faithful to you, looks into your eyes and swoons."

"Yes, I was once seduced, exactly as you've described. There's this young man, Bia, who would not let me be. I still believe he truly loves me. Yes, he had gone further than seduce me. He wanted to marry me, have seventeen children with me, and give me all the best that this life could offer in marital chastity. He's a fantastic person, brilliant, a Catholic like me, with an interesting ancestral history. But, you see, his kind of seduction and the virtues don't mix. So, I'm not for Bia, I'm for someone else. I've already told you he is a Tremendous Lover and no person loves as he loves. He's ever after me, he gives me all of himself.

"Yes, Bia wanted to drink from my shoes, he wanted to bury himself in me. But you see, he would still be Bia, and I would still be Chioma. Nothing more: even as he tried to lift me up to higher and greater heights of love and friendship. I believed he could make me happy and give me a fulfilled life. But I wanted something more. I wanted something much, much more, indeed. And my Lover wants much more from me than I could ever give any human being. And even if I didn't give him all he wanted from me, still he would love

me, having died for me that I may have life and have it
abundantly."

"Who's this mysterious lover of yours, who died for you,
if I may ask, Chioma? Who is he? I'm jealous. And how could
he have died for you and still lives to love you?"

TWENTY-TWO

i was disturbed by what Nkemdi had said at the talk, and I
wondered what lay ahead for such a girl in the United States,
especially for one straight from Nigeria where the old
traditions of truth, good and evil are still extant and, to a large
extent, determine the everyday life of the people. Even in the
face of corruption, people have a good grasp of what is right
and what is wrong, not in a legal sense but, rather, in a social,
familial sense. Or was I out of touch with things in my
country? I very much wanted to be of assistance to Nkemdi,
no matter how slowly or painstakingly.

I worried and worried, and when I was weary of
worrying about Nkemdi, I turned to myself, asking myself all
sorts of questions. Where I stand is clear. I stand on the solid
rock of truth as revealed to me in the scriptures and in the
mysteries and traditions of the Catholic Church.

I see myself as a painter. I am used to reality and its
transformations, giving us new images of human experience.
When I paint images of my African heritage, my mind is
boundless, and life takes on new forms as I try to depict the
little things of great significance to me. Suddenly, what was
simple is now magnificently exalted to an extension of our
closeness to God and our expression of his divinity.
Everything I see, I see with the beautiful eyes of faith, and all

is expressed in the most glorious form I can imagine. Nothing is dross: all is beauty. I look at my great-grandmother's kitchen at Okeosisi. I see pots and pans, the smaller ones inside the bigger ones, making a high pile. I see indigo-coloured earthenware pots for water. These are not the pots that hold drinking water; no, they hold only the water used for cooking or washing. The larger pots used for drinking water are kept out of sight in a room in the main house where Ma stores cooked food in cupboards. The floor is not cemented: Ma will not have it. She prefers the clay floor as she had always had it in her own mother's home; a mother who brought her up to see the kitchen as the final testament of noble Igbo traditional cuisine and family conviviality, never to be trampled on.

My Pa lived in the grandeur and opulence of a zinc-roofed edifice built with cement blocks; but for Ma, the kitchen reflects the legends of family celebrations and festivals down the ages. There are windows in Ma's kitchen, high up near the thatched roof, one in each of the four walls, four altogether and each, not more than one square foot in size, which means that Ma's kitchen is often filled with smoke, spiralling upward, seeking escape. Ma cooks on one side of the kitchen with the fireplace close to the wall, with the result that this wall is the darkest, but it is the one against which any child who wants something to chew would lean, with arms outstretched to Ma for a piece of stockfish, or meat, or snail, or bush meat. Ma has them all in her basket safely stowed away higher up on a rack above the fire, and out of the reach of any child's short arms.

I try to paint this, and believe me, with each meal that my Ma cooks, the geography of the kitchen changes, depending on how dry the firewood is, and, therefore, how quickly the flames rise and how firmly they stay; the time of day, whether the sun is high or is hidden from view by the trees, with the heat on the outer walls soft or fierce, making the inside cool or warm; whether it is raining and windy, in which case Ma might leave the kitchen door ajar, or close it, and make do with the insufficient air from the windows. All this I try to capture in my paintings, giving them a life of grace, freshness, and warmth. And even more, in my Ma's kitchen you see love, you touch and eat love, you drink and savour love. All these are in my paintings: one conveying grace, another something of the joy soaked in the vegetables and stockfish of Igbo cuisine.

I paint what is before me; what I 'see' as I paint; what is on my mind; and how my mind transforms what I 'see', I pour into my works in the hope that all who see them might be filled with the love of God and be transported to heavenly places. I paint that all may see their soul through the eyes of my art. You may say this is not real; that it is a twist on the truth, returning us to the question, what is truth?

****

"Who is this lover of yours?" Doris asked me. I was not willing to get into that discussion at the time because it was at the very kernel of my existence.

"Doris, it is not a long story at all and I could answer this question in one or two words. But I need to go into myself to answer it, for I can tell you, Cupid's arrow has pierced my heart, and now my blood flows seeking the vast sea of my Lover's veins. Let us have dinner next weekend and I shall bare my soul to you."

"You're making this thing sound so serious, Chioma, as if it's a matter of life and death. It's only about seduction isn't it?"

"No, Doris, it's not so simple. Dinner next weekend, not at *Nathan Hale*; this time, but at *The Canyon*, 6 p.m. Is that ok?"

"Why don't I give you a call? You know I've got to sort myself out with Mike and as much as he's left my apartment, I still have some feelings for him, and would like to talk the whole thing over with him so that there's no chance, no matter how slim, of his coming back to me. Do I want him to go back to Sutapa? That's entirely his business. I can't help him there. All I'm interested in is myself; to get on with my life, and make the most of it. Look at you, and see what you've made of your own life. Why can't I do just that?"

"Well, you're on my side now. Come and I'll tell you about my Tremendous Lover who has made me the happiest woman alive. Let us meet. It will give you a chance to avoid Mike, if nothing else. Let him know you're getting on with your life and not there waiting for him, giving the impression you might change your mind. He must get it clear that his days with you are over. Dinner, next weekend it is then."

We met at *The Canyon*. Doris was sitting at the bar with a glass of white wine. She looked very much like Sutapa, exquisitely Indian; dressed in a white crepe sleeveless *kameez*, designed with sequins and stones, showing off her lithe, tender arms, her long, flowing hair tied in a bun at the back. I had never seen her look like this, that is, with so much resemblance to the wife of the philanderer - no wonder he fell for her. If so, there was a good chance he might return to the original version of his heart's desire.

Doris had T-bone steak, rare, with baked potatoes and whipped crème, and I had lamb chops and French fries. We both had water. I had expected her to go for her favorite burgundy to wash down the steak and so was surprised to see her choose ordinary water. She must really want to listen to every word I had to say about this lover of mine. I did not want to disappoint her.

"Well, Doris, let me not keep you waiting for too long: my Tremendous Lover is the Holy Spirit."

Doris, did not let me continue: she blurted out, "The Holy what?" much to the hearing of other diners who turned to our table.

I hushed her and asked her to lower her voice.

"Are you serious? Do you expect me to sit here and not raise my voice when I hear something as preposterous as what you have just said? Chioma, I know your Blessed Virgin Mary conceived Jesus by the power of the Holy Spirit, but she never said she was seduced by him. How come your case is different? Are you going to give us another Jesus?"

"Come on, Doris, you know better than that and...."

Again she butted in, "I guessed I was going to hear something I had never heard before and so I decided not to drink wine to be sure that I would be completely sober throughout our meal. You've not disappointed me. Now let's return to your lover."

"Doris, what is love; what do you know about love?"

"Don't be childish; every adult female in this age knows precisely what love is. So don't ask me these questions, just go ahead and talk about your own experience."

"Doris, love is all about giving oneself to the object of one's love. The more you love, the more you give. I'm sorry, I take that back. You have to give yourself completely to the one you love, body and soul; totally, without reserve. You could say no human being is deserving of this love. That is correct, and, in some marriages, you do find total giving of one to the other and the two do, indeed, become one flesh.

"I know all this. I can even accept that the Holy Spirit loves you. But that is the same Holy Spirit who loves me, even if I do not consider him my lover. So, what makes your case different?"

"That's the whole point, Doris, what makes my case different is that I have given all of my life to him, to serve him, to love him, to do whatever he wants me to do, to always seek his company, praying for him to be at my side throughout the day, from my waking moment till I fall asleep. I long for him and seek his face and he rewards me with smiles and kisses so triumphant that they turn all the circumstances of my life into a masterpiece of joy and peace. His music runs through my every act transforming my mere mortal deeds into symphonies of praise and thanksgiving to God, my Creator. He's ever at my side and only takes his leave on those terrible occasions when I temporarily lose my sense of self as his child and offend him. And I suffer, and suffer, until I run into his arms, he fixes his Almighty eyes on me, and I say to him in great sorrow, "Forgive me, my Lord, for I have offended you. I love you; help my lack of love."

"Chioma, are you all right? Is this what celibacy means, tell me?"

"No, that, of course, is not what celibacy means. One could be celibate for many reasons which have nothing to do with sanctity. I refer to my being celibate in order to devote myself to the service of God, the Church and all souls as apostolic celibacy. But let me finish what's on my mind."

"My ears have heard plenty. No one touches you. No one sends you flowers. No one calls you to say, 'I love you.' I guess that's okay. Here I am: the one who does these things isn't even mine. It was all so temporary and now he's gone. What do I look forward to? Another affair? No, Chioma, no, that can't be love. I want something more. I want something greater. I want someone who is mine and mine alone, to whom I would give all of myself all my life. But where do I find such a person? Where, Chioma, where?"

Completely taken aback, I said nothing. How could this transformation have taken place in Doris in the last few weeks of her affair with Mike? It seemed she really longed for my kind of Tremendous Lover, and that was exactly what I offered her.

"Doris, welcome to the home of my Tremendous Lover. He has many mansions for all who come to him. Some are married, some are adolescents; some, single women like you, others single men; but to all who seek him, he opens his heart and gives all his love."

We finished our meal and paid the bill.

"Well, what are we doing here? Let's be on our way. Let's go and find him. I must feel his touch, though, so that I'll know he's there; not your kind of unfelt touch."

The Holy Spirit works: Doris felt his touch and grew in grace!

TWENTY-THREE

My next class was the following Wednesday, just five days after Nkemdi painfully reminded me that humans, knowingly or unknowingly, live at a superficial level where all they seek is personal pleasure, thus elevating the physical body to the status of a god that demands nothing more than beguiling sacrifices of unrequited passions. Nkemdi's contributions at the talk had left me cold and disturbed, coming from a young African like myself. I thought I should invite her to live with my parents. She could have my room since I now lived permanently at Nesbit.

But then evil exists that good may snuff it out. It was in this mood of snuffing out evil's existence that I went to my class. I could not believe my eyes or, as Bobby Benson sang in Nigerian Pidgin, *Wetin mai ei de si mai mot no de fit tok*, which is translated to, "What my eyes see, my mouth cannot say."

There was Dean Dwight Campbell in a navy blue pin-striped suit, probably fresh from the cleaners, well ironed, with no creases and the lines all showing off their elegance. He wore a pink tie! Can you believe it, a dean in a pink tie? To leave nothing out of place, he wore golden cufflinks, perhaps last worn on his wedding day. His shirt was white, and here I can say as white as snow because this was Maryland, but since I am a Nigerian, I'd say as white as the cattle egret or Asaba women's *akwaocha*. As an African, I'd say as white as an Ethiopian woman's shawl.

I could not resist peering down at his shoes and socks to satisfy my curiosity, and I was not disappointed. Gleaming black shoes, quietly reflecting the glint in my eye and matching black socks gave the dean an insurmountable image of confidence and daring. Confidence, I could understand: Dr. Campbell was an accomplished man; but daring, who was he daring this morning, me? What could he have thought I was about to do that his presence would interrupt now? What made me think he looked daring? I may be wrong, but he looked like a man before whom one dared not make a fool of oneself. But was he not the one who had assured me it did not matter an iota if I made a fool of myself? Did he now want his pound of flesh, that is, a pound of my stupidity? Worse still, 'stupidity' might come to acquire a new simile: as stupid as a Chioma lecture.

I did not know what to make of this disturbing line of reasoning. In a way, I was frightened; but I quickly regained my composure. The question of what constituted stupidity was a burning issue, calling into play how the mind impacts on behaviour and, perhaps more importantly, how the mind itself is formed. I felt I should steer the discourse in a direction far from my thoughts on stupidity or evil being snuffed out by good.

I started my lecture without my usual greeting of 'Good morning, all'.

"I've never had a class with so many students and others, most of whom are not registered for this course. I take this to mean that I must be doing something quite good. Or, on the contrary, it may be the case that you've never seen anyone make such an utter fool of herself and you've all come to satisfy your curiosity. Either way, this University will be satisfied; for my lecture will provide a yardstick for measuring brilliance and originality, or of egregious errors of the mind."

The class was as silent as the Nkwo Okeosisi marketplace at midnight.

"I knew my great-grandfather, Chief Akadike of Okesoisi. Before he died, he made me to understand that the noble traditions of our people, the Igbo, and, in particular of his own Akadike family, will live on through me but in a drastically new setting. Whatever this new setting would be, he did not know; of course, he could not have known. And I don't know either. All that's clear to me is that things would be different from now on, that is, after his death. To give real teeth to his belief in me, I was the first person to throw sand into his grave. Traditionally among my people, this role is reserved for the first male child of the deceased. To further drive home the point of how he saw me in the future, he directed that the soil for this dust-to-dust ritual come from a particular piece of land, where a palm tree had mythically grown out of my proverbial umbilical cord. Of course, all this is strange to you, so why do I dwell on it in this lecture, where all of you have come to hear me. To me, it's very simple: the *Nkwu Alo* of my birth, the palm tree that grew out of it, is part of the noble traditions of my people, the Igbo people, and my prayer is to continue to live a worthy, wholesome life that my Pa would have been proud of.

"In this global age, I believe that our splendid African customs and traditions have a lot to contribute to the transformation of the world. How this will be achieved, I do not know; but one thing is clear to me: our splendid African traditions will save the West from itself. And there's a story here.

"Let's use the Igbo as an example. Igbo culture urges the transformation of self for the ultimate transformation of the community, nay of the world, such that everyone acts in conformity with their *Chi*, who directs their life and everyone comes to live a life of great value. Who is "*Chi*"? You could say *Chi* is God; but *Chi* is actually the manifestation of God's will, that everyone acts in accordance with God's will. Thus, I'm a teacher, a researcher, a painter; and Dean Campbell here is a professor of social anthropology, a composer, a poet, a husband, a father, and more; it's for him to define for himself what 'more' is in union with his *Chi*. And for you, my students, the future is unfolding; it's for you to respond to the noble invitations of your soul to a life of grandeur in your work, whatever your work may be. See your work as the reflection of your soul, so that it becomes a noble instrument of joy and peace."

Dean Campbell stood up to speak, stretching his entire frame for maximum effect - he must have been at least six and a half feet tall.

"Well, are we not dumbfounded? I told all of you that Chioma had the courage, the fortitude, to speak the truth to our bland faces and challenge us to examine ourselves, and for this we don't need hours and hours of lectures. Her thoughts have touched me deeply and I hope they have touched you too. Her name is Chioma, which I know means 'Good Fortune'; and that only good, noble things will happen to her; and that her destiny is anchored in the virtues. I could go on and on giving you various interpretations of what 'Chioma' means and I still won't exhaust the library of the meanings of Chioma. In her own words, we now have to look forward to the cultures of Africa to give us a brave new world. Is this philosophy? Don't ask me, ask your teacher.

"Chioma, surely, you know I had no previous knowledge of what you were going to talk about. The students simply said I made a great decision in bringing you to College Park.

They said you talk a lot of sense based on your own life's experiences. They say you're so young and yet so profound in knowledge based on the ordinary events of your life. What comes through is that nothing about life is a mere trifle; that a lot of good lies in our everyday living waiting to be discovered. Your staggering appeal comes from the way you look at things and see what we don't see; listen, and hear voices we don't hear; and from the way you eat words, digest them and gain richly in knowledge; whereas the rest of us just chew them and they come out of our system as undesirable nonsense. I'm satisfied with what I see and what I hear. I just hope I see, and perceive; hear, and listen. Thank you."

Dean Campbell got up to leave but a student halted his departure with this question:

"Mr, Dean, are we all to become like Ms. Ijeoma? Is that what you are asking of us?"

"Ah no, how could I ask that; just be yourself, only see Ms. Ijeoma as a living testament, a treasure, leading us to a novel transformation of American thinking."

I could not have anticipated this. True, I try to develop my ideas based on what I see and experience. And in this course without an outline, I have decided that the students should meet whoever I am, whatever I am, however I may be understood, in my lectures, with my soul sitting squarely on my eyes so that they can look at me and know me fully. As it was turning out, my PHL 217 had, as its centre-point, the person Chioma Ijeoma, as seen through the eyes and minds of her students!

"What are we talking about then, sir? To be like Chioma and think like Chioma, we all need to go to Okeosisi, the land of her great-grandfather, Chief Akadike, for that's where her spirit lies; where her noble African attributes come to life. It's at Okeosisi that Igbo culture may meet American thinking. So, Sir, ahoy, let's all be off to Okeosisi, borne on the wings of Chioma's *Chi*."

That was Ralph Baldwin suggesting the students all take a trip to Okeosisi to live with the Igbo culture first-hand. He continued,

"We're told that 'Chioma' means 'Good Fortune'; 'One's destiny as designed by the gods', or, in modern terms, God; 'The paradigm by which a person is described and understood'; 'One's character in its pristine, unsullied form'; if 'Chioma' means all this and more, then it is clear to me that we are now part of Chioma's *Chi*; that we're all wagons hitched on to Chioma's train; that we belong to her and she to us; that she'll take us where her own *Chi* takes her. All told, we now belong to her and if there's such a thing as destiny, then our destiny is her destiny. So let's go to Chief Akadike's country, to speak to his people, to commune with them, eat what they eat, drink their water, bathe in their streams, and, dance their dance, float in their air, lose ourselves and above all, to come to know who we are, to discover ourselves in our new Akadike-Igbo-American creation. I await my re-creation."

Dean Campbell was witnessing a revolution of minds; how all this could be, he could not tell. I was speechless. My skin tingled in utter amazement. Life was not like this. Who could have arranged this, the Holy Spirit? Could he saddle me with such an arduous task as to take charge of a gallery of young boys and girls in trouble-infested Nigeria?

Dean Campbell came to my rescue. "Oh yes, Ralph, your suggestion is fabulous. But would it be fair to Ms. Ijeoma?

How do we, as you said, 'hitch our wagons to her train'? What if her train is not going anywhere and, even if it was going somewhere, would it be going to Okeosisi? What about all this talk of her *Chi*? You know *Chi* is sacred and unknowable. All we can see are the results of his actions: if good, we rejoice; if bad, we grieve, but we should rejoice too. We cannot change our *Chi*; we are born with it, we die with it."

Ralph would not be persuaded to give up his idea. "Mr. Dean, Sir, I don't disagree with you one bit. It's just that we have come to know Ms. Ijeoma so well in just six lectures or so, and somehow, we—think I speak for everyone. . . "

"Yeah, yeah, yeah!" was the loud cry of the whole class.

"Well, Sir, I can continue. As I was saying, we've never experienced anyone like Ms. Ijeoma before. She makes us feel we can soar and gain full knowledge of ourselves with our feet firmly planted on American soil the whole time. Now slowly, and noticeably, she is beginning to define us in a new light using the ordinary thoughts and norms of her Igbo culture. We don't know how she is able to do this. All we know is that we want to live as she lives, to do as she does."

What do I do now? It was getting worse. How did I get into this mesh? Am I caught in a net, like a fish, and I am now to be roasted on a charcoal fire by the river? Five students rose to speak at the same time. I asked the only female amongst them, Alicia, to tell us what she had on her mind.

"I don't believe in this *Chi* thing. It doesn't matter anyway, because we all know Ms. Ijeoma is a special kind of human being, and we'll go wherever she wants to take us, even blindfolded. So it's entirely up to her. If she thinks that we can get the best of both worlds of American and Igbo thought, particularly in the area of truth and morals, all well and good."

The whole class clapped in a wild eruption of uncontrolled delight. I shook with anxiety. How was I going to manage all this? Other contributors went along the same lines. Bia, had found his way into my class. Much to my embarrassment, he started speaking before I could say anything.

"I have been to Okeosisi and witnessed the burial rituals of the great Akadike. You should all get up and not just hitch your wagons to Chioma's train: you should all be in the driver's seat and let Chioma be the one to hitch her wagon to your train. Then, you will go where you will."

More "yeah's" filled the air. All that mattered then was that everybody was ready to leave for Okeosisi either as a leader or a follower. Still, I did not know what to do. Dean Campbell did not want to say anything further. The whole class was silent. I waited for a while to gather myself together, regain my balance, breathe in more fresh air to drive away my stress. Clearly, this was a case where I would be pardoned if I made a fool of myself, or, would it be as the dean had said, "Even if you made a fool of yourself, we would still count ourselves lucky for what we have learned: for, if you can make a fool of yourself, then being foolish is admirable."

Bia's presence in my class threw me off guard. I just did not know what to do. Presently, I was able to find my voice.

"My dear students, you're trying to make me into what I'm not. This is not a case of humility on my part to garner more praises from you. I've heard you and the much that I've heard has filled my ears with much joy, but has given my heart a colossal burden. How can I carry all of you along? To learn that you would be as I am is indeed terrifying, for I look at myself and I feel so little for there's so much to do, so many virtues to imbibe, so many wells of knowledge to drink from. I feel an insatiable thirst for the grace of God. As you all already know, I'm a Roman Catholic. Many of you tell me you don't believe in anything. So, all in all, you and I are on different frequencies of religious fervour. When you, therefore, speak of my *Chi* being the train that will carry your wagons, I ask myself wagons of what? What are you bringing with you on this trip? Or are your wagons empty"

"Yeah, you got it: they're all empty; you just tell us what to load them with and we'll be off." That was the wild response of a couple of students, all of them bearded, at the back of the class.

"Okay, you have been of immense help. Where do we go from here? I can tell you: as you know, empty wagons will travel faster on the rail of life; in fact, I'm very relieved you say your wagons are empty, and that you are not bringing anything with you; you are leaving everything behind. Let's approach our learning the same way. Come to class, like me, clearly prepared to deal with the ordinary philosophical questions life throws at us everyday, trying to solve them; no, 'solve' is not a suitable word: I think it's better to say we tease them into little chewable bits, so that we can digest them, that they may offer nutrition to our hungry souls. Philosophy is good for the soul.

"What about me, though? You want to go to Okeosisi? What will I do when we get to our destination? How do I integrate you into my own *Chi*, since that seems to be what this whole course is turning into? Am I the one to do the integrating?"

A loud voice from the left flank screamed: "Our *Chi* will find your *Chi* and they will do all the integration that's necessary once we are all bound together, or once we all band together. This way, we don't have to worry about a thing."

"All well and good," I continued, "please bear in mind that our train will enter Nigeria and travel the whole length of southern Nigeria before entering Okeosisi. It will thus encounter hills of danger and frustration that may delay, or even derail, our journey."

Before I continued, Cheryl, who always sat in front, but never opened her mouth added: "Ms. Ijeoma, I think you worry too much. Have you forgotten that your name means 'Good Fortune'? Well, whatever happened to good fortune? I'm sure the wind will be on our side and move us swiftly through whatever obstacles we may encounter. Whatever we meet in Nigeria as we go to Okeosisi, we shall put it down to your *Chi* and our *Chi* working hand in hand."

****

This *Chi* personality was now a serious philosophical question, one I could not get into right here in Maryland. It would have to wait till we got to Okeosisi.

It was left to me and Dean Campbell to make the arrangements for the travel in summer, just six weeks away, and to decide the credit hours to be allocated to the expedition. Obtaining Nigerian visas for the students now took pride of place.

All ten students who would travel with me were at the Nigerian Embassy on M by 23rd Street, Washington, D.C., at 9.00 a.m. on the appointed day for interviews for visas to

Nigeria. Many more students had wanted to come; in fact practically the whole class of fifty-something students had wanted to go to Nigeria, but I had insisted that at any given time, I wanted to be able to see and manage whatever number of students I had in my care. I thought I could accommodate ten students and no more, and so they balloted and we got our ten.

A college official would accompany us as a representative of the university and take care of all formalities and public relations. Since I would be in my own country, I needed an official, an American citizen, to speak for the University whenever this was necessary. Dean Dwight did not want to come with us; he had his hands full, he had said. Then I tickled him by offering to call him Dwight throughout the trip if he came, and I said that I would continue calling him Dwight on our return. He fell for the trick.

****

God help me. I hope I know what I am doing. Why are things going this way? Why am I being saddled with so much responsibility? Why do I agree to everything thrown at me? And why do I invite some of it myself? How can I cope with all this? Here was the dean of a postgraduate school in a university coming with me to see my great-grandfather's birthplace, a place he sees as the light of the world. Suppose he is disappointed, and the students with him, what would I do?

Yes, in Opus Dei I seek holiness through my work, I offer it to God asking him to make my work holy, and I ask him to help all those I meet through my work and in other things I am able to do to be holy as well. Please, God help me! St. Josemaria, pray for me; Pa Akadike, pray for me.

May 2006

Unbelievable! The Nigerian Embassy was elated when I accompanied Dean Campbell—he is not yet Dwight to me— and Jean, Cathie, Rosemary, Cheryl, Dawn, Barbara, David, Bill, Gordon and Jeff to file their visa applications, that they swept strict protocol aside and gave them visas inside of seven days. Ambassador Alhaji Isa Mohammed, had been in Washington for five years, unusually long for a Nigerian official, and had met me at an exhibition of my paintings. He had told me that if I ever needed his assistance, I should feel free to call him on his personal line. He gave me his card and I had left it at that.

I was often invited to the embassy when Nigerian officials came visiting but I always sent my RSVP to say my school work would not permit any absence from school. I hated meeting government officials. I did not know that my name was top on the list of Nigerian students to be followed closely. Well, they followed me closely all right, closely enough to know that I was at College Park and would be taking a group of my students to Nigeria, even before we made our applications for visas. I hoped I would not get trapped in some diplomatic hoopla.

Cheryl was the first to be interviewed. Ordinarily each student should have been interviewed alone but the Embassy said I could be present throughout all the interviews, but that I wasn't to speak. Fantastic! I would get to know what was going on.

"What's your name?"

"I am Cheryl Petrovic."

"I see you are an English major taking a course in philosophy with Ms. Ijeoma. Why do you want to go Nigeria?"

"Sir, I don't really want to go to Nigeria as such. I want to go to Okeosisi, birthplace of our professor's great-grandfather, Akadike."

"Let me rephrase the question, then: why do you want to go to Okeosisi?"

"To learn about Ms. Chioma's roots, sir. I want to learn something about *Chi*."

"*Chi*, what's that?"

The visa officer, Mr. Usman Katsina, did not know what *Chi* meant.

"*Chi* is one of the most basic concepts in Igbo philosophy. The way I understand it, it means the coming to the fore of one's life force. I want to go to Okeosisi to see if I can discover my own *Chi*."

"Well, you'll go all right, but please promise me one thing, that you will come back and tell me what you've learnt about your *Chi* and the Igbo of my country. Well, I wish you a happy stay in Nigeria and may your *Chi* guide you wherever you go."

"Sir, you said you knew nothing about *Chi*; how come you know my *Chi* can guide me wherever I go?"

"Oh, there's God and I can easily transpose *Chi* into a deity that can watch over you everywhere. That is a common feature of African cultures, whatever may be one's religious persuasion."

I could not believe that a visa officer could go into all this talk. But, then, this was not just an ordinary trip for tourism. It is meant to be edifying, instructive, challenging the mind to know itself.

All ten students were interviewed in my presence. Dwight's interview was hilarious; as he told it, it went something like this:

"Good morning, Dr. Campbell, please let's sit over there in the sofa; it's more comfortable.. You say in your application that the purpose of your visit is to eat out of Ma Nneoma's kitchen, to savour traditional Igbo meals. Who is Ma Nneoma, please."

"Thank you sir; Ma Nneoma is Ms. Chioma's great-grandmother. Chioma never stops painting her great-grandmother's kitchen. In fact, some of the paintings are among her best and have sold well here in the US. So, I want to see this kitchen, and eat of the meals from this centre of culinary creativity. In particular, I want to eat Ma Nneoma's *ugba*."

"What is *ugba*?"

Mr. Katsina did not know *ugba*, prepared from the oil-bean seed.

"Thank you, sir; if I knew much about *ugba*, I probably would not be going to Okeosisi. You must have studied Chioma's works, especially the one depicting her great-grandmother's kitchen as Mary's kitchen at Nazareth. Well, the Jews do not have *ugba*, and the other foods which Chioma creatively ascribed to Mary's kitchen, but she was trying to tell us that her Ma's kitchen gives you the food of life, the bread of life as it were. I love those paintings: they are captivating."

"Yes, I've seen Chioma's works. In fact, we have two of them here in the Embassy. I would have taken you in to see them, but the Ambassador is having a meeting where the paintings hang. Yes, Ma's kitchen makes you voraciously hungry. You want to enter the kitchen and eat up everything there, even the smoke and the walls. But after one meal of *ugba* what else is left, what else would be new?"

"Thank you, sir, the way I see it, Ma can prepare *ugba* anew every day of the year and not repeat the same recipe. I may be wrong but I wait to be proved so. Of course, I have my students with me, their own experiences would also be heart-warming."

"The embassy is very interested in your excursion and the Nigerian Government will do all that is necessary to assist you. We see your trip as interesting and valuable, and, we don't want you to encounter any undue troubles; so we'll come in with pretty good assistance."

"Thank you very much, sir. Thank you."

When the interviews were over, we retired to a nearby restaurant for a quick bite, a sandwich washed down with one's favourite beverage. Dean Campbell left us and drove back to College Park in a great hurry to tell the president, Dr. James Mansfield, how the interviews had gone.

"Ms. Ijeoma, you love wine, I can see. What else forms part of your regular eating delights, from all you tell us about your Ma's cookery?" Rosemary wanted to know.

"Sorry to disappoint you, Rose; I live in the U.S., don't forget, so I eat everything you would eat. American cuisine is wholesome you know. I'm guided by what you would find in Amy Vanderbilt's cookbook when I have to help my mum prepare a meal, but that was before I went to Nesbit Centre.

Now, I don't cook much, but I do help out in the kitchen from time to time. So I miss my Ma's food, which you cannot get here in the District."

"Nesbit Centre, where's that?" Rosemary asked.

"It's an *Opus Dei* Centre devoted to the professional and academic formation of women so that they can better strive to live an exemplary Christian life in their daily ordinary work or duties. Some of us work and earn a living, you would call them professionals, I guess. I simply call them workers. Others are students in different universities in the district. We have medical doctors, teachers, university professors, of whom I am one; we also have a lawyer, a dentist, a banker, a cosmetologist and a musicologist. Altogether, there are twenty of us - workers and students alike."

"Why don't you live on your own, in your own apartments, or houses? Surely, you, of all people, should live in your own house?"

"Oh, yes, I can afford a house, you're right. But you see, Nesbit Centre is home for us where we also dedicate ourselves to organising apostolic activities for students and professionals. Some of us - those I call the workers, and some of the students - have chosen to live a life of apostolic celibacy. Each of us, through her work, tries to communicate true Christian spirit to everyone she meets, in an effort to help them strive to live a holy life in the daily circumstances of life, thus sanctifying the world - a home for the children of God. Well, I think the best way to introduce you to Nesbit is to invite you to one of our activities, or, better still, I'll get you to give us a talk on a subject of your choice, at a get-together, where we can all freely and truthfully speak our minds and comment on whatever you have said."

"You have used the word, 'truthfully', Ms. Ijeoma. You know there's a whole big philosophical debate on what can be described as 'truth'. 'What is truth?' they now ask."

"Indeed, you're right, Rosemary. The world seems to be turning away from the pursuit of truth. Why don't you give us a talk on this at Nesbit when we come back from Nigeria? What do you say?"

"Why not? Perhaps, after Okeosisi, I might gain such fresh insights into human nature and human life that truth becomes a lot more profound for me. Yes, I'll gladly come to Nesbit for the talk. But this celibate life of yours, do you think you know what you are doing? How can you be celibate in this age of passionate sexuality and personal comfort? Is it not too drastic a decision? You know the world is moving fast, too fast if I might say, and one needs to go along with it and not sit there holding on to the pillar of insipid chastity, when one could have a swell time and grab all that life can give. Well, I'm talking too much. I'm sure you know what you're doing; are you not Chioma, Good Fortune? You must know what you're doing. Perhaps, through you, we'll all learn what it means to be chaste, to be pure, to forgo mere earthly pleasures and seek something more rewarding. You just have to show me what beats good, old, man-and-woman healthy sexuality bubbling with terrific pleasures."

"Indeed, Rosemary; good, old man-and-woman sexuality is fine, it is wonderful, or you and I would not have been born. But there's something else, and I've chosen this something else. We'll explore the two worlds: you'll tell me about your sexual exploits, and I'll tell you about my celibacy. We'll compare notes. You'll tell me everything you do, and I'll tell you everything I do."

"But it looks like your stories will be more about everything you don't do."

"No, Rosemary, I do a lot, believe me, with my Terrific and Tremendous Lover. I'm sure he beats yours hands down."

"Come on, who is this unseen lover of yours? You're putting me on."

****

Here I was again, having to speak of my Tremendous Lover.

TWENTY-FOUR

Dean Campbell called and asked me to see him in his office immediately, saying that it seemed to be a matter of life and death. Well, as far as I could make out, he was the one who spoke. What could it be? He had never called me before. I rushed to his office wondering if his call had anything to do with our trip to Okeosisi. What could have gone so disastrously wrong as to constitute "a matter of life and death"?

"I'm sorry to call you so peremptorily, but I had no choice given what faces us right now," the dean said.

Ordinarily, I would have asked to know what it was that faced us. But my dad had drilled it into me, before I started teaching at College Park, to always listen to the very end of the story, whenever I sensed that someone had something important to tell me. Knowing that I was by nature impetuous and impatient, he studiously and relentlessly burnt the nuggets of abrupt conduct from my character till I was of a more temperate mien. Every now and then, though, the old me shows up much to my embarrassment and discomfiture. This would not be such an occasion when my mouth flies far ahead of my thoughts. I heard the dean out.

"Chioma, your people, the Igbo, are known for their communal spirit with everyone being their neighbour's keeper, especially when you meet one another in foreign lands. Well, in the next room I have a student, one of our own, who says she knows you rather well. She's pregnant and she says that she feels like there's a rope tightening more and more stringently around her neck and that right now, she just feels like using the rope to hang herself. Ordinarily, I would refer her to our counselling services but she seems so desperate that I think she needs good old Igbo common sense and home truths. I mean, she needs someone who speaks her language, someone who can enter her soul, into its dark recesses and crannies, and root the devil out. You yourself have dealt with a restless pursuit of selfish desires, which left no room for age-old norms imbued with grace and virtue. You have overcome the stifling and overpowering American pop culture allowing your character to blossom in its purity and green charm. What am I trying to say? Please use the enormous powers of your personality to find out how you can best help . . . oh, I'm sorry I forget her name now; please help her, help her in every way you can. You know, to me, you are not just a member of staff, you are our spiritual guide. Remember, our *Chi* is interminably linked to you, Chioma. I believe if there is ever a solution to a problem, you would find it. Well, let me introduce you to, oh, goodness, how could I forget her name so soon, yes I have it, it's Nkemdi.".

"Who?" I exclaimed in surprise.

"Nkemdi," Dean Campbell repeated. He opened the door and just before I stepped in, he pulled me back

"Just to let you know, I would still have to make an official report to counselling services under the dean of students. I am hoping that once you've seen her, those characters over there at counselling won't have much else to do. Let's go."

It was Nkemdi all right! She looked utterly dishevelled, like someone who had been visited by a thousand *Ishi para gbuo*, the goon god of ruinous vengeance. She wore a red dress made all the more red by her fiery eyes, which spoke of countless bitter, sleepless nights. It was a long, flowing gown, much like a hand-me-down from a tall, legendary priestess. Her shoes were the only fashionable article of clothing: black leather, high-heeled shoes, with sturdy soles for balance. They raised the gown somewhat above the floor to keep her from tripping.

I took one look at her, then ran to her across the room and helped her tie her hair in a neat bun with my scarf. I firmly and stubbornly held her to my breast as she tenaciously tried to free herself. She was weeping uncontrollably. And I too wept, like a child. I could not bear the sight I beheld. I had regarded Nkemdi as someone who knew her mind and spoke it freely and forcefully. How could she have got into this mess?

This was not the place to delve into Nkemdi's problems, and so I took her to my office. I had a class in an hour and so had some time to spend with her. I told the dean that I would take care of the situation and thanked him for his candour and sagacity. He smiled.

"Chioma, you say I'm sagacious, what does that mean? Please tell me."

"Sir, do you want me to tell you the meaning of the word, 'sagacious' or do you want me to tell you why I think you're sagacious?"

Again, he smiled. "Okay, let it be. I'll see you in a while I take it, certainly before the close of work today."

"Oh, yes, Mr. Dean, I'll see you, I promise."

Turning to Nkemdi, he said, "Well, Nkemdi, I told you, Chioma will take care of everything. You're in very good hands now."

Dean Campbell took delight in paying me rather superfluous compliments I knew that. He had audacious, if uncanny, confidence in me. I must admit, however, that I had never given him cause to doubt my abilities in any way, and I pray that I never give him reason to think, or act, otherwise.

I left with Nkemdi to my office. I really did not mean to talk to her there and then. I wanted her to rest, regain her composure, and, with some luck, be able to laugh at herself. It is absolutely important to me that we be able to laugh at our folly whenever we are in a bind. I am forever laughing at myself and asking my friends to do the same.

I tried all my old tricks to move Nkemdi to be more upbeat. I told her that it was not the end of the world, and that it could have been worse; she was ordinarily a very lucky girl, and her luck was not about to change. I drew her attention to her name, what it meant: there is always something good left for me; mine is never finished; I shall always have a surplus; 'my cup runneth over'; my tomorrows are greater than my todays. Still she was inconsolably cheerless and could not be cajoled into being positive about her situation.

I took Nkemdi to class with me. I did not want to leave her unattended, or alone, although she assured me that she would not just get up and go. I thought that she should be with me for all twenty-four hours of the day; or, at least for the remaining sixteen hours till the following morning. I planned to take her to my parents' to spend the night there with me. I would have to inform the director at Nesbit, Chelsea, and get her okay before I go to spend the night with Nkemdi at my parents' away from Nesbit.

Nkemdi sat at the back of the class. What, with all the guys whistling their admiration, she managed one smile, then another, and I could sense that she was gradually beginning to gain her composure, the most important step to being cheerful.

As is often my wont, I used a commonplace occurrence as the topic of the lecture, namely, a name, in this case, *Nkemdi*. I told my class that she was a physics major at College Park with interest in philosophy. Anyway, nothing more need be said, or it would not be philosophical.

It was a month or so before our departure for Okeosisi, so I thought any opportunity would be welcome to drive home the meaning of Igbo names. And this chance would not pass me by.

"What's in a name? 'That which we call a rose by any other name would smell as sweet.' So the immortal Shakespeare tells us. Tell me, then, what is in a name."

I could not believe my ears: a student, whose name I did not know, answered: "Ask the Igbo to whom a given name is the person come alive, the very manifestation of the individual, who, it is believed, lives out a life described by that name."

He continued and I did not interrupt him: "Yes, as far as Shakespeare was concerned, names and things were separate and distinct, and a name was merely how a thing was to be recognized as that particular thing. Thus, a rose could well be called feather, or rice, or thorn, for that matter. It still would not make any difference to the qualities of the rose. It would still smell as sweet. But that's not the Igbo belief — every name given to a child is a representation of what is happening in the world when the child is born, or what the parents, or grandparents, are experiencing in their lives at the time, in which case they think the child comes at that particular time as living testimony of their history. Or the name could be a prayer for what they are expecting at that time, or what is essential at that time in their lives.

"Thus, a name's not just a way of identifying someone as distinct from others but as a way of identifying someone with something in particular, something of such great significance it is hoped the child would live out this dream. Yes, a name's a dream, brought to fruition by the child. But this is not all; a name can serve as an idiom, to be understood by one's adversaries as a clear indication that whatever might be their intent, or grand design, against the child's family is unmistakable and discernible to the child's parents and ancestors. Thus, the machinations of the enemy would be met with unmitigated resistance. If the enemies want war, they should be prepared for a bloody destruction of their own folk, no quarter sought, no quarter granted. It would be a fight to the end. And this is true, not only of the Igbo but of other ethnic nationalities in Africa. But since Nkemdi is an Igbo name, I've used the Igbo as my reference in this contribution. And I know a thing or two about the Igbo."

What was going on? I asked myself, astonished at what I had just heard. How could this student know so much about the Igbo, even to the point of knowing that Nkemdi was an Igbo name?

"My goodness! This is absolutely unbelievable! This is fantastic! It is unimaginable! I cannot believe my ears. You truly amaze me. I'm happy to be alive to see a day such as this, when philosophy assumes a human face and a human personality. Philosophy thus gives meaning to anthropology. All that's left is for us to dress it all up in new garb and give it a new name, breathe life into it and we can all watch it stand up and walk! Wow! You are too much. Please, tell me your name and don't say it's *Nkemdirim*."

"No, Ms. Ijeoma, my name surely ain't Nkemdirim, it is Jack Clifford."

I had to interrupt him: "Sorry, Jack, but remember that we have agreed not to use slang in our discourse, in our contributions. Remember, philosophy deals with exactness, the accuracy of language. Okay? As you all know, I'm one for free and total expression, difficult as this may be."

Jack was apologetic and continued: "Yes, Ms. Ijeoma, you're right. We agreed after a long argument, though. This is what Wittgenstein's work is all about, to have a logically perfect language. And I think the Igbo have such a language. But I would have to research on that to prove my point. I do know, however, that *Nkemdirim* is also an Igbo name meaning, 'may whatever is mine remains mine'; or 'may I not miss my own share of good fortune'; or 'may I hold fast to whatever is mine'. Of course, there may be other renditions of the meaning or what it signifies."

I was dumbfounded! My class was turning into something else. I managed to mutter in response: "Thank you, Jack. Could you tell us how you have come to know so much about the Igbo. As we agreed in the beginning we keep nothing from one another and live our philosophy in the everyday events we come across. Please we are all ears, are we not?"

"Yeah, we're not only all ears but our very beings are aflame with suspenseful joy," Kim responded.

"Well, my great-grandfather, Mr. Arthur Preston Greenfield, lived in Nigeria from 1918 to 1927, nine years he later referred to as the peak of his working life in the British Colonial Government. He even regarded them as the happiest days of his life. With the help of Chief Akadike Okeosisi, of Okeosisi in Ijeobi County, he wrote one of the definitive books on British colonialism, namely, *Politics and the Colonial Experience in Nigeria 1870-1920*. He left Nigeria with his two sons, my grandfather, Peter, and his brother - you can guess his name - Paul. My grandfather, Peter, immigrated to the States in the forties when my dad was ten or so and settled in Amherst, Massachusetts. I was born in the eighties when my dad was already in his late fifties. So, how do I know so much about Igbo names? My great-grandfather wrote another book, unknown to anyone, with the assistance of Chief Akadike. I'm sure..."

I was astounded! I could not bear to hear this, so I quickly interrupted Jack's explanation.

"No, Jack, that's not possible. My great-grandfather never kept anything from me. Never! Impossible! And he just could not have kept this book such a secret from all of us Akadikes. No, I do not believe this. No, no, no."

"You're right, Miss Ijeoma, Chief Akadike did not know he was actually helping my great-grandfather, my very own Pa, to write a book. In those days, they talked and talked far into the night when your Pa came visiting Pa Arthur over the writing of *Colonial Experience*. And my Pa would write down everything Chief Akadike said and then ask him to translate it into Igbo. So, practically, the *Colonial Experience* book was replete with a lot of Igbo names, proverbs and idioms both. My Pa later published a book of Igbo names and their meanings including a large dose of traditional Igbo idioms and proverbs. It was like a *vade mecum* for British colonial officers in Nigeria.

"My Pa made some money from this and, in his will, left clear instructions that all the funds were to be paid to your grandfather, Professor Maduka, to be used to build a school in Okeosisi on the death of Chief Akadike, in his everlasting memory. The funds have grown to about five hundred thousand pounds after seventy-three years, from an initial investment of one thousand pounds in 1929. Your grandfather should be getting the funds about now. Certainly it would be in the Akadike kitty by the time we travel to Okeosisi. I would like to suggest that we help in the actual building of the school while we're there? Oh, I almost forgot, I have a copy of the book, *Meet The Igbo in Their Names*."

This was just too much for one lecture. The whole class was in another world, and we did not know how best to continue. I had forgotten all about Nkemdi as Jack held us all spellbound for a long while with his monumental tale taking me back once again to my Pa. I had to use all of my willpower to keep myself from weeping with joy. Gosh! My Pa was something! I quickly reviewed what Jack had told us in the context of the African soul: understood as distilled ideas that live as persons. The idea becomes the person in a communion of souls. One could proceed from here to the case of the word being the person.

TWENTY-FIVE

I was free for another two hours before my next class, and although I try not to deal with any personal matters at work, I thought Nkemdi's situation required that I put aside this tenet and attend to her.

"Ms. Ijeoma, life is terrible. What do I do now? This man promised me heaven and Hawaii. Now, it's neither heaven nor Hawaii. He says he's going back to Ghana, and that if I loved him, I should come with him, marry him, and live in Ghana. He knows I want to study physics and go on to a Ph.D. Now, how do I fulfil my goals? I'm done for, am I not?"

My mind flew to Bia, oh my goodness!

Before she continued, I stepped in. "What man are you talking about?"

"You know him. He says that he knows you and you know his mother and that you are a friend of the family."

"Is it Bia? Bia Graham? Is it? Oh my God, how could he do something so disgusting? This is very bad of him! How could he be so immoral with you?"

Nkemdi was beside herself with grief: she had come to me seeking relief from her pain, but here she was further straining her already frayed nerves, which were ready to snap and bring her life to an end. She fell across me, crying uncontrollably; her emotional condition was precarious.

I felt my feet, so I was alive; for they tell me that if you can feel your feet, it means you can stand, and if you can stand, it means you are alive. I massaged my legs and kicked my right foot up into the air. This had the effect of jolting Nkemdi, and she stood in stolid silence and bewilderment.

"Ms. Ijeoma, please tell me about Bia. Were you friends? Did he jilt you and now wants to possess me like one of his rock albums? He's into rock and never misses any concert given by the very best of the rock stars, I mean, of course, Genevieve Armstrong, better known as Geneve. You know she was here recently, barely a month ago and Bia took me to see her and her band. It was cool, truly extravaganza stuff."

"Come on, Nkemdi, you're not here to talk about Bia or Geneve. It's because Dean Campbell thought that I would be able to help you that he asked me to see you. And that's all I'm concerned about."

"I'm sorry, Ms. Ijeoma, it's just that Bia talks a lot about you. He has asked me to marry him. But I could as well have an abortion. Must I marry Bia because I'm pregnant? Why, wouldn't another man marry me in the future just because I have a baby to care for? Isn't a baby a wonderful gift from God? No; no abortion. Ah no. I'm sorry Ms. Ijeoma to be causing you all this *wahala*."

"Nkemdi, I don't want to give you a lecture or berate you, but you know what you've done; sleeping around with a man is not the sort of story you would like to tell your parents or the good people of Umuoji Development Union, Lagos, who are paying your fees here. You said you don't know a thing about the States, now see what you've done. How can your present plight help your studies?"

It was time for my lecture, and I wondered whether I should leave Nkemdi alone or not.

"I'll wait for you here," she said, "and then we'll go and take in a movie or something like that. I'll be fine, I promise."

****

Does the saying not go this way: "You do not know who you are until something you do not expect happens to you?" It is how you deal with this emergency - this unforeseen event - that helps form your character. I also know quite a bit about habit, and why it is essential to form good habits which then become the way we live without our being totally aware of what we are doing. I think I know how to parry the blows life throws at me. But none of these quite prepared me for the shock of the news Nkemdi just gave me. I must, therefore, search my memory, my conscience, nay my very soul, to be able to return to a state of equilibrium.

First, I must confront my memory. Is there something in there that I would like to forget, but cannot? Or, put differently, have I memories of the past which, when recollected, predispose me to act in a manner not consistent with my present purpose in life? Should I, therefore, make every effort to keep such memories consigned to the attic of my being, stowed away, never to be reopened? No, I remember what Pa Akadike had said to me, that I must keep all my memories alive, no matter how much remembering them might upset me because I would need them in the future.

These and other thoughts roasted my brains with the hot coals of passion. Ah! I get it, passion, yes, passion: I have been taught that the consequence of a distorted will is passion, that by servitude to passion habit is formed. In this case, I admit there is some element of passion, surely.

At a time, I could say I had loved Bia. That is a truth I cannot deny. How do I deal with this memory, a memory that has immediate impact once it is recalled? I feel so disappointed in his conduct with Nkemdi. They have found themselves in the present mess for not following God's will about sexuality,.

I must understand what memory is all about. Why should I want to forget anything that has happened to me? Granted, some things are not as pleasant as I would have liked. Is that why they should be forgotten? I want to keep all the knowledge I have and be able to remember everything with instant recall. I also want to remember everything my great-grandfather, Pa Akadike, told me and taught me, all safely ensconced somewhere in my brain, especially now that he is no more. I remember, with great pride and joy the day my Pa died as if it was yesterday. And I also remember with great joy the period of my life when I thought Bia and I would be married and have seventeen children! There is nothing untoward in this, simply wholesome feelings of frolicking delight. If all is fair, why do I feel my knees buckle at the news I just heard? That is to say, is there a deep-seated feeling for Bia somewhere in me that could well up under certain circumstances?

I have decided it just does not matter: I shall always have memories that my mind retains, which I am not aware of but which become extant when they are triggered by certain events. This, I cannot change: it is not under my control. It is what I do when such memories come into play that matters. And here the matter rests.

****

I had suggested that I meet with Nkemdi and Bia at my parents' home so that I could help them see that they had acted irresponsibly, doing things the consequences of which they were not prepared to shoulder. I hoped we could talk and try to find an immediate answer to Nkemdi's plight. Mum was expected home by 7 p.m., by which time all should have been sensibly resolved and I could then tell her what we planned to do - about Nkemdi living with her. I had phoned mum about this, with a subtle hint about Nkemdi's condition.

I was home a little earlier than we had arranged so that I could take care of anything around the house that needed to be attended to. My younger sister, Ngozi, the last of us, and Akachi, the third child, now a freshman at Catholic University of America, were home and were excited to see me, not having seen me for over a month. It was evening, a cool evening in June. The leaves fluttered in the gentle wind, and the enchanting smell of summer filled the air with all the power of love and gaiety. This would surely provide a warm and engaging atmosphere for lively conversation. There was a gentle knock on the door: cowardly, made by someone not sure of his welcome. It was Nkemdi. She looked pitiable.

"Come right in, Nkemdi where is Bia? I thought the two of you would come together."

"That was our original plan, Ms. Ijeoma, remember? Bia and I were to take the No. 1 Ride-On bus that stops just outside your house. Then he called to say he'd be late, but didn't say how late, and I wasn't in the mood to ask him any questions, so I left it at that. I guess he'll still come. Please tell me, why do we girls get ourselves into this sort of mess? Bia says I should trust him. Now, see where it's got me. Will he keep his word?"

A knock on the door; it was a bolder, more assertive knock, one that shouted, "I'm the lord of the manor here." That was Mr. Bia Graham.

"Sorry, I'm late. I had some catching up to do on my reading. I'm giving a seminar tomorrow, and I still had a lot to cover or I would have come with you, my one and only. Yes, I didn't give you any specific time when I could come just to keep you in suspense to make you love me more and not leave me. Sorry, Chioma, I am an ass, how are you? Hope you're not too cross with me."

"Bia, I'm fine. I had taken you to be a well brought up young man who would struggle to live the virtues and be of high moral rectitude. Well, I was wrong. You have not shown any respect for yourself or for Nkemdi"

Face downcast, all he could manage was: "I am truly sorry all this happened. It was not in my plan at all, and I cannot say it was deliberate. I was simply carried away by lust, and now look at the mess I have caused."

I cast a glance at Nkemdi and her face had retribution written all over it. I imagined that she wished Bia could be made to suffer for his indiscretion. But then, I thought it over: what about Nkemdi herself; was she not equally at fault?

We slaked our thirst and were on our way outside, to the garden. Bia had been here several times before, when he came over to see my parents; but I think in his new-found paternity mood, he had gained a whole new view of life. He talked about the grass: green, luxuriant and well cut; the white birch trees kept smooth and virile by the peeling off of besmirched pomp revealing their natural innocence; the lilies singing songs of purity to his impassioned soul. Mum had taken great pains over the years to grow cream-white daylilies, and Bia was particularly taken with the crème Francis Fay and another colour group called 'eyed, custard candy'.

Bia tried to contrast the ugliness of sin with the beauty of the garden: he felt totally distraught about having given free rein to his insidious passions. He felt a deep sense of remorse as he studied one flower after another telling us how they shone with the beauty of living love between man and woman. I had never seen it that way, but then I did not need to make many comments. I simply said that we could all better understand why not even Solomon, in all his majesty, was as gloriously adorned as one of these sparkling lilies. Indeed, the custard candy was magnificent, far too beautiful for words and Bia captured its essence when he said:

"Chioma, this flower here will forever symbolize my love for Nkemdi; the pink colour of the main body of the petal is me, on the outside, and the deep burgundy, entrancing centre with golden flashes on the inside is Nkemdi. I shall watch over her and ever live in her inner soul. As the centre of this flower attracts attention to itself, so will Nkemdi keep my interest all the days of my life. Please forgive me, Nkem, for causing you so much pain as a result of my indiscretion. It will never happen again that I lust after a woman. I promise you that I'll live in holy chastity in our marriage."

I could only respond with "Amen", furiously remonstrating with Bia to keep his promise in the future and be faithful to Nkemdi.

Nkemdi said nothing and had said nothing since we had gone into the garden. We left for the park and were in the woods in ten minutes. It was time to get everything straight, for us to be clear about what Bia's plans were for Nkemdi and for himself.

"Bia, this is not at all proper," I began. "It's not an issue to be treated lightly at all. Premarital sex is horrendous, and I am not the one who says so; it is the church, the same Catholic Church that you and I attend. Search your soul thoroughly and make your peace with God in the Sacrament of Penance, if you have not done so already."

Both Bia and Nkemdi responded that they had gone to Confession and were doing some works of penance.

"That's wonderful, and we pray for strength for you in your firm resolution to live a life of chastity. In any case, I hope you'll be able to take good care of Nkemdi and your baby. She says you'll have a court wedding in a month or so and a Catholic marriage some time after. Believe me, I wish both of you well. My major concern is for your souls; that you love each other; respect and follow God's plans on sexuality, marriage and the family."

"Chioma, Nkemdi now knows you were my own gal. I don't want her to have the feeling that she's my first choice for a wife. She knows that that honour belongs to you. You see, there's this barman whom I meet at the bar where I go for drinks on Friday's; whenever he serves you beer, he hollers,

'Here's my best for you!' whatever the beer was. Then another guy asks for the same beer, and yet another guy asking for the same beer, and they'd all receive the same response, 'The finest beer coming up!' So I asked him how each bottle could be the finest coming up and he said: 'What do you think, mate? It's obvious, isn't it? If you have ten things and sell one, then of the nine left, one's going to be the finest, won't it? And when you are down to two, still one of them is the finest you have, until you're down to the last, which, without any doubt, is the finest you have. That's the way it is.'"

"You know, Bia, in response to your story, let me tell you one - a favourite story of my mother's. A guy walks into a store, sees a card he likes, with the caption, 'For My One and Only'. He asks the salesgirl if she has more of the same card, she answers yes, and he says, 'Give me ten of those.' He goes off and over the next week, not months, mind you, manages to give out those 'For My One and Only' cards to ten of his girlfriends. I guess each of those girls would truly believe, as he had made her believe, that she was his 'one and only.' Are you telling us that Nkemdi is your one and only of many 'one and only's'? How many other girls are on your dating list, waiting there, twiddling their thumbs in anxiety if not exasperation? Please tell us, is Nkemdi the only girl for you, or is this marriage simply a matter of expediency? If so, I'll make sure Nkemdi keeps the baby and gets on with her life without you. My mum will gladly look after her and the baby. So go ahead do what you want to do but leave expediency, convenience, and practicality out of this matter. This is serious. We're dealing with at least two lives here, Nkemdi's and the baby's."

Before Bia could say a word, Nkemdi jumped in, saying:

"Ms. Ijeoma. you may say whatever you want to say, I'm going to marry Bia, even if he has twenty other 'one and onlys' as you put it; even if there are other girls out there biting their nails and chewing gum after gum in desperation. As long as Bia wants to marry me, I'm sure as hell gonna marry him. Yes, I know I'm not his number one, but I can easily make him treat me like I was. Don't forget, I'm having his baby."

Bia took over.

"Chioma, thanks a lot. I knew I could always count on you. You must rescue me from my predicament. I'm lost, done for. If my dad hears of this pregnancy business, he would skin me alive. He just can't stand any talk of boy-gets-girl-pregnant. It violates what he holds most sacred. As for my mum, she'll just collapse and might need revival at a medical centre. And what about God whom we have so gravely offended? He who loves me so much that he delivered himself for me onto death on the cross; what about him?

"Why did I do it then? Please don't ask. I must be out of my mind, wouldn't you say? Ever since you turned me down, I've not been myself. But that's not a good excuse for what I did."

"You're right, Bia, it's not at all a good excuse"

"I agree, Chioma, it's not a good excuse at all. God has called you, and you've followed him. You're ever so true, so pure, so direct. Yes, you were my *numero uno*, the ultimate. But as the barman said, after the best, the next best becomes the best. Anyway, in our case I thank my God. I've accepted that he wants you for something much more fulfilling than what my dry heart could ever dream of offering you. His love is immeasurable, awesome indeed."

"You're quite right on that, Bia, God's love is tremendous."

"I've come to realise, as you have always said, Chioma, that God wants you for himself. I'm happy that you responded fully and can now help drowning souls like Nkemdi and myself. So, it's all settled. I'll marry Nkemdi, no matter what. We just need some assistance which I believe your mum can provide before we get married. We don't plan to live together before the wedding. I'll travel to Nigeria, to Lagos, to meet her parents and with my dad leading the way, we shall complete all the formalities of the traditional rites in a manner which even the fastidious Akadikes would approve of. Nkemdi insists on this, that my people meet her people, and seal the bond in a truly African way. Fantastic, won't you say."

I did not know what to say to Bia. I felt very sorry for him. At least, he knew they did the wrong thing and was prepared to make amends and to take care of Nkemdi. It remained for my mother to broach this matter to his mother, a dear friend of hers. All seemed solved, and we could all get on with our lives. Nkemdi would have to live with my parents to enable her to escape, for the time being, from what she had told me was Bia's constant temptations.

After a salutary hour or so, in the garden, we moved indoors to listen to Geneve's music, and take our minds off the present problems. In his true, effervescent self, Bia jumped up in dance, without a care in the world, totally oblivious of our discomfiture.

Mum was home later than we had hoped, but we waited for her so that she would see Nkemdi in the flesh and make her final decisions. I already gave her the hint that she would be caring for a young friend of mine who had threatened to abort her baby.

"Hi, mum, welcome home. What kept you so long? How was your day? Here's Nkemdi, Bia you already know."

"Good evening, ma," Bia and Nkemdi greeted mum simultaneously, Bia looked like he wanted to disappear.

"Ah, thank you, my children. How are you? Chioma, dear, have you guys had anything to eat, or are we going out for dinner? Just say so, 'cause I'm fagged out and won't mind going to our favourite Thai restaurant. Sorry, I'm later than I had planned. These legal cases just keep piling up, fresh evidence all the time, new leads open, old leads close; you pursue this and then you reach a cul de sac, and you have to back up and start from scratch. I'm sorry. Nkemdi, do you like Thai food? And you Bia, what do you say?"

"Mum, Nkemdi here has never eaten Thai food. She doesn't even know what it is. I don't think Bia fancies oriental foods very much either. Don't worry, I'll fix something for all of us. You can just settle down on the sofa, put your feet up, and I'll whip up your favourite dish of steak and mashed potatoes and salad. We'll have rice with some steak too."

"Okay, Chioma dear. Let me get out of this stuffy suit and be more comfortable." Mum went upstairs and changed into an *adire* caftan, over a turtle-neck.

"Chioma, your mum is so beautiful, so pleasant. Seems the two of you are like sisters. You're so casual with her. Oh, you're a very lucky daughter."

"Yes, indeed, Nkemdi, I am a very lucky daughter. I thank God everyday for my parents. They are so good to me and to each other."

Mum came down, and asked Nkemdi and Bia to join her in the garden. It was somewhat chilly and mum had to fetch sweaters for them as they were dressed in simple cotton, summer clothes. I had returned to the kitchen to prepare dinner, and could not clearly hear what they were saying, but every now and then I thought I could make out the words 'baby' and 'marriage'. I guess mum must have been pressing Bia to know his plans for marriage and for the baby. I whipped up a meal that would be pleasing: mum's steak was rare, mine, medium-well, and Bia's and Nkemdi's, well done. I called out to mum and they all joined me in the dining room. The conversation on 'baby' and 'marriage' continued for a while.

Then mum threw the bombshell.

"Nkemdi, Chioma tells me that you will be living here until after the marriage to keep from continued violation of your body. I have another idea. Bia, what about you having your wedding in two weeks' time so that you could both live together in your parents' home? I know you have a large room, Bia. It can comfortably accommodate both of you. I'll see our parish priest and seek his approval for the date, but I don't anticipate any problems. The traditional rites by native law and custom can be done at any time afterwards. What is uppermost in my mind is that you both live together in love and marital chastity. What do you say?"

"But, mummy, we don't have any money and I don't want to trouble my parents. Yes, rent, utilities and food would be free, but there are still other expenses especially when the baby arrives....."

Mum cut Bia off.

"Come on, stop this manner of reasoning. Didn't you think of all this before putting Nkemdi in the family way? Are you so irresponsible as not to have considered all these expenses you now complain about? Of course, your parents will not be happy with what you've done and may feel like scalping you. But your parents are there for you. They've looked after you till now and I'm sure they won't abandon you now. At the worst, your father will give you a loan and you can pay him back when you are able to do so. Surely, your parents will take great pride in caring for their grandchild at no cost whatsoever to you and Nkemdi. Yes, you'll have to pull your weight somewhat and support Nkemdi. I'm sure you're proud of her and we'll all chip in to help. You'll never be alone. Never! Just concentrate on your thesis and that would be all. By the way, you do realise that you won't be cosy-cosy with Nkemdi from now on until after your marriage. I mean, no sexual intimacy, not anymore. "

I knew Mum was by nature helpful and understanding, but I did not think she would go as far as this and arrange Bia's wedding so soon without giving him much of a chance to say no. I felt very proud of my mum. She takes charge and does not brook any nonsense.

It was agreed: mum would see the priest and pick a date as soon as possible so that Bia would have an early wedding, and not go out of his mind waiting for his 'one-and-only'. Of course, mum would work all this out with Usha and Kweku, Bia's parents. But first, Bia must explain to them what he and Nkemdi had done and, with true sorrow and remorse, ask their forgiveness. He should take Nkemdi to meet his parents and together plead for their pardon and blessing. Mum never ever wanted to see a young girl suffer from the indiscretions of a carefree man.

Dinner over, we all returned to the garden for our dessert of fruit salad.

TWENTY-SIX

I had not seen Sutapa for about two weeks and was getting worried about her. We talked a lot on the phone, but nothing beats face-to-face conversation, where the warm aroma of a delightful friendship envelopes you, you look into your friend's eyes and walk to eternity, all in an instant. So, I went to see my dear friend in her home, after Mass, one Sunday afternoon. She was not looking too well, and I did not have to ask why.

"How wonderful to see you, Chioma. I'm in deep trouble. I'm not well. I'm losing my mind. I'm losing myself. There are some people I recognise, some faces I remember, and some places that I know. The rest escapes me. I'm blank . . ."

I did not want Sutapa to continue telling me her woes. I could not bear to hear of any new agonies, particularly as I feared Mike was the cause of all this. How little we know of the enormity of the pain which we inflict on our loved ones through avoidable acts of indiscretion. And the consequences of some indiscretions are not easy to forgive or forget. Oh my God, please do not let my dear Sutapa lose her mind. So I left her. In unbearable sorrow, I drove back to College Park

****

"What's happened to you? Look at you, Sutapa, you must have missed me. See how untidy you look. This is not like you at all. Look at your hair, what's wrong with you? I'm back. I'm back to you. I've made a fool of myself.. Sutapa, Sutapa, Sutapa, don't you hear me?"

"Who are you?"

"Who am I? Sutapa, aren't you Sutapa? Please tell me, am I in the wrong house?"

I was in their home during this encounter; it was my first time to see Mike with Sutapa together since their separation. Carmen had rushed out to meet her erring brother, having carefully herded the children into their rooms so that they would not see their dad. She had come to take care of the children, at my instance, when it became clear that it might take quite some time for Sutapa to return to her normal self.

"What are you doing here?" Carmen stood between her brother and his home.

"You said you weren't ever going to come back. So, tell me, what you have come for? Just take your ugly self out of here before I call the police, and I mean it. See what you've done to this great woman, now she does not remember many things and can barely take care of herself. The kids are in bad shape, and I'm all they have right now. So, please just go before you do more damage. Oh my God! Men, you men, you're all dirt, nothing but dirt. Goodbye, silly brother."

He was forced to leave. After Carmen explained to me what was going on with Sutapa, my pain grew worse. What if she did not fully recover? What if she lost all memory of her past life? Many 'what if' questions flooded my tired brain, none of which I could answer. I asked Carmen to tell me what had happened in the past two weeks or so since I had not seen Sutapa.

"Chioma, it's not too bad really. It's just that we don't yet know how much of her memory Sutapa has lost and the type of memory loss that is now apparent."

"What do you mean by 'memory loss'? Please don't tell me this may be permanent." I was visibly frightened.

"Chioma, I said it's not too bad. She has been to the doctors; they've done many tests, and all the results are inconclusive. All they can tell from the brain scan is that the part of the brain that deals with emotion has suffered some deterioration. That's about all we can make out of all the medical and technical jargon they threw at us. They say, in lay man's terms, what happened to Sutapa was as a result of an unparalleled shock that sent her memory into immediate withdrawal from perceiving or recalling certain events."

"I wonder, what sort of events is she able to remember? Well, at least she knows who we are, and the children too."

"So far, she seems able to recognise a good number of faces, names and places, but not Mike: she does not seem to know who Mike is! He was here to see her, telling her he was back and all that repentant rubbish men tell their wives when they have made fools of themselves. But she didn't recognise him. I ordered him out of the house, and he's been back now every day ever since and each time Sutapa asks him, 'Who are you?'

"That's very disturbing, isn't it?"

"Oh yes it is, but we remain hopeful. Once Mike leaves she returns to asking me, 'Who was that?' and I would tell her that he was the man she was married to. And she would ask, 'Am I married?' I would remind her of her dear children, Devan and Tara, and that they had a father. And do you know what she would ask me, 'If I have children, does that mean they have a father?'

"How do you answer such a question? This must be worrying."

"So far, I've tried not to answer this question. I fear that it might throw her into a frenzy, and make her condition worse. To compound everything, each time Mike leaves, she would not remember ever seeing him. So, each time she sees him it is like the first time for her. It's always, 'Who are you?'

"You're fast turning into the psychologist-in-residence."

Carmen laughed at my suggestion and continued: "The doctors told us not to force her back into her past, that she would make the necessary recovery and find her own way through the maze she's in right now on her own. And I'm doing what the doctors advised. So, she knows Dev and Tara are her children. She calls them by their names, and remembers everything about them quite independent of their father, and even helps them with their homework."

"That's wonderful. Things will surely be fine again, one day."

"Yes, indeed, Chioma, just like that, one day, things will return to normal. Sutapa should have returned to her classes, but the doctors have given her one month leave to be extended, if necessary, if she does not show sufficient improvement. The college authorities are understanding and have provided every possible assistance she has requested."

I was having this talk with Carmen when Mike came calling as was his wont every day. Carmen was going to send him away, as usual, but I prevailed on her to let him stay for a while because I wanted to hear whatever it was he thought would make him acceptable to Sutapa once again.

"Chioma, Carmen, you have no idea what's happening to me. You can't begin to imagine the sort of pain I'm suffering right now, going through the agony of losing my identity by not being recognized by the one person with whom I have an identity."

I was getting hot under my blouse; but for my practice of abiding in the presence of God in all things, great and small, I would simply have concurred with Carmen that Mike should just be thrown out to visit his own vomit. But, again, I thought, perhaps, some good might come of our listening to this fool bare his chest. I winked at Carmen, and we both let Mike continue.

"As I was saying, you don't know what it means to lose your identity. Chioma, you're an artist just as I am. Suppose your agent brought you a painting, one you don't recall ever painting; he tells you it's been evaluated and that it would sell for over five million dollars, and he needed your okay to offer it to the auctioneers for bidding, what would you do? Would you say, 'That's not my work, so take it back to wherever you got it from'; or, 'Leave it here in the studio and I'll think about it.' Tell me, which would it be?"

Of course, I was clear in my mind what I would do and answered Mike that I would ask my agent to take the painting back to wherever it came from. Only if he continued to insist that it was my work, would I ask him to leave it in the studio, and that I would think about it.

"Yes, Chioma, I know that's what you would say and, in your case, that particular painting might never see the light of day. It would probably lie in your studio until your death, unknown to the world, leaving the rest of us all the poorer for not seeing this masterpiece. And after you have left it in your studio, what would you do? Would you not pore over it and try to figure out just how come you don't remember anything about this work staring you in the face? If you don't remember painting it, wouldn't you remember your own style, your peculiar colours and your own signature on the painting? Won't there be features you would recognize as typical of your work?"

"Mike, don't worry about what I would or would not do with this hypothetical painting. Sutapa is not a painting; a work of art of God, yes. So, please, leave off this line of reasoning."

"You're right, Chioma, Sutapa, my wife, is, of course, not a painting, but a work from the hands of Almighty God, the greatest artist of all. I'm only trying to find a way to communicate to you my present sense of loss. So, please, let me continue with my hypothetical work of art."

I did not know what else to say but to keep quiet and let Mike go on. He was in great pain and continued without any break in the trend of his thoughts; but I was not paying much attention to him.

"And suppose after all this probing, thinking and analysis, you still can't remember when you did the painting, would you not go mad? Would you still think you're a normal human being? Okay, we all know you did some paintings at a period you considered the 'dark period' of your life."

Yes, I remembered the period when I did those horrid works

and I did not want Mike to remind me about this. Not now.

"What about this period, Mike, what has it got to do with this sordid act of yours?

"Chioma, please don't get me wrong. I'm not at all saying it has anything to do with my action. Please bear with me for a while, so you may better understand my plight. Now tell me, without the input of Jeff, who identified the work as something to do with Ifa, the Yoruba god of divination, and your mum, who saw it in your studio, among many others like it, not to mention the role your *Uzo* played in the whole thing, do you think you would have been able to come out of your so-called dark period? Do you think you would have regained your normal balance? Would you not instead have gone mad? Tell me, please tell me."

Mike was right, surely. I would have gone mad if nobody had been there to help me because I would not have known who I was or, put differently, I would never have dreamed that I could have done such a painting, which to me was hideous; then, I would have come to the conclusion that my mind, my whole self, was equally monstrous. And I would not have been able to live with that. I might have gone mad, yes. I told Mike so.

"Now, Chioma, Carmen, please give me a break. Sutapa is in a better position than I am. If she never regains her memory of who I am, she would be able to go on and live her life fully and successfully and even happily, perhaps even more happily than ever before. As for me, if Sutapa does not regain her memory of me, then I have lost the notion of who I was, or who I am."

I really did not mind if Mike just disappeared from the face of the earth. But I must try and be charitable and friendly:

after all, he was still Sutapa's, husband. My interest in his words was reawakened.

"If Sutapa did not know me as her husband, then, I won't know myself fully, for it's only the other who can validly tell us in truth about who we are. That's how parents tell their children who they are and teach them who they are. The child grows up knowing herself in the context of her father and her mother. Only later does she begin to discover her own identity."

Mike was right and I began to feel some of his pain. "Imagine then how she would feel if she lost this identity," Mike rhetorically asked, "without any reference to her biological or even adopted parents. Now you can begin to understand my excruciating pain, with a million pins impinging on my brain and ten million nails seeking space in my heart, each more piercing than the others. My past is me, and if Sutapa does not know who I am, with whom could I share this large chapter of the book of my life? Oh, God, am I going mad?"

I left with the excuse to see Sutapa, sorrow and grief must have been written all over my face. Mike and Carmen saw it all, and I wanted to spare them the discomfort of attending to me under the present circumstances. I had never met sin as I did today. The only real suffering I had endured until now was when Bia put Nkemdi in the family way. But that was a different kind of sin, not the type that buried you alive here on earth while patiently waiting to do the same to you in hell.

I have always known how terrible sin was, especially mortal sin that was indeed mortally destructive. I had never come face to face with such a disaster.

Here was Sutapa, beside herself with grief, losing a vital part of her memory; for as much as Mike thought that he had lost much of his identity, Sutapa, would also lose that part of herself that depended on Mike for manifestation. She would not remember who her husband was, who the father of her children was, and all those wonderful years she and Mike had together. And now Mike, feeling as though his world had come to an end, suffered even more.

Carmen came looking for me to tell me that Mike had fainted after I left, but soon came to.

"This whole thing worries me more than I had ever imagined," Carmen confessed. "How do we get these two people back together? What about Doris, have you set eyes on her?"

I told her that Doris and I had met for lunch at *Nathan Hale*; and that she was fully repentant and had sent Mike packing, which was why he ran back to Sutapa.

"That silly brat, no better than a sleazebag."

"Oh, please Carmen, this language does not sit well on your lips. Don't forget, whatever her faults may be, it was Mike who ran into her arms; and Mike is still your only brother, and my friend."

We returned to the living room and I turned to Mike; "Now, let's play a game: Mike, don't say anything about your being Sutapa's husband. Let's . . ."

"You must be out of your mind to make such a shallow suggestion. Sutapa is all I've got. How can I possibly act as though she wasn't my wife? Forget it. I'd just as soon be dead." Mike would not hear me out.

"Mike please, let me finish. You've put me through the most painful experience of my life so far. Pa Akadike had told me that I would suffer immensely. At the time, I could not make out what that meant. But after this messy behaviour of yours, and all that has followed in its wake, with my meeting sin at first hand, amongst those I count as friends, that is you and Doris, I now understand that the worst suffering is when you suffer because of your friends, sharing in their pains; going through whatever it is they are going through.

"I have begun to better understand the meaning of self-giving. It demands so much of the soul. I pray all this does not leave me dry, devoid of feeling. So, please, Mike, listen to me. My only joy is your happiness. You have repented of your sin. I'm not God. I am not sitting in judgment over you. I don't like what you've done. I hate what you've done. But I don't hate you."

Mike was listening attentively and I continued:

"Now, what I have in mind is for you to act as if you were meeting Sutapa for the first time, and that you want to take her out on a date. It sounds whimsical, but you'll have fun, I reckon. Look, you already know what Sutapa likes: all her favourites, her favourite perfume, dress styles, foods, everything. Now, just start all over again, and woo her with all your love as if she's the first date in your life; only this time you're starting with an advantage: she doesn't know that you know her, and know her very well. I bet she'll come around and one day, one day you just can't begin now to imagine, she'll recognize you and fall in love with you all over again."

Mike seemed attentive quite all right, but his eyes darted this way and that in apparent wonder and I felt he was not following what I was saying. And so I asked him:

"What do you say? What have you got to lose? Carmen says she has all the time in the world to care for the children and also assist Sutapa in her total recovery. Carmen will act as the matchmaker."

"Well, what do I have to lose? Nothing, really. Let me hear you out. Please go on."

Feeling more confident and assured I continued: "As you know, Sutapa doesn't remember ever seeing you. This is to your advantage, as each date would be a new date for her. And the children, thank God, through the deft ploys of Carmen, have not yet seen their daddy. So, you'll go back today. Tomorrow, bring your wife her favorite flowers and invite her to dinner, to her favourite restaurant that offers her favourite dishes.

"Spend your money. Spoil her. Lavish all of your sentiments on her, and sweep her off her feet. Ah! somebody tells me every woman can be swept off her feet; you just need the right broom. You already have the right broom. I wish you a romantic whirlwind."

Mike appeared convinced: he thanked me, giving me a 'high-five' for my suggestion, wondering how I could have come up with such an ingenious scheme. Carmen was impressed as well.

Try as I could, the strong words of Sutapa just could not leave my mind. I wondered if there was any hope that things would return to their original tempo. Sutapa had said, and I remember the words as clearly as though they were said now:

"No, Mike cannot r-e-t-u-r-n to me. He can come back. He can visit, he can do whatever he likes, but he cannot return to me because I am not the same Sutapa he left behind. Whether or not I know it, I have changed. My soul is changed. My spirit is changed. Even my body is changed, as my thoughts now draw lines on my face, leaving me looking dry and forsaken. I am sorely wounded. No Chioma, just forget about Mike returning to me. There is no longer a me for him."

But I am ever full of hope. I believed my scheme would work

****

Do they not say "Sow the wind, reap the whirlwind?" I guess what they have in mind is that when you sow evil, you shall reap an avalanche of evil. But what happens if you sow good?

Well, Mike went out sowing seed after seed of love, furrow after furrow, for a rich harvest to accrue, believing that one day Sutapa would walk up to him and say, "Mike, where have you been, I love you." He took his dear wife to places and then more places, wooing her, serenading her, giving her the best any husband could dream of giving his wife. For the first time, Mike gave Sutapa all of himself. He dug deep into his heart, and discovered himself anew and swathed his loving wife with the freshness of sublime tenderness.

TWENTY-SEVEN

Bia and Nkemdi were married within the first trimester of Nkemdi's pregnancy. Nkemdi wanted her wedding photos to flatter her slim, svelte figure. No one could tell that she was expecting a baby. It was only the family present, anyway; and they all knew what was going on. I personally picked the flowers for the bridal bouquet: yellow roses, chrysanthe-mums, white lilies, festooned with ferns from our Nesbit garden, and arranged them into a flowing bouquet that could have been the proud subject of a Van Gogh painting. My sister, Ngozi, was the chief bridesmaid. I was filled with indescribable joy as I watched Bia, not forgetting that we were to have been married and have seventeen children together. But the gods and God thought differently and called us to different vocations.

****

July, 2006: The trip to Okeosisi

After two weeks of assiduous preparation, it was time for our journey to Okeosisi. Our flight was to depart at 6pm from Dulles International Airport, Washington, D.C. on the first leg of the flight to Lagos. We all agreed to meet on campus, at The George Graham gymnasium at 3pm, allowing sufficient time for check-in and baggage searches and any other unforeseen details at the airport. Dean Campbell was his usual self: mixing humour with skilful administration, he called out our names. We each answered "present", indicating that we were with him at the chosen venue. When he got to my name, he started singing a Bob Dylan song, a favourite of mine, *My Back Pages*. None of us had ever heard the dashing dean sing, and we were pleasantly surprised he sang so well. He completed the first stanza, and I heartily joined him in the second. Then it was a party, everyone joined in and we sang our hearts out. *My Back Pages* always reminds me of my Pa Akadike.

How did this man know I liked this song? And to befuddle my mind all the more, how did he connect the song to my love for my Pa? Do I give myself away so readily? Where did I leave the clues that guided him to come to this knowledge? I must find out. I do not like anyone having the better of me when it comes to my likes and dislikes. I have nothing to hide, really, but I do not like the idea of someone snooping on me.

The college bus took us to Dulles, and we completed all the formalities in good time with an hour to spare. Rosemary started playing her i-pod, softly at first and then somewhat more loudly to the irritation of a man sitting opposite her.

"Hey Miss, is that damn thing for your ears or for mine?"

Rosemary did not hear him, and he repeated his question: "I said is that thing you're playing for all the travellers here at Dulles?"

I stepped in and asked Rosemary to turn down the volume of the music and apologized to the gentleman on her behalf. He stood up, thanked me and said,

"My name is Ted, Ted Hall, and I'm going to Lagos. And you, where are you off to?"

I studied his face to see if I could make out the type of visitor-to-Nigeria he was likely to be—a tourist, a businessman, a university professor attending a conference, an anthropologist conducting research. I took a look at his hand luggage and saw that he had a computer and a slim bag with him. He was about forty or, if he was any younger, in his mid- to late thirties. He wore a blue shirt with pockets on both breasts. His shoes, I thought, gave him away: he must be a businessman out to make a good impression, for his shoes were as shiny as those of a Wall Street capital market investor.

"I'm off to Lagos, also. I live here in the District. And you, which company do you represent and what sort of business are you considering bringing to my country?"

Ted smiled. "Oh no, I'm not a businessman at all. I'm returning to Port Harcourt where my wife and three sons live.

I've been away now for two months here in the States. I'm a writer and have just completed my fifth novel to be published this fall. And you, what do you do? What's taking you to Nigeria?"

"I have been here for about seven years. I graduated from Georgetown and I'm now teaching at College Park. I have with me ten students in their sophomore year, who are going to see the birthplace of my great-grandfather, Pa Akadike. They are enrolled in my philosophy course and want to know something, first hand, about the Igbo culture, during their stay in Okeosisi. We'll be there for two weeks."

"Wow! Can you beat that? I've never heard of US students coming to Nigeria as a group for anything, what with all the terrible news of armed robbery and '419' scams, the bad roads, traffic jams, and so on."

"With all this *wahala* why are you still in Nigeria, Ted, if I may ask?"

"Oh, my wife's a Nigerian, an Efik, from Duketown, Calabar, and I've grown to love it there. Your people are simply wonderful, friendly, boisterous. You know what I mean."

"Yes, Ted, I know what you mean. My grandma on my mother's side is from Duketown also. Maybe my grandma, Adiaha, is related to your wife, somehow. You know, Duketown is a very small place and everybody knows everybody else."

"What's your grandma's maiden name?"

"It's Henshaw, Adiaha Henshaw."

"No, I don't think your mother is related to my wife. She comes from the Effiong family. The Henshaw family is very well known. One of them is a big-time lawyer in Port Harcourt, Mr. Etim Henshaw."

"That's my great-grandfather."

"Really? By the way, you haven't told me your name yet."

"I'm Chioma, and Mr. Henshaw is my great-grandfather; his daughter, Prof. Adiaha Maduka, is my grandmother."

Ted and I chatted for about fifteen minutes and it was soon time for boarding. My students were all agog with the excitement of the adventure ahead of them, and they quickly joined the queue to the boarding gate as though they were lining up for heaven. Rosemary stayed close to me and would not let me be, wanting to know more about Ted, even after I told her that he was a happily married man. She said Ted looked like her type, one who would spoil her and take her to the finest restaurants. I told her that whatever her schemes may be, she was not likely to see Ted again as he lived with his family in Nigeria.

Rosemary seemed to have won the battle when Ted came over to the group, introduced himself, and wondered if we could give him the story of our life at Okeosisi when our trip was all over. He said he would write it up for *The New Yorker*, and that it would help project College Park further into the limelight. I had not thought of this, but it was not up to us to say yes or no: it was up to Dr. Campbell. And knowing him, the dean would not do such a thing as consent without the permission of his students, as he never wanted to infringe on their freedom. Each person could, of course, do as he or she wished, as far as he was concerned, but only if decent behavior was the norm. I could have broached the subject to him, but it was clearly too early in the day for us to be considering writing rights for the trip. So, I simply told Ted I would be in touch with him. He gave me his business card and mobile phone number.

We boarded the plane, all of us in the fourth row from the front, seating three students on the right aisle, four in the middle, and three on the left aisle. I sat on the right flank, between taciturn Barbara and gregarious Jeff. Dean Campbell had the option of flying business class, but did not want me out of his sight. He said he would be monitoring my *Chi* as we flew, and he would chart our progress as I slept or laughed or stood up to use the toilet. Also, he wanted to keep an eye on his students. But no sooner had the plane attained its maximum height than the dean fell into a satisfied sleep. He had to be awakened for dinner and, not knowing where he was for a short while, he looked like a ghost. He sat directly behind me and confessed that he had a fear of flying and had taken two *Jack Daniels* before the flight to put him to sleep. He was happy the whisky worked!

I had said my prayers before we took off and continued praying till we ascended fully. In that time, I had said two rosaries and was quite happy with myself knowing we were in the good hands of my dear Mother Mary. I had a picture of her with me, a copy of one of my favourite Filippo Lippi's paintings. Barbara saw this, held it close to her chest, in the manner in which The Blessed Virgin held her son, and slept off. Unbelievably, she did not wake up till we were about to land in London. Dean Campbell had a little more whisky and was not in any position to follow my *Chi* anywhere.

Jeff kept waking and sleeping. Rosemary came over and asked him to move to her seat so she could spend some time with me.

"Come on, Rosemary, give me a break. This is the only chance I've got in the whole bazooka world to be close to *Chi*, and you want me to give it up? Come on, buzz off."

Jeff was not agreeable. I sensed he was still half-asleep and did not want to be disturbed. He dozed off again, and I pleaded with Bill, who sat next to Rosemary, to take my seat. He agreed.

"So what is it this time, Rosemary? What is it that can't wait till we get to Nigeria?"

"You're right, Ms. Ijeoma, there's something that can't wait. I want to have a black baby. Now, please tell me, can you arrange for me to marry a charming guy from Okeosisi? Better still, do you have any cousins who might be interested in a blanched white face like mine? Please, Ms. Ijeoma, I really want a black baby and so I want to marry an African."

"Is that all you want, Rosemary? Are you sure that's all you want, because you can ask for more; we have everything good at Okeosisi. All I have to do is post a notice in the town square inviting applications for marriage to one of the most fascinating girls I've ever known, Miss Rosemary Stevens, aged nineteen, five foot seven inches tall, second year university student, of rich parents, Mr. and Mrs. Carl Stevens, boat-builders of Newport, Connecticut."

"Ms. Ijeoma? How could you think of such a thing? It would be very odd, wouldn't it?"

"Well, you're the one who suggested it, aren't you?"

"Yes, I agree; I might be crazy, but I'm not stupid. What I had in mind was something private, something personal that you could work out with some of your more charming relatives with your brains and acumen."

"Okay, Rosemary, I shall do all I can to help you. But tell me, what sort of qualities do you seek in this Okeosisi husband whom you would have known for no more than a week or so?"

"Ms. Ijeoma, I'm telling you now so that you can set to work once we land in Okeosisi.."

"What about Dean Campbell?"

"What about Dean Campbell, Ms. Ijeoma?"

"Shouldn't he be in on this, seeing that we are all in his custody?"

"In on what? Are you out of your mind? This is between us. Ok, let's just say the young man can join me in the States. Only you and I need to know."

I laughed a magnificent laugh, when I realised that Rosemary was really serious. I was consoled that at least she wanted marriage, not just a fling that would produce a baby. A baby is precious and requires not only love but also careful planning. We agreed that if Rosemary found anyone she thought she admired, I would help the love-pair along. My grandpa, Maduka, had taught me, a long time ago, ever since I was twelve or so, that there was no point in arguing about anything that was not likely to come to pass, or that was still far in the future; that there was no point in making enemies over mere possibilities.

"Rosemary, if you should meet someone you like, please let me know."

These were my words to my student and, unbelievably, she was thrilled at the thought of finding the love of her life in Okeosisi. I returned to my seat and Bill to his. No one had heard us; so, Rosemary's secret was safe with me. I looked back, Dean Campbell was still asleep.

We landed safely at Heathrow airport, dutifully checked through immigration, groggy though we were. It was just after 6 a.m. and we went about looking for seats where we could continue sleeping. We found a bay that would take all of us and we made good use of the uncomfortable, but welcoming, sofas. Dean Campbell came up to me and I greeted him "Good morning, Mr. Dean."

"I thought we made a deal that on this trip I would be Dwight to you?"

"No, Sir, the deal was that I would call you Dwight only after our stay in Okeosisi, that is, at the end of the trip."

"Aren't you being too fussy, Chioma? We're not at College Park, and we can be relaxed with each other. Don't ever forget I came to the University of Maryland because of you."

"Please Dr. Campbell, I thought we have gone through all this before; that is to say, you're not to make me feel any responsibility for your life. You took the decision you took and I know I'm part of it, but I'm only a part. You have the freedom to do as you please, and as I said to you before, I am humbled that you found so much good in me, so much so that you put almost unlimited confidence in me. Anyway, Sir, it's too early in the morning for this psychological analysis draped in academic lustre. Please, let me sleep."

"Sleep, go ahead and sleep. Your job begins from here onwards."

"I thought my job began the moment you broke into that Bob Dylan ballad, *My Back Pages,* taking me back to my Pa. Ok, let's make a new deal. If you would tell me how you got to know that I like that song, and that it always reminds me of my Pa, I'll call you Dwight."

"No, Chioma, not now; I think I need to get some sleep. Does that give you a clue: some more sleep?"

It was too early to trouble my poor head, but I tried not to look stupid. The dean had given me what he thought was a clue that I would understand: 'some more sleep'; what could this mean, or suggest? Then it hit me, 'some more sleep' reminds me of my teenage years at Georgetown when my byword was, "I need to get some more sleep." I slept a lot; in fact, I still sleep a lot at Nesbit and I am ever struggling to sleep less.

When my Pa passed on, I wrote on his tombstone, "Get some more sleep." Then my siblings and I sang Dylan's *Back Pages* over, and over again, and I continued singing this at Georgetown. I believe the Dean had heard me sing this song many, many times, because after painting, music was my passion. But how did he know about 'Get some more sleep' on my Pa's grave? I just put it down to the age of the Internet when everything one did could be made available to the whole world, and almost anything I touched got circulated on the web.

"Ok, Dwight, you win. You seem to take so much interest in my affairs, why?"

TWENTY-EIGHT

After a peaceful and relaxed five-and-a-half hour flight, we landed at Murtala Muhammed International Airport Lagos. I was the first of our group to get off the plane, and as soon as I stepped on Nigerian soil, I knelt down and kissed the ground. Everyone else, including Dwight, followed suit.

We made our way through the long arrival walkway and finally came to the immigration section. A police officer, an inspector of police, with a sign that read "Welcome College Park", walked up to me and asked if I was Ms. Ijeoma. Certain that I was, he then took all of our twelve passports, submitted them to the immigration officer and asked us to follow him to where he had reserved seats for us while we waited for our luggage. He then returned to give back our passports. I thanked the genial inspector, Mr. Emeka Okafor, most warmly, and we made our exit.

****

Dwight and I knew long before our arrival in Nigeria that, at the instance of my grandpa, the chairman of Okeosisi Local Government Council had made security arrangements for us to be accompanied on our travels by police officers. However, President Mansfield and other university authorities had not insisted on this. One day, soon after the students mooted the idea of the Okeosisi trip, Dr. Mansfield had called me into his office.

"Good morning, Ms Ijeoma. Please come over and sit here beside me. What would be your pleasure, tea or coffee?"

"Coffee, sir."

"Decaf?"

"No sir, the real thing."

"With or without milk?"

"Black sir, black like me."

"Please tell me: what it is about you that has moved the students to such torrential delight that at the mere mention of your name they start dancing?"

How does one answer such a question? "I'm sorry sir, you'd have to ask them. I just do my job and leave it at that. They're the ones who have responded, as you say, in 'torrential delight'. I would not describe my lectures - if you could call them lectures - as capable of causing 'torrential delight'." "You've got it, Chioma; hope you don't mind my calling you by your first name, Ms. Ijeoma."

"You may, sir: I don't mind at all."

"Fine. You said you don't rightly consider your lectures as lectures. Tell me, why do you think they are not like formal lectures?"

"Sir, I simply deal with knowledge as it develops, as it is formed. I try not to deal with knowledge after the fact, after all the 'knowing' is over; and then I try to understand what has been described. I enter into knowledge as I enter a room. Better still, I treat knowledge as I treat a buffet: all the foods are laid out before you, and you just take what you want. The same choices are available to everyone who comes to the buffet, and everyone creates their own knowledge out of the foods."

"If you continue along this line of reasoning, are you saying, Chioma, that you make your own knowledge out of what is before you, and that from the same materials, different people create their different types of knowledge?"

"Yes, sir, but with some qualification: as you know, sir, in a buffet dinner, many foods are served. Of course, if you and I pick the same items, then you and I have the same knowledge. It's only when our plates have different items that we have different knowledge. But it's not quite like that either: for there may still be differences in quantity of one food or the other and this could make for differences in knowledge."

"Is this the exactness for which you are well known among your students? They say you're Ms. Exactness."

"I have not been exact. I simply entered into one room of knowledge, and there are millions of rooms. As you well know, sir, there are all kinds of buffets."

"Now tell me about Okeosisi and why the students think they will absorb the Igbo culture by going there. What they actually say is they will drink full of the Igbo stuff."

Here I was before the president of my university, a man I had met only once, and rather briefly at that, and he was drilling me. Well, I gave him his fill and told him all I could about my great-grandparents, Pa Akadike and Ma Nneoma; and Pa Etim and Ma Eno Henshaw; my grandparents, and my parents. I was with him for almost an hour and he was all ears.

"Well, Chioma, let me just say how happy we are to have you. Your students have paid you the ultimate compliment: they think you're the best and they love you so much. They all want to wear your skin and be African if that could be. We're very, very happy with you. You've brought Africa closer to us. More so, the way you live your life as an Igbo has transformed so many of us, of course, unknown to you. *Ndewo.*"

"How do you know the word *Ndewo*, sir?

"Yes, I know that *Ndewo*, means 'thank you', or a general word for greeting people when you visit them. I have been studying Igbo with the help of a video programme out of the University of Virginia at Charlottesville. They have an Igbo village, built and kept exactly like what obtains in Igboland. You've been there, I presume?"

"I haven't sir."

"Please find time to go there, and then tell me how it compares with the scene at Okeosisi."

I wondered what this conversation had to do with assuring the good president that the students would be well taken care of at Okeosisi. I got the feeling I was always being subjected to one test or another. Well, I shall just be myself, and whoever wants to know who or what I am, will get just that: Chioma, daughter of Onyebuchi and Okeadinife Ijeoma, grandchild of Adiaha and Maduka Okeosisi, great-grandchild of Nneoma and Akadike Okeosisi; a painter, with a strong leaning to music and dance, a woman, living a celibate life in the midst of this crazy but fantastic world.

****

Our luggage came off the conveyor belt one by one, except Bill's suitcase, which took a long time arriving. It was the last item to be delivered, and we had given up all hope of getting it. When Bill caught a glimpse of its red handle, sticking out before the body of the suitcase itself revealed its identity, he jumped up in wild joy, and started singing *My Back Pages* all over again. I tried to restrain him from dancing, but the genial inspector, who was enjoying this whole spectacle, persuaded me to let him be. So Bill sang and as he danced, we all joined him right there in the airport building. I had a feeling my summer PHL 217 experiential course had commenced in earnest. Alleluia!

The inspector walked us to a twenty-seater Toyota bus with three security men in civilian clothing on board. Altogether, there were fifteen of us in the bus including Dwight, who left everything in my feeble hands believing I could deal with any situation that may arise. We drove to our hotel, Silver Valley Hotel, one of Nigeria's finest hotels known for its distinctive hospitality and exquisite Nigerian cuisine. It was about 8pm, and we were all hungry and sleepy, the meal before landing was a mere appetizer. We checked into our rooms and agreed to meet for dinner in the *Cockcrow* restaurant in thirty minutes time. Like clockwork, everybody was there on time. In fact, I was the last person to show up.

It seemed the aroma of the foods and the friendly ambience of Cockcrow woke us up, whetting our appetites. The waiters pulled three tables together so that we could all be together. I sat next to Dwight. Everybody was avoiding him, and I did not like that, so I kept him company. We tried to mix it up so that two ladies or two men did not sit together. But it did not quite work out as we had seven women and five men.

I explained the menu to everyone and they enthusiastically chose the Nigerian cuisine. Cheryl and Bill went for fried rice and *dodo* and beef; Jeff and Rosemary preferred boiled rice with beef stew only, no *dodo*; Dwight was taken with snails, he had never seen them that big, so he had potatoes with snail in gravy. No one else had snail. Dawn, Dave and Cathie opted for yam chips and *dodo* with fresh fish stew. I had fried yam chips, some fried rice, beef stew and dodo. There were other Nigerian foods on the menu but I thought the ones I had suggested would be far more agreeable with their stomachs, green in Nigerian gastronomic repertoire.

Feeling adventurous, Gordon, Jean and Barbara wildly chose *iyan* (pounded yam) and *edikaikong*, saying they liked the dark-green colour of the vegetable soup and the whiteness of the yam. Black and white, they said, made a formidable pair. We all laughed. As she ate her meal with gusto, Barbara wanted to know everything about the *edikaikong* vegetable soup. She dived into the soup, got a spoonful, filled her mouth, and started chewing. She took some more, and then some, without touching the *iyan*. I pointed out to her that she would enjoy the dish more if she ate the yam with the stew. But she would have none of that, telling me that although black and white made a good pair, black was the real stuff while white came for the ride as the white yam was not exciting. To Barbara, dark-green *edikaikong* was simply black.

To prove it, she ate of the yam and said, "You see what I mean, the thing is tastelessly white." Those eating yam chips or boiled yam did not agree with Barbara, so she tried the yam again, this time chewing it more slowly. She took some more and ate it, without the stew. She found that well-chewed yam was delicious.

"My goodness! What a mistake I made." She ate the yam with the stew and bellowed: "Don't mind the colour. It's what's inside that counts. College Park and Lagos have found union in white yam and black stew."

I told Barbara that my grandma made the best *edikaikong* in the world. Everyone knew I was not much given to hyperbole, so Barbara shouted for joy saying that she looked forward to my grandma's dish. Other diners looked in our direction, some raised their glasses in salutation, others joined us for drinks, and the dinner took a riotous turn.

I raised my glass in a toast to everyone:

"Welcome to my country. Welcome to Nigeria. Welcome to Lagos. May your stay with us, with me, be fruitful, filled with gratifying adventure. And may we see a new day for Igbo and College Park inter-connectedness. Cheers, ladies and gentlemen."

I wondered where I got 'inter-connectedness' from! It was not my style. They all broke out in uncontrollable laughter when I said it. Dawn took me up on this.

"Chioma is using awkward words now Does she want to confuse us? Is this a sign of things to come?"

Dwight came to my rescue. "Chioma must have got this word from me, for I haven't stopped talking about the inter-connectedness of cultures since we started planning this trip. Chioma has heard it a thousand times, I'm sure. I like it because it reflects the problems involved in bringing people together. We can all, therefore, better appreciate that what we're doing here, in going to Okeosisi to live the Igbo culture, a bunch of college kids who've never left the States, is something fulfilling and heart-warming. So, Dawn, Okeosisi will not pose any difficulties. The difficulties lie with us, in our hearts, and in our capacity to love."

Talk of love then filled the air: love of life; love of the earth; love of the human soul and love of food. We all believed that whatever was good elicited love. Above all, we sought love in one another. There was no point in seeking to be embedded in Igbo culture if we could not be fully

American at the same time. The talk over dinner truly warmed my heart. I admit I always try to find something good in whatever I see, in whatever I meet, and in whatever is thrown at me. But here we were, feeling like we owned the world, that the world was ours; that there was nothing we could not do to promote good. I looked at Dwight, I looked at my students, and I felt that this evening must count as one of the happiest of my life; for it seemed to me my group was beginning to understand that loving meant giving to the other, giving oneself without reserve.

TWENTY-NINE

After breakfast, we took a short tour of Lagos. So much had been said about the horrible Lagos traffic that everybody wanted to go to the really ugly parts. I had hoped this would not come up, that we would just check out of the hotel and leave for Okeosisi straight from there. But I was a lone voice; not even Dwight could save me. I prayed that nothing untoward would happen as Jonathan, one of the guards, took us round to gain a first-hand experience of some of the worst traffic jams in the world, something I would not wish on anyone.

We went up Bank Anthony Avenue through Ikorodu Road to the Third Mainland Bridge on our way to Falomo, where I hoped to attend Mass at the Church of the Assumption at 12.30 p.m. The traffic was moving at a snail's pace, but by the time we crossed the bridge, we resumed normal speed. We wondered why the bridge did not have a high railing, at least seven feet high so that cars would not fall into the lagoon. To buttress this point, the students pointed to damages to the railing where colliding cars may have turned over into the water. This disturbed our group as they got the impression that the government, who built the bridge, had little consideration for human safety. I did not make any comment as I totally agreed with them

Gordon did not like this one bit. "Chioma, are your authorities so callous and unfeeling?"

"We are not, Gordon. It's just that some of our public officials are so corrupt that they put their own interests first and care very little about the people."

I could have said more but that might have provoked more comments from others. Dwight was calm and was his usual diplomatic self. Thank God the air-conditioning in the bus worked perfectly so there was no irritating heat to add to our discomfort.

We were on time for Mass. We had planned for Jonathan to take the rest of the party to two museums on Awolowo Road, *Charms* and *Onyinye*. But once they saw the Church, they all wanted to be with me and not leave me by myself. I was filled with joy.

Mass over, we joined the maddening traffic at Falomo where cars were bumper to bumper, moving inch by inch. No sooner had a car moved forward, creating one inch of space, than five other cars would try to inch their way into this space, but only one car would make it, and the four others would wait until someone somewhere moved ahead and then the whole scramble would commence again. If it were only cars struggling for space, it would have been more tolerable. But on this day of all days, there were trailers and tankers on our right, on our left, in front of us, and behind us. Our driver, thus, had to be exceedingly cautious, allowing the heavy trucks to move on. We did not want to use the police siren so as not to attract any more attention to ourselves: we decided to experience the madness of Lagos traffic in full. It was a tourist experience! Everyone in the bus was quiet, amazed that nerves already frayed by the heat did not explode in this relentless 'go slow'.

There may be no serious accidents. How much damage can you do at 10 kph? But there are scratches and scrapes.

Finally off Falomo, we headed to Obalende bus stop. To the first timer, Obalende is a sea of colours and human beings, all involved in one activity or another. A great place to paint a watercolour! After we satisfied our curiosity at Obalende, we headed to Oshodi through Apapa. It took us exactly thirty-seven minutes to negotiate a distance that would have taken no more than two minutes. The buses parked right in the way of traffic to pick up passengers, and would not move until they were filled, paying little or no attention to the traffic wardens who controlled the traffic flow.

Dwight asked me how we moved around in Lagos, how we kept appointments, how we lived. It just seemed impossible to him that humans could conduct business, have happy families, and live healthy lives in Lagos. He wanted to know whether Lagosians were happy people or not. I told him that, in fact, they were and that those who lived in Lagos would not, for their life, live anywhere else in Nigeria; so used have they become to the fast pace of life in boisterous Lagos!

People do get around in Lagos, it just takes more time. If people are late to meetings, no one would hold it against them. To get to work on time, people wake up at impossibly early hours to beat the perennially insufferable 'go-slow'. And after work, they would stay back in the office until late, again to avoid the 'go-slow' of home-bound traffic. The result was that many people had no social or family life. They get home very late, have something to eat, and then hit the bed only to be off again very early in the morning. There may be lateness to work, absenteeism, and yes, there were many fake illnesses certified by equally fake doctors' reports. But on weekends, Lagos dances with numerous parties and celebrations that make the city wear a garb of fantastic delight. And many families find ample time to enjoy the weekend together.

Dwight wondered if he could stay a few days in Lagos to learn how humans could live happily in such chaos. Somehow, he could see joy on the faces of many people, even with all the noise. As he saw it, unhappy people did not talk much, did not make much noise, and did not argue much either. Did I not say my PHL 217 course was 'experiential'?

From Obalende, we headed to the frenzied Oshodi bus stop with massive numbers of people buying, selling, bussing, travelling, sleeping, and stealing, leaving one with the impression that this was the home of total confusion and chaos. We could not believe our eyes.

"And you say Nigerians are poor? Do you see the mountain of effort in this place? Do you see this super-bowl activity all in this heat? Gosh! people with this high octane turbo drive energy can't be poor, man. No, they are not poor, just disorganized and maybe not educated. But poor, no way!"

Rosemary spoke the minds of the rest of us, for we were totally astonished to see thousands and thousands of people all huddled in such a narrow strip of space. Lagos was truly indescribable! We drove for about forty minutes on the Oshodi 'flyover', and then headed towards the airport finally turning to return to the hotel. It was 6pm, and we were worn out and famished, although we had each had a packed lunch of hamburger, fries and hot dogs. Some preferred *akara* (deep-fried bean-balls), others, *moi-moi* (steamed bean-cakes). Dwight ate *akara* with me.

Over dinner, where everyone had their heart's desire, we talked and talked about Lagos, with even a daring whisper that we should go to one of the night clubs. Of course, that was out of the question: it was only our second night in Nigeria, and I was not sure I could take care of everyone in the rather raucous atmosphere of a Lagos night club. But that the idea was broached at all pleased me: it meant that we must be enjoying ourselves. Would it not be wonderful to dance here in Lagos? I made inquiries and was told that yes, there could be dancing in our hotel, in the *Castle*. Eventually, we did not go anywhere;, not that we did not want to dance, but we had lost track of the time as we buried ourselves in delightful conversation, going from Lagos to Washington, D.C., to College Park to Nesbit and back to Lagos.

My group found Nigerians pleasant and longsuffering, believing that their boisterous energy and verve would get them out of poverty, out of any ugly situation. Dawn spoke up:

"A new age will dawn in Nigeria, in this new millennium, it is close. It is beating in the hearts of the ordinary person. The traders at Osh....."

I helped her out: "Oshodi."

"Yes, thanks, Ms. Ijeoma. The good traders at Oshodi will save Nigeria. Mark my words. I've never seen what I saw today at Oshodi. A people this tough will go places. Poverty is reborn. It has a new face, and now it will learn to put on some flesh and grow. Yes, the poor people of Nigeria will turn out to be its greatest wealth for they are the ones who have the heart to give of themselves. They are vulnerable and weak and in all things, it's the weak who can change things. Do you know about Pope Leo the Great, Ms. Ijeoma? You're a Catholic, you should know about him."

"Yes I do, Dawn. He was the man who stopped Atilla from invading Rome."

"Yes, He was the one all right. And do you know that Atilla had been warned, by someone I can't remember who now, to beware of the man who bears no arms. The man who carried no gun was Pope Leo and he saved Rome, without waging any war. So, watch the poor of Nigeria. They will make this country great."

Others offered their own thoughts, wondering how the poor could achieve so much, not enjoying much freedom themselves. Well, we knew Dawn was not a prophet and that her words might not come to pass. Still, I found some comfort that Nigeria might not be lost, after all, if others,, like Dawn, saw something good in us.

Dwight filled us with critical apprehension when he wondered aloud, "My goodness! How could Nigeria be like this? I can't understand this. Here is a country with so much talent; some of its best brains are in our universities in the States. And in this country, you have everything. What happens to the oil wealth we have all read about? Does money solve problems? Nigeria has shown all of us that throwing money at problems does not necessarily lead to any improvement in the life of a people. What is needed is a vivid vision of what freedom is all about. As Amartya Sen tells us, development is freedom, people being free to pursue their dreams. Nigeria is full of dreams but what happens? They flounder, they perish and all is lost. Look at those women at Osho . . . ."

"It's Oshodi, Dwight," I said. It seemed this word posed problems for them, Dwight included.

"I'm sorry, look at those women at Oshodi selling all sorts of things. Imagine mobilizing them into a co-operative and getting them to do something really big, something big like living out their dreams, then come and see where Nigeria would be. Fantastic. I believe in the Nigerian woman. Give her a chance and she will move the world. And soon she will have that chance; just wait and see.

"Look at you, Chioma, we're here because of you, because of your *Chi*, how about that? Need I say more about the Nigerian woman? Take your people places, Chioma. Mobilize the women. Get going. Your research might have to change. We'll discuss some more when we get back to College Park. I think you're called to great action. Just pick up the gauntlet and get cracking."

What do I say? Here was Dean Dwight laying a heavy load on me yet again, when the one he had given me was as yet unfinished. In fact, I had not started my fieldwork when this trip was thrust on me.

"Dwight, there you go again. Before I finish one thing, you give me another. I'm only twenty-three, not quite experienced, and you are saddling me with this heavy load. Please give me a break, let me settle down into my life at Nesbit Centre and then I'll try and catch my breath and see what next I can do. But if College Park plans to collaborate with the Nigerian woman in her quest for freedom, as Sen sees it. I'm your arrowhead. But, please, as we say here in Nigerian pidgin, *Ai beg yu, mek ai rest smal befo yu kil me wit so so wok,* which in English means, 'you should let me rest awhile so that you don't kill me with too much work.'"

"There you go, Chioma, you just want to throw me off track, but you won't succeed. I'm still Dean of the Graduate School, and I have every intention to challenge you beyond your obvious strengths to fully bring out all that lies in you. I'm afraid, though, that you are your own best motivator. And you can always move in a different direction as you see fit. No, it won't be *so so* work as you said. It will be *so so* brains.

"Now, who said there's a place here where we can all dance Nigerian highlife, reggae and juju? What are we waiting for? I've been talking too much."

"Please Dwight, could we put off dancing till we get to Okeosisi? It's already past nine and we have to be up early tomorrow morning by six for the long journey ahead. You've not been on our roads before. I assure you, they're quite tricky, with a lot of treacherous potholes. Please, I beg you *'mek we go slip',* that is, let's go to sleep."

He took one look at me, saw my tired countenance and said we could retire for the night, but not before he held me to a promise of reggae, juju and highlife music at Okeosisi. I went to bed giving thanks to God for a satisfying day.

I was able to attend Mass in the morning at St. Mark's Church, close to our hotel. I caught about six hours of sleep and was ready to herd everyone into the bus at 7.30 a.m. after a fast but hearty breakfast. And we were on our way to Okeosisi.

Although our bus was brand new, the Chairman of Okeosisi Local Government Area, Chief Madu Akubueze, wanted to be sure that nothing would interfere with our safe arrival at his area of authority, no matter what. So he sent a second bus to accompany us all the way. But we were all in one bus, the one that met us at the airport, but with the amiable Inspector Emeka Okafor as driver this time.

THIRTY

We left at 7.50am, our spirits were high, filled with eager expectancy for Okeosisi, wishing the journey was just an hour, not most of the day. After an hour we were at Shagamu ready to join the expressway to Benin and Asaba. There was no sight to catch our attention, just rolling woods with Nigeria's ubiquitous roadside mechanics intruding into the peaceful landscape.

"Where are we?"

Dwight wanted to know where we were at any given time, the highway codes, everything, like a typical American. I searched through the map and told him we were close to Ijebu-Ode, on the A121 dual carriageway, travelling east to the ancient historical city of Benin. The questions and requests came in a flurry: adventurous Barbara who would go anywhere and try anything wanted us to stop briefly and take a walk in the woods; boisterous Jeff, who loved wild flowers, asked if we could collect samples of different plants. One of the security men, Ben, looked at me with an expression that said, "no way". Of course, I was not going to allow any stops at this stage of the journey. We had another six or seven hours ahead of us before reaching our destination. We drove on and the conversation was non stop.

Dawn regaled us with stories about her parents, now divorced, her mum teaching and living at Berkeley, and her dad, a Canadian living in Vancouver. While her dad had remarried, her mum was still single. As far as Dawn saw it, divorce was the best option for a marriage gone awry - without love, without romance. She wondered why people bothered getting married in the first place; to her, it would be much better if couples just lived together, maybe have children, and then either of them could just get up and go any time. I asked her what would become of the children in such a situation. She said it did not matter, once the child knew the father and mother and could live with either, with the one who could more comfortably afford it while the other parent provides some assistance.

This produced a lively discussion, some for and more against the suggestion. Dawn gave us more details of her family. Her father had married his secretary with whom he had been having an affair for quite some time, unknown to her mother, who trusted him with all her heart. Why did her father behave in such a dastardly unbecoming manner? Why did he not just go and live with his lover? Why put her mother through this torture? If there were no marriages, would her mother be so trusting, giving herself so completely to this man who betrayed her trust and let her down? Would she have put her entire life in his hands? Could she not have loved him without going into this bonding matter?

As far as Dawn was concerned, marriage was for cowards who wanted someone else to take charge of their lives for them. She was certain she would never marry. She would live her life, love whomsoever she pleased, and if he loved her back and his company gave her joy, then she could live with him, or he with her, if this was convenient and thrilling. There was not much new in this way of thinking. Many people in the States felt the same way. I was therefore surprised when many of the students took exception to this thinking and laboured to talk Dawn out of it.

Rosemary was the most candid. She thought it was far better to love, marry, be disappointed, divorced, and marry again, than not to give oneself completely to one's lover; otherwise love would be a mere commodity to be bought and sold in the market of carefree convenience. For Rosemary, life was not worth living without passionate love whatever its consequences may be. Saying he spoke on behalf of the guys, to their quiet delight, Gordon weighed in with his views, in support of Rosemary, that he would give his life for the woman he loved. We all clapped, cheering loudly.

But Dawn persisted; she was not convinced by this argument for total, undiluted love.

"Look at my dad: I saw him as a good man, as someone I could count on. After he left mum, I could never trust him even with all his ardent avowals that he was still my dad and that I meant everything to him. I asked him if that was the case, if he thought my life worthwhile with both of them apart? What was it that that silly woman has that my mum doesn't have? Mum is beautiful, charming, and a very pleasant person. And dad too, pleasant and apparently trustworthy; how come he says I should trust him when my mum cannot trust him, when he treated mum so badly?

"What makes a man wear two faces, or even three: one for his wife, one for his family, and another for his paramour? I'm sorry that I sound so sore. It's just that the one man who, I thought, was trustworthy turned out to be just a jerk. What do I do? How could I trust a man who comes to me with all those high-sounding words about love and trust, all that rubbish? Come on, love is for losers."

Gordon would not have this and reasoned with Dawn that her dad probably made a big mistake in leaving her mum, and perhaps, right then, he would like nothing more than to get back together with her mum.

"You're damn right, Gordon: you have a discerning mind, alright. Dad flies down to San Francisco at least twice a month begging mum to have him back."

"I told you, your dad's not so bad. He just made one stupid mistake, that's all and now he regrets it. I doubt if that would ever happen again. He must have learnt his lesson. At all events, he's still your dad. You can't change that; so you better learn to live with it."

"Learn to live with it you say, Gordon. Sure, that's just the point: I've learnt to live with it and I've made the necessary adjustments like not wanting to ever be married."

"Well, you're wrong, mighty wrong. There are many other children from marriages gone more sour than you can imagine, and they are all getting on okay, living normal, healthy lives."

"I don't believe they are happy, though. They go through the motions of life without really knowing much about the vast world of love out there. I believed in love until my dad left my mum. I now live with my mum, and I'll try and protect her from other invading male marauders."

"Life's not like that, Dawn," Gordon resolutely continued. "We make our mistakes, we suffer the consequences; and if we're lucky we pick up the pieces, and try and put them back together. They never make a perfect fit, though. Wounds leave scars. Who do you think is scarred more, Dawn, your dad or your mum? Tell us. I bet it's your dad who's suffered more from his guilt, and he'll suffer even more if your mum doesn't forgive him and take him back. So, why don't you give your mum a call as soon as possible, or e-mail her and tell her all that we've talked about on this trip and say one of the benefits of your trip, was the resolution of your family crisis; and that she should give your dad a chance again and regain her former gaiety, charm and cheerfulness. What do you say?'

Everybody joined in, "What do you say, Dawn?"

I could not believe what was going on. Here we were, being truthful with one another; playing the analyst with Dawn, and helping her resolve her problems. Loving and not loving are big issues. I just hope we can keep this up and be our brother's keeper. Then I could shout, "Wow!"

Dawn said she would think it over, and when we got to Okeosisi she would know what to do. With no more questions asked and no stories to follow, we turned once again to the journey.

By now we had passed the town of Ore and there were helpless lepers on either side of the road, begging alms, in one of those horrendous spots where the maddening potholes had deepened into a formidable gully that engulfs vehicles. Our visitors asked who the lepers were, and I did my best to present things in the best possible light under the circumstances. I had prayed that it would rain, so that there would be no beggars, and physically- and mentally-challenged women and men on our way.

Cathie could not take it. She came across to me and asked me who they were, why they were there, why nothing was being done for them, what kind of a country Nigeria was? She wondered just how much it would cost to take care of these helpless people. Trying not to get her involved in something that would probably be way out of her depth, I told her it was not as easy as that; and that taking care of the physically challenged required far more emotional commitment than she could possibly sacrifice in the short period she would be in Nigeria. Still, Cathie wanted to do something, no matter how small. We agreed to try and work something out, so that she could make her contribution, in her own way, to ease the suffering in my country.

We were soon in Benin. I tried not to raise any issues about the pride of place the ancient city of Benin held in Nigerian history, fearing that they might just want to spend the night there. And I would not blame them: I wanted to stop in Benin too. But my fears were just that—fears; nothing came of them.

Jean, the most sensitive and perceptive of my students, asked how much longer the journey would take and I said another five hours or so; that crossing the Niger and Onitsha could be fraught with anger, frustration and charlatans out to make a quick naira. She suggested that if that was the case we should continue on our way and eat our lunch in the bus, saving time thereby. I heartily concurred, and we continued but not before some of the guys had to go use the bush as toilet, as we had rehearsed before the journey. We looked out for a good petrol station with running water so that some of the ladies could use the toilets. They did not like it much but they took it quite kindly. It seemed no matter how difficult the terrain, my guests accommodated the pitfalls, the dirt and squalor. One thing that kept pounding in their hearts and what they considered to be the whole purpose of living was the sort of dreams that Nigerians have, and how Nigerians would live out those dreams. They would accept anything, but a life without dreams.

I was sad and miserable at the lack of security in my country, necessitating our travelling with three well-armed security men, their powerful pistols well concealed, and an extra bus in tow.

****

The journey from Benin to Asaba, through the new Benin bye-pass was so smooth that we all fell asleep and were in front of the great River Niger by two in the afternoon. Ever since my childhood, I had been captivated by the Niger, always singing songs to her, listening to her enchanting voice as the dawdling waters swept the drowsy shores. I felt like telling our guests something about the Niger but resisted the urge, for I was very fond of the Niger and my tale might last until we got to Okeosisi. Anyway, the story was always better told with the mighty river in commanding view, eliciting warm and powerful feelings of Africa's romantic glory. However, all did not go by just like that, without some questions asked. Dwight wanted to know if the Niger conjured up in me any particular history of my people.

Where do I start? The Niger gave my country more than its name, it gave her the oil-rich Niger delta. As I gathered my thoughts on how best to phrase my answer, Dwight must have thought that I might start weeping so he handed me his handkerchief. But I said, "thank you," and gave it back to him. He guessed that the story would cause a huge emotional upheaval in me and would not be told during this particular journey. I said nothing, my face giving away the emotional turmoil welling up in me.

Everybody watched in disbelief: they had not seen me in such a strongly emotional state before; and I did not know that the Niger could evoke such supreme passion in me. Without my knowing it, I must owe a lot to this river; for, it seemed, my spirit resided in her depths. I wondered: was there something Pa Akadike had not told me about the River Niger? Had he any ancestral links with the people who lived along its shores from Sierra Leone to Timbuktu to Onitsha, or in the Delta region?

How do I find that out now that my Pa was gone? Perhaps my grandpa might know. I should ask him.

Somehow, I found sufficient composure to tell my students that the Niger was to me a powerful literary and artistic force, and that, quite possibly, I had some ancestors, artistes amongst them, who gave me their remarkable ingenuity in painting and music. They left it at that, with a measure of empathic union with my spirit.

We stopped for drinks and food near Oraifite, and the security officers also had a chance to get a bite and stretch their legs and weary backs. We were now on the last leg of our journey to Okeosisi, and when I announced that we would be there in an hour or so, pandemonium broke loose, everyone jumping and stomping on the floor of the bus.

In an hour, we were in my hometown. When we got to my compound, I stepped out, kissed the ground near my Pa's grave then we moved on to greet my large family eagerly awaiting our arrival. They were ecstatic and I prayed,"Thanks be to God."

We were warmly welcomed with a dance normally reserved for dignitaries, *abigbo*. The sound of agile music filled the evening air, lifting our spirits to great heights. Massive drums were beating, their pulsating reverberations pounding the red iron gates of the compound with gloved fists of tender joy. The dancers, about thirty in all, in their colourful attire of *george* and white round-necked singlet with white handkerchiefs knotted around their necks performed their routines with the grace of galloping giraffes.

My grandpa and all the young men in our compound came out with shouts of *Unu abiala, ndewo nu o!* meaning, 'Welcome to our home, thank you for your presence.' The music and dancing continued while we went to our rooms in my grandpa's house.

THIRTY-ONE

It was 5am. My alarm had gone off and woken me up with a start. On this our first day at Okeosisi, I wondered how the day would turn out. I was nervous. I said my morning prayers, and that calmed me, having placed all the day's events and occurrences in God's massively able hands. Still, I had my own part to play. A voice I could not make out beckoned me to my Pa's grave. It was dark outside, and since I was mortally afraid of snakes and other reptiles I had to call on one of my older relatives, Denis, to come with me and stay by me.

"What are you afraid of, Chioma?" Denis asked. "You know this whole place is safe and nothing can happen to you while you are here. Don't forget our Pa is still very much alive. He lives with us and protects us. So, you go on to the grave, and I'll go back to sleep. Go ahead. Don't be afraid."

I was at Pa's grave-side, and lit a lamp to give some light. My Pa's personality completely took hold of me, and all my thoughts were directed to the communion of saints for, I believed, my Pa was up there with them.

"Pa, please, pray for me. Here I am at your grave-side, so early in the morning, without any particular thoughts in my mind except that I'm so nervous, hoping that this whole summer course here at Okeosisi will go well. If anything goes wrong, the University of Maryland at College Park would be the laughing stock in the university community in the US, and nobody will take me seriously anymore. You've got to help me. Please tell the Most Blessed Virgin Mary to come to my aid. No, you've got to do better than that; you have to get her to help us, not just me, but to help all these wonderful students to have fun here and learn a new way of life."

I returned to my room and commenced my meditation, my conversation with God; with profuse thanksgiving for bringing all of us safely to Okeosisi. I prayed for the success of the huge project we were undertaking by coming to Okeosisi.

"My God, I've been saying to anyone who cares to listen that my people, the Igbo, might have much to offer in this global age where cultural transformations, unforeseen through the ages, will now be manifest. The world we know is changing so fast there's no telling what tomorrow will look like. All is novel. All is unknown, but, I pray, not unknowable. What am I to do? How will it be possible for these students to be different from what they were when they came here, that one could say they've been transformed?

"The job is enormous. No, I don't mean that it's too much work for you, my God; of course, not; nothing is too big or too much for you. What I fear is that you might expect too much from me, a huge challenge I cannot meet. I'm feeling I just might let you down this time. My most loving Mother, I pray you to ask your loving son, Our Lord, to do what he did at the wedding feast in Cana, in Galilee: change water to wine, except that this time it will be changing these my wards from American-Americans to Okeosisi-Americans; that is to say, that larger and larger holes of Igboness be drilled into the hard core of their American-ness, day after day, slowly but inexorably until the fourteenth day of this visit when we leave, filled with the soft soil of Okeosisi, right from the area where my *Nkwu Alo* lives and thrives.

"Yes, Lord, this would be like your turning the water of American materialism into the wine of Okeosisi selflessness. That's what this whole course is all about, Lord: a new philosophy forged right here where you gave me my Pa."

My mind moved on to my work as an artist and I continued my prayer.

"Lord, in this global landscape, new kinds of artists are appearing all over the place. Some offer us softness and tenderness in natural colours; some others are surreal. They say what we see is not really what we see; that art reveals nature to us; others imagine things and just put them all on canvas; some just splash paint on whatever surface they fancy and they say it shows the flow of the mind. Where does Okeosisi come in, Lord? We need our own art to show that we too belong to this world, that this world belongs to all of us;

and that what happens to one region has effects on other regions.

"Lord, you've given me a talent for art, and I paint as you guide me. How do I translate this ability into a real culture that represents my mind and my African self? Please, train me to transform the world with my art that it may travel far and wide and open peoples' minds to a new way of thinking that would make them see the world differently."

With God by my side, I was at peace with myself. A cool breeze, rushing through the louvres, bathed my face, and flowed into my heart, filling me with the air of courage and enterprise for the day's engagements. I went with Grandpa and Grandma to Mass and we were back before our guests were up and about.

****

"Grandpa, what's all this I see behind the house?"

"Ah, my sweet Chioma, it was meant to be a surprise for you. I'm happy it is. Let's walk across, and I'll tell you all about it."

We walked up to what I discovered to be a tennis court and a swimming pool.

"Chioma, my child, you see, you make things happen. Immediately I learnt that your students would be coming here not just on holiday but for research, I thought it would be a good idea to provide adequate facilities for recreation so that they would be able to relax and have fun. In fact, what was uppermost in my mind was that they have fun, that they enjoy the visit and have fond memories of Okeosisi. So, I got your uncle, Onyekwere, to build what you see before you: a swimming pool, a tennis court and a basketball court.

"As you can see, the basketball court is not of competition size. You know your uncle Onyekwere is a civil engineer, a man of means, not like me, a poor professor. He agreed without any fuss, and do you know what? He came up with a brilliant idea. He said, "*Dede*, let's do this as a real project such that our Igbo children in the US, who are dying to come home, and whose parents don't have the time to bring them home, can come here and spend some time learning aspects of Igbo culture, in particular, the Igbo language. There's so much we can do here in Okeosisi for our children. So, this is just for starters; let Chioma's students have fun, and then we'll develop a solid programme for our children in foreign lands, keeping them close to their indigenous culture. I'll have the whole thing completed in seventeen days."

"And, Chioma, indeed at two o'clock in the morning on the fifteenth day of operation, all was ready. The labourers worked in shifts, night and day, for twenty four hours, non-stop. The whole place was lit up and it was even brighter than day. Onyekwere himself was here to supervise the work, and he too gave a lot of himself, getting little sleep. The swimming pool was finished first, believe it or not. I had thought the tennis court would be number one, but it was the last. It gave us some problems, but not so the swimming pool. The pool was filled with water two days ago and everybody in the compound jumped in, swimmers and non-swimmers alike. In fact, it was mostly the non-swimmers, for only your uncle, I and three of the workers can swim.

"So, here we are, let's thank God for making this possible. Your uncle will be here before you leave, exactly when, I don't

know yet. He'll call, I suppose. Of course, he can just show up.
This is his house. So, my dear, welcome to the Akadike
holiday resort."

"Grandpa, this is just too grand. My students will be wild
with joy when they see all this. And Dean Campbell too.
You've just blown my mind with the idea that Uncle
Onyekwere would like to see us develop this into a study-
holiday project for Igbo students in the US and abroad who
would like to see their native land for the first time, perhaps."

"Well, it involves a lot of work yet, my dear; planning,
getting government approval, building up a library, getting
good personnel and so on. But surely it will be done. This will
now be my retirement enterprise."

My grandpa had arranged that our guests be awakened in
the morning at 7am to rousing sounds of *ekwe* and *ogene*
followed by breakfast at eight. But this being their first
morning at Okeosisi after what would be, by all expectation, a
not-too-pleasant night, he asked the musicians to delay
playing until eight. Breakfast would then be at nine.

This gave me sufficient time to say my rosary, read from
the New Testament and from a spiritual book, *The Holy Spirit*,
by Edward Leen. I also helped in the kitchen, with some
cooking and washing up, though Grandma did all she could
to discourage me. She loved spoiling me, giving me her best
anytime we were together, especially now that she had not
seen me for about five years since Pa's funeral. Still, I insisted
on helping out, in any little way, to keep up my struggle in
humility. I did all this as unnoticeably as possible, so that the
house-help, ever close by, would not come in and take over.

Two kitchens were in operation, Ma's traditional kitchen,
which was in the family compound, separate from my Pa's

main house, and Grandma's contemporary kitchen which was on the ground floor of my grandparents' house. There was some distance between the two kitchens so one had to choose what food one would eat and then simply go to the kitchen that served that particular dish. Since we did not know the preferences of our guests, both kitchens simply served their particular specialties. It was now almost nine o'clock and no one had come out for breakfast. Did this mean they were still enjoying their sleep, or that they slept in fits and starts and were by now gleaning some straws from the forest of deep sleep? Well, Rosemary was the first to come out of the house. We had agreed to congregate outside, in the *obiriama*, in the morning to greet the members of the household and then proceed with breakfast and the day's activities.

"Good morning, Ms. Ijeoma, how are you?" She said to me.

She then went round and greeted everyone. She tried the greeting in Igbo, *"I bola,"* but it did not quite sound like the real thing. However, undeterred, she continued until she came to Ma who sat her down, clasped Rosemary's palms in hers and patiently put her through saying *"I bola"* with the correct accent. Having learnt the right pronunciation, Rosemary went round again and greeted everyone, amidst candid laughter.

The students started to come out of the house one by one. Dawn, then Jean, David, Bill, Gordon and Barbara together, and finally, Cheryl, Cathie and Jeff. Dean Campbell was not yet in sight. He was a deep sleeper and a keeper of late nights, he had told me.

Totally unexpectedly, everyone dashed toward Ma all at once as if a coveted prize was to be won by the one who got to her side first. Rosemary beat everyone to it and instantly squatted by Ma's right side, before a seat was brought to her. As Ma's chair was next to the wall, there was no room for anyone on her left side but she moved her chair, allowing Dave, the second person to get to her, to sit on her left side. The others jostled to sit as close as possible to Ma, who was beside herself with joy.

Her exalted seat seemed to have conferred on Rosemary the role of spokesperson for the group because she stood up and addressed her fellow students:

"You good people here, this is our first morning in Okeosisi, great land of great men and women. We're all awake and well and we thank our stars. Look up in the sky tonight and try and find yours, give it a name, and that's the name you will bear till we leave. So, no more Cathie and Dawn and Jeff and so on; it would be Dodo, or Didi, or Dada, according to the name of your star. Today will be a great day."

"Come on Rosemary, or Rasandra, as you will be called after you find your star," Dave said, "let's have some quiet, please. The night is still ways off and we are dying to have our first meal at Okeosisi. So, please, let's eat."

My Ma's kitchen had three of our relations, all of them women, cooking, with my grandma, Adiaha, giving instructions every now and then with Ma watching, taking in the imagery of the moment as the flames robustly heated the pots, which responded with a symphony of rising and splashing juices. Five pots were put to cook - one with yams, another with yam porridge, another with beans, yet another with beef stew, and the last with water, put to boil, for pap.

Ma usually cooked with firewood: she could never for the life of her agree to use a cooker, gas or electric. She said she had only one life and that she would live it as closely as possible to the way she met the earth when she was born, the way it was in her childhood. Of course, she did not live her life that way; she meant it only in so far as it concerned her kitchen. After all, she watched TV, had a refrigerator, running water from the borehole and electricity from the generator. Grandma would taste food from a pot and ask that more pepper be added, or a little dash of salt, or water, if the contents were drying up, this may be followed by removal of some firewood to lower the intensity of the flames.

Grandma had a way with salt: she would put some in her left palm, spread it out with the fingers of her right hand and then tease the grains into the pot, grain by grain, it seemed. She did not take to salty foods, and she got all of us not to add salt to our food at the table. It would be interesting to see whether my students would find the saltiness of the foods adequate, for she hated nothing more than to see someone add salt to food she herself had prepared.

It was quite a study for my students to see the big pots sitting on the oversized rings, burning firewood underneath. They had seen this sort of spectacle only in the movies, in Westerns especially, since none of them had ever been a Boy Scout or a Brownie. Ma always had a good supply of dry firewood which was sure to produce virile fire to cook a meal quickly. All was set for an African breakfast made in Okeosisi.

For those who cared for some, there was boiled yam served with beef-stew, yam porridge cooked with shrimps and dry fish, black-eyed beans-porridge served with beef-stew, and pap, which had to be made in small portions because pap does not keep well. I had some pap, just to show my guests what it was like.

To complete the breakfast menu, Grandma brought some milk, whole and skimmed, fresh fruits, paw-paw, bananas, pineapples and guava from her own kitchen. There was already coffee as well as tea. Grandma had baked two cakes, a fruit cake and a chocolate mousse cake.

Grandma had wanted to bring out all the foods in serving bowls from which we may serve ourselves. But the guests all loudly shouted, "No, Grandma." Dave then continued "We'll help ourselves straight from the pot," to which Jeff added, "Hey the pot's the charm"; followed by Dawn, "Straight from the pot."

Rosemary said a prayer, "Eat the food, eat the soul of the food; eat the pot, eat the mind of the pot, eat the fire, eat the living love in the food," and we all responded, "Amen."

The food was served right from the pot, or as we would say in Okeosisi, straight from the fire. Who had what? Let me try and remember. All I know is that they ate all the food Ma and Grandma had cooked. Nothing was left. Dave, our college basketball star, with a voracious appetite to match, ate the most. Rosemary must have had him in mind when she said, "Why don't you go ahead and eat the pot?" He kept coming back for more and more beans and stew until his tennis ball-stuffed cheeks were reflected in the bare bottom of the pot. He then moved on to yam porridge. But here, he had competition: Cheryl, artistic, of aristocratic bearing, although she never told us anything of the antecedents of this aristocracy, loved yam porridge, just like that. She did not eat much, but she would not let Dave enjoy more than just one helping. Did she think this was her last meal of yam porridge?

Jeff, boisterous, gregarious Jeff, just let Dave lead on and had a generous helping of boiled yam with stew himself. Who else? How could I forget Rosemary, the charming irrepressible one, poetic and great lover of wines. She helped herself to a bit of everything. She started with a little pap, no more than five spoonfuls, and added some honey, sliced guava and pineapple. She then moved on to yam porridge. For some unknown reason, yam porridge appealed more to the girls than to the boys. Dawn, Cathie and Barbara all ate a lot of yam porridge. Gordon and Bill were more finicky and wanted to stick with just coffee and cake but Rosemary would have none of it insisting that everyone had to eat something from the boiling pots. As she said, "Our souls have a new life in 'dem dere' pots."

Grandma personally served everyone, and while we ate, she and Ma watched us with intense interest. Ma could not carry on a conversation in good English so Grandma Adiaha translated what Ma said in Igbo to us, in English

"My children," she began, "my own wonderful ones, young lions and lionesses of tomorrow; bearers of good fortune; the future hopes of your people, God bless you. You have made us very happy with your presence here in Okeosisi. Chioma tells me you've come to learn certain things about our noble African culture that would help transform the world. They say the world is becoming more and more like one village. Well, your presence here gives credence to this view. For you will surely take much of Okeosisi with you when you return to America such that America would be a little like Okeosisi. And we, having lived with you, would become a little bit more American in our own Okeosisi ways. Thank you, my children. I am blessed with twenty-nine great-grandchildren and now God has given me ten new ones - you. You are my own children, my great-grandchildren, and

I'll give you your new names here and now so that I can call you by the names I myself have given you."

The students did not quite grasp the significance of all this but went along with Ma all the same. They were all quiet.

Grandma then proceeded to call the students one by one, the girls first, then the boys. Ma had said the girls would bear a name with *Chi* in it, since she had been told that one reason they had come to Okeosisi was to discover the *Chi* of Chioma, her own personal god, as it were. That way, they would all share in Chioma's *Chi*. The girls leaped in wild excitement and teased the boys saying that the boys had no gods to give them a special identity; that the gods preserved the best for women who bear their children.

Dave spoke for the men: "Mama, we beg you, give us names that contain *Chi* also. The gods first made man before woman. Please, Mama, give us our own *Chi*."

Ma agreed with joyful laughter; in fact, she regretted her error in thinking only of the women. This provoked rich banter and deep, penetrating discourse that would last all morning running into the afternoon, to lunch time.

Ma began with Rosemary whose presence was felt all the way to the Okeosisi forests.

"My dear daughter, I call you Chigozie, meaning, 'May God bless you.' And I say, God will bless you all the days of your life."

"Amen, thank you Mama." Rosemary answered.

Ma proceeded to give them their *Chi* names, one after another. As she was naming Jeff, Chibuzo, Dwight strode into the *obiriama*.

Dressed in casual wear, a safari shirt over khaki shorts, he walked straight to Ma's welcoming arms, stretched to their full lengths, as soon as Dwight said 'Ma *itele*', meaning, 'Ma, you have woken up', or, in ordinary parlance, 'Ma, good morning.' With the zeal of a matriarch, whose wandering children have finally come home, Ma responded *'e, nwam, etelem'*; *'yes, my son, I have woken up.'*

Where did Dwight learn Igbo? I wondered. Perhaps, he will tell us later.

Ma then continued: "I give you a new name, *Ezechishiri, The King That God Crowned*. May your crown be ever studded with diadems of joy and peace. May your face light up all the earth. And may your students gain full knowledge of this world, and give us a new life in the city of love."

Ezechishiri, answered 'Amen' with wild enthusiasm, his arms lifted up in the air. Grandma then fetched him a cup of coffee and Ezechishiri added sugar and milk to his taste, and served himself from the pots of beans and fish stew.

I walked over to Ezechishiri. "Wow! It's no longer Dwight; it's now *The King That God Crowned*. I bow to you, my king."

"Come on, Chioma, knock it off. Ma is very loving and kind. I thank her with all my heart. Now, on this visit, I plead with you, just leave me out of everything, and I mean 'everything'. Your grandpa and I have already struck an abiding friendship, by e-mail: do you believe it, friendship by e-mail, and an abiding one at that? Well, it has happened, and, now, all I want to do is to sit with Maduka, your grandpa and drink full of the good wine of his life, especially his experiences at Ibadan and Ife. So, I leave our students in your caring hands. Yes, if you need me, I'll come in and lend a hand; but, please, Chioma, if you say I'm your 'king', and you, my 'subject', then kindly let me be, and leave me with Maduka. I'll tell you all I would have learnt when we are back at College Park."

Just then Grandpa walked in, embraced Ma with warm greetings, and practically dragged Ezechishiri with him to my Pa's mud-brick house.

"Oh, Chioma, let me put your mind at rest; once you agreed to come to College Park, I started to learn Igbo, using the internet. I know your greetings, with correct pronunciations and all, and Maduka here will teach me some more."

My head was now spinning: my life at College Park would incomparably test my mettle.

THIRTY-TWO

Dave, now Chudi, started it all. He asked Ma the significance of *Chi* in Igbo life and belief systems.

Ma's eyes lit up. Her voice was solemn and solid, as if she wanted to make certain that everyone heard her, even though what she said was being translated by grandma, and it was only her voice that would be heard. In fact my grandma's voice was softer than Ma's. She told us a story handed down to her by her grandparents who received it from their grandparents. So, she said, it must have come from antiquity. Not a sound could be heard: we were all transfixed by Ma's countenance which made us understand that the story she was about to tell us was one of great import like the one story of a lifetime. Ma proceeded:

"There was once a man, named Agu, meaning lion. He was tall and strong, a noble warrior and a fierce fighter, the strongest man in his village and the best wrestler too. Nobody was able to pin him down with his back to the ground. He was always able to twist himself, curl himself till his head touched his toes, and go into several somersaults without stopping. He led his village to victory in all their wars against distant villages, and so his village came to own a lot of land in far away places.

"One day, he set out to visit his daughter who was married and lived with her husband and children in a place called Alaoma, meaning Good Land, a Blessed Land. Agu never reached Alaoma. On the way, a little boy no more than fifteen years old, wrestled Agu to the ground. Three times they wrestled and three times the boy threw Agu down. He lay prostrate on the ground. Agu did not want to live to hear this little rat, as he called him, tell tall tales of how he defeated him; and so, drawing his sword, he plunged it into his own chest and bled to death.

"The little boy was astounded and disappeared. No one ever saw him again, but he left his bag and farming tools on the spot where Agu was found dead, his sword still deep in his chest, and his hands firmly clasped around the weapon. The villagers recognized the bag and its contents as belonging to one Ndubisi, meaning Life Comes First, an orphan, without any known relatives, who helped people on their farms. He could not be traced, and it was not known how Agu came to kill himself until the chief priest of Ala, went to their oracle. It was pronounced that a boy named Ndubisi had wrestled Agu to the ground, and Agu had killed himself in shame.

"No one believed this. A more powerful oracle had to be sought and its verdict obtained. The result was the same: that Agu had died at his own hand. All the oracles in Igboland were consulted at great expense to the people of Ala, who by now had sold almost all of the land they had won in the wars in which Agu had been their leader. Afterall, they reasoned, they would not have owned those territories without the valour and courage and strength of one man, their own Agu, their lion.

"All the elders put their heads together and agreed to cease inquiries into the cause of Agu's death. They accepted that Ndubisi had thrown him down and Agu had killed himself honourably. But how could such a boy, a mere urchin, cut down a huge iroko like Agu? The question was reduced to one concerning Agu's existence and Ndubisi's existence too; how were these two existences related? And what determined the existence of one and not the other? The twelve elders agreed to meet again in eight days time and each would tell the others his dream for they believed the answer would be revealed to one of them in a dream.

"On the appointed day, they met. One after the other, they had nothing to say until it got to the turn of the last man who turned out to be the one who identified Ndubisi's bag and on whose farm Ndubisi had last worked. He stood up, a short man he was, he looked rather frightened. He cleared his throat, and as he was about to speak, Ndubisi appeared from nowhere and told them that his real name was not Ndubisi but Chi, and that he was a spirit, and he could come and go without anyone seeing him; that he worked on the farms just to help people; that he was not born the way humans were born. Then he rose into the air, right before everyone.

"The elders were about to run away, but the oldest among them implored them to be men of courage, saying that they must all sit and see what was happening. Ndubisi was about ten feet in the air. He said he was Agu's *Chi*, who gave him his soul; took care of him and endowed him with enormous strength and valour; that he had been with him in all the battles and had always saved him from harm. He said further that Agu had always listened to him, co-operated with him and did as he had commanded. Not once did Agu go against him. And so Agu always found great favour with him, Agu's *Chi*.

"On this fateful day, Agu was going to his in-laws, to where his daughter was married, to make trouble with her husband who had sent her home. Agu's *Chi* advised Agu not to go, that it was not good for a man to go to his in-laws to fight, that he should find a way to bring the erring husband to his senses and make peace with him. He agreed that he would make peace, and not fight anyone. When Agu's *Chi* saw him fully dressed, armed with his peculiar battle-sword, which he had given Agu for use only in battles, he knew Agu did not heed his advice, that the visit would end in a fight. Well, Agu's *Chi* had to find a way to show him that a man does not forsake his *Chi*. If he did, then he would be responsible for whatever happens to him. That was why he appeared to Agu on the way, as the little boy, known to all in his village, and he wrestled Agu to the ground. Three times, Agu challenged Ndubuisi, and three times Ndubuisi beat him.

"Of course, Agu did not know who Ndubuisi really was; that he was his life source; the one who watched over him and determined his future; and secured everything for him. Agu's *Chi* thought that Agu would be able to read meaning into Ndubuisi's throwing him down and then see this as reason to return home, especially as his *Chi* had warned him in his sleep, in the first place, not to go to his in-laws. *Chi*'s plan was that after throwing Agu down, he would just disappear; but Agu drew his sword in vaulting pride and came after Ndubuisi. Still eager to save Agu from certain death, *Chi* whispered in his ears, over and over again, a well-known saying of the people: 'My son, he who fights and runs away, lives to fight another day.'

"Agu heard the words but could not make out where or whom they came from. Undaunted, he charged after Ndubuisi in an attempt to kill him, but Agu did not know that it was just not possible. He should have realised that Ndubuisi did not throw him down using mere human powers; he should have suspected that the voice that spoke to him in his sleep, and that later warned him to go home so that he could live, was at work, and that it was not the voice of a mortal. But he went after Ndubuisi, after his own *Chi*, totally unknown to him. He did not know a man does not fight with his *Chi* and live. *Chi* vanished into thin air when Agu tried to plunge the sword into him and directed the sword into Agu's chest instead. Agu screamed, 'The God of Good Fortune has deserted me!' as he lay in his own blood.

"After telling the elders the story of how it came about that Agu killed himself, Agu's *Chi* ascended into the clouds and was hidden from view. There was still one elder who was about to speak before Chi made his sudden and dramatic appearance. Since none of the eleven elders had come up with anything that happened in their dreams, all ears were now open to hear what Nna Ama had to say, and he did not disappoint them. He said he had received a message in his dream: that a man must obey his Chi, and co-operate with him in everything; that if he did this, then, his Chi would lead him and guide him and protect him and fill him with everything that is both materially and spiritually worthy; and that when a man becomes too proud and full of himself, his Chi would abandon him to his own fate; that is, pride and arrogance drive Chi away."

Ma added that other communities close to Okeosisi have similar renditions of what Chi was all about but that farther-off villages have their own tales of the origin of Chi, who he was and how he came to be the determinant of one's fortunes and life history. Whatever one believed about Chi, however, Ma made it clear that pride and arrogance were the death of any man because Chi cannot tolerate pride: so, he always destroys a proud man.

Bill, now called Chima, asked Ma, "What happened to Agu's Chi after he disappeared, after Agu died?"

"I'm sorry, Chima, my child, you know your name means, as I explained to you, 'Only God knows everything.' So, indeed, Chi knows everything. And you know what, everything includes what happens now, what will happen tomorrow, what will happen next week and, as you might now guess, what happens at the end of time, and in eternity. That is to say, Chi belongs to today and to eternity at the same time. That is what makes Chi so powerful. What does this mean for us, the living? It means Chi is with us all the days of our lives. If we die a good death, our Chi takes us to his place, a very grand place and we live with him. And if we die an awful death caused by our evil ways, or evil deeds, our Chi abandons us, and we can never be reunited with him. Our suffering is that we never see him again. Now, Chima, I think that completes the whole story of how Chi governs our life, and directs it to the good."

Ma once again repeated what she had said before: that everyone's Chi is great, and if we just go along with our Chi all would be well because Chi sees to our well-being and takes care of us.

We were all stunned and did not know how best to proceed. It was beginning to look as if Ma would be the one guiding us to a healthy amalgamation of the two cultures, Igbo and American. All we needed to do was to try and interpret things in our way, with Ma's help. But not on this morning of mornings; we had had enough Igbo philosophy for one morning, I thought. But it seemed my students wanted to resolve this Chi issue right there and then. They moved over to my grandma, Adiaha, and sought her views. Grandma begged off with the excuse that she was Efik, and that if she had anything to say, it would be when we all went to Calabar, where she was born. Grandma knew only too well that Calabar was not in our itinerary. This was classic Grandma response, merrily tactful.

THIRTY-THREE

"Hey, what's that hoop I'm looking at? Don't tell me it's for basketball."

That was Jeff, now Chibuzo, God-is-the Way, who had caught sight of the basketball court some distance from Ma's kitchen. He ran out, not quite believing his eyes. "Yeah," he exclaimed, "it's a goddamn basketball court!" I genially reminded him of one of the rules we imposed on ourselves: not to use foul language. He apologized profusely promising that it would not be repeated.

By then, everyone was out of the kitchen area, everyone except Chigozie, who sat resolutely beside Ma, unwilling to be coaxed out of her peaceful comfort. Ma kept on talking to her in halting English with Chigozie nodding her yes's and no's.

When the others ran to the basketball court, they discovered the tennis court and the swimming pool.

Chinemere and Chudi wanted to shoot some baskets but I tried all I could to dissuade them from starting because we had an appointment to see Igwe, the King, at one o'clock in the afternoon. We had just over an hour to be ready and we needed thirty minutes to practise how to conduct ourselves before Igwe and through all the protocol of the palace. Chudi and Chinemere dunked a few baskets, and we returned to the *obiriama* where Grandpa Maduka was ready to begin his lesson.

"Let me begin by saying that Igwe is a king. We don't have the time to go into the fall of the Nigerian kings during the colonial era of our history. Very much unlike the Yoruba and the Bini, who have had undying impressive lines of *Obas* from long before European and British incursion into Nigeria, the Igbo are more republican in their social and political organisations and accorded respect and reverence to elders of noble character and intellect and of great accomplishments. Some Igbo communities had kings, who exercised supreme majestic powers as endowed by the Almighty *Chukwu*, the god of heaven and earth, who created all things and rules over all things but not co-terminus with the Christian God, for the Igbo notion of Chukwu predates the arrival of the first missionaries who transported Christianity to our land. Before you leave, we shall find time to take a look at the Igbo Chukwu and the Christian God and seek, in their striking similarity, the reason behind the solid foundation of Christianity in Igboland."

This was a good beginning, but my friends - I now called them friends after Ma had given them Chi names - had their eyes on the basketball court. Their minds returned to what Grandpa was saying when he kept clearing his throat over and over again to get their attention.

"Our own community here in Okeosisi ranks among the few in Igboland that had recorded history dating hundreds of years of majestic kings down to the present Igwe Ikemba II now on the throne of our ancestors."

This struck a note of joy in their hearts, and they all yelled, "Great! We'll all be princes and princesses after this visit."

Grandpa was pleased, laughed loudly in agreement and continued: "Regrettably, with the advent of colonialism, the powers and authorities of our Obas and Igwes were obliterated."

"Oh, how terrible," my friends sounded a bit dejected. "Well, we'll still be daughters and sons of a king."

"Indeed you'll be," Grandpa affirmed, "for our kings have undeniable authority in upholding our indigenous traditions. In this, their role is virtually supreme, and we are glad it is so, so that our customs and traditions may thrive and not be lost to modernism, more so to globalization. I guess that's why you are here: that your encounter with our culture may be a wellspring in you that continuously fills you with fountains of joy in all that we hold dear, so that you may always seek to live intimately within Igbo culture and find refreshing energies in its cool waters."

They all rose to their feet in wild exultation as if they had reincarnated with African souls.

"I'm sure you can now easily understand why we show great regard for our dear Igwe and bow before him when we are in his presence. It's central to all that I've said that you come to understand his place in our life and accord him the same respect and regard he receives from us, his children."

"Grandpa, we're his children too, by adoption. I hope he'll see us like any other child of Okeosisi. I can pretty well imagine the University of Maryland having a campus here at Okeosisi after we leave, and wait till we tell them back home what we've seen so far, and it's only our first morning. We want to live here."

That was Jeff (Chibuzo) putting Grandpa at ease as to how they view their experience at Okeosisi, which would translate to their respect for Igwe Ikemba II.

Grandpa proceeded to demonstrate how we should bow before Igwe, boys and girls alike, and told us that we should not speak in the presence of Igwe; and that someone, that is my good self, would speak on behalf of everybody, and that we should all remain standing until Igwe asks us to sit down. He went through the ceremony of the presentation of kola nut which Igwe will give us, and what we were to do. After that, we were all set for the palace.

It was a fifteen-minute drive to the palace, but it seemed like an hour to me for I was genuinely apprehensive as to how things would turn out. Grandpa did not go with us. I led the students, but to show that the Akadikes gave me their solid support, two elders from the family accompanied me. This protocol had been transmitted to Igwe by my grandpa before our arrival, and he had got Igwe's approval.

On our way, there was much talk and laughter as we drove past the market, the Catholic Cathedral of Our Lady Queen of Apostles, St. Stephen's Anglican Church, schools, a huge forest, dusty dirt roads, urchins lined up to fetch water from a reservoir. Finally we were at the palace.

We were cordially ushered into the Eastern parlour, where Igwe received those who he considered as family, those closest to him. Here, Chief Ogadinma, Igwe's principal chief, welcomed us with profuse expressions of warm and affectionate regards. He took us to our seats only a few feet from Igwe's seat-of-honour on a raised dais. He asked how we were; how well we slept on our first night at Okeosisi; and how we found the place, to which I responded pleasantly. He said Igwe would be with us shortly, and just before he finished speaking, Igwe made his majestic entry with six chiefs leading the way. We immediately bowed, and at the top of our voices greeted Igwe, bowing and repeating I-GWEE, I-GWEE, five times. He acknowledged our greetings with several hearty shakes of his royal whisk. He sat down, and Chief Ogadinma requested that we take our seats.

Igwe asked for some kola and Chief Ogadinma presented him with a tray of twenty-four kola nuts. Igwe touched the tray, and the chief proceeded with his prayers on behalf of Igwe. He first spoke in Igbo and then rendered it in English; basically, that it was Igwe's prayers that we have a happy and fruitful educative experience in his kingdom and that our visit may forge even closer ties between Maryland and Okeosisi.

Igwe, through Chief Ogadinma, asked us to take one kola nut each. We did so and then the chief asked one of the palace officials to break one kola nut. Only one kola was shared into tiny bits, hardly big enough to be picked up by hand, and we each took a piece and chewed it. Igwe was glad that we seemed at home with the kola and nodded his head in satisfied joy.

This was not the first time my students had tasted kola nuts. On our way from Lagos, I had bought some from a persistent hawker at Benin, washed them and shared them out. It was bitter, but I told everyone that they should learn to like it because they would be chewing a lot of it in Okeosisi. I did not, however, explain the significance of the kola nut in Igboland.

Then came time for me to address Igwe. I had written the address down and made sure that the language was regal, befitting a king. But I did not read it, I had practised it so well that I knew every word by heart.

"Great Igwe of Okeosisi, Eze, Lord of all Kings; Face and Power of Okeosisi, Killer of Lions, King anointed by the god of life, Light of the People; Fierce Lightning of the Skies; Big Soul of Man, I salute you. I greet you. I honour you. Forever and ever I shall serve you with all my strength. I shall fight any fight, climb any mountain and cross the oceans, to bring honour to you, great one, and to Okeosisi, great land of my birth, land of giants."

Igwe nodded his greetings and twisted his royal whisk. I continued.

"I bring you my students, ten of them, they will introduce themselves shortly. Great Igwe, these wonderful young women and men through their own initiative decided to come to Okeosisi to learn something about the Igbo culture, and how it could be rendered into a philosophy of the global age. The whole class that I teach wanted to come here, but, only ten of them could conveniently travel with me. Great Igwe, King of the Forest, whom leopards see and they run, history is being made at Okeosisi by this visit. We pray it won't be the last, and that it is a sign of greater things to come.

"Great Igwe, these young men and women were impelled to come here by the name I bear, the name my great-grandfather, Pa Akadike, gave me, that is, Chioma. They say they want to live in the world of my *Chi*, since they see me as a symbol of the Igbo mythical force of life. Majestic Igwe, it seems we are entering into a world the meaning of which is just not clear to us, for I myself don't quite know what to make of the philosophical concept of *Chi*. That's why my students have come here, Great Igwe, to this your noble community, and we are now in your able royal hands to bear us up and carry us with you in this land of my *Chi*."

Igwe's retinue clapped in enthusiastic joy, while I continued standing until the Igwe motioned to me to enjoy the comfort of my seat. He smiled in sublime satisfaction. All was quiet for a minute or two, then Igwe motioned to me to get up. He looked intently at me for what seemed like eternity. Beads of perspiration dotted my face, visible indicators of my stirring discomfiture. What could I have done wrong? I wondered. Igwe must have noticed my state of patent worry.

"Wonderful, my child, wonderful; Chioma would you please tell us this story again, how the students want to be embedded in your Chi and how they see Chi as the cornerstone of Igbo philosophy. Please, let us hear it again in case we miss the point of your address."

Well, surely His Majesty got it all right: what he said was the kernel of my address. Maybe, he wanted to hear it from the tender innocent mouths of the students themselves. Wonder of wonders! As if they read my mind, my students all stood up, moved from their seats and surrounded me holding hands, forming a circle with me in the centre. And then they asked me to tell His Majesty what I had said earlier, that they were with me fully and that they all spoke with my voice. I was more relaxed, more at ease. I smiled.

"Great Igwe, my students, as you can see for yourself, have surrounded me saying I'm their voice and so I repeat everything I said earlier exactly as you have ordered me."

I then proceeded to tell the great Igwe once again the whole story, not one word changed. We continued standing, and he motioned to us to sit down. He addressed us from the higher seat on the dais, which had all the paraphernalia of a throne.

"Thank you, Chioma, thank you my children, for now you have made yourselves my children and I adopt all of you by the *Chi* names our own Ma Nneoma has given you. Now tell me your names, one by one, and on Nkwo Okeosisi, I shall make a pronouncement on today's unforgettable events. Again, I most kindly welcome you, my children."

The students stood up one after another saying the names given to them by my great-grandmother, Ma Nneoma. At the mention of each name, the great Igwe showed his appreciation and joy with a flick of his kingly whisk.

Great Igwe, all smiles, left us amidst our show of obeisance and warm respect with more bellows of I-GWEE, I-GWEE, I-GWEE from my wildly excited students. Chief Ogadinma invited us into the royal gardens, and we all stepped outside. I had been to see our great Igwe on only two occasions before this, and had not been taken round the grounds. So what I beheld on my visit with the students was, indeed, a marvellous surprise.

There was a hedge of hibiscus interspersed with red and yellow roses; an orchard of oranges, guavas, mangoes and lime. Portions of what must have been a forest were retained and, here and there, were *udara*, iroko and flowering flamboyant trees.

The good Chief Ogadinma invited us for drinks and what he called 'small chop' - cheese-and-ham sandwich, fresh tomato, cucumber, onions and egg sandwich; tuna sandwich, chicken sandwich; steak sandwich, and, of all things, beans sandwich. I had never seen beans served with bread as sandwich, but this was so cleverly done and the beans held on firmly to the roll and did not fall out of its secure anchor. I tried this and loved it.

It became the choice of the boys in particular, Chudi and Chinemere enjoying it the most. Chika and Chibuzo, the veggies among us, had the vegetable-egg sandwich. We also had salads, and those who went for chicken and steak or cheese-and-ham sandwiches found the spicy salad invigorating. There was a wide choice of fruit drinks, soft drinks and *Graves*. Chigozie and one of the boys, Chima, helped themselves to some wine. I had water instead of my usual white wine. When it was about time for us to leave, Chief Ogadinma gave us bags and bags of fruits from the orchard. We thanked him and then went to our bus.

We were on our way home. It was about four o'clock on a hot afternoon, and, unexpectedly, the students asked me to take them to the sports field in one of the schools we had driven past on our way to the palace. I did not like this idea as I wanted to go home so that I could do my meditation, while everyone else took a rest. However, I had no choice but to go onto the sports field, and sweat with the rest of them in the scorching heat. I just could not make out how these newcomers to tropical heat were able to bear the high temperatures and oppressive humidity. Were they so enthusiastic about Okeosisi that the surge of their superior adrenalin overcame all regard for comfort and ease? My students truly astonished me with their immeasurable love for me, my people, and my place. I prayed it would all end well.

In their decent clothes, they rolled and rolled on the field. I could not believe my eyes. I tried to dissuade them from this frolicking, which left them all dusty and dirty, their clothes brown with clay. But they would not listen, simply saying they wanted to wear the Okeosisi clay.

Chima ran over to me. "Ms. Ijeoma, you know if you just add an 'o' after the 'i' in my name, it becomes your name, Chioma, and yet the two names mean two different things. And we all want to be like you. Do you think by the time we leave the gods would have added the 'o' to my name?"

I smiled, and slowly, my joyous smile grew to mild laughter. This course was becoming glorious, and I felt enveloped in the warmth of friendship. I gazed into space, day-dreaming, transported into a world where people lost their selfish identities and gained a new existence in the spirit. We are all different: with, or without, an 'o' in our names. How wonderful it would be if we could just change ourselves and become someone else we desire to be simply by adding a letter to our names. We can change, though; all we need is a personal conversion. It is quite easy and yet so difficult if we do not want to. Did St. Augustine not give us this classic statement about our passions: "Lord make me chaste but not yet."

"You're a great guy, Chima, you know. You're wonderful as you are, as God made you. You're a tennis freak; you love your beer, and you're cheerful. What more do you ask from your Chi? Your name, Chima, means 'God knows everything.' Don't you think that's a striking name? If you'd always remember that God knows you as you are; he knows we're having this conversation and he's listening in on what we are saying right now. I'm sorry, that's not philosophy and I'm supposed to lead you through the alleyways of philosophy as lived by my people, the Igbo. Don't forget I'm not an expert at this."

"Ms. Ijeoma, just watching you this afternoon at the palace of your king . . ."

"We call him Igwe," I said.

"I'm sorry, Ms. Ijeoma. At Igwe's palace today, just watching you I got the distinct feeling that you're very much like your great-grandfather; he lives in you, it seems. Don't ask me how I can tell. It's a long story. It began in Georgetown, then on to College Park, and now Okeosisi. Someday soon, the whole world will come here to know this place."

"Thanks, Chima. That's very kind of you." That was all I could say, not quite knowing how to respond to this prophecy.

It was time to go, we did not have a time table but I wanted us to get home so that we could all swim, play tennis, and shoot some baskets. I shouted out instructions, but no one listened to me. They proceeded to pull tufts of grass from the field. They wanted us to go over to the market and buy clay pots in which they could each grow their grass in separate pots.

I agreed and we went to the market, Nkwo Okeosisi, not to buy any clay pots, but to gain some insight into the boisterous and colourful atmosphere of Igbo local markets, not much different from Oshodi. It was late in the day, and as it was not a market day, not many goods were on display. Still, my students were enamoured of the wide variety of fruits and vegetables all of which they had eaten either fresh or cooked in one or more of Ma's tasty dishes. Now they had the chance to see more of *ugu, ukazi, oha, onugbu, okra, ogbono, nkwu,* cooked in vegetable soups. Oranges, bananas, pine apples, and guavas, were in plentiful supply and we bought some. Chima cheerfully peeled an orange and ate with much relish. Not to be outdone, Chigozie went for guavas being hawked by an athletic and zestful lad, no older than seventeen or so. She came over to me smiling joyously and whispered, "I think I've found my great love from Okeosisi," and proceeded to ask the lad his name. He said his name was Ikenna. Chigozie went further and asked Ikenna his surname and he said it was Ahamba. Moving over to me, she exulted, "How about that, Chioma; how does Mrs. Chigozie Ahamba sound to you?"

"Fantastic, Chigozie. All you need now for your marriage is to obtain Ikenna's consent, since you would be the one proposing to him, and a sworn declaration from his parents stating their son has their permission to marry you. All that can be concluded in a week and you can arrange for Ikenna to give up hawking, return to college, gain a university education and then immigrate to the United States. In the alternative you could return and live with him in Nigeria."

Chigozie burst out into wild laughter much to the amazement of the rest. "Come on, Chioma, love does not run so fast."

"Well, don't forget I'm simply helping out. The whole enterprise is of your making."

"Let's go home, Chioma; let's go back to Ma Nneoma and Grandma Adiaha. I think we've all had a swell time here in the market."

Evening beckoned. You should come to Okeosisi on an evening in early July, just like today, at that time in the rainy season when thunder and lightning reign supreme over the atmosphere. The students said they would like to bathe in the Okeosisi rains and prayed for a heavy downpour before they left. But the sky was not about to grant their wishes today. Although the clouds were gathering, and they all had their necks stretched to the full, heads tilted backwards, eyes beckoning raindrops, it was still hot and dry - no lightning, no rumbling thunder, only clouds. We agreed it would be a good evening for swimming.

We returned home with our tufts of grass. Grandma Adiaha found some pots and cans, old and abandoned coffee mugs, mortars, and other odd containers that now proudly housed the Okeosisi grass we had collected. We wrote our names on our pots, and we hilariously tried to match our names to the features of the containers. Chibuzo, 'God is the Way', had a clay pot with a corrugated lip, which he called *Uzo*, 'The Way'.

Everyone was interested in my own 'grass pot', an old calabash from Pa Akadike's days. It was used for practically anything that required the use of a container - to fetch water from one bucket to another; to fill up a jar of Palm-wine wine; to serve as a dish for *ugu* leaves as they were picked one by one from the stems, or for okra, or *ukazi*. In its old age, with cracks here and there, it had been left out in the garden, collecting soil and rain and insects and seeds sprouting to weeds. I picked it up, cleaned it, and planted my grass in it. I wrote my name on it and was taken to task to cast my name into poetry in a poem depicting the life of the pot, all in two or three lines, or so. I managed to write:

> *Nothing good ever dies*
> *what's abandoned is not lost*
> *nature's pot's eternal clay*

I placed my pot on the cardboard bearing these words. While the others swam, I excused myself and went on to share the day's experiences with my God. I was thankful that all had gone well, meditating on the major themes of the day, namely, the meaning of Igbo names, the nature and significance of *Chi* as told by my Ma, and the close association between the Igbo and the earth.

THIRTY-FOUR

"We thought you were with us, Ms. Ijeoma. Where have you been? I turned, and didn't see you."

That was Chidinma's way of saying she missed me, and I obliged her with a soothing reply, "I was praying for you."

"Come on; don't start with this your prayer business. Before you know it, you'll have me going to church. No way."

Chidinma was aristocratic, coming from a line, she said, that dated back to the heyday of the Austrio-Hungarian empire. Friendly and adventurous, she was an apostle of individualism anchored in science, knowledge and reason. Faith and religion were anathema to her supreme intellect. Every now and then, I would try and rub in the innocuous issue of prayer, not so innocuous to Chidinma, however.

"Tell me, Chidinma, why did you let Ma give you this lovable name that means God is good? You could have begged off, and Ma would have gladly respected your wishes."

"You're being difficult, Ms. Ijeoma. I love Ma, and, as you can see, she's now our very own Ma. She has become our own great-grandmother, not just yours. We're sure there's nothing she would do for you she wouldn't do for us. The only difference would be that you have more frequent access to her, that's all. And, as you know, love doesn't suffer as a result of distance. It suffers as a result of neglect and lack of consideration. And we're sure we'll ever live in Ma's thoughts. So, whether or not I go to church, I'll keep

Chidinma as my name. And you know I don't pray. Surely, the good God....ah! That's it, am I not 'God is good'? Surely the good God knows my needs and would take care of them. I don't have to pray. Well, I suspect you prayed for me. So go ahead, pray, but leave me out of it."

"Chidinma, you're one hundred per cent right. My Ma loves you with the same heart with which she loves me and you're now her own great-grandchild just as I am. You all make me so happy that I wish there was something personal I could do for each of you."

"We're here with you, Ms. Ijeoma. You are worth your weight in gold. What more could we ask for?"

Chidinma came over, embraced me and held me so close that I felt her ribs. Then she said, "Go on, Ms. Ijeoma, just be yourself and we'll follow you and be like you."

I wondered: did this mean she would follow me to the Catholic faith? Well, I would take her up on this in time.

This 'being-like-you', once an allegory, was fast becoming the trumpet sound of my class, PHL 217. How frightening!

****

It was getting late, and the mosquitoes had started buzzing, sand-flies surreptitiously following them. Everyone was getting bites. I had forgotten that we should all use our insect repellent. I then brought some, and we rubbed them on our exposed arms and legs, while we sought refuge behind the veranda with mosquito-proof netting. This meant we could not gather round Ma in the evenings. In any case, Ma always retired early for the night, not later than 8pm. My grandma did not really want to sit with us as she felt that her ordinary, daily Igbo-Efik habits had been corrupted by long sojourns in Europe and the U.S. What we wanted was Okeosisi as

Okeosisi in its pristine glory, which meant we had to seek the company of the elders of whom we had plenty. But at this time of the night, none of them was awake; so, we had to rely on ourselves for company.

Grandma Adiaha had laid out a table of sumptuous meals, in one of the many verandas, with mosquito-proof netting, a wide variety of food from her inexhaustible kitchen: plantains — fried, boiled; rice — white, jollof, and fried; boiled yams; potatoes, couscous; gravy; fresh fish stew; peppered steak with onions and paprika; lamb chops; pork chops; grilled gizzard; salads, and for dessert, a fresh fruit cocktail. Grandpa came in with some wine — his South African specialties of Cabernet Sauvignon and Chardonnay. For me, or rather considering my taste, he brought my favourite *Pouilly-Fuisse*. There was beer: Gulder, Star; different kinds of juice, soft drinks and malts. We were not really into malt drinks, but Grandpa always served malt drinks for non-alcoholic tastes.

This was dinner on a grand scale, but not to my grandma, who regarded the kitchen as her favourite laboratory where she could carry out experiment after experiment on the compatibility, or lack of it, of various dishes from different Nigerian ethnic groups. She saw the kitchen as a poetic landscape, as art, as music; and from day to day she would serve the same dish but not in the same way. With different spices and sauces, Grandma would turn an ordinary meal of *fufu* and *uha* soup into a masterpiece of subtle and sublime flavours, reflecting the grandeur of simple human skills. To her, cooking was all art and composition. She was excellent in cooking, and it gave her immense joy to entertain. My mother was nowhere in Grandma's class when it came to kitchen affairs: Mum was ever too much in a rush to give the kind of distilled and fulfilling attention that poetic meals required. My grandma had no equal in cooking.

We found it difficult not to taste a bit of this and a bit of that which all ended in a heavy plate of satisfied appetites.

"Grandma, this is simply fantastic. Thank you ever so much for taking so much time to prepare all this. Oh, this is all the philosophy I need, Grandma. My heart and my brains now know the meaning of life: life is love, and love, and more love. That's all the philosophy I need."

That was Ogechi, who had said so little since we arrived in Nigeria and had spent much of her time gazing at this and that in total bewilderment. She was prone to mistakes and was usually very apologetic for them. She could not contain her joy, translating Grandma's cuisine into biscuits of lively love. Ogechi, literally meaning 'God's Time', or, more fully rendered, 'God's time is best', lived true to her name: this must be God's own appointed time for her to give us a talk on love as philosophy.

Ogechi, who did not eat chicken, noted that Grandma did not include chicken in the meal, and she was thankful for this, seeing it as a mark of love. She was thrilled that Grandma's cooking was lean, stripped of any fat-inducing calories. More than this, she saw in Grandma's cooking, the qualities of a passionate woman who loved her family with all her heart, and gave her best to anyone who called at her home. She said that Grandma did not just cook; she created satisfaction and joy for her guests who tasted her meals. Ogechi went on about how Grandma used the kitchen as an instrument of an apostolate—an apostolate of friendship and pleasant conversation; how Grandma served God better in the kitchen than any priest served him at Mass. I had not known she was Catholic and I immediately told her she was making one of her mistakes again. She laughed and reminded me not to forget what Cardinal Wolsey said when his king, King Henry VIII, condemned him to death. Cardinal Wosley said that if he had served God with half the zeal that he had served the King, God would not have given him over in his grey hairs.

How do I correct Ogechi, whose time for speaking had come? Chinemere quickly came to the rescue.

"You got it all wrong, Ogechi; the best prayer Catholics have is the Holy Mass, and the best anyone can do in this life is to be in a state of grace to be able to receive Our Lord in Holy Communion. Nothing beats that. Nothing."

I did not wish to encourage this line of talk because we had all agreed not to discuss any particular religion except in a philosophical context, and what was going on now did not seem philosophical to me. Chinemere must have read my mind and then saw an opening to thank Grandma for her exquisite cuisine, cooked with delicate care and love. Ogechi had the last say, expressing her regrets for the kind of analogy she had drawn. She said that she did not intend to preach heresy; all she wanted to do was to give Grandma the highest praise she could think of. We teased her and left it at that.

Drinks flowed. Grandma sat with the boys and Grandpa with the girls, not bad if you ask me, but they did not say a word; they were only moving from glass to glass to refresh the drinks. The cabernet found good company in Ogechi, and in tennis buff, Chima. The chardonnay sat well with Chika, the comical and fearful vegetarian, and with the adventurous Oluchi and our basketball stars, Chinemere and Chudi. Beautiful and perceptive Chinwe joined me in savouring the dry and spicy *Pouilly Fuisse*. The others had soft drinks.

It was after nine o'clock in the evening, but we were still wide awake, the conversation was still flowing, and no one had taken more drinks than they could hold. I was pleased, very pleased, because we had exercised our freedoms wisely. Chima thanked Grandpa especially for the 1996 Stellenbosch Cabernet that was served. He paid him great tribute for being a distinguished wine connoisseur who kept that distinct 1996 vintage till then. He said his great-grandfather was a vintner who had large vineyards in South Africa. The business, a family affair, passed on to his grandfather and his brothers and sisters, down to his own father, and uncles, but then his father immigrated to the United States where he, Chima, was born. His dad loved wines, he said; and, as far as he was concerned, wines were the greatest gift of God to discerning humans.

We retired for the night with thoughts of the gifts of God. I said my prayers, thanking God for a wonderful day. Then I went through what and what I had done that day, what I did right, what I did wrong and what I could have done better, begging God for his mercy with a firm resolution to do more things pleasant in his sight, things not only good, but excellent.

THIRTY-FIVE

I reflected on the grass episode all through the night. I just could not believe that all this was happening without any compulsion on my part; that is to say, it was the students themselves who came up with all these ideas, as if they had been born with them, as part of their personality, simply waiting to be manifested here at Okeosisi.

I took these thoughts to my morning meditation.

When I ran into Chief Ogadinma after Mass, in the morning, I saw it as a God-sent sign and asked him to come and have a talk with my students on the Igbo fascination with *ala*. I narrated the story of how they had kissed the ground and uprooted the grass from the field and transplanted them. More than this, they each would take a bit of soil to the United States, and let the grass grow there in their respective homes. Chief Ogadinma could not believe his ears, but was so exhilarated that Okeosisi was being transplanted to the United States that he immediately agreed to come with me so that we could all have breakfast together in our historical *obiriama*.

No one except my grandparents, with whom I went to Mass, had been privy to my scheme to give my friends a thorough grounding on the significance of what they had done the day before—their spontaneous involvement with Igbo ancestry as demonstrated by their immersion in the land — and to let them know that the land was their land.

I helped Grandma and Ma cook a good meal from ingredients grown in the family garden behind Ma's kitchen. And so we all went out to the garden. Some of us brought vegetables, *utazi*, and *ncha anwu;* others, pepper for peppersoup; some plantains; others fruits, oranges, bananas, and paw paw. Robust and voracious Chinemere picked some *ugu* leaves for vegetable soup: he wanted pounded yam for breakfast, and Chima concurred.

With assistance from our large family, the cooking was done swiftly, and we were ready for the land-given breakfast of yam with peppersoup, pounded yam and vegetable soup, plantains with fresh palm oil stew, and fruits. Chigozie liked her fresh oranges squeezed just for the juice, but the others ate theirs, having peeled off the skin. Paw paw, was a delight for Chudi, and he had a lot of it. Chief Ogadinma, who was enjoying all this, had boiled plantain with some peppersoup, and was ready to proceed with the talk.

He said I had told him that the students had formed an association, a union with *Ala Okeosisi,* and that they all wanted to be one with the land of Okeosisi. He expressed his profound delight with this development which was unprecedented in the history of our land. He said that he was so filled with joy that he believed he would not see another day like this, and so he would share with these new friends of Okeosisi what he knew about *ala.*

"*Ala* has a huge significance in Igbo culture and I can't begin to enter into its meaning in the short time you're going to be here. In fact, it's not the sort of thing we talk about: it's rather an idea, even a philosophy of Igbo life, a truth, which a father transmits to his children more by habit and nuance than by talks and admonition.

"We live on the land. We build on the land. We live off the land. Our farms are cultivated on the land. Our forests are on the land. Everything depends on the land: the sky would not be the sky if there was no land. We know it as sky because there is something else we step on called land. The sun beats the land, makes it hot, the air rises and cools down; clouds are formed and rain falls on the land, makes it wet and cool and soon it's hot and dry again.

"Above all, we return to the land when we die. Perhaps, on this land where we are all gathered, we have the dust from bones after millennia of imperceptible degradation. So what today is dust was once human life, human body. The dead are with us; the past is with us. Our ancestors are with us. Our land is with us; it is the air we breathe.

"Thus, to take someone's land is not a simple matter of taking a piece of territory or his possession in material terms: it is snuffing the air out of him. And some of the land is hallowed, not in terms of holiness or the oracular, but in terms of history; a place where history was made, whereby a people come to acquire their name and character. Regrettably, these days, our lands are not that sacred any more: they have been sold to the unstoppable gods of progress and modernity. And why not, some ask.

"The spirit of a people lies in their land. Ask yourselves: why were you born in the United States and not in Africa and you, Chioma, why were you born in Africa and not in the States?"

Ogechi came in with a ready-made answer:

"Passionately loving the world, I make the entire new world of Okeosisi my world. This land is my land, Chioma has made it so. Chioma, am I wrong?"

I could not believe my ears and my eyes: my students, now my friends, swooped on me and they all surrounded me and held me firmly to their friendly bodies telling me how much they loved me, how much they were now indigenes of Okeosisi, to the extent that they said they would live out their lives in Okeosisi if it were possible.

I could not get my thoughts together, and just sat there, in their midst, flooded with intense joy, as they continued to express their undying love for my Igbo culture.

The amiable chief continued."I can't believe that it is me who has created this unforeseeable expression of true human brotherhood and oneness shown by your students, Chioma. I must tell Igwe about this. I wonder what he would do. My goodness, how can we repay you for this supreme love you have shown us? He turned to the students and said:

"You can now better appreciate the advantages of world travel. It has brought you here, freed you from the moorings of a particular culture and social milieu, and you all avow that Okeosisi is the place to be, all because of one person, our own daughter, Chioma. So, what am I saying? Are your age-old attachments to your land now obsolete? No, because land, more than anything else, is character, values, and hallowed nobility. Understood thus, you can immediately see the inviolability of the human being - a being of character, of values. So, let us love and serve our land, this good world of ours, through all that is noble and worthy, so that all who meet us may want to know us better.

"You met our daughter, Chioma, and she has held you spellbound and you've followed her here to know at first hand the culture that produced her, the Igbo culture. My children, God bless you all."

I then called my students friends, as they could actually see into me and know that I was completely overwhelmed by the tremendous love they had shown me in their immersion in Okeosisi culture. All of this, I could not have foreseen. My evening meditation thus overflowed with thanksgiving to God for this cultural integration, as my students, now my friends, were slowly being immersed in Igbo life. I felt extremely fortunate.

The days were rolling on; one great, delightful day after another not so great, not so delightful day; one ecstatic day after another not so ecstatic day. Our freshly crowned 'king', Ezechishiri Campbell, joined us at meals, telling us stories upon stories of his childhood and school days in Boise, Idaho. This gave us some insight into his personality, something he could not have considered doing at College Park. Respectfully, we made no comments, and simply listened in delightful wonder. What a man! we all felt. And he insisted that we call him by his new royal name, prefaced with 'dean' and, every now and then, he would come down in one of Grandpa's Igbo traditional wear. We would all shout our praise with EZE, EZE, EZE; that is, KING, KING, KING.

I was profuse in my thanksgiving to God for sending His angels to take such good care of us, our security guards notwithstanding. So far, no one had come down with malaria, or any of the other ailments associated with travel in the tropics like diarrhoea, vomiting, unexplained fevers, or excessive dehydration. I just could not relax completely, but I tried not to let anyone read this from my countenance. I looked ever so cheerful, no matter the riot going on inside of me.

But Chigozie, from time to time, would come over to me, look deeply into my eyes and start a talk on her own idea of the philosophy of the Igbo and would say something like, "Ms. Ijeoma, you're deep in thought, imagining all sorts of things: don't worry, all will be well. You're a great lady and if we've come here to be with you in your Igbo culture as part of PHL 217, to learn a new philosophy that will have meaning in our lives. Thus, all the fun we're having would count for our success. Don't you think this beats any dry, fossilised, crazy philosophy with little use in our daily lives?"

I was very fond of Chigozie and was happy in her company. I had not forgotten she had hoped to secure a boyfriend, nay a future marriage partner, here at Okeosisi. Every now and again, I thought she might delve into the subject of the love of her life. She continued:

"You know, I never forget that Hegel saw philosophy as the owl of Minerva that spreads its wings at the fall of dusk; that philosophy comes in to explain and help us understand that which has already taken place. We're here in Okeosisi, with the Igbo, living as the Igbo live, eating Igbo food, sitting on Igbo grass, dancing to Igbo music, sleeping and waking up having dreamt Igbo dreams. Come to think of it, Chioma, we go to sleep and wake up in Igboland: that must count for something. It means when we go to bed to sleep, we join the communion of your ancestors until we wake up, and do we wake up to the American air? No, what we have is the sun at Okeosisi, and we breathe clean Okeosisi air into our American lungs. No, I don't think we can fully grasp what we gain by being here with you, emphasis is on WITH YOU.

"Fortunately, we'll still have you when we get back to College Park, or else, if we were to say our goodbyes here, I bet some of us would stay here with you. I certainly would stay here just to be with you."

I got various versions of this quiet compliment from my other friends. However, only Chigozie seemed able to come to me just when I most needed someone to lift my spirits and confirm that no matter what happened, they had all had such a good time, that they believed their experience would transform them, not only when they got back to the US, but for as long as they lived.

THIRTY-SIX

ı had called Angela twice after we got to Okeosisi, but I was so happy that I wrote to tell her all that had happened to us so far—how the whole experience was like a dream to me, totally beyond my wildest expectations. Due to the slow postal service in Nigeria, I sent the letter by courier service, or else it would not get to Washington before our return to the United States.

I began to think of her and all that she had done for me. I recalled how she had strenuously endeavoured to make every iota of the spirit of divine filiation come alive in me, leading me to strive assiduously to live with the joy of knowing that I was a child of God. She slowly and lovingly led me to see the cross in the form of all those little irritating, provocative and seemingly unbearable incidents of everyday living, in things I cannot stand and which bring out the worst in me; in the contradictions I continually face. These will always be there! Angela showed me that the occasions on which my defects tried to get the better of me were, in fact, opportunities for my sanctification; that my deficiencies were my cross, and I should always struggle to overcome them.

She was ever after me to try and control my great love for wines, something that runs deep in my family. My success in this relentless effort would depend on my recollecting myself and living in the presence of God in all things, at all times, being humble and showing charity to others, particularly to those I do not find so likable. Whenever the demons of my pride reared their ugly heads, I would make every effort to squelch them with a self-vouchsafed mortification, through doing such domestic tasks as scrupulously scrubbing our bathrooms on my knees, vacuuming our conference hall, dusting the upholstery and washing the windows, or doing the laundry for the Centre. I make steady progress but fail even when conditions are not really testy. It is a never-ending battle.

Then, there are the crosses which God allows in his infinite wisdom and love; crosses such as illness, death in the family or of a friend, the massive evil of '9-11' or the terrorist acts all over the world. What do we do with these? How do we take them? What purpose could they serve? Angela had gradually and resolutely guided me through the significance of these horrendous circumstances; instilling the sense in me that this unimaginable level of evil immediately urges us to do all that is good so that evil may be drowned in a world of good. Whatever happens, she said, I must not lose my happiness which comes from knowing that I am a child of God.

"Be ever cheerful," she would tell me; "go deeper and deeper into prayer and hang on to your faith; for God, your Father, would never do anything to hurt you. Rather, whatever you were confronted by, was meant to draw you closer and closer to a state of increased sanctity. Of course, you must continue to offer up voluntary mortifications daily, again, in the simple and ordinary circumstances of your life. So much joy comes from penance, making the face of our Lord shine in all we do."

"Chioma," she would lovingly call me, "we can all be better. Being the great painter you are, I need not remind you of the steep challenges you meet in your works which you have so triumphantly transformed into masterpiece after masterpiece. Be a masterpiece of God by accepting the cross; seeking your sanctity in suffering. But don't forget, also, that our joys have an element of the cross in them; in the care, the efforts, diligence, patience, and in the virtues that produced the joys.

"Remember," she would say, "embrace the little things. Life is full of simple, ordinary things. Dance in them and make everyone happy in doing little things. Make people smile, especially those who would irritate you or annoy you."

These thoughts were on my mind as I sat with Florence for my "chat".

****

Ms. Florence "Flo" Onyejekwe, the Director of Onyinye University Centre, Enugu, an *Opus Dei* Centre, paid me a visit in the company of another resident at Onyinye, Dr. Patricia Egunjobi, the vice-principal of Brooksides Girls' Secondary School, Enugu, founded and run by some women faithful to Opus Dei. They made weekly trips to Owerri and were on their way there to meet some university students who were receiving spiritual, social and doctrinal formation. In accordance with the arrangements we had made from Nesbit before our trip, they had come to be with me to offer me the assistance I needed with fulfilling my vocation to serve my God in apostolic celibacy.

I told Florence my students were thrilled with Okeosisi beyond belief: they felt at home and, in fact, had come to adopt it as their own. They now had Igbo names and felt integrated into the Akadike family. Above all, they gave me to understand that I had exposed them to a whole new existence in a world, where the spirit reigned supreme over our actions. If things were so wonderful, why then did I feel the weight of the cross at this auspicious time?

Then it struck me: my students have become my responsibility; it was not simply a question of their being adopted into the Igbo culture, they had, as it were, involved me in their lives, and now their welfare was my welfare. I shared these thoughts with Florence, recounting to her my sessions with Angela, and telling her how fearful I was, as though I had been thrown into a battle without appropriate weapons.

"Thanks, Chioma; this is good news. You have found that your brains and intellectual powers do not immediately help you out of this huge load laid on your weak shoulders. God has endowed you with a lot, from all we're told, and now you're being challenged as never before. That is your cross now, and it's in handling these students in their daily life that you will be fulfilling your vocation to offer yourself completely in apostolic service. Yes, I know you will not be able to help the male students directly, because you will not maintain any personal contacts with them. Still, you could introduce them to an *Opus Dei* Centre for men where they can receive social and cultural formation. In time, who knows, they might seek to know more, and be guided through spiritual formation. The ladies, of course, now belong to you; you can bring them to Nesbit, and you will know exactly what to do, as they will be with you. They all love you, you tell me. They will love you more, yet."

We spent about thirty minutes talking and I felt light and fully invigorated; ready to see, not only to the academic, intellectual and cultural life of my students, now my friends, but also to their spiritual development, as much as possible. I knew this would be a huge task, but with God's grace, I was prepared to give of my best.

Pat had gone to meet Grandma in the kitchen, and after my chat, Flo and I joined them to prepare a quick meal of rice and beef stew, which we ate heartily. They still had a few minutes and were able to meet my students and hear their experiences first hand. Rosemary,(Chigozie), told Flo that she would visit her in Enugu to see what their centre was like when she came to Nigeria the following year, 2007. This was totally unexpected, out of the blue. I wondered what Chigozie had in mind.

We had drinks together, and then I took them to Grandpa, Grandma and Ma. Grandma practised her Yoruba with Patricia and was quite excited to learn that Patricia was born in Ife and had studied chemistry at Obafemi Awolowo University. Patricia would have loved to spend more time with my folks, but they had to return to Enugu that same day, after leaving Owerri, and the roads were quite tricky, filled with potholes that could cause life-threatening car accidents.

I called Angela that night, and told her just how happy I was with Flo's and Patricia's visit.

THIRTY-SEVEN

It was the day of receptions for me and the students: one by the Local Government Council, at ten in the morning, followed by another at one in the afternoon sponsored by the elders of Okeosisi at the home of Chief Ogadinma, the first among the chiefs of Okeosisi, a genial, amiable man who helps sweeten the taste of discord, discontent or malice in Okeosisi, with a large dose of graceful aplomb. We would have lunch at the chief's home and be entertained by the different dance groups of our town. I did not like meetings but my grandpa had somehow managed to distil out of me my loathing for them with the insight that even the stupid have their say, and we must listen to them. I could never stand listening to those who said one thing when they meant something else altogether; or people who kept on waffling, not making much sense; or those who were there just for their own interests, while pretending to be on the side of the public good. I had found my place with the few relentlessly tough and honest ones who spoke the truth, looked you straight in the eye and would shout, yell and pound the table, all to get to the bottom of things.

However, my grandpa had taught me that if I wanted to carry out an apostolate with people, I would have to take them as they were, just as they came, in their real flesh and bones. He said if we wanted to change the world, then we would first need to know what it was we were changing; or, as he put it, "know your enemy." As he saw it, if I hated being at meetings, then I would never quite know what it was I wanted to change. We argued a lot about this but in time I began to see reason, and started liking meetings, receptions and those other occasions when people got together trying to outdo one another in feeling good.

But our meeting with the local government council was something I had looked forward to; if for nothing else, to offer our immense gratitude to the chairman, Chief Madu Akubueze, who had seen to our every need and comfort. What we did not count on was that the state governor would be there as special guest of honour and would use the occasion of our visit to shore up his failing administration.

In my daily chat with my friends that morning, I had told everyone to pay little attention to all that the politicians would be saying and they readily agreed, as they were used to the ways of politicians in the United States, who would promise our college the moon and the stars only to deliver a mere doughnut at a school rally. So we did not take anyone seriously. They made their speeches and I thanked the chairman and it was all over; or so I thought.

The governor threw us a fastball: he called each of our guests by the name Ma had given them without any mention of their American names. He cleared his throat and gave us this wonderful surprise: he had learned that Professor Maduka Okeosisi was building a school with funds provided in the will of Mr. Arthur Preston Greenfield, one-time resident of Okeosisi Province, in the hey-day of our colonial history; and that Mr. Greenfield's great-grandson, Jack Clifford, was one of my students. He expressed his profound gratitude to Mr. Greenfield and then continued:

"I have been in touch with the governor of Maryland, Mr. Nelson Haynes, and a couple of other heavyweights in Maryland, in New York and New Jersey, and with seed money which my state will provide, we shall build a university, a joint project of the collaborating parties, Azara State University and the University of Maryland. We have provided ample land for the university and with the approval of the National University Commission, we hope the enterprise can take off by next year. The rest are mere details. My main interest is to join forces with Maryland in a number of educational projects. Chioma has done so much for our people, and now I see that she's doing the same for your people, so that we are now one.

"To make this all the more defining and definitive, you came here wanting to know the Igbo as well as the Igbo know themselves, and all in the unbelievably short time of fourteen days, here in Okeosisi. You've all given us a new world, and in a way, you've given the Igbo culture back to us for us to know ourselves better, and be what would make our ancestors proud of us. In the short space of fourteen days, you've called into question so many facets of our customs, discovering in them the philosophy of being, of *Chi*. I can't believe what's happening here. Time will tell, when the whole thing explodes to our mutual delight."

Ezechishiri was asked to speak, but he declined, and asked me to speak on behalf of the University of Maryland at College Park. I called him aside and remonstrated with him as protocol demanded he make the speech in response to the governor, I added that I was still a Nigerian with a Nigerian passport!

"Chioma, forget it, if you want an American passport, you can have one when we get back. I am Ezechishiri, yes; but I want to remain totally incognito here. I would like your people to know that you are the seal between us and them; that we owe all this to you, to your talents and forthrightness, which has opened new vistas in the minds of our students, so much so that they wanted to be like you, to be Igbo. No, the world belongs to you, so go ahead, speak, say anything. I'll take notes for President Mansfield, if he should ask me for a copy of what you said. You know he's kept copies of all your speeches at College Park. Anyway, go on. You'll be fine."

Totally unprepared for this responsibility that fell to me, I thanked the governor in words which I did not know where they came from. They must have been longing for a day such as this to make their appearance; to tell the world that they existed, that they had a life, and that although they had been locked up in the attic of my mind, they were just waiting for the good governor to say those incredible words, to create this amazing atmosphere for them to be released from their moorings. They clapped and did not stop clapping until the governor and his party left.

It was time for us to leave for the party with the elders but not before Chief Akubueze came to sit with us and chat with each person individually. When he got to Chima, there was mild consternation for he started speaking Igbo to the chairman. I could not make out what he was saying; we were all wondering where he picked up Igbo from. Surely, it could not have been from Okeosisi in barely ten days! So where did he get this knowledge from?

What happened next was that both Chima and Chief Akubueze stood up and started dancing to the music of *abigbo* with rhythm and gusto. What was going on? It turned out that the chief's son, Ama, was a student at the Catholic University of America in Washington, D.C., and was a dear friend of Chima's. When the idea of our trip was mooted, Chima got Ama to teach him some Igbo, the sort you needed to exchange pleasantries and for greetings at parties. He practised for several hours and until we were in the presence of the chief, none of us could have suspected that Chima spoke a word of Igbo. And then he showed us his mettle.

Dwight could not contain his joy, saying if he had two lifetimes to live, he would have lived out one as an African. In fact, he added that in his next life he would come as an Igbo, to which Chief Madu Akubueze bellowed, "Amen", with all the power of his lungs. The whole event ended with thunderous shout after thunderous shout of 'Amen' from everyone.

Chima would have no rest: we all wanted to know what he said to the chief that moved him to dance. He replied that he had told the chief in his best Igbo, "Let's join the abigbo dancers." His dear friend, Ama, had taught him the dance and how to say the words correctly. Once he heard those words, the amiable chief jumped up and started dancing, then he joined the chief and the party reached a crescendo.

This trip was moving from one mountain top to another, and it seemed my friends kept seeking out one more mountain after another, to my utter amazement.

We arrived late for our party with the elders. The chief who had accompanied us apologized profusely on our behalf, heaping the whole blame for our lateness on his broad shoulders. Chief Ogadinma received us with eight kola nuts and the eldest amongst our hosts said prayers in Igbo. This is because no respectable Igbo man would pray the prayer of the blessing of kola nuts in any other language. For the kola god understands only Igbo. He later translated his prayers to us after the kola had been broken and the pieces shared out.

Since we had spent the morning listening to one goodwill speech after another, our hosts did not wish to inflict any more speeches on us, but simply guided us through our lunch, accompanied by drumming and dancing to abigbo for our entertainment.

THIRTY-EIGHT

it was our last day at Okeosisi, a miserable day for me. I woke up not wanting to wake up, that I may not have to face this day of all days. I just could not imagine anything wonderful happening. We had all been so thrilled with the wonders of the ordinary things of Okeosisi in the two weeks we were there. How do I put my thoughts into words?

We had spent all our time in one little town, now transformed by the new age after the Nigerian civil war, but with some of its ancestral relics still intact. Modern buildings were all over the place, and the forests where my Pa used to take me to, were now schools, hospitals and offices.

My childhood days were no more, and so I did not expect
that those things that made my childhood so special would be
there to welcome me and invite me into their angelic homes.
They were all gone. All I had left were my Ma, my
grandparents and my relations—many of them quite old. For
how long would I have this solemn life of sublime love? Oh
my God, why do things change like this to the point where we
no longer recognise anything of what we were once used to? I
could not bear my sadness and prayed that it may yield to
cheerfulness and delight. This seemed like a tall order, as I
did not even have the inclination to pray for the cheerfulness I
so desperately needed. Was I now to live in this misery?

****

Grandma woke me up for Mass. She must have guessed I
needed all the prodding I could get on this day when I was
not downstairs in time. She sat next to me, and I could sense it
was no easier for her than it was for me.

"My dear Chioma, you don't have to worry. Don't forget
that the good God brought you and your students here. Are
you now saying he made a big mistake in arranging this trip,
using you as an instrument for endearing friendships, such
that we now find ourselves in an entirely new era of
collaboration between Okeosisi and Maryland? Just look at all
that has happened here in the past two weeks, all filled with
joy and love. Could you have imagined something so
enchanting when you were at College Park? Please, don't be
sad. Rejoice, I say rejoice, for you have been able to
accomplish what none of us ever dreamed of. Rejoice, my
dear, rejoice."

It was after five in the morning, and as much as I could
hear Grandma clearly, my thoughts were on my disconcerted

state, and I did not feel courageous enough to be cheerful.
How could I be expected to be cheerful, all the grace God
gives me notwithstanding. This seemed to be a case of "Lord,
let my will be done. Please leave me, let me be as sad and
miserable as I can be."

But my grandma held me so closely to her heart that her
heartbeat was pleadingly pounding on my misery-infested
chest. What choice did I have? I could not tell Grandma I
would not go to Mass. And so I washed my face, brushed my
teeth and joined her and Grandpa for Mass.

Back home after Mass, I still wished this day could be
skipped in the annual calendar long enough for me to find
myself back in College Park without any punctuating pains of
unbearable and excruciating goodbyes and farewells. But I
was mistaken: the day would not go away. The sun still shone
brightly; the sky was above our heads, the clouds were
spiralling, turning white then dark, as usual. Nothing was out
of place, telling me not to be afraid and not to be miserable.
After all, had I not said that nothing good ever ends? Why
should I not put this into practice right now? And so, after
about ten minutes of these thoughts, my spirits were up, and I
rushed off to Grandma to help her prepare breakfast.
Chigozie caught up with me and provided another pair of
hands. She sensed that I was not my usual happy self and
tried to lift me up.

"Chioma, what's your headache? What are you so
miserable about? Look at it this way: we're no longer students
taking a course from you, we're your friends, and we've made
Okeosisi our motherland, your Ma, our own Ma too. We'll be
back next year, all of us, we've decided. We'll come and live
out our lives as authentic Igbo women and men. Anyway,

that's another story. For now, you should be so happy that all of the universe could not contain your joy.

"Have you ever heard in the states of a trip such as we have undertaken with you? Are you the only Igbo professor in the United States? For that matter, are you the only Igbo professor at College Park or in the University of Maryland system? You know you're not. So, don't you think being with you so close as to be absorbed into a whole new culture is something greater than all the philosophy you could teach us?"

My gloomy canopy was being gradually but inexorably lifted by Chigozie's poignant words. I was still filled with delicate sadness, but I would be an ungrateful fool not to respond to Chigozie's sincere promptings. At all events, I was still the leader of the group, and I was expected to be in full control of everything. If anything went wrong, I would be held responsible. Then I wondered: what was so terrible about being held responsible? What if I was the object of lack of responsibility? These thoughts were not comforting enough, so I made up my mind to put all of my energy into this last lap of the thrilling race for philosophical and cultural union. Thanks to my Pa, whose voice kept beckoning to me to climb the heights of difficulties, I was able to follow his advice and brought the course to an invigorating end.

We had a slow day, everyone doing whatever they wanted to. Ma and Grandma served some of their special dishes, now that everyone was quite taken with Igbo cuisine. *Ugba* with *usu* was the thrill of the evening, washed down with choice drinks, from white and red wine to cold beer and soft drinks. Some of us wanted the *usu*, prepared from melon, to be securely wrapped, to be taken to the states.

Everybody in the compound was present for dinner —
Grandma, Grandpa, Dwight, my great-uncles and great-
aunts, my cousins from different generations and the village
elders. There was not much talk as we were all somewhat sad
at the thought of parting. Then, out of nowhere, Dean
Ezechishiri Campbell gave us the speech of his life.

"My dear students, I can call you all by your Igbo names,
Chinwe, Chima, Chinemere, Ogechi, and with the right accent
too, I believe. Grandma here nods her approval. And you told
me you will continue bearing these names when you return to
College Park so as to give real meaning to your Igbo links.
You even told me you not only bear Igbo names, you can
trace your ancestry down to your Igbo forbears. And you are
all white, as white as Grandma Adiaha's signature
handkerchiefs. Tell me, is this not the globalization of
cultures? Igbo names and culture living nobly in white faces,
in white souls?

"We came here looking for an Igbo philosophy that would
make a unique contribution to the global age. We were
wrong, we now know, for there is no new philosophy. It's all
out there, in the traditions handed to us down trough the
ages, the traditions of virtue, of knowledge and of research.
Surely, we can clarify and make more poignant the ideas we
have received from past philosophers in the light of new
knowledge—scientific, sociological, political, or whatever.
Still, we must not forget: philosophy is for human beings and
not the other way round. So, whatever makes humans more
human, more true to their calling, is much needed in our
world today.

"We sought to change the world with new concepts of life
and living. We have met the world in Okeosisi. It is us. Yes,
each one of us needs to change. A new conversion awaits us,

and challenges us to rid ourselves of all the dirt of subjectivism and relativism. We need to discover who we are and be who we are supposed to be.

"There's an ad for a watch—one of those Swiss masterpieces of detailed, arduous and refined craftsmanship. Let me talk about the ad. It shows a beautiful woman, as charming as they come. She has on a black chiffon dress - V-neck, long sleeves. Her arms can be seen under her transparent dress, the right folded over the left, hugging her bosom; her hair is somewhat ruffled, as though she was awakened from relaxed slumber; her face is turned sideways, to her left, looking apprehensively into the distance.

"To the left, in the direction in which she is looking, are the words that, I think, are meant to portray the image right before you, 'Who will you be in the next 24 hours?' I was struck by this question, and now I frame the rest of my talk around this profound question. It does not ask, 'Who will you be tomorrow?' No; it specifies 24 hours because, I suspect, each hour, each minute, each second counts, and you are inveigled to start checking off the seconds once you drop the magazine, using the watch to help you keep count of the steps in your transformation that comes with each passing second. At the end of the twenty four hours, when all that time is gone, down to the last minute, the last second, as recorded by the watch, who will you be?

"The lady looks so perfect she could not be any more perfect: who will she be then? Will she be so transformed by wearing this watch that she would become someone remarkable, someone like a dream? But she already has the watch, she's wearing one. So, who can she be? Someone spectacular who from one 24-hour period to another gets better and better? Would she be transformed by owning this watch? Hell, no! She would transform her world, if, at all, by being the sort of person who recognises those same qualities which best describe this watch.

"So, like the ad asks, who will you be in 24 hours? Except that in your case the question is, 'Who will you be after 336 hours with Chioma in Okeosisi?' We all have the answer now, don't we? In our case, we recognized Chioma as someone unique, for her *Chi*, her Good Fortune. You wanted to be part of her Chi, to enter her world. Could you not have entered her world in the United States? No, you didn't think so: you supposed that you had to come to Okeosisi for that, to gain access to her mind; to her natural Igbo landscape; to breathe the air of her Chi, consume the foods of her mind, digest them and gain new blood for your blanched souls. Yes, living with Chioma in Okeosisi has done it for you. You are all transformed beyond your wildest expectations. And College Park will no longer be the same. And I might add, Chioma has done it for me too; I believe I'm transformed, no less than you are."

* * **

We packed our personal belongings and stowed our Okeosisi soil and grass in our suitcases, well sealed in large, brown envelopes. Dean Ezechishiri had obtained prior approval from U.S. Customs for us to bring home the 'practical materials' of our PHL 217 course. And we were off to Lagos, then to London and finally to Washington, D.C. We were not the same persons who left this same airport two weeks ago: we were better people. Chigozie did not meet the love of her life in Okeosisi. She was close to me, and discovered herself thereby.

"I now know who your tremendous lover is," Chigozie had said as we boarded the bus for College Park, "and from being near you, I truly believe you're very much in love with him. I can't imagine any human being giving you all of his love as he has done. I want to have this kind of love, and I think I'm going to get really attached to you so that you could bring me into your life at Nesbit. You're one hell of a fantastic person, and I think it's your lover who has made you so."

"Thanks be to God who has shown me so much love and has given all of himself to me," was all I could say in response, hoping that Rosemary meant every word she said about coming to Nesbit.

THIRTY-NINE

I wanted to keep Mike searching his soul, to be able to deal with his dear wife not recognising him, while suffering the withdrawal problems caused by Doris abandoning him. I thought the best way to get Mike to look deeply into himself was for him to give a talk. The opportunity offered itself when a group of students with whom I have get-togethers suggested that I give them a talk on Eros. I was astounded.

Usually, we discussed cultural matters with a moral emphasis, and all I did was simply direct the discourse to keep it focused. I would introduce a topic, talk for about five minutes or so and then the students would take over. It was a mixed group of fifty students or so: Some were students taking a course I taught, others came from other departments on the strength of what their friends might have told them about our get-togethers. In time, I was able to do apostolate with some of the female students amongst them on issues of morals and the virtues.

I jumped at this unique opportunity and immediately thought of having Mike give the talk on *Eros and Human Freedom*. He was not readily agreeable, but on second thought, he went along with me. Our get-togethers held at 7pm and Mike found the hour suitable.

It was an unusually warm September evening. Gold-and-red variegated autumn leaves blew into the lecture hall. We did not pick them up, the colours added lustre to the lecture. I introduced Mike and he quickly strode into his talk.

"My dear students, we all live in the same physical world, the world of matter, of the senses, of sensations. A few months ago, I fell victim to a disordered will that led me to the sinful world of misdirected Eros. I misconstrued love, and descended into wild passions that had little to do with the truth of being. And now Chioma wants me to talk about the real thing, the real Eros; Chioma is always after the 'real thing'.

"The first question I would like to deal with is, what do I mean when I say I love you? You will agree with me, I hope, that to deal with this matter, I would first have to know who I am. Who am I? Some of you know me to be an artist, seeing things with forty eyes at the same time; to see layers and layers of the same face, each layer revealing this aspect and another layer that aspect of the same face. Therefore, you find you don't have just one face but many faces of the same structure in front of you. So, which of these layers is real? The answer is that they all are. Which is the real thing? Each is the real thing. So when I say 'I love you' what exactly am I saying?"

I hoped Mike would not go the way of those artists who see art as 'real' as the human spirit is real; to whom reality is only a certain perspective on nature.

"I must, therefore, be quite clear in my mind that my love is real, for a real person; because I am not dealing with a work of art."

We were enjoying ourselves and no one was fidgeting in their seat yet. I liked this. We had agreed beforehand that Mike would talk for about twenty minutes, allowing ten minutes at the end for discussion.

"When we look at some works of art, particularly surrealist art, one comes to the conclusion, 'This is impossible.' What then happens? If we could only let loose our intellect and try to flow with the painting before us, we might find that we begin to experience a certain pleasure which the abolition of reason brings.

"So, why look for meaning where the whole purpose is to release one from meaning? Why look for walls when the architect wants you to float in the air? Therein lies the problem of dealing with reality in the mind of the artist. But let's not forget, that the work of art is entirely a creation of the artist, whatever may be the sensations transferred to the beholder."

As an artist, I could not agree more with Mike; but life is not all art. So I waited to see how Mike would weld all this artistic talk into the love of Eros. It was our practice that get-togethers last no more than thirty minutes, and although this was an invited lecture, I hoped it would not drag on for long or the audience might get restless. But my fears were put to rest: after thirty minutes everyone seemed absorbed in Mike's words. He sensed our interest and began to wax even more eloquent.

"Why am I saying all this? What has this got to do with Eros, and loving? Everything and I mean everything, for, as I said earlier, there's the tendency for us to give our own meanings to love, to be surrealistic about things that have real life and real meaning, and which lose their very essence when they're given a new existence in their life of new meanings."

I was really enjoying the talk and could not help nodding every now and then, to indicate my complete agreement with Mike's trend of thought.

"Dear friends, we don't live in an impossible world; however, we may perceive this world of ours. Chioma is a painter, and I'm sure she has given many talks about her own works and her perception of nature. And I'm sure she'll tell you that, sometimes, her hands tend to have an existence of their own as she paints, as if she has no control over the movement of her fingers that express her thoughts. She will tell you that her thoughts flow into her hands and they respond to this energy without her deliberately wishing it so. She must have told you all about a painting of hers, *Anyanwu*, meaning sunshine, which she made while in a state of apparent spiritual darkness, and she cannot quite recall what she was doing. All this shows that the human spirit expressed in art has immense dimensions, almost without any boundaries."

Mike was right. I had told him about *Anyanwu*, and that he could use it whenever he pleased as an example of darkness gaining control over our thoughts in a manner we cannot readily understand. Besides, I had also discussed this painting in great detail at our get-togethers. How then do we move from this vast, immeasurable world of the mind and memory to our real world of sin and virtues? Mike provided some answers.

"Sexual behaviour has little to do with true love. There are those who, with all of their body and soul love the one God. The rest of us have to make do with showing our love, often of a mediocre quality, to a human person. Love is so singular that it is rare to find a human being who would love another as Christ loved his Church and gave his life for it. I hope you do not mind a little bit of religion here and there."

Where was Mike heading? He had been speaking for close to forty- five minutes. I hoped we would soon get into the real meat of the talk. And he did not disappoint us.

"This now brings me to Eros, the subject of this talk, for it is the ultimate expression of love, so demanding, so passionate, so all-encompassing that the person in love feels possessed by a maddening spirit of such mountainous proportions that he seeks to be absolutely lost in the person of the beloved and thereby be infinitely dissolved into her essence that his life may have meaning, worthy of being lived. This was the Greek understanding of Eros, the god of love and sexual desire. One would say, Eros is love, true and pure. Thus, life becomes understood only in the context of the beloved. 'I'm glad that you exist' becomes the signature song of the lover for his beloved, and all he desires is the good of his beloved. Because he is free to choose, and knowing that it is in his freedom that he can reach the perfection of his own being, he gives himself to the beloved in total merging and continuity of beings. This, to me, is what Eros means, and what it's all about."

We clapped in agreement, thrilled at this exquisite presentation of sublime human love. Mike was not done yet and gave us more from his enchanting library.

"Christians say God is love. This is clearly understandable for he created us in his image and wants us to be like him, giving us all of himself even to the extent of coming as a man to save us from our limitations, and appropriate for us the full measure of our being as his children. Is this not Eros, this total giving of self to the other, for the good of the other? Must the expression of sexuality involve sexual intimacy? Did the Christian son of God not express his perfect sexuality in the act of total obedience to the will of his Father? Did his mother not do the same, for the sake of the kingdom of God, lived and fully expressed in his son? Did the early Christians and the martyrs not live Eros?

"So, what went wrong? Can we trace the history of how Eros got corrupted? Let me say right away, I don't know. All I know is that slowly, and inexorably, humans paid more attention to the needs of the body and tended to satisfy their sexual appetites, without due consideration of the nobility of the body as the living abode of the human spirit, turning what was noble love into disgusting lust."

This was where I thought Mike would bring us into his personal life, and as much as I longed to hear the whole affair all over again, straight from the horse's mouth, I feared this horse's mouth was so full it might just spew out all of its insides on to the unsullied floor.

Mike returned to the beginning, like the good lecturer he was: but I was not prepared for how extensive his foray into his life would be.

"I spent some time in the beginning on art and the artist, and how art came to be considered as an instrument freeing the mind from the shackles of reality. Not only art, but according to this mode of thought, anything goes, and all that matters is the individual person acting out his or her individual ideas of life. Reality becomes a matter of opinion.

"I lived this dream of individual freedom without any qualms whatsoever. I got close to someone I had known for some time, a regular visitor to my home, and a dear friend of my wife's and mine. What was once a healthy chaste relationship between Debbie and me degenerated into lust and sheer uncontrolled desire. This was the beginning of the slide into shameless debauchery."

I knew he was referring to Doris. All my old anger and disgust returned and, once again, I felt like breaking Mike's head. But I knew the whole story, and my rage was not as intense and vicious as before. I really did not want to hear this all over again. But I had asked for it: I invited Mike for the talk. Recalling Doris riled my senses, even if she had left Mike, and we had made our peace. Still, I am human and these feelings of gross displeasure do not easily disappear into thin air: they stay around for a while.

Mike went on telling us about 'Debbie'.

"Debbie encouraged me to the hilt: in fact, it turned out that she was all out to wrench me from my firm marital anchor. What we didn't count on was that all the clichés of life were not mere clichés; they were real. Yes, reality actually exists. I wonder, why we were so foolish, thinking we could live on the highs of love and not drop down into the valleys, sometimes? In our case, Debbie was the one who came to her senses first: She told me to pack my things and leave! I could not believe my ears. The day after she asked me to leave, I returned to her apartment to find she had changed the locks on me, with a note that she had sent my things to my home address. I nearly died."

I felt the same way; he should have died and be gotten rid of. But he did not die, he was right here in front of us giving this talk.

"I went to my house to pick up my things and then suffered the biggest shock of my life. My wife, Sutapa, did not recognise me. I thought she was just so mad at me that she did not want any part of me, and so had constructed the whole thing to make it look like she had gone wacko. She would, of course, not let me stay in the house, and I didn't ask that favour of her. I took a room at a motel, hoping we could sort this out.

"But Sutapa did not recognize me, I knew from Chioma that she was fine in every other respect. I was lost, not having any identity as far as Sutapa was concerned. Until now as I speak, Sutapa does not know who I am, I mean she does not know me as her husband. I think my unexpectedly deranged behavior shocked her so severely that her brain cells that stored the memory of who I was, suffered an immediate seizure, and I was neatly erased leaving no other damage to her immaculate intellect.

"Believe me, reality exists and it is far sweeter than make-believe, for that is what surrealism leads us to: make-believe. A make-believe world can exist in art, in our writing, in our imagination, but we cannot live in a make-believe world. Our world bears us up when we walk or else we would slip and fall. Debauchery, lust and erotic love, have nothing to do with the Eros of the ancient Greeks, or with the real love that nourishes human souls. I will live on Eros and give all of my love to Sutapa if . . ." .

What was happening? Mike had stopped speaking as if his tongue was frozen. I turned and saw Sutapa moving toward the front, toward the table where Mike was seated. Nobody stopped her. And now, wonder of wonders, Sutapa gamesomely walked up to Mike, warmly embraced him and held him as firmly as she could. Releasing her hold, she flung back her luscious hair, looked straight into her husband's eyes and kissed him with all the Eros she could muster.

The hall erupted with the thundering power of a tornado. We had never seen this before. Right here before our eyes, a long lost love was being re-kindled. Eros has come to life right before us, and has taken us in flight to heavenly places, to our Tremendous Lover.

"Ladies and gentlemen, this is my wife Sutapa. I think she now knows who I am. Oh my God, I'm alive again. My world is complete. And I can go on living. I can fly to the sky, and catch my own star, that lights my way. And Sutapa here is that star. I have her again. Oh, I am a man again, with a past, a present, and a future, I hope, with my Sutapa."

Mike sat down and drew Sutapa onto his lap, buried his head in her bosom, and kept muttering, over and over again: I am sorry; I love you; I am sorry; I am sorry. . . .

We fell dead silent once we saw this elegant lady walk up toward Mike. When he said she was his wife, the same one he had been talking about in this get-together, we practically slumped in our seats, in utter bewilderment. And as he held Sutapa close, you could hear the air softly whistling through the tightly-shut windows, accompanying Mike in his song of love. Our astonishment turned to indescribable joy and we all stood up clapping, hugging one another, singing any song that came into our ecstatic heads.

****

I gave two get-togethers based on my trip to Okeosisi at Nesbit and it was one 'wow' after another, much to the delight of our director, Chelsea. Funke and Amaka were present and have been coming to our means of formation at Nesbit ever since.

I wrote to thank Florence and Patricia and, through them, sent greetings to the entire residents of Onyinye University Centre, Enugu.

I was all over Angela with my joy, fear, and struggle to overcome my defects, including some signs of billowing pride which, to my great relief, she surgically dissected out of me.

Sutapa welcomed Mike back to their home, and their marriage blossomed.

I spent a weekend with my parents, my brothers, Zoputa, Akachi, Kelechi, and sister, Ngozi, who was extremely delighted that I was a faithful of *Opus Dei*, urging me to use my position as teacher/painter to bring people closer to God. Mum and Dad were beside themselves with joy. My brothers, Zoputa and Akachi plan to spend the summer of 2007 at Enugu with Grandpa Maduka.

Doris and Chigozie started receiving spiritual, cultural, social and doctrinal formation at Nesbit and, by arrangement, with priests at the National Shrine of the Immaculate Conception. All my other friends kept their Igbo names. Chinwe, Chika, Chidinma, Oluchi and Ogechi remained close to me, and came to Nesbit whenever I invited them. Chinwe and Oluchi wanted more and, without much prompting from me, came to live at Nesbit, just like some of our student residents who were not Catholic.

I introduced my male friends—Chudi, Chima, Chinemere and Chibuzo—to Fr. Paul Carter, and they were frequent guests at his get-togethers at the Desmond Centre for Social and Professional Development. I kept in touch with them at College Park and gave them all the assistance they needed with their studies.

Nkemdi had a baby girl and she and Bia planned to return to Nigeria where he has been appointed a lecturer in the Department of Biochemistry, University of Ibadan. We had long talks together on faith and truth, and we became very close.

Susanne Capello kept up with her doctrinal formation at Nesbit and regularly brought a good number of students to the programmes for spiritual and cultural formation at the centre.

Constance Ferguson wanted to go to Okeosisi on her own, but I promised I would travel with her when I could manage this.

I asked for water more frequently than I used to, instead of my favourite white wines, especially at dinners with guests and on other occasions when my paintings were celebrated. I still love wine and would offer it to any of my guests who so desires.

Dwight changed his name to Ezechishiri, officially, and was called Chishiri Campbell. He did not mind that many of his friends and colleagues just could not correctly pronounce his name. True to his word, he gave get-togethers for my students, and their friends, on his visit to Okeosisi, and his friendship with Grandpa Maduka and Grandma Adiaha. So many students wanted to attend that poor Chishiri had to give get-togethers twice a week to accommodate their wishes. He told us thrilling stories of Nigeria from the fifties to the eighties; in particular, what life was like at the University of Ibadan (UI) and Obafemi Awolowo University (OAU). I felt proud that there was a time when Ibadan and OAU could be said to be 'as good as they come'. He strongly believed that all was not lost, and that these two institutions, OAU and UI, would be resurrected to a brand new glory in post-graduate research in Nigeria.

I liked this a lot, and many of my students told me they would go to OAU for their post-graduate studies, because I would be there, for a while, for my Ph.D. fieldwork.

I went to my first class in the fall of the 2006/2007 session. I could not believe what I heard. The world is no longer one I can master, or is it?

"We're here to go to Okeosisi next summer, Ms. Ijeoma, all one hundred of us. We've arranged for the ten students, whom you took last year, to live with your *Chi*, to take care of us. We were told you took only ten students because you wanted to be able to keep an eye on everyone. Now there'll be ten others who can watch over us. And Dean Campbell said he'd come too. We hope we'll still make intimate contact with your *Chi*. From what we gather, your *Chi* comes alive at Okeosisi and infects the souls of anyone close to you. We hope you'll like us enough to consider us as your friends and then we'll be as African as you are."

****

Can it get any better? Is this world not wonderful, full of unimaginable thrills and joys? Can I capture all this in my painting? Can I cope with this avalanche of activity? Oh yes, I am exceedingly happy and my joy is complete! Oh my God, I love you; help my little love. I now know myself better and can serve you in the world, turning my dreams into torrents of love, in total self-giving.

FORTY

October, 2006

Geneve enjoyed coming to Nesbit: she had been to dinner a number of times, in disguise, so no one could recognise her. We took her round, through the gardens, the library, and the theatre, yes, we have one that seats about fifty. I took her to our rooms, including mine, and finally, the oratory. She went into the oratory, knelt in prayer for about ten minutes, moved to the front pew and sat there directly facing the tabernacle. She sat there for a long while; she must have totally lost track of time, as she was ten minutes late for her concert. I went up to her and told her it was time for her performance. She followed me outside to the corridor and then shocked me with her question.

"Did you say my performance, Chioma? What performance?"

"We are all assembled in the theatre waiting for you to come on stage. Your band-mates are all set up ready to go."

"I don't know what's going on, Chioma, I'm shaking and I don't think I can sing."

What could be the matter? I saw that Geneve was not her usual 'I'm-in-control-of-the-universe' self. She looked forlorn and wilted. Something must have struck her in the oratory. I took her to my room to give her time to calm down, away from inquiring eyes. It was then she told me:

"Chioma, there's so much peace here, I'd give anything to live with you, close to you."

I did not like this at all: things were not supposed to go this way. I had had enough of this 'close-to-you' affection from my students, and just when I thought I was gathering myself together, here comes this megastar to complicate my life. I tried to steer the conversation in a different direction.

"Sing first, Geneve—you'll find your range—then you'll have some wine in the garden, and then we'll talk more intimately about Nesbit. But for now, let's sing. By the way, I have some new lyrics for you, especially for you. You might want to consider them for your next album."

"Well, Chioma, you got me there. I'll go out and sing two tracks from my new top-selling album, thanks to your lyrical talents, all written by you. Oh, before I forget, we already have a check for you based on our colossal record sales from which we pay you royalties. This should project you as the new queen of musical lyrics. I think the check is in six figures, and there'll be more to come with greater sales. They'll give you a call and bring it to you here at Nesbit, your residential address. To the theatre then, let's sing our hearts out!"

And sing her heart out, she did; and more. I introduced Geneve and the audience went wild in fervid joy. Accompanied by three members of her group, Bonndde, Collins on rhythm guitar, Blunt on bass guitar and Barrymore on drums, she swiftly and adeptly shifted into overdrive. We had done all we could to keep the whole event quiet, and had invited only thirty students from around the District with strict instructions that they should not come with any of their friends. Only invitees were allowed in. It seemed we succeeded; the theatre was filled to comfortable capacity and no more.

Now that I saw Geneve performing at close quarters, I could better appreciate her beauty and poise, her supple body that easily folded, twisted and turned like the golden-coloured silk gown that draped her exquisite body.

"My first number: *'Where did you find me?'* is one I'd like to dedicate to Dawn, now known by her Igbo name, Ogechi. We met a few days ago, and she regaled me with stories of her holiday in Nigeria, in a place called Kosi. She promised me she would take me to her new home in Igboland any time I was ready."

Where did you find me
living my life all by myself
unknown to anyone
my mum so loving
where did you find me.

Looking at pictures
and turning the pages
from Degas to Delacroix
dancing their ballet
smoking their pipes
where did you find me.

My heart's aflame
with burning desire
grinds me in the morning
to shout in wonder
where did you find me.

My mum in excitement
seeking fulfilment
to grant you contentment
how did you find me.

Take me then stranger
bear me to your tent
tremendously loving
now you've found me.

We jumped from our seats, stomping the floor in satisfied excitement clapping endlessly as if we were beating Barrymore's drums.

I remembered Grandpa Maduka, dancing *ese* at Pa's funeral. Immediately after Pa was laid in the grave, the performers began in full force. The fast undulating sounds knocked out of the wooden slit-drum, *ekwe*, urging the big, heavy drums to explosive, throat-deep resonance transported Grandpa into mountainous heights of commanding nobility. Responding to the gripping beat dripping with valour, Grandpa burst out with unmatched zest and zeal trying in some way to pay distinct homage to his deceased father: telling the world as profoundly as he could through dance just what kind of a noble man his father was. He sent many complex messages in his vigorous steps of marked dexterity.

After watching Grandpa's inspired dance, I swore to myself that I would study dance as art, that I would immerse myself in the culture of dance, and paint dance. I knew that if my feet would not carry me and fully respond to the music of my heart and my soul, my eyes would come to the rescue.

Geneve moved our spirits, and like Grandpa dancing *ese* without any practice, we all got off our feet and stomped the floor in wild dance, moving in any way we could move. The *ese* vibrated in my ears, and mixed with Geneve's resplendently powerful voice. The combination lifted me high in triumphant joy. And my eyes danced.

Geneve gave us six or seven of her earlier hits and for her show-stopper, ended with a song I had written for her, *My Eyes Dance*.

> *I walk down nature's way*
> *birds fly over my head*
> *trying to land on my feet*

and there build their nests
'cause my legs cannot dance.

Freshly hatched
my feet their playing field
they run here and there
drumming their songs in flight
coaxing me to move and dance.
Iroko forests
their solid trunks

the seat of the earth
all twisting and turning
all the world's gone dancing.

Burst out I must
what weighs me down
where are my hands

my head on shoulder
still bearing my eyes.
Blasting rhythms fill my veins
my face my limbs encounter
in the living waters
of that Tremendous Lover
Who makes my eyes dance.

Printed in the United States
By Bookmasters